Blood
in the
Woods

J.P. Willie

A HellBound Books Publishing LLC Book
Houston TX

A HellBound Books LLC
Publication

www.hellboundbookspublishing.com

Printed in the United States of America

Acknowledgements

Cover and art design by Joey Brana
For HellBound Books Publishing LLC

Edited by Xtina Marie

This novel is dedicated to my family and childhood friends.

Friends come and go in your life, people die and love sometimes fades away, but true horror is forever.

J.P. Willie

INTRODUCTION

Fearless Reader, the story you're about to embark upon has taken over seven years to reach publication. After countless rejections from literary agencies and publishing companies, *Blood in the Woods* has finally made it into the hands of avid readers like you.

Although it is evident that evil lurks upon the very pages of this novel, like a lion stalking its unwitting prey, the malevolent is not all this tale has to offer. This bittersweet, heartfelt and vivacious anecdote is about family, first loves and the unbreakable bond of friendship.

I hope this novel not only terrifies you, but also inspires you to reach out to a loved one and tell them how much you love them; maybe you'll pick up a phone and call a friend you haven't spoken to for years. For some of us, our friends mean more to us than we ever mean to them. And if you have children, this novel will make you cherish them all the more.

Just remember, you'll find no monsters or werewolves lurking within these pages - only devils of the very worst kind.

- J.P. Willie

PROLOGUE

THE GRAVEYARD: 1975

On a deep-south Louisiana country road, a young boy by the name of Jerry Jones Jr. patrolled up and down Rhine Road on his yellow, 1975 *Schwinn*. His slim body leaned from side to side as he pedaled back and forth, humming to himself an out of tune rendition of KC and the Sunshine Band's *Get Down Tonight*.

The boy's curly hair (most people would call it *nappy*) tightened as the wind pulled it back slightly, as he waited for his three friends; the Benson boys.

The Benson's father just happened to be one of the wealthiest men in all of Hammond – Jerry thought he was an architect or something, but all he knew for sure was that the man drew really neat pictures for people to build houses by.

This particular evening, Jerry and the Benson boys had decided to take an adventure – a detour to the local graveyard that sat but three miles away. The kids at school had been talking about it for weeks, and of course to kids in their early teens, a graveyard was not just a chilling place to be, but also a location you'd gain notoriety for visiting. And so, today was the day that Jerry was to earn his fame for being one of the only boys in school to have set foot in the place, the old boneyard's reputation was a fearsome one which kept all but the most hardy at bay.

Jerry watched as the Benson Boys approached on their bicycles, his heart pounding with excitement and nerves.

Unbeknownst to them all, they really should've stayed home.

The boys rode toward their destination, making a sharp turn onto a small dirt road lined by a bunch of oak and willow trees that stood tall and proud on both sides of the street, their branches hung halfway over the road, providing the boys welcome shade from the murderous Louisiana heat. Taking the turn a little too fast, the front tire of Jerry's *Schwinn* almost lost traction. Skillfully, he regained balance, keeping himself from being thrown over the handlebars like a man from a skittish horse.

The graveyard rested upon a small hill and contained twenty to twenty-five graves, many of the headstones illegible. It was well shaded by the surrounding woods, which served to give the place an eerie appearance.

The second they stepped into the graveyard, Jerry noticed something strange; the place was unnaturally quiet – a pretty bizarre occurrence, since birds, wildlife, the wind – *something* – should've been moving around in those woods.

As the gang made their way further in, avoiding the creation of any noise, they spotted a dead bird, laying upon on a gravestone to their right.

It looked like a crow, although it was difficult to be certain since the thing had been completely gutted. The bird's lifeless, black eyes stared up into the beautiful fall sky as if it were searching the heavens for someplace to go. The poor creature's intestines were draped across a gravestone, and it looked to Jerry as if someone had tried to write a ghoulish message with them. A cool breeze blew through the woods, making the feathers on the dead bird flutter as if for one last attempt to take flight, and each of the boys felt goose bumps on the backs of their necks, like ghostly fingers were caressing them.

"What the hell happened to it?" Daniel asked, his eyes fixed on the bird's ruined corpse and the visiting flies that buzzed around it.

"No idea," Jerry replied as he studied the thing with morbid fascination.

Keith, the oldest of the Benson brothers, squatted down next to Daniel. He poked at the bird's guts with a long stick, scattering the flies.

"Stop that!" Alvin shouted at him. "That's nasty! You might catch a sick disease or something."

Keith and Jerry giggled as Alvin chastised his older brother, broad smirks on their faces as he rounded on them. "I wanna go home," Alvin whined. "Doesn't this place feel weird to you? It's *too* damn quiet; I can actually hear myself think." Keith and Jerry snickered again. "*Everything* surrounding this graveyard is just as dead as *it* is." He pointed a trembling finger at the dead bird.

Jerry stood up. He did have a peculiar feeling about the place, but he was trying to play it cool; no way was he going to be the chicken shit who let the old graveyard spook him. "Yeah, let's go. There's nothing special here. You ready, Keith?" he said.

13

"Sure." Keith stood up and threw the stick back on the ground.

Keith happened to glance over to his left and noticed something in the far corner of the graveyard. "Jerry... Daniel..."

"What?" both boys answered in unison.

Keith pointed to the far left side of the graveyard, his mouth gaping. "Look," he whispered in a voice that didn't quite sound like his own.

There, in the corner of the graveyard, were twenty-odd dead birds, all stacked on top of each other. From what the boys could make out, most had been gutted the same way as the first one they'd seen. It also became obvious, upon further investigation, that some had their eyes gouged out, heads torn off and their guts stuffed inside their beaks.

Someone had been getting their sick, twisted kicks torturing and mutilating birds in the graveyard and whoever it was had been at it for quite some time – some of the birds were decomposing, their thin, fragile bones stabbing through what remained of rotted flesh.

Jerry's brain spun, images skittering across his racing mind as to how the cruel deed had been done; the bird laid upon a headstone, it's delicate body struggling, beak attempting to bite the hand that held it firm, a knife pressed firmly to its breastbone. A faint *pop* would sound, as the knife went in, the poor bird squawking in agony; and its torturer would enjoy every second of the creature's pain as he yanked out his victim's innards with quick, expert precision...

Jerry snapped himself out of it, knowing full well that the vision he'd just conjured was going to keep him up tonight; the very thought sent chills down his spine.

The sun began to slink towards the horizon and the darkness of night prepared to cover the graveyard. The boys were still far from home, and Jerry knew his father would be bringing the stick to his rear end if he didn't get home before dark.

"Let's go," Jerry mumbled, he craved the safety of home.

As the boys made their way towards their bikes, sounds drifted in from the distance – *voices* – the first noise they'd heard since their arrival at the graveyard.

Frozen with fear, they all listened to the voices – coming through a tad more clearly now.

"Do you hear that?" Daniel asked.

"Yeah, I hear it." Jerry whispered.

"Shh!" Keith hissed at them.

The voices didn't appear to be getting any closer, but it did sound like more voices had joined them; if anything, they seemed to be moving away from where Jerry and his friends were standing stock-still and terrified.

"They're in the woods." Keith played the tough guy, "let's go take a look."

"I can't move, guys," Alvin was first to admit. "I'm too scared." Alvin was the youngest and the puniest of the brothers, and hence the most skittish. "What if they catch us spying on them and beat the shit out of us? What if they call the cops on us for trespassing? Or what if they're a bunch of backwoods psychos who will kill us like – *them*?" He nodded towards the stack of mutilated crows and squirmed at the thought.

"Quit being such a chicken shit, Alvin," Keith growled.

"Quiet!" Jerry spat. "Alvin, you can stay by the bikes. Me 'n Keith will go take a look-see. Okay?"

"Okay." Alvin nodded, his face flushed.

"Daniel?" Jerry added, "can you stay here with him?"

"Sure." Daniel couldn't hide his disappointment;

15

Middle Child Syndrome was a motherfucker.

"Cool." Jerry turned to Keith. "Let's go – but don't make a sound, got it?"

"Got it." Keith agreed.

The two made their way through the graveyard, trying their damndest to make no sound at all, towards a natural depression at the far end that went down a good fifty feet and was lined by trees and bushes all the way down to its bottom.

The voices were getting louder as the boys approached, Jerry and Keith dropping to their knees to get a better view of what lay through the dense bushes.

And there, Jerry observed something he knew he'd never be able to forget for as long as he lived.

There, at the bottom of the slope, there was an opening that led to a rock quarry, not entirely dissimilar to the one Fred Flintstone worked at. At the entrance of the quarry there was a small group of people – six in all – dressed in black hooded robes and standing in a circle. Jerry also spotted several more hooded individuals gathering fat sticks from the wood's line.

The boys couldn't see any of the hooded people's faces, and weren't entirely sure that they wanted to. The hooded people were talking amongst themselves in hushed tones, and Keith and Jerry couldn't make out anything they were saying, they were still a good ways away from the weird assembly.

"What the hell are they doing, man?" Keith kept his voice low.

"No idea," Jerry replied, "but we need to get out of here before they see us."

The boys stood up too quickly and Jerry's shoulder caught on a dead, kindling-dry branch of a tree, snapping it. The branch made a brash popping sound like a bone breaking, in an instant giving away Jerry and

Keith's presence.

"Dammit!" Jerry growled, angry with himself at being so damned clumsy.

Terrified, Jerry stared over at the gathering of hooded people, all of whom had heard the noise as sure as if he'd shouted a jolly *hello!* over to them.

Three of the black hooded figures turned as one and faced in his direction and for a fleeting moment, Jerry imagined he'd actually made eye contact with the one in the middle of the three.

In the blink of an eye, the hooded guy took off, sprinting toward Jerry and Keith at full-pelt.

"Run!" Jerry screamed, his voice shrill with terror.

The boys took off, feet pounding, hearts thumping, making it back to Daniel, Alvin and the welcome sight of their bikes in what felt like a matter of seconds.

"Go!" Keith screamed at his brothers.

"What's going on?" Daniel stammered, nonplussed at his brother's ashen face. "What the –?" But before he could finish, Jerry, Alvin and Keith were already on their bicycles and well on their way along the road. Daniel jumped on his bike and raced after them, not knowing what he was running from.

*

The front door of the Jones household flew open and Jerry darted into the living room, yapping loudly about what he'd just witnessed in the woods.

This caught the attention of Gayla, Jerry's older sister, who was on the sofa with the telephone stuck to her ear; she was busy gossiping with her friend, Jennifer, who just happened to live three miles from the very graveyard her brother was babbling about.

"Hold on, girl, Jerry just came running in yelling

about something crazy again. Let me call you back, okay?" Gayla hung up the phone without saying goodbye.

Household drama wasn't an everyday occurrence at the Jones residence, theirs being a strict yet loving – Christian-based home. Church happened every Sunday at the local *Church Of Christ*, located in downtown Hammond; very much your typical southern Baptist teachings – *sinners will burn in the lake of fire for eternity, the devil will always be at your heels, ready to tempt you and turn you from Christ, you must repent – repent or burn...* the whole Fear of God thing going on, so the Jones kids pretty much minded their P's and Q's.

Gayla stood up, tugging at the hem of her short-shorts, which were riding snug up in her crotch and ass crack. She then focused her attention towards the kitchen where Jerry was red in the face and ranting to their mother about everything he'd witnessed.

"I'm telling you, momma, there were people wearing black robes! And there was a pile of dead birds! And *somebody* killed them!"

"Jerry Jr!" Teddie Jones interrupted her son. "Why in the world were you playing around in that graveyard when you know you shouldn't? Just you wait 'til your daddy comes in, he's gonna tear your butt up!" she spat.

"Momma, they saw us. They chased after us, but we got away."

"*They* saw you! Who saw you?" Teddie asked, concern creeping into her voice.

"I told you - the men in the black robes," Jerry replied, gasping for breath.

"You see what happens when you go looking for trouble, Jerry Jones? It finds you! What if they are vicious criminals, Jerry? What if they come looking for you and those Benson boys? Maybe they already know who you are. And just maybe they'll come chop us *all* up in our sleep! There's some crazy people living in this world, Jerry, and they do unspeakable things to nosey boys like you!"

Jerry Sr. walked into the house, covered in sawdust from head to toe. He was a big man – six-foot-three without his shoes. His chosen hobby was the one that he figured would bring him closer to Christ – carpentry – and that took up much of his non-work time. Jerry Sr. had a thick, bushy mustache that hid his upper lip entirely and drew attention away from the rest of his facial features, but still he was a strikingly handsome man. He dusted himself off as best he could, sat himself down, and asked his dear wife what the problem with Jerry Jr. was *this time.*

And so, Jerry Jr. began his tale once again, all the way from the beginning.

Gayla wandered into the kitchen after ten minutes of listening in and sat down opposite her father at the kitchen table. She could always tell when something was bothering the old man about a situation, and whilst her father could handle any type of problem, she felt that somehow this one was different. It wasn't fear or horror she saw in his eyes, it was more a look of deep concentration, as if he was distracted.

Jerry gazed up from the table, looking his son square in the eyes. "I'm going to tell you this only one time, Jerry. Only once," his voice remained calm, yet inexorably stern. "Stay away from that place. And never – and I mean *never* – go back. Do you understand me, son?"

Struck dumb by this uncharacteristic demeanor, Jerry nodded his agreement.

Gayla studied the expression upon her father's face, still trying to read him. She possessed a God-given

19

talent for reading people and later on in life, she would pass that ability to one of her sons; but for tonight, she just couldn't figure her father at all – no matter how hard she tried.

Jerry Sr. reached his hand over to his daughter's back, rubbing it in small circles. "It's alright, Sissy, it's alright," he said.

Jerry Sr. knew full well what the hooded people were doing by the graveyard, but most importantly, he knew who – *what* – they were. He couldn't tell his children the terrible truth, their youthful minds wouldn't be able to comprehend the true horrors of what lurked in the town. Heck, he couldn't even tell his wife!

Teddie was prone to overreacting and theatrics, which Jerry Sr. didn't feel like entertaining right now. *Yes,* he thought to himself, *he would tell several trusted members of the church – of course he would, he* had *to.* There were the weekly meetings in which they discussed the comprehensive bible study curriculum, possible upcoming humanitarian aid support to the less fortunate countries on their ever-growing list, as well as who would host the next Saturday night pot luck at their home. Jerry was a man of God and a leader within the church, and he firmly believed that you must *always* protect the ones you love – and at any cost. And it was not just protection from the deranged and depraved, the killers and rapists, or those harmful lyrics within popular songs that could sway a person away from the Lord – no, Jerry Jones's defense applied on every level as a father; protect them from pain, be it mental, physical, or emotional; Jerry Jones was a proud, stoic man who would willingly give up his life for any of his children.

Just as Jesus had died for all mankind.

Having well and truly instilled the *Fear of God* into his son, Jerry Sr. went to bed that night with fear in his

20

own heart. He lay upon his bed, eyes wide and mind racing.

He prayed hard.

Not because he feared God – but because more than anything in the world, he feared what lurked in those woods.

CHAPTER ONE

COMING HOME: 2008

There were several reasons why I thought I would be dead long before Jamie.

I have witnessed the true revulsion of war, encountering bodies twisted and strewn in hideous, unnatural ways while serving my country in Afghanistan; man's horror wrought upon his fellow man while supposedly seeking peace.

Also, there was what happened in the Woods.

I'm standing here in my old driveway thinking about my best friend, Jack's sister, Jamie, who just passed away two weeks ago; she was sideswiped by an eighteen-wheeler as she was coming out of the Wal-Mart parking lot in our hometown, Hammond.

Memories of her as a young girl keep flashing in and out of my mind like an old, flickering film clip, only with color and occasional sound. I remember well all the times she used to bug the hell out of Jack and I, always diming us out to our parents whenever she found out some dirt. Even though she got on our nerves back then when we were kids, we are all wishing to God that she was still with us right now. Jesus, I can only imagine how much Jack must be missing her. The beauty mark she had under her left eye seems to be the image that burned its way into my mind like a hot iron; Jamie was the only girl I knew with one of those marks besides some erstwhile celebrities, and now my wife, Corrie.

I remember when Jamie was working at a Corndog stand in the Hammond Mall, a few years back, and giving away free food to my kids. Nachos, corndogs and strawberry ices had stuffed their greedy bellies that day and I remember asking myself, *am I starving these kids or something?* as I watched them scarf down greasy corndogs like prison inmates scoffing their final meal before the chair. I'd continued to stand at the counter and make small talk with Jamie while my unruly heathens finished their plates.

It breaks my heart now to know that although my children met her and will always remember her presence, Jamie's own child, who is a year old, will never lay eyes on his mother's face again, or even get to know her. I don't know what else to say besides my heart goes out to him, and I know deep down in the remainder of my soul he'll be loved and well taken care of for the rest of his life.

The smell of the air here always puts my body at ease as it chases itself, the cool chill of it descending deep down into my lungs. It actually feels as if I'm being cleansed of all the poison my body has been exposed to over the last thirteen years; the smells of the pines, honeysuckles and magnolia bushes remind me of the days that Jack and I roamed this street without a care in the world – it amazes me that our sense of smell as human beings is so directly linked to our memory, and how catching a whiff of something or having an unwanted stench invade your senses can set off one of two different chains of events. One is a swarming overflow of blissful memories being feelings of happiness; maybe the occasional replaying of a significant event in your life. The other is the complete opposite, which in turn is filled with regretful memories and feelings of sadness, accompanied with the rerun of something traumatic that occurred in your life.

To this very day, I can't stand the smell of burnt pork.

One Father's Day, while serving in Afghanistan, I had to medically evacuate several soldiers who'd been hit by a suicide bomber while riding reconnaissance in their vehicle. Once we'd got the injured soldiers transported out by helicopter, we were instructed to clean up the rest of the bomber and retrieve as many of the remains as possible. Lo and behold, less than fifty feet away from where I began my search I stumbled upon the bomber's singed, mutilated, severed leg next to a building wall. The smell of the burning flesh that clung to the charred, protruding bones seared an everlasting imprint on both my senses and brain as I stood there under the scorching sun, breathing in the scorched stink of a dead coward.

But, unbeknownst to all around me, the aftermath of Mr. Suicide Bomber's morning excursion wasn't the first time I'd been subjected to violence, death, or the disturbingly macabre; I'd learned all about those right here where I'm standing – Rhine Road.

I can hear the crickets chirping in the distance, the same song they've sung since I was a small boy. The frogs are calling for their mates with stylish vocals, which to me sound horrible, all while the calm wind blows ever so gracefully through the tall, majestic pines. I'm here tonight not only to reminisce about the

24

wonderful times I had while growing up on this street, but also to face the demons that have been haunting me and my dreams for the last thirteen years. Demons that kept me up at night more than the earth-shaking crash of mortar fire, or memories of random firefights combined. I have to do this thing for me, and no one else. I must come to terms with my past so that I may move on with my life.

As darkness begins to set in on Rhine Road, I watch the last sliver of daylight slope below the trees that stand directly in front of me. While I disregard the owls as they begin their nightly operas, I focus my attention to my old backyard and see that my basketball hoop is still exactly where I left it all those many years ago. Weeds and grass have wrapped themselves all the way up to engulf the backboard and now it resembles a basketball goal that Swamp Thing would shoot hoops on. I guess whoever moved into my grandparent's old house recently never got around to tearing the old bastard down, as unsafe as it looked. So here it is, like some lonely survivor of a Great Basketball Holocaust, becoming less and less visible to me as the darkness slowly swallows it up.

I shut my car door, walk down the old driveway and can't believe it's still partially paved with the remnants of the asphalt I remember so clearly. Weeds and grass are winning the battle over the pavement, though; green growth shoots out from the uncountable cracks that crisscross the lingering blacktop, like some oozing infection exuding from beneath the earth.

Snap!

I quickly turn around and with nervous eyes examine the woods directly behind me across the street. Something – or *someone* – was in there. I pause in total silence – listening, waiting and watching the woods.

Nothing.

Maybe it was just a raccoon, or some other furry creature chasing down its prey? A deep sigh of relief releases itself from my lungs and I turn back to resume my walk along the driveway. I postpone my trip a second time; my eyes blur and a faint vision of my old mobile home comes into focus on the flickering screen of my mind. It feels as I am suffering a hallucination, which is purposefully attempting to distract me from my purpose of being here.

Deep inside my imagination, I envision the trailer's long, white body stretched sideways across the yard, separated by rust-colored lines that run vertically every fifteen feet or so, and my old bedroom window that seems to scream for my attention. I spent many rainy days and sleepless nights gazing from that window upon the star-filled skies, or the torrential downpours that often took place upon the weed-riddled lawn. In my mind, the front porch, which hosted many stunts with hippity-hops from my brother and I, stood its ground under the cheap outer screen door that firmly connected itself to the blistering white entrance of the trailer - it's funny how I can remember what my trailer looked like way back then, yet I can't remember where the hell I put my car keys on a daily basis. I made so many wonderful memories growing up in that old trailer with my mother, Gayla, and our brother, Hunter; often times I wish I could return to those days, but of course I can't.

I take another deep breath of the fresh country air and feel it sweep down through my body. My chest begins to swell and a solitary tear rolls out of my left eye and trickles down my face. Wiping it away, I close my eyes and think back to 1989, the year I made some of my fondest memories as a child, and the time I began living some of my worst nightmares.

CHAPTER TWO

A TRIP DOWN MEMORY LANE: 1989

I was eight years old and rocking a killer mullet hairstyle. I was scrawny as hell, (weighed in at a whopping *seventy* pounds) and hyper as a field mouse on cocaine. I always wore spandex shorts of some sort, most of which were purchased by my mother from Wal-Mart. I never really wore a shirt much, so naturally I exhibited a nice tan almost all year round. I owned a blue bicycle that I rode everywhere I went – it was like my own *American Express* card; never left home without it.

Much later in life, I was diagnosed with *Attention Deficit Hyperactivity Disorder*, good ol' ADHD, but during those days growing up in the Deep South, despite diagnoses of hyperactivity having dated back to the late '60s, a kid like me was just considered a little badass with no home training.

Of course, that wasn't true; my mother was a great parent. She raised and disciplined me well to her utmost and did the most amazing job as a single mother. Shit, it's not easy raising children, period, especially those who are into every damned thing possible like my brother and I. My mother had been living on Rhine Road since way back in the '70s, many of her adolescent years having been spent here until she met my douchebag father in '78, married his no-good ass in '80 and moved from Rhine Road out to Robert, Louisiana. She had me dragged out of her stomach – *literally* kicking and screaming – via caesarean, and then came back to Rhine Road in '81.

That's right; you can't say I was ever wet behind the ears. No pussy ever slapped me in the face on the way out.

Our trailer was located about a hundred feet to the right of our grandparent's house – that's *Memaw* and *Pepaw* to my brother and I. Their home consisted of solid white slate rock—which produced a bright gleam of white only the clouds could envy—that supported your typical blacktop roofing. Inside, there were three bedrooms, one bath, a kitchen and a decent-sized living room. Momma told me once that Pepaw single-handedly ran all the plumbing—including the sewage—electric circuits and wiring throughout the house when it was being built. Pepaw was a latter day *Bob the Builder*, so to speak; it's sad that most men don't come handy like that anymore – hell, I can barely tighten up a screw in the rocking chair for my wife without my blood pressure rising! But Pepaw was special; one of the world's last real, great men and that's the God's honest truth.

Over the years, Pepaw had built his own shed, with matching white slate rock and all, just behind the house, and I recall seeing him in there, constantly practicing his carpentry skills on some piece of lumber he'd acquired from somewhere or another, and I remember watching him wipe sawdust away from that bushy mustache of his, shooting a smile back at me as I watched him work.

You see, Pepaw and Memaw were helping take care of us financially, since my no-good excuse for a father claimed he wasn't making enough money to send child support. We all knew that was horseshit.

My parents had only been officially divorced for two months and momma was too busy raising my brother and I to get a job; deep down, in the very fiber of her being, Momma felt that it was her sole responsibility and mission in life to raise us. I couldn't have agreed any more, if she had not been there for us, there's no telling if I'd actually still be alive today. Despite the divorce and the constantly present financial hardships, we as a family were extremely happy. Never were we upset, or depressed, especially about the divorce, although I suspected that my mother cried many tears behind closed doors, without my brother or I ever knowing for sure. That's how she protected us, by not letting us see her pain. Momma always had a smile on her face for us kids, no matter how bad she was hurting that day, or wondering how the hell she was going to be able to survive on her own; my dear mother always seemed to shield us from any of life's sorrows – and it worked, we never felt a thing.

Pepaw moved to Rhine Road in 1970 from Vivian, Louisiana after accepting a job with the Shell Oil Company out of New Orleans. Momma told me that when she'd moved to Rhine Road it was nothing more than a dirt road in the middle of the countryside. Over the years, the road was extended to about a mile and a half long and deep ditches were dug up on both sides to help decrease the flooding during the rainy months. Lining the man-made trenches stood the mountainous trees which casted a cool gaze upon the residents and offered a place of refuge from the unforgiving Louisiana sun. When I was younger, around six or seven years old, they made me think of oversized tree people watching a Mardi Gras Parade on a bright February afternoon, the wind swaying them from side to side as if they'd drunk too much bourbon.

Of course, Pepaw had to commute long drives to and from New Orleans, but Momma told me he liked the drive and actually appreciated the solitary peace of his monthly trips.

Most of Pepaw's time wasn't consumed in New Orleans behind a desk, but on oil rigs across America and in the middle of the Atlantic Ocean. He'd started off as a roughneck, but worked his ass off over the years and now spent his months in Saudi Arabia, Iraq and Yemen, always bringing back stories of the strange people he met there for Hunter and I, and gifts for the ladies. I remember well him telling me about children my age carrying machine guns in Saudi; in the not-so-distant future, I'm sure we wasted some of those kids after 9/11 – but let's not get me started on the war in Afghanistan, or we'll be here all damned day. All in all, Rhine Road was a quiet, peaceful street and that's why my mother and Pepaw always came back to it.

During the year 1989, houses were sprouting up faster than the weeds up and down the street. A sub-division that Alton Benson (the local real estate snob) had just finished construction on—christened *The Oaks*—quickly became a hot commodity. Even though the street was beginning to build up nicely, this was still the country and the sub-division wasn't all that big. The street names in The Oaks were named after Benson's sons, Daniel, Keith and Alvin. All three Momma knew personally, but they were even better acquainted with my Uncle Jerry. Momma said she eventually fell out of touch with them over the years; she wasn't the only one having kids and trying to survive life.

Rhine Road quickly filled with new faces and personalities. A mid-thirties couple, Matt and Julie Green, had moved into the house across the street from my grandparents'. They relocated from Mississippi and had two children, Kyle and Lucy. Kyle was about six years older than me, but Lucy was around my age. Then you had Mr. Littleton, a cripple confined to a wheelchair, who was accompanied by a sweet lady named Miss Lynda, a single mother with a child named Alex.

One day, I was hanging out with Alex, trying to catch minnows in one of the ditches by Pepaw's house and I'd asked, "How do they actually do it? His pecker doesn't even work!"

With a sly grin, Alex had responded with, "He just sucks on her tits and plays with her cooter; I've walked in on them a few times!"

At that, we laughed until it hurt.

Alex was a puny kid, not skinny like me but like a white version of the Ethiopians we saw on the TV documentaries. He was blonde, and had freckles all over his face, and his damned ears stood out like he was a wingnut or something. The poor kid was also incredibly impressionable, and I could get him to do pretty much anything I wanted him to.

During those early years on Rhine Road, Alex was the only person I could call a friend, but sometimes I fucked with him way too much. I recall one time convincing him that killer ninjas lived in the woods behind his house, and the poor little bastard couldn't sleep for weeks. Miss Lynda eventually picked up the phone, dialed Momma and asked her if she'd tell me to lay off the killer ninja bullshit since Alex couldn't sleep. What can I say? *Ninja Gaiden* was my favorite game at the time and I was obsessed with all things ninja, so why not make up a scary story to scare the shit out of someone? It wasn't my fault that I had a wild imagination, and although the numerous times I messed with Alex's head, he remained my first real friend on Rhine Road.

Around this time, Momma was dumb enough to convince Pepaw to get me a BB gun. I know, *you'll shoot your eye out* was the well-worn saying that stuck with those confounded things ever since *A Christmas Story* hit the theaters, but I loved it and can still see perfectly fine with both eyes. Anyhow, we owned a dog named Trixy – some kind of mixed breed that we people down south refer to as *shit-eaters*. If it wasn't a purebred, it was a shit-eater and boy, Trixy was a shit-eater, all right. She looked to be ninety percent Chihuahua and ten percent French bulldog. She was cute as could be though, and her white underbelly was always dirty, while the rest of her was black as midnight.

One day I happened outside to shoot my trusty BB gun and noticed a big-assed brown mutt digging in the bushes to the right of our trailer. I quietly reached into my pocket and pulled out my plastic cylinder filled with ammo. The tiny brass bullets were just itching to strike the mangy mutt and my heart was beating loud with excitement. I had yet to actually shoot anything with my gun, besides imaginary ninjas, so I dropped a brass ball down the end of the rifle and heard it set into place. I pulled back on the charging handle and pressed it firmly back down, thus arming the gun. I brought the BB gun up into firing position, looked down the sight and aimed center mass on the shit-eater who was still apparently trying his damndest to dig all the way to China. During this brief time of preparation, Trixy came into my peripheral vision from off to the right; she'd come around from the side of the trailer, and walked directly in my line of sight, her wide, brown eyes staring in my general direction. I began to pull back on the trigger and my sight steadied on the shit-eater who was oblivious to his fate. I felt my heart racing with the sheer thrill of the anticipated kill; even though I knew deep down that the BB wasn't really gonna kill shit. Then, all of a sudden, Momma opened the front door of our trailer; she'd been watching my hunting expedition from the window. "Be careful, Jody, don't hit Trixy!" she called over.

But it was too late.

I squeezed the trigger before Momma's sentence caught my attention. The brass BB departed so weakly I could practically track its path with my own two eyes. I watched the BB exit the gun's cheap barrel and I watched with rising panic as it flew towards Trixy...

And split second later, my poor dog took friendly fire to the rib cage. High pitched yelps and howls filled my ears and I looked back at Momma, who simply stared at me with grave disappointment, while in turn I cast her a look of honest regret.

Meantime, Trixy was giving an Oscar-winning performance for her injury. She took off yelping and hollering up our driveway and then banked a hard left onto Rhine Road, still yipping with pain, finishing up her journey by sharply turning up Pepaw and Memaw's driveway, and that damned dog didn't shut the hell up until she dove under the damned house. I felt totally ashamed of myself, I could only wonder what the poor neighbors thought was going on, and wished I could tell them all that it had been an honest-to-God accident. Trixy's performance had been epic and while deep down I wanted to laugh to avoid an ass whupping, I had to give my own Oscar-winning performance and remain story faced and immensely *sorry*. Let's just say I was able to pull an Emmy and only got a small ass chewing from Momma, but poor old Trixy never trusted me again.

Sorry, girl.

CHAPTER THREE

THE McSPADDENS: 1990

A year or so passed on Rhine Road and nothing really seemed to change. One day, I saw a little girl walking down the street with an incredibly tall man, and once they got a little closer, I realized the little girl was Jamie McSpadden. I remembered her because the year before, I'd played on the same softball team as her brother Jack. She also had a beauty mark under her left eye that gave her this radiance and the kind of face you just couldn't forget. When they noticed me staring, the two slowed down a little at the end of my driveway.

"Did you guys just move here?" I asked.

Jamie was about five or six years old at the time and she just nodded her head by means of a reply.

"I didn't, but she did," the man told me, his voice warm and kind. "I'm her grandfather; we were just taking a nice stroll down the street while her mommy and daddy finish unpacking. Her brother Jack is at his cousin's house and is staying there tonight; he'll be along tomorrow. You two boys should meet," he finished with a smile on his face.

"I already know Jack. We played on the same softball team last year," I told him.

"Well that's good," he replied, again with a warm smile. "I guess you boys won't have any problem making friends, since you already know one another." With that, he took hold of Jamie's hand. "We should get back home, though, nice meeting you," he concluded and continued his way along the street.

While I stood there squinting, I watched the two of them become more distant as they traveled further from my gaze and directly into the deep haze of the sun. I felt a twinge of excitement run through me; finally there'd be someone else to hang out with besides Alex.

Not more than a day later, I was inside playing *Mega-Man* on my Nintendo when I heard a knock on our trailer door. I don't know if you've ever lived in a trailer, but when someone knocks, it's like the whole damned place shakes with each knuckle rap. I jumped up and dashed from my room at breakneck speed, and out into the narrow hallway, making as much noise as I possibly could. I flew through the cramped kitchen, planning to be the first one to the door.

Then, seemingly from out of nowhere my mother appeared in front of me and opened the door just as I got to it.

"Renee!" she yelled at the top of her lungs, "*oh my God*, I can't believe you guys moved here! Come on in."

"Who is it, Momma? Who is it?" I asked, jumping up and down and trying to see over her shoulder. Momma just ignored me and motioned for the McSpadden family to come inside. Mrs. Renee stood there on the stoop with a smile on her face for a moment, and then motioned her kids inside our trailer.

Renee McSpadden was a pretty, blonde-haired

woman who stood about the same height as my mother and who always seemed to be smoking a cigarette – later in life, she'd quit cold turkey and shock the shit out of us all. She always gave off a good feeling when you were around her; it was akin to being around a person you'd known your whole life, even if you hardly knew her at all. Although my mother didn't realize it at the time, while watching Renee courteously put out her cigarette before entering our trailer, she was going to remain best friends with this woman for the rest of her life.

Jack came up the stairs into the trailer first, his hands behind his back and looking like some detective as he checked our place out. The kid was just as scrawny as me, but had blonde hair that looked untidy, as if it had never once seen a comb. He wore a pair of black spandex shorts just like mine and when I looked down at his feet I noticed he was bare-foot. Jack finished scanning the house and turned his head in my direction. "Jody!" he screamed.

I guess he was excited to see someone he knew. I mean, anyone who has ever moved to a new home knows exactly what I'm talking about. For a nine-year-old kid, moving to a new place can seem like the end of the world – but not for Jack McSpadden, it was just the beginning of a brand new and infinitely exciting friendship. We exchanged a few cursory words and then darted our asses out the front door of the trailer to the swing set in our front yard.

Once I became friends with Jack, Alex became real jealous. He would shoot us dirty looks and throw rocks and shit at us while we were on our bikes riding past his house. Every now and then we would allow him to play with us but in the end, we knew we would lose him along the way; quite possibly the straw that broke the

37

camel's back for Alex and I was when Jack beat the shit out of him in my front yard.

It had started off like any other day when Jack and I were together. We'd talk about video games, sports, guns and whatever else was on our minds at the time. Alex, who hadn't gotten the hint that we didn't want to play with him anymore, decided that he was going to walk over to my yard and show us his new karate moves he'd learned in the class his Mom had signed him up for that spring. The next thing I remember is Jack putting Alex in a headlock, then picking him up and slamming him hard into the ground. Alex let out a sharp screech of pain, which sounded to me kinda like a huge mouse squeaking, when his ribs cracked against the ground.

"You give up?" Jack yelled, tightening his hands on the back of Alex's neck.

"I give, I give!" Alex whined.

"You got him Jack! You got him!" I said, all the while jumping high up in the air like some freakish cheerleader.

At that very moment, I heard Alex's mom screaming at Jack from across the street, "Let him go, Jack! Let him go *right now*!"

Once Jack heard the yelling, he let Alex go. Alex stood up, crying fat tears with snot bubbling from his nose, and took off running back to his house, his arms flailing in every direction.

"I'm going to call your father, Jack!" Lynda yelled once more from across the street. "And you're going to get in *big* trouble, you bully!"

"Eat me!" Jack yelled back at Alex's mom.

I sat there dumbfounded for a minute or two, simply processing what had just transpired; Jack just said the words '*eat me*' to an adult.

"Holy shit," I said out loud.

The phrase seemed to just tumble from my mouth from shock; I'd never heard a kid talk back to an adult like that before, not once in my nine years on earth.

"You little *bastard*!" Lynda screamed back, her face red with frustration.

And the second she began striding purposefully across the street toward us, Jack was already hauling ass back to his own house, seeking the protection of his own mother. Lynda stopped just as she reached the edge of my yard, raised her fist into the air to shake toward the fleeing Jack. She looked back at me, shaking her head in disappointment (like it was my fault her son got his ass whipped), turned around and went home.

From that point on, Alex was never allowed to play with us again, which really didn't matter to me because he moved to New Orleans about three months later. After that, Jack and I became best friends and were always doing something that made our parents crazy whenever we got together. If we weren't pulling dead animals out of ditches, throwing rocks at houses, putting dog shit in mailboxes and beating on front doors then running away, that only meant we weren't together that particular day. We quickly gained a reputation on the street as the little *motherfuckers* of Rhine Road, and we were still only nine years old; and what our neighbors didn't know was that over the next couple of years we were only going to get worse. Jack and I didn't care what anyone thought of us at all, we were proud of our title, and considered it rightfully earned.

My Pepaw had a dog he'd named Rambo, one of the ugliest dogs ever to step foot on Rhine Road. He was a brown shit-eater that always had thick, oozing eye boogers cemented in the corner of his eyes. His tongue had sort of a blackish color to it and always carried an everlasting smell of shit; but to a kid like me, he was the absolute coolest dog on the planet. Rambo and I did everything together, we were virtually inseparable, apart from the one time he was taken to the pet hospital for over a month for God knows what—Pepaw said he ate something that he shouldn't have—and I missed him like hell. Eventually, Rambo made a full recovery and returned home. And for me, there was nothing much better than having that dog and Jack by my side; I was happy and safe, oblivious to the evil that lurked so very closely all around me.

CHAPTER FOUR

EVIL HAS COME

Lewis Rhine marched up the Jones's driveway late one afternoon. He was a firecracker ready to explode, the anger clear on his face for all to see.

Boom, Boom, Boom!

The intrusive clatter he made on the front door carried all the way into the kitchen, where Teddie was making dinner. She stood up, hoping it wasn't her daughter with news of yet another injury obtained by one of the boys, but Gayla always used the back door that connected directly to the kitchen. Teddie tugged off her apron, turned down the burners on the stove and made her way toward the front door.

"Mr. Rhine, what brings you down here to our side of the street?" she said with a big, beautiful smile.

"Mrs. Jones, I need to talk to your husband right away. It's a matter that needs to be discussed right now. Not tomorrow – but today."

Lewis Rhine was a crusty old man with a bristly mustache that slunk on his face and which always seemed in need of tightening up. His glasses dug deep into his lower brow and the smell of dairy clung to his farmers' overalls.

"Sure, Lewis, I'll go get Jerry. Would you like to come in and –"

"No," Rhine interrupted, "I'll wait here on the porch, if you don't mind."

"Sure, wait here."

Moments later, Lewis took two steps back as Jerry, the biggest man on Rhine Road, stepped out onto the porch.

"Well, well. I've been living on this street for quite some time now, and this is the first time you've ever made it all the way to my house to chat, Lewis. It must be something very important," Jerry said to Rhine, with a calm yet stern voice.

"It's your goddamned dog, Jerry!"

"Rambo?" Jerry said, puzzled.

"Yes, *Rambo*, if that's what you call the little sumbitch."

"What's he done, Lewis?"

"He killed two of my goddamned cows, that's what he's done!"

"What?" Jerry was shocked by this revelation. "Rambo couldn't have killed any of your cows, Lewis. That's impossible; he isn't even fully grown yet."

"But I saw your damned dog do it!" Lewis exclaimed, now sounding like a lawyer stating his case to the jury.

"You saw Rambo attack your cows?" Jerry quizzed the man, even though he could pretty much tell Lewis Rhine was lying straight to his face. Rambo might have been named after Stallone's hard-ass, but that dog couldn't harm a fly, let alone a pair of dairy cows. It was a lie, and Lewis was trying to blame anything and anyone for his financial loss.

"How were they killed, Lewis?"

"Their fucking hearts were eaten out of their damned chests, Jerry."

"Their hearts were eaten out of their chests," Jerry repeated. He knew full well that wasn't physically possible, a dog could rip out a throat and gorge on the meat, not waste its time gnawing through ribs. And besides, Jerry had seen Rambo playing with his grandson that morning and there was no blood on Rambo at all, not one drop.

"Bottom line is they're dead, and it's gonna cost me a good chunk of dough to replace them. And that goddamned shit-eater of yours had everything to do with it! There was blood everywhere in my damned barn – it's taken me all morning to clean up the mess your dog made."

"Did you actually *see* it happen, or are you just assuming this is what happened?" Jerry remained calm.

"I'm not *assuming* anything, Jerry! I woke up last night when I heard the thing rustling around in the barn. Right around midnight it was – and I ran out of the house in my damned underwear. I got to the barn just in enough time to see your ugly ass shit-eater running off toward the road."

"And you're one hundred percent certain it was Rambo, Lewis?" Jerry snorted his derision. "This is just absurd."

"I wouldn't be here if I wasn't sure, Jerry," Lewis said, sarcastically. "And I don't care how far-fetched this sounds to you. It was a full moon last night; I could have spotted a wild hair on a man's ass standing two hundred feet away."

Jerry's heart all of a sudden felt like it was falling into the depths of his stomach. He placed his hands on the doorknob to steady himself from falling onto the porch. He then looked back up and met Lewis Rhine's face.

"You alright, Jerry?" Rhine said.

How could Jerry not have seen it sooner? How could he be so stupid? The truth hit him like a power surge in a thunderstorm. He'd been caught off guard – maybe because he hadn't heard about *them* for quite some time. Nevertheless, Jerry knew in that instant precisely what had killed Lewis Rhine's cattle, and it certainly hadn't been Rambo.

"Jerry?! You all right, big guy?" Rhine's anger turned quickly to concern, "You look like you've just seen a ghost."

"I'm alright, Lewis, I'm alright. Guess I just lost some wind."

"I know how that is," Lewis said, calming down. "I can hardly bend down to tie my own boots nowadays without my back going out on me. Old age, I guess," he added with a knowing nod.

"Yeah, I know what you mean," Jerry said. "Look, Lewis. I'm sorry about your cows. It's terrible that happened, and I know this is gonna set you back some, financially. But, if it was my dog, I can assure you that it won't happen again."

Once more, Lewis Rhine's face turned bright, cherry red and rage poured from his mouth. "That's *it*!? You're just going to let the little shit-eater run around like nothing ever happened? You need to put him down, Jerry! *He slaughtered my damned cows!"*

"Not gonna happen, Lewis," Jerry said calmly. "That would break my grandson's heart. Since my daughter got divorced, the kid's been playing with that dog every damned day. I can't do that to him."

"Well that's just another reason to kill the little shit-eater! You don't want a dangerous dog like that playing with your grandson, do you, Jerry?" Rhine growled, his eyes squinty and mean.

"Like I said, Lewis, I'm sorry about your cows an' all, but I'm not going to kill Rambo. I'll gladly pay you the money you need."

"I don't want your goddamned money!" Lewis spat. "I want that shit-eater put down so he doesn't do this again!"

"I promise you, Lewis, it won't happen again. You have my word."

Defeated, Rhine backed away – physically as well as mentally – "Well, if I catch your dog anywhere near my herd again, you won't have to worry about putting him down, 'cause I'll put a bullet right between his fucking eyes myself! And *you* have *my* word on that!" He took a step backwards, ready to be gone from Jerry's stoop. "So unless you want your damned dog dead and to meet me in court, keep that thing off my goddamned property!" And with that, Rhine turned on his heels and stormed off the porch and back toward the driveway.

Jerry didn't say a word. He just stood there on the porch and watched Lewis make his way down the driveway to his pick-up truck. Jerry knew what he had to do now. He looked over to his daughter's trailer and saw his grandson playing with Rambo in the front yard. They looked like they were having the time of their lives, and it reminded Jerry of his own time as a youth. He took a deep, wheezing breath, turned around and went back into the house.

"We have to put Rambo in the shelter," Jerry said, walking straight past his wife and directly toward his car keys that hung on a nail on the wall in the kitchen.

"What? Why, Jerry? What was Lewis yelling about on the porch?" Teddie asked, as her eyes wide.

Jerry shrugged, non-committal. "All I can say is that Lewis Rhine will be back in a month. And when he does, he's in for a big surprise," Jerry told his wife. Teddie just listened; she knew when her husband had something to do it was best to step back and just let him get on with it, a lesson learned when they'd first got together, way back in the day when Teddie had been just sweet sixteen. Jerry walked over to his keys, grabbed them, picked up the phone, and called his daughter.

Gayla was busy cleaning the kitchen when the phone rang, her mind running on blank; the boys had tracked mud all over the kitchen floor again, dashing in and out of the trailer. This had become an everyday occurrence for her since the sporadic rains had arrived, and every day Gayla did the same thing to ensure a tidy home. Resting the mop against the cheap laminate counter top, she walked over to the ringing phone.

"Hello?"

"Sissy."

"Yeah, Daddy."

"Bring Jody inside the house," her father's voice instructed, "I have to take Rambo to the shelter right away. I'll explain everything to you and your mother later. Just tell Jody the dog's sick, and he has to go to the veterinarian for a while."

"Okay," Gayla said, very slowly, her mind burning with a dozen questions at once, but she didn't dare ask any of them; she knew her father just as well as her mother did.

"I know he'll be upset, but I'll talk to him about it later. I have to go. Love you. Bye."

"Bye," Gayla said, and hung up the phone. Of course, she didn't know what was going on, but she did know that it couldn't be good. With a heavy sigh, Gayla walked to the front door and scanned outside for her son.

"JODY!" Gayla yelled at the top of her lungs. Her son came running full-pelt around the corner of the trailer, and Gayla smiled upon the beautiful creation she'd made. Even though she wore two smiling scars across her belly from both her boys' cesareans, she wore them with great pride.

"Yes, Momma," Jody panted.

"You need to come inside for a minute, Bubba."

"Ok, Momma. See ya later, Rambo!!" Jody yelled back to his dog, who was occupied taking a mountainous shit in the middle of the yard. Jody ran up the steps of his porch and darted past his mother into the trailer, a trail of muddy shoe prints in his wake. Gayla looked at Rambo with a heavy heart and sadness in her eyes and then closed the door.

Several hours passed by, but as soon as Jerry was back from dropping Rambo off at the shelter, he parked his car and made his way over to his daughter's trailer. He knocked on the door and Gayla opened it, welcoming her beloved father in with a hug and kiss to the cheek. Jerry looked around the house and saw both of his grandkids sitting on the floor playing with their toys; the tearaway Jody, and his sweet baby brother with golden blond hair, Hunter, who was just as cute as could be. Jerry sat himself down on the couch with a forced smile playing across his lips.

"Hey, Pepaw," Jody said, then went right back to playing.

"Rambo's going to stay in the animal hospital for a while," Jerry told the boy, "He might come back, and he might not. But if he doesn't come back, I'll get you a new puppy."

Jerry had told the shelter, located in the small town of Ponchatoula, to go ahead and put Rambo up for adoption. Of course, he wouldn't tell his grandsons this – he knew better – and he fully intended to get Jody a new dog if the kid really wanted one. Hunter was still too young to even care about the dog; he had more than enough imaginary friends to keep him company.

"No, that's okay, Pepaw. Rambo's going to get better fast, and he'll be back in no time," Jody said with smile that radiated innocence. It really hadn't occurred to him that his beloved dog might not come back.

"Alright, Bubba, I'll talk to you later," Jerry said with a wan smile. He ruffled the boy's hair and let out a sigh of relief that telling his grandson the bad news had gone smoothly, even if he'd had to flower it up a little.

"Gayla," Jerry spoke quietly, "when the boys are asleep, come over to the house, I need to talk to you and your mother about today."

Gayla eyed her father with suspicion; it wasn't like him to be so cryptic. "Sure. They'll be knocked out in bed in a couple hours or so – I'll call before I come over," she said.

"Okay then, Sissy, I'll see you later," Jerry got up from the couch, bent down to give his grandsons each a kiss on the cheek and then stood back up. Immersed in their imaginary worlds, the two boys didn't notice, and Jerry just smiled. He envied them, that youthful ability to have that special inner place where nothing in the world seemed to matter. He smiled once again at his grandchildren and walked out the door.

"Okay, you two! Get your butts in bed and go to sleep!" Gayla yelled through the paper-thin doors to her sons' bedrooms. Muffled giggles followed, giving away their after-bedtime fun. Most likely Jody would have been running out of his room and into Hunter's, making those sticky fart sounds with his hands and laughing up a storm along the way.

Eventually, both Jody and Hunter fell asleep, after two more yellings and one threatened ass whoopin' with the belt. Gayla waited until she was sure they were both deep in slumber, then slid out the door and over to her parents' house.

And so, Jerry told his wife and daughter about Lewis Rhine's accusations. Teddie and Gayla just sat there quietly, mouths half open, not saying a word and trying to make sense of what Jerry was telling them. And, although Jerry told them what happened so far as Rhine's crazy theory about Rambo, and that he'd had to put the dog up for adoption, he stopped short of telling *everything* he knew.

Jerry didn't tell what *really* was killing Lewis's cattle.

He kept that particular nugget all to himself and his conscience, and let his family go on believing that nothing terrible was going on, just a crazy old dairy farmer and a dog that may or may not have been worrying his damned cattle.

***

A month later, Jerry was watching football on the TV; the New Orleans Saints were losing again, this time to the Green Bay Packers, and the exponential rising of his blood pressure signaled now was a good time to turn off the game. There came a sudden, panicked knock at the front door; it had happened again.

Jerry placed the remote down on the arm of his chair, rose up and answered the door.

"Hello, Lewis. How've you been?" Jerry smiled at his somewhat not unexpected visitor.

"Don't give me your bullshit, Jerry! Your dog has –"

"My dog has done absolutely nothing," Jerry

interjected, "I dropped Rambo off at the shelter the last time you were here accusing him of killing your cattle, Lewis."

"What?"

Clearly, the man knew the jig was up. Jerry Jones had outplayed him and all he could do now was stand there and look at his feet.

"I don't know what your problem is with me, Lewis," Jerry said quietly, "But I hope it's resolved now. Like I told you the last time you were here, my dog did not kill your cattle. I believe it is something far more than just an animal that's responsible."

"Well, who's responsible then?" Lewis demanded.

Rhine's entire demeanor had changed now; he'd thought he seen Rambo running away that night a month ago when he'd found his cows all chewed up, but perhaps he'd been mistaken in the heat of the moment. He really didn't know what killed them that night; it was obvious that Lewis Rhine had seen what he wanted to see. Plus, he'd never really liked Jerry Jones. He was jealous because the man had more money and a better life than he, so who better to blame than the person you detest? Now, though, Lewis Rhine was scared; he didn't know what was responsible for the killings, and he just knew that it wasn't about to stop anytime soon – Lewis Rhine was up shit creek without a paddle.

"That's something you have to figure out. Not me. Why not try using your brain? Have a nice day," Jerry growled and slammed the door shut just inches from Lewis Rhine's worried face.

Jerry leaned his back against the door, let out a sigh of relief and waited for his unwanted guest to go away, pleased that the confrontation was over and that his plan had worked. He knew, though, deep down in his troubled soul that dark forces were working their way into the country area where he lived; he thought back to 1975, when his son had said he'd witnessed something sinister within the woods. He recalled the myriad meetings with all the church leaders and most of all; he remembered the fear that had come along with all of that.

Jerry was forced to come to the conclusion that something evil was now present on Rhine Road.

That night, Jerry made his way into his bedroom, tiptoeing silently past his sleeping wife, who's light snores purred from between her slack lips. He took off his clothes, climbed in alongside her and before he closed his eyes Jerry prayed hard for his family. He prayed for God to protect them from the malevolent things that he knew were skulking about the town, and he prayed even harder for his grandkids, begging the Good Lord to watch over and protect them.

"And if anything should happen, Lord, let it happen to me. Amen," Jerry ended.

No more than two weeks later, Rambo showed back up to the house.

Evidently, the well-meaning person who'd adopted him had forgotten to keep him locked up, and the dog found his way back to his old home on Rhine Road. Jody was ecstatic and Jerry stood on the porch, shaking his head back and forth at the joyful reunion.

"Can you believe that dog, honey?" Teddie smiled.

"He sure did like it here, didn't he?" Jerry stated.

"The little rascal ran all the way from the Kentons' house, and that's at least six miles away. They only adopted him five days ago and he's already escaped," Teddie said, with a big, soppy grin on her face.

"Call the Kentons, honey, and see if they want him back," Jerry instructed.

"Already did. They said we could keep him if we

wanted to."

"Look at little Jody's face. What do you think?" Jerry matched his wife with a smile that seemed to stretch from ear to ear.

This would be the last fond reunion between the boy and his best friend, for a month later Rambo was struck by a car out on the street and died twitching in the gutter.

CHAPTER FIVE

NIGHTS LIKE NO OTHER: 1990

My brother Hunter really was something else.

Let me tell you, that boy had so many nicknames while growing up it was ridiculous. One day it was Hunter-man, then Pudge, then Roo-Rha-Pooh-La-De-Da and finally Ra-tou-ka-ly. Don't ask me how my mother came up with these ridiculous names, because honestly, I have no idea.

Hunter was an adorable child with golden blond hair; he was also very short and had a cute little speech impediment. The kid was four and a half years younger than me, but that never slowed him down one iota when it came to playing; he was hyper like me, and a tough little shit to boot. So much so, he once beat the shit out of a kid of my age with a water hose that he found from under Memaw's house. That kid took off running and hid under Memaw's porch for over an hour, too scared to come out, all because of Hunter.

There were no other kids of Hunter's age on Rhine Road, so he was always playing with me after Jack and I were done for the day. I remember this one day we were outside playing baseball and Hunter had pissed me off because he wouldn't let me have a turn batting. Naturally, everyone wants to bat; no one ever wants to play the outfield all day. So, when he continued to refuse to share I bent down, grabbed a crayfish hole and threw it at him. Now, if you don't know what a crayfish hole is, take a trip down to Louisiana and look around for towers of hardened mud that resemble little dirt fortresses. Crayfish extract the soil, bring it up to the surface and build a nice little home for themselves. When the pellets and globs of mud dry, they're hard as nails and that's what struck Hunter in the hand and sent him charging at me like a crazed bull.

Well, that little bastard sucker-punched the shit right out of my left eye, and instantly it began to swell like someone stuck a dark purple balloon under my skin. Hunter and I stood sobbing in the backyard, Hunter's weeping a little more dramatic than mine because he thought he'd blinded me, until our cries got the attention of our mother. Momma came outside, beat the shit out of us both for fighting, and then made us – literally – kiss and make up. Then she'd had the nerve to come back outside with the camera and take a picture of the two of us crying on the porch like two little schoolgirls. There's one thing I can say now that I couldn't say then; we were some badass kids.

Bill Murray was our favorite actor at this point in our young lives, and so Hunter and I would stay up to the late hours on the weekends with Momma, and we'd watch either *Meatballs* or *Stripes*. Those movies were just so damned funny – Bill would work his magic on screen with his wild, out of control hair and make us all but piss our pants with laughter. Those times helped out Momma a lot too; the divorce had taken a pretty nasty toll on her, and she was fighting some kind of depression. On school nights, there was no Bill Murray with Momma, we were put to bed at eight sharp, but Hunter and I would still mess around in our rooms 'til about ten, and I think that secretly, Momma knew that we did.

Anyways, when the weekends would finally roll around Momma would sit on the love seat, which was on the left side of our living room, beneath the sliding window that looked out into our backyard. Late at night when you looked out that window, it was so dark that you could barely see anything, not even Memaw and Pepaw's house, which was only a hop, skip and a jump away. A typical night on Rhine Road was normally pitch black; I often imagined it to be akin to the darkness that *Jack the Ripper* and his friends used to hang out in. Every time I had to take out the trash, I would haul ass to the garbage cans at the end of the driveway, throw the bags into its respected can and beat feet back to the trailer like some dribbling, hideous monster was right behind me.

There were no streetlights, therefore when the sun went down, you went down as well. Living on Rhine Road wasn't like living in the big city where there is constant noise and glowing lights to keep you company during the night. The only type of light you got in Hammond at night was when there was a full moon, and of course that only came around once a month. To me though, those nights when the moon was full made being outside even creepier than the inky darkness alone. The moonlight had a way of making cold shadows out of every little thing it touched, giving off a bright glow that illuminated like some weird, ghostly luminescence. It always looked to me like snow was on the ground when the moon shone its brightest, and I remember how the phone lines used to cast long, stretched out shadows on the ground to make it look like railroad tracks ran through your yard. And the only thing that could be heard on those soulless nights when you stood still was the sound of God's creatures stirring in the darkness.

So, this one night, we boys were sitting opposite our mother on the big couch, all comfortably positioned for a night of fun and hilarity with one Mr. Bill Murray and around 11:45 the Hunter-man passed out. My little brother actually fell asleep sitting up, and momma whispered from the couch, "Lay him down, Bubba. Pudge is knocked out. He's had a long day."

"Okay, Momma," I whispered back.

I did as she asked and laid Hunter carefully down on the couch, and then I was back to watching our favorite comedian.

"ARMY TRAINING SIR!!" Bill yelled to the man standing on the stage behind the podium. This was at the end of the movie, and my most favorite part. They would twirl their rifles in the air, do some cool choreography, sing the *Why did the Chicken Cross the Road* song and that would be about the last laugh of the night for me. So, as the credits started to roll and John Candy marched his group of shitbag soldiers off into the sunset, Momma looked over to me.

"You ready for bed, Bubba?"

"Not really. What's coming on after this?"

"I have no idea, Bubba. I didn't get the TV Guide out of the mailbox today. I'm pretty sure – it's nothing – good," she said, while yawning.

"Okay. I guess I'll take Hunter to bed with me now, then," I said, getting up off the couch, stepping over the scattered toys that Hunter had left right below my feet.

I stopped, stretched my back a bit and bent down to

pick Hunter up when I heard something.

Thump... Thump, Thump, Thump... Thump...

I looked over to Momma, my eyes asking the obvious question. Momma quit yawning and sat up, straight as a board on the couch. She turned off the TV with the remote and looked back at me as I stood there in the middle of the living room with my head cocked slightly to one side as I tried to figure out where the hell the sound was coming from. The loud, rhythmic thumping was coming from outside the trailer; it had a constant, irritating groove to it that repeated itself and oddly enough it made me want to dance around in a circle like a war painted Apache in the old westerns.

It stopped.

"What on earth was that, Jody?" Momma asked, finally breaking the silence between us.

"I don't know, Momma," I replied, my heart thumping wildly in my chest. "What do you think it is?"

"Shhh –" she hissed.

Thump... Thump, Thump, Thump... Thump...

There it was again.

That same rhythmic beat we'd just heard moments before, like some kind of otherworldly heartbeat that the night was producing all on its own. It sure as heck didn't sound like someone bumping *Soul II Soul's Back to Life* on the radio at a high volume, but something altogether more.

Momma got up on her knees on the couch, pulled the sliding window to the right as hard as she could and poked her head out of the window and into the darkness. She scanned the yard from left to right and then looked up at the dark sky. The clouds were thick and bloated and blocked out the moon as if God himself had covered it with a blanket. A thunderstorm was definitely approaching, and by the look of things, it would be arriving in Hammond shortly. As soon as the window was open, the cool wind from outside blew through my hair and the thumping sound became even louder. It made my heart race like I was running a marathon.

"Is that drums, Jody?" Momma asked me; I could see the eerie beat was making her feel uneasy.

"I think so. Is that what you think it is too, Momma?"

"Yeah. That's what it sounds like to me," She said quietly, not wanting to wake Hunter. "But who the hell is banging on drums at this hour? Jody, go check the microwave and see what time it is," she instructed.

I took off like a bat out of hell and ran into the kitchen to check the time on the microwave's built in clock. My heart was racing as I looked at the blinking green timer as it flashed on and off, displaying *12:02.*

"Well, what does it say, Jody?" Momma called from the couch.

"Two minutes after midnight."

"Oh," she said, calming down a tad. "It's probably drunken high school kids back there in the woods past Hilton Road, beating on tin cans or some such." And so saying, Momma shut the window all the way and turned back around. "They'll stop soon, there's bad weather coming. But if they don't, somebody will just call the cops on them. They got a lot of old folks that live back that way and they don't like being disturbed this time of the night."

"What if it doesn't stop, Momma?" I asked.

My heart was beginning to slow back down after the big rush of whatever it was that had washed over me like some cold fever. It might have been fear, or excitement, I don't know, but it certainly wasn't the last time I would get this feeling.

"It'll stop, Bubba." Momma reassured. "Like I said, it's just a bunch of drunken teenagers making a bunch of racket – nothing to be worried about." Momma said, with one of her special smiles. "When your Daddy and I were dating, we would go in the woods and shoot rifles in the middle of the night at the trees. I used to think it was so much fun; this type of thing is just a stage kids go through. Let's just be happy that its tin cans they're beating on and we don't have bullets flying through our windows."

I gave Momma a little grin and turned back around to pick Hunter up. I lifted him gently off the couch and made my way toward his room. Even though he was a short little thing, my brother's ass seemed to weigh a ton. I kicked the door to his room open, wobbled over to his bed and dropped him down on it with little ceremony. I tucked the kid in nice and tight, turned off the light and exited the room.

As I was shutting his door, I looked back over to Momma, who was poking her head out the window again and listening to the drum beat that wafted over on the darkness. After a moment or two, she pulled her head back into the trailer, looked at me and blew me a kiss goodnight. I jumped up and pretended to catch the imaginary kiss that was soaring my way. We both smiled at each other and I walked over to my room, which was next to Hunter's and I opened the door. I walked over to my bed, un-tucked the covers and climbed in, getting myself nice and cozy under my newly purchased *Super Mario Brother* bed sheets. I closed my eyes and tried to get to sleep, but all I could do was listen to the sound of those drums; I could still hear them in my room and even though it was faint, it was still there. I did try to think about something else, but my mind was filled by that haunting beat.

CRACK!!

Lightning struck outside my window and turned the

inside of my room turn a bright, electric blue. At that moment, I stopped thinking about the drums and pulled my covers up to my chin, and rain began beating down on the trailer, sounding like a million needles falling from the sky. I glanced nervously over to my closet to make sure it was closed… and it was, thank God.

As the rain came down ever harder, the last thing I remember was its thrumming pitter-patter sound as I drifted off to sleep.

***

We finally got the hell out of school for the summer, and I couldn't have been more excited about getting out of the fourth grade, the main reasons being I couldn't stand my teacher, and all the kids in my class annoyed the shit out of me.

I had recently been diagnosed with a severe under bite by the orthodontist three weeks before school let out. I was told I'd have to wear braces for about three years as I was starting to look like a piranha, so Momma took me in fast. Memaw and Pepaw forked out the dough, and they slapped those shiny bastards on my teeth quick, snap and in a hurry. And so, thanks to those damned braces, all the kids in school began picking on me, and to top it all off, I had to wear fucking headgear as well.

I guess the kids all thought it was pretty hilarious watching me walk around school with a football-type mask on my face. They'd all point and laugh at me, so I'd reach into my mouth, un-hook one of the rubber bands that was attached from my braces to my headgear and I'd shoot it directly at their faces. Of course, I always got caught doing that and the teacher, or teachers in some cases, would start yelling. Then I'd go to the office, they'd call Momma and I'd go home to get my ass beaten.

And that was how the last week of fourth grade went for me, but deep down I really didn't care. Fourth grade was about to be over and the summer was here.

Finally, on the last day of school, the bell rang and I took off out of the classroom, passing all the other kids, busting out the main doors of the school like the place was on fire. The buses were lined up around the flagpole, and I stopped to scan for my bus number – 7-H. I looked from left to right, and finally found it, the first bus in line, so I ran up to the door and it swung open. I looked up and there sat Ms. Kenton, the meanest bus driver to ever drive the streets of Hammond, Louisiana. She had hair that stuck up in the air like she had just been electrocuted, and a set of lips that put *Steve Tyler* to shame – I always had to hold back from laughing every time I set my eyes on her.

"You ready for the summer, son?" she asked me with her raspy voice.

"Yes I am, Ms. Kenton," I replied; I was looking at the ground at this point, because if I made eye contact with her, I knew I'd be done for – the laughs would just burst right out of me.

"I could tell. You ran up here so fast you almost took the doors off the bus."

"I'm just glad it's summer time, that's all."

"You and me both," Ms. Kenton spit out. "Now get on the bus!"

I said no more and did what she told me. Once I was on, I went to my assigned seat at the back of the bus and sat down. Shortly after that, the bus began to fill up with the rest of the kids and we were off.

"Sit down and stay in your *SEATS*!!" Ms. Kenton screamed at the top of her lungs.

All the kids on the bus ignored her and continued to do what they were doing. I was staring blankly out the window when John from the seat behind me tapped me on my shoulder.

"Guess what, man?"

"What?"

"I got spit ball pens!"

"*COOL*, where did you get them from?" I asked.

"I made them in class today. Everybody was outside at recess, but I stayed in the bathroom to make them," John explained.

He lifted his backpack up off the floor and placed it in his lap. He opened it and pulled out three empty BIC pens. He had pulled off the little black cap from the end of each one, removed the points from the tips and had carefully taken out the plastic ink tubing from the inside. He took the pen from the middle and handed it to me.

"Thanks, John," I said, taking the empty pen from his hand.

"You want some paper?" John asked.

"Sure, give me some."

"Not a problem, I got a whole notebook full!"

He reached into his backpack and pulled out his notebook, ripped a sheet of paper out and handed it to me.

"Thanks," I said, "Now watch this."

I ripped a small piece off and stuck it into my mouth. I chewed it up until it was a nice little hard ball. All the kids behind me started getting excited because they wanted to see me whack somebody with the spitball.

"Watch little Suzy Thompson up there on the second row," I said, feeling like Billy the Kidd.

I lifted the empty pen up to my lips, aimed at my target's head and blew with all my might.

SPLAT!!

"OOOWWWW!!" Suzy shrieked out loud.

The spitball had smacked her square on the cheek and all the kids started laughing their asses off.

"You got her, Jody – you got her!" John laughed.

"Watch this one," I said, scanning the bus for my next victim, "Chris Rogers, two rows up."

"Do it, do it, do it," John exclaimed, squirming back and forth in his seat with eagerness.

I chewed another piece of paper, lifted the empty pen back up to my mouth, aimed at Chris's head and blew.

WHACK!!!

"Who did that?!" he yelled, "Who did that?"

"Holy shit, Jody, that one smacked him dead on the ear."

"Stop laughing! He'll see us and figure it out," I said.

"No he won't, he's a dumbass. He failed the fourth grade – again."

"No way?" I was completely shocked.

"Yes way, he probably can't even spell his own name," John said, making us all crack up again with uncontrollable laughter.

"I dare you to hit Ms. Kenton, Jody," a sweet voice said.

The laughter stopped, and the back of the bus fell silent as if the Grim Reaper himself had just joined us. This suggestion had come from one of the quietest kids on the bus – Angela. She was a pretty blonde-haired girl with sparkling blue eyes who had just moved to Rhine Road about two weeks ago. She'd moved from Mississippi because her father had got some new job in Hammond that paid him better money. She lived at the far end of Rhine Road, in a big red two-story house. Her family was really quiet, and extremely religious from what Momma had told me when I asked about the new family on our street.

This was the first time Little Miss Quiet had chosen to speak to me and she'd had the nerve to ask me to hit the meanest bus driver in the world with a spitball. Everyone in the back of the bus was shocked as well, I think because no one had ever heard her talk before.

"You want him – to hit Ms. Kenton – with a spitball?" John sounded nonplussed.

"That is what I said, wasn't it?" Angela snapped back with more than a little bit of attitude.

"You must be out of your mind, Ms. Kenton is pure evil! She'll kill all of us if you do something like that. You'd have to –"

"I'll do it," I said, interrupting John's speech while looking into Angela's eyes. She was looking back into mine and my heart started beating faster than a galloping pony. My body began to feel hot, and I pulled my shirt from my neck to get some cool air down there, and it felt like everything around me was moving in slow motion. Angela's cheeks turned red, and finally she broke the stare to look down to the floor.

"Hello? Are you going crazy, Jody? Ms. Kenton will eat you alive if she sees you!"

"Well – I'd best not get caught then," I said with bravado.

I slipped another wad of paper in my mouth and chewed it up until I got a nice-sized ball. Once more I raised that empty pen to my mouth and aimed at the back of Ms. Kenton's head. Everyone fell silent again and I looked over at Angela who was on the edge of her seat watching me with a big smile on her cute face. I focused back on my target and aimed a lot higher. I knew I'd have to blow pretty hard to hit the driver since she was all the way up front, and if I didn't aim high enough the spit ball would fall short.

"Here we go," I said, and I blew with all my might.

SMACK!

"Aaahhh!" Ms. Kenton screamed and yanked the steering wheel hard to the right.

The bus jolted and half the kids screamed for their lives. I tried to duck down into my seat, but Ms. Kenton had turned the wheel so hard, the momentum lifted my feet off the floor.

"We're going to die!" Ben Matthews cried out from two seats in front of me as the bus came to a screeching, juddering halt on the side of the road.

We were all flung forward into the seats in front of us, unceremoniously falling back into an upright position when the bus finally came to a halt. Kenton stood up, and walked down the middle of the walkway. Every kid was quiet, sitting nice and straight and showing Ms. Kenton the most respect she'd seen all year. It looked to me that her lips had gotten a little bigger, her hair standing even straighter up off her scalp as she reached behind her head and grabbed my spitball from the back of her neck. Slowly, deliberately, Ms. Kenton brought the offending projectile around to her face and studied it like it was a piece from some heinous crime scene.

"Holy shit, Jody," John whispered, "you hit her in the damned neck."

"I want to know," Ms. Kenton said calmly, clearly trying hard to hold back from screaming, "Who hit me with – *this*?"

She'd almost made it without yelling – almost.

"It came from the back, Ms. Kenton. Somebody hit me on the ear with one," Chris Rogers whined.

I thought silently to myself, *Momma is going to beat the living shit out of me for this,* as Ms. Kenton inched closer to the back of the bus. Chris Rogers, that whiny little bitch, had given Ms. Kenton a direction in which to check now.

"Angela," Ms. Kenton asked sweetly, "do you know who did this?"

"No, ma'am," Angela replied, still looking down at the ground.

I could tell the gal was nervous, but she made it through.

"How about you, Jody? Do you know who did this?" Ms. Kenton asked me.

I could tell she was studying me hard, so I had to play it cool. I took a deep breath and said the first piece of bullshit that came to my mind. "No ma'am, I don't even know what that is – looks like a booger to me."

After that comment, the majority of the bus laughed, including me.

"You know what this is?" Ms. Kenton yelled. "Don't play dumb with me, boy! I don't care if this is the last day of school! This will not be tolerated! If I catch anyone doing something like this again next year, you'll *all* be suspended for a whole year from this bus. Do you understand?"

Everyone nodded their heads in agreement and Ms. Kenton threw the spitball to the floor and stormed back off toward her seat.

"Oh my God, Jody," John said, letting out the breath he'd been holding, "you almost got busted."

"I know. That was way too close," I replied, "but did you see the look on her face?"

"Yeah, she was pretty pissed off," John said, and then we all laughed our asses off again.

We were finally on Rhine Road, and Angela was preparing to get off the bus, collecting up all her belongings before exciting one last time before the summer. As the bus slowed down, she walked by me and touched my hand with hers – by accident or purpose, I couldn't be sure – and my heart raced all over again. We looked at each other one more time, for just a split second, and then she was gone and even though she was just down the street from me, it seemed like Angela with her pretty face and sparkling blue eyes was a million miles away.

As the bus set off I gazed out the window and Angela gave me a small wave. I returned it and sat back down in my seat with the biggest, dumbest grin on my face.

About five minutes later, the bus door flung open and I set foot onto Rhine Road for the summer. I crossed the street and ran into my front yard, where Hunter-man was waiting for me on the swing.

"Whatchya doing, Hunter-man?"

"Nothang, jus' swingen," he said with that endearing speech impediment of his.

"You want to go play under Memaw's porch?"

"Yeah!" he shouted.

"I'll beat you there!" I threw my backpack down on the ground and took off running without a care in the world.

Later that night, we were watching *Ferris Bueller's Day Off* and it was getting to our favorite part of the movie; where Ferris jumps up on the float and sings *Twist and Shout* while the entire city danced along in the background. Tonight, though, Hunter decided to join in with the dance sequence, he jumped off the couch, ran into the middle of the living room and started spinning in crazy circles. He then thrust his hips back and forth like he was doing the nasty while me and Momma sat on the little couch, laughing uncontrollably.

"Shake it Hunter-man, shake it!!" she said and clapped her hands along with the beat, and of course I joined in. My little brother danced that entire song while me and Momma laughed at how cute he was and

Momma said he looked a like a four-year-old *Elvis Presley*.

Once the song was done, Momma and I clapped and cheered for Hunter and with a huge smile on his face, he ran over to Momma who covered him with kisses and lifted him back up on the couch.

"It's about time for you boys to go to bed."

"Aww, Momma, can't we stay up a little bit longer?" I asked in that whiny way kids have when they're over tired.

"No, ya'll have to go to sleep. Memaw is taking ya'll to the mall tomorrow to get some new play clothes for the summer."

"This stinks! The movie isn't even over yet!"

"I know, Bubba, but you do need to get some sleep. You know Memaw is an early bird and she'll be over here bright and early for you boys."

"Aww, alright," I said. I picked up the remote from the floor, pointed it at the TV and thumbed the off button.

Thump... Thump, Thump, Thump ... Thump ...

There it was again.

It was back.

The drum line in the darkness, beating that same rhythmic beat as before. I looked over at Momma and saw a look of fear in her eyes for the very first time in my life. She looked back into my eyes and I guess she saw that I was feeling the same – she motioned me over to the couch.

I ran across the living room and joined her and Hunter. We sat there silently for a short while, just listening to that strangely hypnotic beat.

The drums would stop every now and then, offering the briefest of respites before picking up once more, their tribal beat resounding through our little trailer; I was scared, and I knew that Momma was scared too, even though she never actually admitted as much until I was much older. Momma reached up to the side window and pulled it open, poked her head out into the night and looked up at the sky.

"It's a full moon," Momma said as she ducked her head back inside the trailer. She looked sternly at Hunter and I. "Go to bed, boys. Everything is going to be okay. It's just those damned kids again."

Momma was lying to us. I saw the fear in her eyes, even though she was trying hard to hide it.

The sounds that came from the night made my imagination run wild with all sorts of weird bullshit; Crazy renegade Indians, deranged cannibalistic hillbillies that lived in the woods, shit like that. Although, I guess the real reason I was so scared was because I saw the true distress in my mother's eyes, a look which was so incredibly foreign to me. I looked across at her, nodded and grabbed Hunter by the hand. I walked him to his bedroom, told him goodnight and then went quietly to my own room.

As I opened my door, I glanced back at Momma and she was on the phone, looking out the window and up at the night sky again.

I said nothing, and went to bed with my imagination running wild.

CHAPTER SIX

SUMMER OF TRUTH

"Hello?" Jerry's voice was disoriented; the shrill ringing of the telephone had woken him from a deep sleep.

"Daddy, I'm sorry I'm calling so late, but do you hear those drums in the woods?"

"I don't know what you're talking about, Sissy," Jerry replied.

"Could you meet me out by the shed in a few minutes?" Gayla asked.

"Sure, let me get my slippers on, and I'll meet you out there," Jerry replied as he pulled the covers off his body and rolled out of bed.

"Okay. See you in a few. Bye." Gayla hung up the phone and went down the hall to peek in on her boys. They were both knocked out cold, so she turned around and headed toward the front door.

Jerry was already standing outside by the shed with his arms crossed and listening intently to the drums by the time Gayla showed, his shadow cast by the full moon making him look like a giant from some kid's fantasy novel.

Gayla could tell that he was studying the situation, and was a hundred percent in tune with everything going on around him.

"You do know what's going on here, don't you, Sissy?" Jerry spoke quietly.

"No, Daddy, I don't," Gayla admitted, in a hushed voice.

"Have you been watching the news?" Jerry asked her.

"Not really. I'm busy with the kids during the day, and at night we watch movies."

"It seems we have a serious problem in Hammond," Jerry said. "The world is changing again, and as the Bible tells us, it's only going to get worse before the End of Days. The unthinkable will become normal, and evil men and women will roam freely all over His earth."

Gayla said nothing, just stood in the silvery light of the full moon and listened to her father.

"As a vigilant parent to you and your brother, I have protected you from certain things since the day you were born," Jerry took a small pause, as if to select just the right words, "You protect the ones you love, Sissy. That's what it boils down to. Do you remember the time your brother told us about the men he thought he saw in the woods? The ones he said were dressed in black robes?"

"Yeah," Gayla replied, her mind racing. "You never really told us what that was all about, though. I'd pretty much forgotten about it over the years."

"And do you also remember the little incident with Lewis Rhine?"

"Sure do. But you never told me what that was all about, either."

"I never told you – or your brother – the truth about

71

what happened that day in the woods, because I didn't want to scare you. Both of you were too young to understand at that point in time, but now you do need to know the truth."

"Well?"

"It was Devil worshippers that your brother saw, Sissy," Jerry said calmly, as if he were merely discussing the weather, "disciples of Satan himself."

Gayla's mouth dropped open at this, she'd never heard her father speak of such things before and it was kinda scary.

"He saw a group of them that day in the woods with the Benson boys. I didn't want to believe that it was really happening; we'd been discussing it in the church for about a year before your brother saw what he saw. The church advised that we keep an eye out for ourselves and most importantly, our families and children. So that's just what I did, Sissy. I tried my best to keep you all away from it," Jerry let out an audible sigh, "But now that you are mature enough to understand, and have kids of your own, I figure I can tell you without scaring you too much."

"I'm glad you're finally having this discussion with me, Daddy," Gayla said softly, "so, what *did* happen with Lewis Rhine?"

"They cut the hearts out of his cows, Sissy," Jerry said, his voice catching in his throat. "That's why I took Rambo to the shelter, because I knew it would happen again on the next full moon, and that when it did, Rhine wouldn't be able to say a damned word.

"So, as you can hear," Jerry raised a hand and pointed toward the woods, "they are very active on the full moon. That is when they perform their ceremonies and sacrifices." He lowered his hand quickly, as if fearing the wrath of the drumbeaters. "Those people are different from *Satanists*, though. Satanists believe that people should live out their lusts and desires, enthusiastically exploring the *seven deadly sins* with other consenting adults. They believe children and animals are the purest expressions of life, and are to be held sacred and precious." He paused, as if for thought.

Gayla stared, wide-eyed at the father she thought she knew so well. Since when had he become such an authority on the dark arts?

"Devil worshippers, on the other hand," Jerry continued, "will happily kill in the name of the Devil. Devil worshippers are immature and unstable, believing that Satan is a dragon that lives within the earth and is pleased when blood-filled rituals are offered to him.

"Devil worship appears to be becoming very popular across America these days. Many sick, twisted people are flocking toward it to do bad things in the name of the Devil. And I'm afraid that they are giving Satanists – along with others who practice alternative religions – a bad name." Jerry brought his hand up to his mustache and ran his fingers through it.

"Everyone who walks this earth has a right to choose their own religion, Sissy, but one man's religion can be another man's excuse for depravity. What better place for a vicious, cruel, evil-intended mind and heart to be in than a so-called satanic cult? How many times have you heard a killer say that the Devil made them do it, or even in some cases, God?" Jerry asked his daughter.

"I could probably name a few who've said both," Gayla replied.

"Exactly! It's simply a way for evil people to evade responsibility – by blaming religion. People can make their religion fit whatever their hearts desire, they step away from the guidelines and make it their own. To be honest, more people have been killed in the name of

Christ than Satan; did you know that, Sissy?"

Gayla didn't respond.

"Tell me, what does any religion, either Christian or Satanic, have to do with an already evil individual?" Jerry asked.

Gayla thought about it for a second, and then replied, "Nothing."

"You're right. Such a person is already evil and intent on doing evil things. You can't blame that on any religion, people like that already have darkness in their souls and there isn't anything anyone can do to change that. The only person who could save them is God, but as the Bible says, God has a plan for us all. The devil can only touch you if God lets him, and the book of Job tells us that." Jerry stroked his 'tache once more, as he always did when immersed in thought.

"I have a feeling that bad things are going to start happening around here, Sissy," he said. "There are folk in Hammond who are only too happy to use Devil worship as an excuse to do terrible things."

"Like what, Daddy?" Gayla was truly scared now, she'd never seen fear in her father's eyes before, and it was terrifying.

"A talk show ran a show on Devil worship the other day, and it was very disturbing. The host claimed that children are being sacrificed to the Devil in many towns across America. He said that babies and children are killed, and that many law enforcement and high-profile political figures are in on it."

Gayla couldn't believe what she was hearing. This was all horrifying to her, but somewhere deep down in her soul, it seemed like she had known all of this already. She was scared for her boys, and for sure didn't want them anywhere near the woods, or those people who were banging so relentlessly on their drums.

But, they didn't just walk around town wearing a *Hello... I worship the Devil and kill kids* tee-shirt. No, they'd be so incredibly secretive about it, sort of like an evil version of the Freemasons; one never knew who was *in* until they approached you to join.

"I can't believe this, Daddy," Gayla said, shaking her head.

"Everything is going to be okay, Sissy, I promise you. But there is one thing," Jerry said.

He then turned away from the woods to face his daughter. "There was a twelve-year-old girl kidnapped from Albany two days ago, and no one knows where she is. As you well know, Albany is only just up the road from us and that's why I asked if you had seen the news lately.

"The Hammond and Albany police departments are looking for her, but I don't think they will have any luck." Jerry's eyes saddened, a tear glistened in each.

"The police also found the cemetery behind the Hammond High School desecrated. Bodies pulled from graves, graffiti spray-painted on the tombstones, you name it – it was destroyed." Jerry rocked back and forth on his feet, as if trying to not let the drums distract him from finishing his story. "I think God is trying to tell me something, Sissy, and I strongly believe that those drums we're hearing have a lot to do with what's been going on." Jerry raised his arms and placed his broad hands on his daughter's shoulders. "Not all Devil worshippers have evil intentions, Sissy, but the ones around here – I think do."

"What?" Gayla asked, but the word only came out as a whisper.

"Keep an eye on those boys of yours, Sissy, but don't tell them what we've talked about tonight. You don't want to scare them; they're too young. But you do need to warn them to stay away from strangers – and those woods." Jerry kissed his daughter on the forehead, a tender, fatherly kiss. "Now get back inside before the boogey man gets us." He offered a wry smile, a fond, shared memory of more innocent times gone by.

"Of course," Gayla smiled back through her confusion, "I have to pick up the house anyways."

"Those boys sure are something else, aren't they?" Jerry asked as he turned to go.

"They sure are, Daddy," Gayla replied.

"Goodnight, Sissy."

"Night, Daddy," Gayla said, and headed toward the trailer.

Jerry paused awhile and stood in the pale moonlight and watched his daughter make her way back to her home. He tilted his head to the nighttime sky and admired the stars that God had seen fit to spread across the black velvet of the heavens. He muttered a small prayer beneath his breath for the missing twelve-year-old girl, and for his own family; no matter how much the world changed, or how weird things got, you always had to find a moment in life to admire the beauty around you – and that night, Jerry Jones did just that.

CHAPTER SEVEN

THE OFFERING OF AMANDA

It had been about an hour since Amanda Parsons of Albany, Louisiana, had heard the last beating of the drums.

She was blindfolded with duct tape wrapped around her mouth, wrists and ankles. She was in some strangers' van and she was hoping that *they'd* forgotten all about her.

She could hear the racket outside, a bunch of scary yelling and chanting, and no matter how hard she tried, Amanda couldn't stop crying – the cloth blindfold was soaking wet with her tears.

All she could think about was her mother, father, the cute teddy bear she'd been given for her twelfth birthday, and her little brother, who was only two years old. Why hadn't she just listened to her parents when they'd told her to be home before dark? She'd been having way too much fun with her friends at the park to think about such things, and as it transpired, it was pretty much dark when she'd finally headed home.

She'd been about a block away from her home when the silver van pulled up beside her and two men dressed all in black had jumped out, grabbed her, and carried her into the vehicle.

Amanda wondered just how long she'd been missing now. It was difficult to tell, almost as if time had stood still in the cold, hard interior of the van. Was it days? Weeks? She honestly didn't know, for minutes felt like hours to her, the hours, like days in a never-ending nightmare. As Amanda sat sobbing in the van, she noticed the duct tape around her wrist and ankles was working loose. It didn't matter to her though, as she had finally come to realize she was never going to make it back home to her family. Whoever the people who had snatched her were, they clearly had no intention of letting their prize go.

Suddenly, the side door of the van slid open. Amanda jumped back, startled. The van shook as people clambered in, and three separate, distinct voices could be heard; two of which were definitely male, the third a female. Amanda heard the driver's side door shut, and a moment later two more male voices joined the group.

"Start the van. The witching hour is almost upon us," spat the female voice. The driver started up the van, and in a matter of seconds Amanda was on the way to a new destination.

"She is such a beautiful piece of flesh," the woman said as she stroked her fingers across Amanda's cheek. "We were watching you for a couple of days, Princess. We decided to take you instead of one of your friends, you were just so much prettier than them," said the woman in a cold, heartless voice.

At that moment, Amanda felt a hand upon her thigh. It made its way to her zipper and began undoing the button to her pants. Amanda tried her best to resist.

The woman yelled, "Hold her down, Goddamn it!" Amanda kicked and squirmed with all her might, until she felt the cold steel of a knife press up against her throat.

At this, the little girl froze.

"Move one more time, Princess, and I'll cut you from ear to ear," snarled a man whose breath smelled like something dead and decaying.

Amanda quit moving as they cut the duct tape from her ankles and slid her pants all the way down to leave her in nothing but her panties. She felt sick to her stomach and began to dry heave, but nothing much came up.

"Now, now – look at those cute little panties. Can I have those?" asked the woman.

Amanda shook her head vigorously.

"No?" said the woman. "I think I'll take them anyway, *Princess*."

The man who held the knife to Amanda's throat took it away from her neck and slid it down her midline. Amanda felt the knife on her inner thigh as it cut through the elastic of her panties. She was completely horrified; the only people who had ever seen her naked before were her mother and father, and that had been when she was much younger. Now, Amanda knew that there were at least two strangers looking at her vulnerable body, and she felt ashamed.

"There is nothing quite like a child's innocence. So pure... so very perfect," the woman purred, running her hand up Amanda's bare inner thigh. "Now, this might feel a little bit funny to you, Princess. You might not like it – but honestly, I don't really care all that much."

***

"We're here," said the driver, "cut the bullshit and get her out of the van."

The door to the van opened and a new voice spoke up, a low, rumbling voice that resonated through Amanda's terrified mind – she assumed that this participant had been waiting for them to arrive. "Get her inside the house and prepare her for the ceremony. We don't have much time," it said.

Someone grabbed Amanda her by the wrists, with another grabbing her ankles. The two men jolted her up into the air, and away from the cruel, cold floor of the van and carried her like a suckling pig on a stick toward an old, run-down house.

Amanda heard the door to the house close behind her, and she felt someone cutting the duct tape from her wrists. She had a fleeting moment of relief; she could finally move her arms, but before she could even stretch back, someone ripped her shirt off with a violent yank. The only thing she wore now was the blindfold, still tied tight around her eyes and the duct tape over her mouth. Her legs shook from exhaustion and fear and she wanted nothing more than to fall to the ground. But Amanda couldn't even do that, for someone had placed a hand under her armpit to prevent her from dropping.

"Sit the fuck down, you little cunt!" shouted the man with the deep voice.

Amanda's heart felt like it was about to explode, but she knew she had to stay strong. So, she did as she was told, and bent down until her hands felt the floor, slowly bringing the rest of her body down after them.

"You all have three minutes to change, and then it begins," instructed the chilling, ever deep voice.

Everyone in the room nodded their heads and began. Amanda heard the rustling sounds as they quickly stripped naked.

Unbeknownst to the little girl, each one of the individuals in the room had a duffle bag, which contained the thick, heavy ceremonial robes they would wear for the night's ceremonies.

What is going on? Amanda asked herself, so many memories running through her trembling mind; the time her mother read her *Little Red Riding Hood* before she went to sleep – *"Mom... is the Big Bad Wolf real?"*

"No, sweetheart. He's not real."

"If he's not real, then why did they write a book about him?"

"It's called make-believe, sweetheart. People just make these stories up from their imaginations."

"What's imagination?*"*

"Just go to sleep, baby. We'll talk about that when you're a little bit older."

"But, Mommy, I am five.*"*

"I know, sweetheart, but let's just talk about it later, okay? Mommy's really tired, and I'm sure you are, too."

"Okay, Mommy..."

"Mommy...?"

"Yes, sweetheart?"

"You would never let the Big Bad Wolf get me – would you?"

"Never in a million, trillion years, baby."

Another memory came to the fore, jostling for attention in her mind; Amanda could see her father...

He was running towards her because she'd fallen off her bike. She had struck the cement hard and split her knee wide open. Her father scooped her up into his big, strong arms and carried her inside the house. He brought her over to the water faucet to wash out the cut.

"It hurts, Daddy."

"I know, baby, but I got to clean it so I can put the Band-Aid on. You have to be strong, okay?"

"Okay... I love you, Daddy."

"I love you too, sweetheart."

Then, as quickly as they'd come, the memories stopped, and Amanda wished she was back in her father's loving arms and safe from the terrible people who had taken her.

Amanda wondered how her parents were – *were they crying? Were they looking for her? Did they call 911?-* all running through her mind when someone removed the blindfold.

It took a few seconds or so for Amanda's vision to swim back into focus. And when it finally did, she wished she still had the blindfold on.

She was standing in an ancient, run-down kitchen. There was dirt and filth everywhere, rusted old pots dangling from hooks in the ceiling and split, molding worktops. The three people who had brought her to this dreadful place were standing directly in front of her. They wore black, hooded robes and silver necklaces with circles and upside down stars in their center. Two of the people wore what looked to Amanda to be real human skulls over their faces, whilst the woman wore a thin, black fabric that barely concealed her face. One of the men stood proudly beside a severed goat head, which lay on the floor in a fresh pool of congealing blood.

Daddy, help me! Amanda's whirling mind screamed as she glanced frantically around. She could hear her father's voice – *you have to be strong, okay?-* and it gave her a much needed boost of strength.

It felt almost as if her beloved father was there with her, but Amanda knew in her heart he wasn't going to swoop in and save her like the superheroes in the movies – Amanda had accepted back in the van that no one knew where she was, even her father.

The woman from the van stepped towards Amanda and lifted her mask, revealing her face for the first time "It's time, Princess," she hissed with a salacious grin and she reminded Amanda of the wicked witch from the *Wizard of Oz*.

The two men circled Amanda as the woman grabbed her wrist and led her through a set of doors that went from the decrepit kitchen and into an equally derelict living room. Amanda didn't understand how her legs were moving, her actions independent of her will, almost automatic and she realized to her shame that she was urinating on herself as she was manhandled forward.

The abductors lifted their hoods over their masked faces, and struck up a dark hymn in perfect harmony and they sounded like an evil church choir as they marched forward with Amanda.

Amanda thought to herself once more, *Please, God, help me! Let this be over soon!*

In the area of the living room where the furniture should have been, there sat a table which had a black sheet covering it. Behind the table, there stood a masked man in a black robe that had devil's horns sticking out on each side of its hood, his face was covered by a small cow's skull.

A row of black candles had been placed along the window seals, including the mantle to the left, their flames jaundiced and flickering weakly.

Amanda felt as if her eyes were going to pop out of her head from the terror that raced through her brain, and she just *knew* that she was about to die. *Maybe if they take the tape off my mouth, I can convince them not to kill me.*

"I'm only twelve years old!" Amanda tried to scream, but it came out from behind the tape as gibberish.

The people laid Amanda carefully upon the table, facing up into the eyes of the horned man. They pinned her firmly by her arms and legs and the room fell quiet.

The horned man began to speak.

"Hail unto my Master, the Devil, the Lord of this world and Prince of Darkness! The Red One of Darkest Brilliance, whose eternal shadow is the light of my life. Surely, I belong to thee in both body and spirit; I have taken thy name as a part of myself, and I rejoice in thy spirit. For in the shadow of Lucifer there is love and warmth, and in the midst of his darkness there is undying light. O mighty black goat of the Wilderness! O mighty serpent of Eden's demise! To Thee I give praise forever and ever."

"Amen!" shouted the group.

Terrified, Amanda tried her best to squirm, but the men had a too firm grasp on her limbs.

"Master, I call thee forth from the bottomless abyss. Master, I call thee forth from the ends of the earth. Master, I call thee forth from the nighttime sky. Come forth from within my flesh and my spirit, and greet me as thy humble servant and friend. I wish to worship and honor thee, to commune with thee and to be still and know that thou art my God."

Amanda felt that the people who held her limbs were uneasy and anxious as the horned man spoke his sinister words, they had the air of little kids waiting for someone to bust open a candy-laden piñata. Out of the corner of her eye, Amanda watched the woman slip the horned man a silver dagger from out of her robe. The knife was about ten inches long and had an ornate skull at the end of the hilt, and glinted wickedly in the dim candlelight.

The horned man placed both hands around the knife's shining hilt and held it high above his head and Amanda's heart beat hard and fast with terror, blood pumping ferociously throughout her body. "I give thanks unto thee, Prince Lucifer, my master; for all that you have done for me. I give thanks unto thee for guiding me, for giving me strength in my hour of darkness," his voice was incredibly shaky now, but he continued, "and for never leaving my side. Thou art truly a most noble and loving God, and to thee I am forever devoted in both spirit and flesh!"

Then the horned, deep voiced man brought the dagger down with all his might piercing the young girl's bare, vulnerable chest.

It was a pain that Amanda couldn't have ever imagined, and she screamed out at the top of her lungs as the horned man repeated his retched task again and again. Everything began to spin and her blood was flying everywhere. The pain was insurmountable.

Moments later, the horned man halted and Amanda, barely alive, heard him clear his throat and shout: "Hail to thee, Prince of Darkness! Lord of the elements, beloved master! He who is of the Darkness, but who brings the light. All praise unto thee, my Prince of Darkness! This offering is for thee! Hail Satan!"

"Hail Satan!" the group repeated.

Amanda was bleeding out, dying, the pain a distant memory now, and as her head fell limp to her left shoulder, she saw the man who stabbed her. As her gaze began to fog-out, she watched him remove the skull mask from his face, and once it was off, much to Amanda's surprise, she recognized him.

CHAPTER EIGHT

HANGING WITH JUSTIN: 1990

It had been about three weeks since I'd last heard the drum solo from the woods.

Momma had been acting a little funny ever since Pepaw had a talk with her a couple of weeks ago. She went to one of the sports stores downtown and bought a silver whistle like the ones the coaches' use during football practices. She told me when I heard her blow that whistle, I had about two minutes to get my skinny ass back home before she started swinging *Mr. Belt* around in my direction like some deranged Viking warrior.

Naturally, I just nodded and went on my merry way. I mean, I was always either at Jack's house or in the backyard; it wasn't like I was going to China anytime soon, so I couldn't understand why she was freaking out about where I was going to be all the time. It didn't matter much to me, though, I just did as I was told and all was okay.

I was over at Jack's house one day and we were

hiding in the bushes and shooting his pellet gun at the transformer attached to the old, peeling telephone pole that stood sentry at the front of his house.

"Bet you can't hit it, Jody," Jack teased me.

He only got to antagonize me because we were best friends, and best friends can get away with digging under each other's skin from time to time.

"Yes I can, fart-mouth. I just need you to be quiet so I can aim."

"Just hurry the hell up! I'd like to get a shot in sometime this year," Jack spat.

We both started laughing at this and I couldn't wait to shoot that damned hunk of junk sat up there on that pole like it owned the whole damned street.

"Aim high! Aim higher!" Jack shouted with glee as I finally took aim and shot at the transformer.

BING!

Nothing happened, nothing at all.

"Damn it," I said.

"Give it to me. You got to pump it up more. The more you pump it, the more powerful it gets," Jack explained.

"Well thanks. I wish I'd have known that before I took the damned shot."

"Get over it," Jack said with a smile on his face.

Jack's hair had grown a couple more inches since we got out of school for the summer, and he now looked like the blond-haired Don Johnson in Miami Vice. Jack put the gun between his legs and began to pump it up until his little arms couldn't pump any more.

"Help me out, Jody," he demanded.

I walked over to him and did my best until the last bit of air went into the gun.

"Damn!" I said.

"I know!" Jack agreed. "That was like trying to push a fat chick into an ice chest."

"I bet it wouldn't be hard to push a fat chick into an ice chest if it had hamburgers in it, though," I chimed in.

"Yeah, fat chicks love food. Remember Stephanie who rode our bus?" Jack asked.

"Yeah, I do. She used to eat paper out of her notebook when she thought nobody was looking; I caught her doing it a couple of times." I began laughing at this point and couldn't help it. "She also said that Coke makes her fart!"

"HA-HA! She only said that because that boy she liked heard her fart one time on the bus, so she blamed it on the Coke she was drinking," Jack elaborated.

"That fart sounded like a little kid screaming – and it smelled like one of those dead raccoons you see on the side of the road," I added.

"Yeah, my Dad rips some pretty nasty ones, too," Jack told me. "Me and Jamie just laugh when he does it because Momma always gets pissed at him. She always yells, *Shawn!!* And then Daddy says, *who stepped on that bullfrog?!*"

Jack and I laughed uncontrollably at that point and fell to our knees, bellowing away.

Jack's dad, Mr. Shawn, was freaking hilarious. Every time I came over to Jack's house, Mr. Shawn would be outside smoking a cigarette on the swing that was attached to their carport. I'd walk up to the side door of the house and Mr. Shawn would say, "It's the Return of the Joe-die."

I would just look at him and give a big smile. I'd seen the last *Star Wars* movie that had come out – *Return of the Jedi* (and I wish it would have stayed that way, too; those new ones are complete poo-berry-stew) – and Mr. Shawn just loved to replace my name with the Jedi part.

He'd said it two days ago at Jamie's funeral, and it brought tears to my eyes. Even when he was at one of his most miserable points in his life, Mr. Shawn still put on a smile and said the Joe-die thing to me; that just shows you what type of man Mr. Shawn is.

So, Jack and I eventually got our giggles under control and focused back on our goal – the transformer. If we could hit it in just the right spot, we could quite possibly cause a badass power outage that would stretch out for God knows how far. We just knew that it would be more than great; it would be freaking *awesome*.

Jack put on his game face and aimed the gun at the transformer. I never admitted it to anyone, but at the time, Jack had a way better shot than me; as kids you have pride, and I was just a little bit jealous about that. While Jack took careful aim at our target, I carefully made my way behind him, squirming so much with excitement, it was like I had fire ants invading my underwear. Jack placed his finger on the trigger.

Squeezed.

The last thing I remember was hearing a pop and something metal flew past my head with a loud *ZOOM* sound.

"Holy cow!" I screamed as we both took off running toward Jack's house.

Whatever Jack was aiming at, he'd hit it, and although it didn't cause a power outage as we'd hoped, he had broken something and we were both just delighted with that.

"Did you hear that thing zoom past our heads?" Jack asked me, beside himself with excitement.

"Yeah, that was so sweet!" I said, still pretty stoked at our achievement, for some reason, Jack and I just had one big hard-on for destruction – don't ask me why, we just did.

We went back into his house to put the pellet gun away, when Mrs. Renee bustled into the kitchen.

"Sorry, Jody, but Jack has to go to the store with me really quick."

"Aww!" I hissed.

"We won't be gone that long," Renee told me, "We're just running up to Eckerd's, it's not like you're never going to see him again. We'll be back in an hour."

"Okay. See ya later, Jack. Bye, Mrs. Renee!"

"See ya," Jack replied.

I walked out of Jack's house, got on my bike and made my way back down to my trailer. Our homes were only like a football field away, but somehow it always felt further when I was going home.

As I rode slowly along, I looked up from the road and noticed some other kid making his way toward me on a bike, wearing a D.A.R.E. t-shirt and red shorts. Once I got closer to him, I noticed it was Justin Richardson, a kid that lived a street over. He was husky, somewhat shorter than me, and had a mop of jet-black hair.

"Hey, Jody!" he yelled.

We stopped our bikes right next to each other in the middle of Rhine Road.

"Hey, Justin," I said.

"You want to come with me to go see an old eighteen-wheeler trailer that's in the woods? It's across from Angela's house," Justin asked me, right off the bat. "It's going to be cool, Jody. Trust me."

"I don't know anything about an old trailer, and I *live* on this street," I said, more than a little put out.

"I was with my Dad while he was picking up some beer at the Kentally gas station, and I overheard some older kids talking about it. They said it's a pretty spooky place."

"Why would I want to go see a trailer an eighteen-wheeler pulls around all day that's stuck out in the middle of the woods?" I was being a complete smart ass about it, but I could tell the kid wasn't picking it up. That's still a great trait I have to this day, and God bless it.

"I don't know. I bet Angela will think you're cool if you go there. I hear you like her."

"Who told you that?"

"Everybody knows, Jody."

"Really?"

"Really. You might even get to see her, too," Justin said, clearly trying to influence me, and by God, it was working.

"My Mom doesn't let me ride down the street that far yet. I can only go a little bit past Jack's house, and that's it," I told him.

"Oh, come on, Jody. I don't want to go by myself."

"You were going there just fine before you ran into me," I countered.

"Please, Jody. Come with me," Justin whined.

I stood there and thought about it for a second. I was trying to imagine the consequences that would unfold if I missed Momma blowing on that damned whistle. I would definitely get an ass beating, but then again, I'd already got plenty of those and was pretty used to them. I never got grounded from Jack, so that wouldn't happen. The Nintendo wouldn't be played for about a day, but I could live with that. *You know what, screw it,* I thought.

"Sure, Justin, I'll go with you," I said.

"Awesome!" Justin shouted.

"Let's just get going before my Mom blows her whistle. If she does, this trip is over."

We took off on our bikes like bats out of hell and headed down the street toward Angela's house, not knowing the horrors that awaited us at our destination.

Now, if there's one damned thing I can't stand about

the summers in Louisiana, it would have to be the snakes. I'm terrified of those slippery bastards. When I was about six years old, my cousin and I were walking down a dirt road close to her house when a big-assed copperhead crossed right over the top of my feet. I froze in place – literally – I couldn't move a single muscle or bone in my body. As the snake rolled over my feet, I looked down and caught a glimpse of his smooth, scaly skin and cold, black eyes.

My poor cousin had to physically place her hands on me to get me to move and when we got back to her house, Momma asked me why the hell I looked so pale. So, ever since then, I can't stand fucking snakes and, unfortunately Rhine Road had a lot of them.

As we went past Jack's house, it occurred to me that there were more flowers on the sides of the road than there were down by my house. Only a few little ones here and there popped up in the ditch in front of my trailer, but past Jack's it was like a totally different street. I had never really been this far down the road, other than when I was on the bus or in the car and in those moments, I wasn't paying much attention to the scenery.

It all felt like a great, big adventure to me, like I was in some entirely new and exciting land. I looked to my right as I pedaled my bike and I saw some of the most beautiful flowers I'd ever seen on Rhine Road, all growing up from a ditch. It was like the flowers here were reaching out, hoping that someone would pick them up from the earth and take them home.

Justin and I rode side by side, not really talking that much and then Justin looked over to me. "I have to pee," he said.

"Well, let's stop so you can pee, then," I replied.

We slowed down and pulled off the road into the long

grass that grew next to the ditch. It smelled to me like sewage, but as a kid your senses are a little bit more resilient than when you get older; even now, when I smell someone's fart, I have to run out the room to get some fresh air.

And don't ever ask me to change a shitty diaper, either. Oh screw that; I know that sounds pathetic and I'm not a dirt-bag father or anything, it's just that my stomach can't handle that stuff. Corrie used to think I was making excuses so I wouldn't have to change our son, until I puked all over our living room floor one day while attempting to change him. Once that happened, my dear wife believed me and never bugged me about it again. I think I inherited the weak stomach from my father – thanks Dad, you scumbag.

As Justin unzipped his shorts and began emptying his little weasel, I noticed something swirling around in the ditch, moving back and forth and making *S* shaped ripples in the water.

"Snake!" I screamed.

Justin was still pissing when I yelled that magic word and he jumped into the air with his tally-whacker still hanging out of his shorts. I mounted my bike and started hauling ass in the general direction of our agreed destination.

"Wait, Jody! *Wait!*" Justin yelled as I took off, leaving him behind.

I had given him the warning, now he had to move fast because I wasn't coming back. I stopped my bike a good two hundred or so yards away from *Snakezilla*, and looked back for Justin, who by now was only about twenty yards behind me. I waited a few more seconds and he came to a screeching halt right next to me.

"Why – the hell – did you leave – me like that?" Justin asked, out of breath from hauling his own ass.

I glanced down and I saw that the poor kid had pissed his shorts, or at least giving him the benefit of the doubt, he had pissed *on* his shorts, either during the scare or the ride over to me. Justin noticed that I was looking at his crotch and he turned a little red with embarrassment.

"It would have happened to you too if your pecker was out when someone screamed snake," Justin grumbled angrily.

"I'm sorry, Justin. I hate snakes and I had to get out of there. At least I gave you a heads up."

"Next time you give me a heads up; just make sure my pecker isn't hanging out," Justin said.

He was smiling now, and I knew that the snake hadn't foiled our plans for seeing the trailer in the woods. We both snickered about the whole thing as we got back on our bikes and headed for the woods across the street from Angela's house.

As we rounded the corner of Rhine Road, which quickly turned straight again after only a few feet, I caught a glimpse of an old dirt driveway that was to our left. It was right at the bend in the road and appeared to be pretty much overgrowing with weeds and grass. Intrigued, I made a mental note of the driveway and moved on.

We kept on pedaling until we got to about fifty yards away from Angela's house, and my heart began beating fast once more, and my sweat felt like it was *pouring* out of my body. I didn't understand why I reacted that way every time I started thinking about her, or even when someone mentioned her name, at times it felt like I was going to pass out.

"You alright, Jody?" Justin asked.

"Yes… I'm fine. Now, where's this eighteen-wheeler trailer again?"

"It's through the woods, over there. You see that

94

board that's been laid across the ditch?" Justin pointed down the street.

I squinted so I could get a better view, and noticed that there was a raggedy two-by-four stretched across the ditch, and it looked like it could collapse at any minute.

"Yeah – I see it," I said.

"That's where we cross over to get to the trail that leads you to the trailer."

"You sure you know where this place is at?" I asked.

I had a funny feeling about the whole thing, now. Either Justin was full of shit and was going to get our asses lost in the goddamned woods, or some of the older kids were back there doing God knows what, and would kick our asses for being in a secret spot that only they were supposed to know about.

"Don't worry, Jody. It's there. Come on," Justin said, and he pushed off the ground with his left leg to set his bike into motion.

"Here we go," I said out loud, and took off after him.

After we crossed over the two-by-four one at a time, there was a good fifty feet left of open field before we hit the edge of the woods. The grass was thick and tall; some of it past our knees, and the field had thousands of tiny blue flowers barely poking their heads up from the earth. I turned around from where I was standing in the field to look back across the street to Angela's house. I didn't see any cars, or the family van in the driveway, so I took it that no one was home at the time. When I turned back around, Justin was yelling my name from the wood line.

"Come on, Jody! I think I found the trail!"

"Alright, alright, I'm coming!" I shouted back, glancing one last time over my shoulder at the thousands of flowers that covered half the field.

I quickly gathered myself and took off toward Justin, who was, by now rocking back and forth with excitement in front of the trail. Once we were side by side again, we looked into the woods.

As soon as we stepped in, the trees seemed to completely cover up the sun and the temperature dropped by at least five degrees. There were three towering oak trees with Spanish moss hanging from them; two were on the right, thirty feet apart, and there were several magnolia bushes straight ahead of us that surrounded the third. Currant bushes also ran rampant in the wooded area, accompanied by several briar patches.

The trail that we were on appeared to be the only path that led through the woods. The ground was matted down flat from either people or animals that followed its meandering, and it looked to me like it was used often. As Justin and I walked along for a minute or two, we noticed a lot of trash along the sides, some of it tossed even further back into the woods; beer cans, Butterfinger wrappers, Coke bottles – you name it. Wherever this trail was going, kids had definitely been back here, partying with junk food and booze stolen from their parents. We walked on a few feet further, until we came to a small clearing that had an old cooler in the middle of it, which was surrounded with yet more trash.

"This must be the spot where everybody hangs out," Justin said.

His voice almost made me jump out of my skin; we hadn't said a word to each other the whole time we'd been following the trail.

"I guess so. This place smells like a trash can," I said.

I took a good whiff of the air, which was a bad idea, and had to stop myself from gagging; it smelled to me like something dead and rotting.

"Where the hell is this trailer? It's got to be around

here somewhere," Justin proclaimed. "Follow me, Jody."

At this point, between the smell of rotting garbage and heady mix of booze, I was getting sick to my stomach and I just wanted to go home. I kept straining my ears to hear if Momma was blowing that God-awful whistle, but so far, so good. I gave myself a gut check and continued on with Justin passing through the clearing, and the further we walked, the worse the stench seemed to get.

The trail itself faded away bit by bit, until it was finally gone. Once it was no longer visible, we had to start navigating our way through all the briar patches that were now blocking our way. The briars dug viciously into my flesh, ripping tiny, jagged holes in my clothes, but I still followed Justin until he came to a sudden halt.

There were hundreds, if not thousands of flies circling the infamous eighteen-wheeler trailer we had come all this way to see. *FRED'S FURNITURE* was written along the side of the trailer in big green letters, taking up the whole side. The reek of rotting flesh had intensified to the point now that I started to dry heave into my mouth. Flies swarmed all about my face, some even shot up into my nose, and I started flailing my arms around like I was some kind of deranged Karate expert defending myself from multiple opponents.

This was all too much for us, and Justin and I took off running into the woods until we were far enough away from all the damned flies to talk without them flying into our mouths.

"Why the hell are all those flies there?" Justin asked me, still swatting away at the air.

"You don't smell that, Justin? Something's got to be dead, that's why all those flies are swarming over there,"

I surmised.

"Of course I can smell it, but I don't see any dead raccoons, dogs, cats... I don't see anything."

"Well, I'm getting sick to my damned stomach, and I'm ready to go home. This was a dumb idea," I told him.

"Oh come on, Jody! Let's at least go take a look in the back of the trailer."

"No! Let's get the hell out of here. I'm not going back anywhere near those flies, or that smell!"

"Quit being a little girl. Are you scared or something?" Justin asked in a little baby's voice.

"No, I'm not scared. I just don't see the damned point. We came, we saw the trailer and now we need to leave. My mom is probably blowing her come-home-now whistle, and I can't hear it from here because I'm standing with you in these dumbass woods, looking at this dumbass trailer."

Because I had said all of that all in one breath and without stopping, I sighed in an attempt to regain the natural flow of my breathing.

"Well, *I'm* still going to go take a look in the back of it – with or without you," Justin stated.

"Justin, come on. Let's just –" but before I could finish with what I was saying, he was already walking away from me, back toward the trailer.

I thought to myself, *well screw him, I'm leaving,* and made my way back through the woods away from Justin, trying to find the one and only path that would lead me out.

But, before I could get through the very first briar patch, I heard Justin scream. Without thinking, I turned around and shot toward him as fast as my feet could carry me.

I was at the trailer within a matter of seconds, out of

breath, standing next to it with my hands on my knees. Justin was standing to the side of the trailer frozen, with flies covering him from head to toe. They buzzed and crawled and formed seething masses on top of his head and as I watched, he leaned forward and threw up; it looked like spaghetti mixed with melted Pop-Tarts shooting out of the kid's mouth, spewing in every direction. The flies quickly swarmed over their fresh meal, all courtesy of Justin's weak stomach.

"Are you ok, Justin?" I asked him.

I was concerned now, because Justin was just fine minutes ago, and it looked like he had lost some color in his face. Without saying a word, Justin looked up and pointed to the back of the trailer. I didn't say anything to him, but I knew he expected me to go look inside. I walked slowly toward the back of the trailer, swatting flies away from my face, and once I rounded the side, I peered in and saw something that would haunt and disturb me for the rest of my life.

Inside the trailer there were two slaughtered calves, lying in pools of their own congealed blood.

My body went into complete autopilot as I clambered up into the back of the trailer without even thinking. I guess I just wanted to see *everything* that was going on inside. And when I finally got up into the back of the trailer, I became confused with the whole scenario.

Black candles had been placed all around the calves' bodies, to form a neat circle around them. Half of the candles were burnt down to the last nub of wax, while the other half looked like they had been deliberately blown out. Both calves had their throats cut, which explained why there was so much blood – but it didn't explain the six Styrofoam cups on the floor that were all stained red on the inside.

I studied the calf to my right and saw that its gums

were beginning to decompose, they were as black as night, and maggots wriggled and jostled over the remaining teeth. And, much to my disgust, both calves had flies covering almost every inch of their dead bodies, from the hooves to the tips of their limply hanging tongues. What struck me the most, though, were the maggots crawling all over the beast's unresponsive eyes; one calf's eyes seemed to be looking back at me from beyond the grave, shooting guilt almost as if I was the one who had done this.

I glanced up from the butchered animal and turned my attention to the very back of the trailer, where there was a huge circle with a star in the middle of it, drawn in blood; obviously that of the unfortunate calves. I had never seen that type of symbol before in my life, and I wondered what the hell it meant– and why someone would draw it with baby cows' blood.

All of a sudden, something grabbed me by the ankle and I screamed at the top of my lungs.

"It's me, Jody. It's Justin."

"What the hell, Justin!? You scared the crap out of me," I yelled at him.

"I'm sorry, Jody – but we need to get the hell out of dodge. I think I heard someone walking around in the woods," he said.

Justin's eyes were wide, and I could tell that the kid was scared out of his mind. Seeing him in that state rubbed off on me, and I came off of autopilot in an instant and once more gagged from the thick stench of death. My heart raced as fear set in, and I was almost to the point of throwing up when Justin and I heard a branch break somewhere in the woods directly behind us.

We didn't even say a word to each other; it was like we were using telepathy as we both jumped from the back of the trailer. Once our feet struck the ground, we took off out of the woods, not daring to look back, and hoping no one was behind us.

We shot out of the woods, coming back out into the field in front of Angela's house, and thanks to the adrenaline that was pumping through our veins, we cleared the ditch with one jump. With one quick motion, we scooped up our bikes and proceeded to haul tail back home.

"What the hell was going on back there, Jody?" Justin asked as he pedaled next to me.

"I don't know what's going on back there, but I'm scared," I admitted.

"Yeah, me too," Justin replied.

"Do you think whoever did that to those calves was still back there? You know, maybe just hanging around?" I asked him.

"I don't know, but those calves had been dead for a while. I swear to God, Jody, I'm not lying to you; I heard footsteps right before that branch broke," Justin said.

"You think someone was watching us?"

"I don't know for sure – but I think so."

"Are you making this stuff up, Justin?" I panted, "'cause if you are, you need to cut it out. You're freaking me out now."

All I could picture in my mind was an image of a tall man with a machete dripping with blood, leaning up against one of the trees in the woods watching Justin and I, as we checked out his two-calf masterpiece.

"I'm so not lying!" Justin yelled back at me, and for some reason, I believed him.

We had both stumbled upon something horrible, of that there was no doubt, and neither of us would forget about it any time soon, but I did wonder if it was just the kid's imagination when it came to hearing someone in the woods; a lot of people imagine things when they're scared – just watch the *Exorcist* alone one night, and you'll see what I'm talking about.

I put the thoughts in the back of my mind for the time being and continued home, not speaking another word to Justin along the way.

As we approached my trailer, I began to slow down so I could make the left turn onto the driveway. Justin zoomed right past me, flying straight back in the direction of his street; we didn't even say goodbye to each other, Justin just kept on going as I wondered just what the hell I was going to tell Momma while I rolled up to the front porch. I threw my bike down, leapt from the ground onto the stairs and jetted my ass up them until I came to the front door. I paused, collected my thoughts and finally turned the knob.

"Momma," I called out, "you in here?"

"What do you want, Bubba?" Momma asked as she walked down the hallway, carrying the vacuum cleaner.

"I have to tell you something, but I don't want you to get mad at me, okay?"

"What did you do now, Jody?" Momma asked me.

She set the vacuum cleaner down slowly, her eyebrows lifted so high they touched her bangs. I knew that look – oh yes, it was the infamous *You're about to get your ass beaten* look that I'm sure everybody has gotten at least five or six times in their childhood. If I didn't speak fast enough, I was going to get beaten before I could even tell her what happened.

"I didn't *do* anything! I was just with Justin, you know, the kid that lives a street over? And we were down by Angela's house playing in the woods across the street, and we found something," I told her without taking so much as a breath.

"Well – what did you find, Jody?" Momma asked.

When I was finally done telling her about the whole ordeal, Momma sprung up from the couch and grabbed the phone.

"Go sit outside on the porch, Jody," she demanded.

I stood up from the couch and did exactly what she'd asked. Once I was on the porch, I planted my skinny tail down on the top step and replayed the whole conversation I'd just had with my mother from start to finish. I tried to remember if I'd told her every last detail that she needed to know, but my mind kept going back to the grisly tableau of slaughter I had just discovered less than an hour ago. I was looking down at the stale blood that had covered my *Nike* sneakers, when my mother swung open the front door.

"I just called the police, and they're going to go over there and take a look, so you'd better not be lying to me, or I swear to God, Jody, you'll never see the light of day again," Momma spat.

"I'm not lying to you Momma. Why would I lie about something like this?" I said.

"Because you were all the way down the street where you weren't supposed to be?"

"I swear to you, Momma. I'm telling you the God's honest truth," I protested.

I was now feeling like I was explaining myself to a court judge instead of to my own mother. I knew I was in the wrong for being down the street so far, but I hadn't done anything *wrong*. It wasn't like I was the one who killed those calves.

"Well, I gave our phone number to the police, just in case they need any more information. I told them everything you told me, so don't be surprised if they stop by the house to ask you a few questions. You didn't forget to tell me anything, did you?"

"I told you *everything*, Momma," I promised.

"And you didn't vandalize anything?"

"No."

"You didn't break anything?"

"No."

"You didn't set anything on fire?"

"No!" I yelled.

"Good," Momma concluded, trial over.

I saw the worry leave her face almost instantly after that last question, and that let me know she believed me. I stood up from the steps and stretched out my back. It felt like I had been sitting in an interrogation room for hours on end, defending myself against a crime I didn't commit. Momma walked up behind me, placed her hand on my shoulder and leaned forward like she was about to tell me a secret.

"Did you or Justin see anyone else in the woods?" Momma asked me.

Oh shit, were the words that almost came out of my mouth, but luckily, I caught them at the last second. I had totally forgotten to tell her about Justin hearing footsteps right before we heard the branch break. I began to open my mouth to tell her, but I suddenly realized that it was probably just the dumb kid's imagination; it had freaked me out for damned sure when he told me, and I could only imagine how Momma was going to react if I told her. I looked up into Momma's eyes and decided to tell her a little white lie. After all, *I* hadn't heard any footsteps, and neither of us actually *saw* anyone.

"No, Momma. It was only me and Justin in there – no one else," I told her.

CHAPTER NINE

THE WARNING

"We're fucking done for, guys! The goddamned police found the trailer and hauled it out of the woods two hours ago! We need to get the fuck out of town fast!" yelled the man with rotten breath as he burst into the back bedroom of the house.

The deep-voiced man was sitting at the edge of the bed, receiving a blowjob from the woman who had assaulted Amanda. She pulled his stiff penis out her mouth and let it fall between his legs, even though it was still fully erect.

"What the hell did you just say?" she spat, wiping the excess saliva from her mouth.

"They found the trailer in the woods – some fucking kids found the damned thing and went to the cops about it."

"How the fuck do you know some kids found it, Scott?" the woman asked.

"I went back there to look for my knife – I left it out there several nights ago."

"So why didn't you try to stop them from getting away?"

"I was too far back in the woods. I couldn't get to them fast enough." There was a short pause, "I'm sorry, Rebecca," the man – Scott – said.

"Did they see you, Scott?" Rebecca asked him.

"I don't know, but I think they heard me rustling around in the bushes."

"You asshole!" Rebecca yelled at him. "You risked getting us caught just because you wanted to go back for a fucking knife?! And then you let some stupid kids find the trailer and *then* get away!"

"It's not my fucking fault, Rebecca! They found the trailer on their own, and then they took off like bottle rockets before I could get to them. If I *had* caught those little shits, trust me, we wouldn't be in the predicament we're in now."

"But you didn't, Scott. You didn't get them – and if we get caught, I swear, I'll cut your throat before they take me away," Rebecca threatened him, her cold eyes that seemed to reach deep into Scott's soul piercing him.

"I'd like to see you try, you fucking bitch!" Scott retorted with teasing laughter.

"Shut up!" yelled the deep-voiced man as he rose up off the bed and pulled up his pants. "We're *not* going to get caught. They're just kids, and I'm sure they're scared out of their minds right now. I bet what they saw today will keep them out of the woods for a while. Now Scott, are you *sure* they didn't see you?"

"I'm positive they didn't. I think when they heard me it spooked them. I mean, they took off really fast, they didn't even look back," Scott stated.

"Good," said the deep-voiced man. "Don't worry about the cops; all they have is a trailer filled with dead calves. How is that possibly going to link them to us?"

"You're right," Scott said, calming down, "they don't have shit on us."

"Exactly. So everyone just needs to calm down."

The deep-voiced man walked over to the right side of the bed and picked his shirt up from off the floor. He shook it off, placed it over his head and pulled it down into place.

"What are we going to do about the kids?" Rebecca asked. "Do we know who they are?"

"Were they boys or girls, Scott?" asked the deep-voiced man.

"Boys," Scott told him.

"What did they look like?"

"One was sort of thick, with black hair that went down below his ears. The other one was real skinny, with braces, I think. Shit, I wish I would have followed the bastards home..."

"No need to worry. I think I know where one of them lives."

The room fell silent as all three stood in the bedroom deep in thought. Rebecca walked around the bed and placed her hand on the deep-voiced man's shoulder.

"What are you going to do, baby?" she whispered.

The man gave her a chilling grin that consumed his entire face and asked, "Did you end up finding your knife, Scott?"

CHAPTER TEN

COMFORT OF MY OWN HOME: 1990

It was around 11:30 at night, and I was sitting on the couch with Momma, watching *Meatballs*. I was still trying hard to erase everything that I'd seen out there in the woods, when something crashed into the side of our trailer.

The trailer shifted from side to side, and we jumped with fright, grabbing hold of the couch as tight as we could. It sounded to me like someone had thrown a bowling ball up against the backside of our home – where the playroom was. I reached over and squeezed Momma's hand, looking deep into her eyes for reassurance. She pulled me in closer and wrapped her arms tightly around me, tighter than ever before.

"What the hell was that, Jody?"

"I don't know, Momma, you're scaring me."

"I'm scared too, but I need you to sit still and be quiet," Momma said. She stood up off the couch, walked over to the window, flung it open as hard as she could and stuck her head out into the darkness.

"Put your head back in, Momma, put your head back in!" I pleaded.

"Who's there?" Momma yelled into the night.

THWACK – THWACK

Something struck the opposite side of the trailer, next to the front door. For a second I thought I heard footsteps running on the stairs, but before I could be sure, another hit rocked the trailer.

"Get the phone off the wall and bring it to me!" Momma demanded.

"I can't move, Momma! I'm scared – I'm *too scared*!" I wailed.

At this point, I began to cry, and that must have pushed Momma's adrenaline through the roof. "Go away, damn it! I'm calling the police right now!" she screamed at the top of her lungs.

I then heard footsteps coming down our hall and as I looked up, I saw Hunter standing there, crying and shaking in terror. "Momee, someone is scatching on my wendo," my kid brother mumbled, which sent me into a *total* panic; my breathing became heavy and I began to feel lightheaded, and the room felt as if it was spinning uncontrollably around me. Momma ran over to Hunter, scooped him up and brought him over to me on the couch as yet more hits struck our home. She then ran across to the phone, but before she could pick it up, something sharp was scraped across the side of our trailer. It made a loud, screeching noise, as if *Freddy Krueger* himself was slowly, deliberately dragging his glove alongside the thin, metal wall.

"Go the fuck away, damn it!" Momma shrieked as I watched her fingers struggle to dial 911.

Several more hits came to the sides of our trailer, rocking it like a canoe in whitewater.

"Jody, I'm scared," Hunter whispered to me.

At that very instant, I knew I had to be strong for my family; I had to protect them from whoever was out there doing this. There was no way I was letting anyone in my family get hurt, and at that moment my fear seemed to dissipate. I felt ready to take on whatever it was that was lurking out there in the darkness.

I pushed Hunter away from me and I scrambled off the couch and headed for the front door. I wrapped my hand around the knob, twisted it and pulled the door wide open.

"No, Jody!" Momma yelled, her ear stuck to the phone.

I peered out into the darkness, and suddenly someone ran into our trailer knocking me to the floor as they entered. My back hit the floor hard, and the air rushed out of my lungs like steam leaving an engine. I gathered myself, looked up from the floor and saw Pepaw standing there with a shotgun.

"Thank God, Daddy! Oh my God – thank you!" Momma said, and began to cry.

"Everything's going to be okay, Sissy. Hang up the phone. Everything is going to be okay," Pepaw reassured.

Momma sat down next to me and Hunter on the couch, as Pepaw ventured back into the darkness to check out the trailer. My little heart was still beating like a racehorse, even though all the craziness had stopped – or at least we *hoped* it had.

Now all I wanted to know was who the hell had been beating and shaking the shit out of our home, and *why*. It couldn't possibly have been kids. I mean, Jack and I were the only ones who terrorized this area, but even we weren't strong enough to shake an entire trailer. And so I kept on replaying the whole event over again, wondering why someone would try to scare us like this.

Momma scooted closer to Hunter and I and rubbed her hands on our knees, trying to reassure us it was all over now. I glanced over at Hunter and saw that he was falling asleep and thought to myself, *I wish I could go to sleep like that*, but knew that there was no way in hell I was getting to bed anytime soon.

I heard footsteps coming up the front porch again, and I turned nervously to watch the door. Pepaw came in, this time with no shotgun, and made his way to the kitchen table. He grabbed one of the chairs, pulled it back and sat himself down on it. "Whoever it was is gone now. There's nobody out there anymore," he said.

"Thank God. Did you find anything outside, Daddy?" Momma asked.

"Well, it looks like something sharp was scraped along the side the trailer. It's a pretty deep scratch, and it goes almost all the way down. I don't know for sure what they used, but to me it looks like it was done by a hunting knife," Pepaw stated. "Now, Sissy, do you have any idea why someone would want to do this to you?"

"No."

"Has Jody or Jack damaged anyone's property around here lately?" Pepaw asked.

"I don't think so. He better not have done something like that!" Momma lashed out. She was giving me the evil eye, and I actually had to start thinking if Jack and I had torn up anybody's property recently. About a week before school had let out, we'd snuck up to old man Nathan's house, which was down the street a ways, and wrote the word *SHIT* on his front door with some spray paint we had found in a ditch. I think Jack even squeezed out the word *DICK* on the side of the old guy's van just before we took off.

Then, just the other day, we stole some people's mail

out their mailbox and threw it into the woods so they wouldn't be able to find it. But no one had seen us, or at least I thought no one had at the time. You see, Jack and I were pretty damned good at covering our tracks and getting away with vandalism and all sorts of other stunts. We had mastered the art of lying at a very early age, and half the people we told the lies to actually believed us. My head thumped with thinking so hard, as I tried to recall all the destructive shit Jack and I had done over last couple of months.

Then, like a bolt of lightning to my brain, I recalled one particular incident.

***

Late one afternoon, about a month ago, Jack and I happened to stumble upon some old smoke bombs stored in his Dad's shed that had been left over from the New Year. I have no clue how we came across the things, but we had, and we knew just what to do with them. Jack ran inside his house and came out a few minutes later brandishing a pack of his Mom's matches that he'd taken from the small drawer under the microwave.

I was so excited about the whole thing and couldn't contain myself as I started jumping up in the air and yelling *Cowabunga!* like I was one of the Ninja Turtles. Jack laughed as he picked his red and silver bike off the ground, throwing his legs over it like he was mounting a horse. I quit jumping up and down like a retard and bent over to pick up my bike, which had no damned brakes. We jetted out from the driveway and took a left onto Rhine Road as we made our way toward Mr. Rhine's driveway. Then about halfway there, we decided to turn around and head back to the Oaks subdivision where there was a kid Jack and I couldn't stand; he was to be our new target.

"You think they're gonna shit their pants when they look in the mailbox?" Jack asked as we rode down the street.

"Oh, yeah. They're going to shit all right. It's not every day the mail in your mailbox turns blue, red, or green. It's going to be funny as hell," I giggled.

"We can't get caught, though. Mrs. Ansen already hinted to my mom that she thought she saw us stealing those flower pots from the Greely's house."

"How the hell did she see us? I thought we got away with that."

"I guess not, but anyways, let me finish –" Jack said, "Momma said if she catches me doing that stuff, I'll be grounded from playing with you – *forever.*"

I could tell Jack was serious. The color in his face drained a little once he'd said it.

"There's no way they can keep us from playing with each other. We're best friends!" I spat out.

"I know… I know," Jack said and stared down at the pavement.

"So let me guess. You don't want to do this, then?" I asked him.

"I do, Jody. It's just that I don't want us to get caught. We're best friends. I don't want to get grounded from you. That would really suck."

"I know it would," I said.

I looked up the road and saw a broken glass bottle on the side. Some jackass must have thrown it out the window on their way home from a wonderful night of drinking and driving.

"Stop up there by the glass, Jack."

"What for?'

"Just stop up there," I said.

As we rolled up to the bottle, Jack braked and I put my feet down *Fred Flintstone* style to stop myself. We got off our bikes, walked them over to the side of the street and laid them down. I made my way over to the smashed bottle and picked up a nice-sized piece of glass. Returning to Jack, I extended my hand to him.

"Why are you giving me a piece of glass?" Jack asked me, nonplussed.

"Just take it."

"Why?"

"Just take it, *asswipe*!" I demanded. What Jack didn't know was that I had an idea that would make us more than *just* friends.

Jack reached out, took the glass from my hand and said with sarcasm, "Why, thank you, Jody. This is the best gift anyone has *ever* given me."

"Oh, shut up," I said, trying to maintain my composure. "Now – I want you to cut me."

"What?!"

"I said – I want you to cut me."

"Are you crazy? I'm not going to cut you," Jack said.

"Cut me right here on the hand. Trust me. It'll be cool."

"Get out of here..." Jack said jokingly, pausing a moment to study me from head to toe. "You're serious, aren't you?"

"Yes. Now cut me right here on the finger. But don't go too deep. I don't want to wind up in the hospital."

I opened up my hand and extended my pointer finger toward him. Jack took one last look into my eyes and grabbed my wrist firmly. He let out a quick sigh of breath and swiftly ran the glass through my finger.

"Ouch!"

"Are you alright?" Jack asked.

"I'm alright – I'm alright," I grimaced, squeezing my

hand tight.

I looked down at my finger and stared at the wound. Bright red blood ran out at a very slow pace, and that meant Jack had cut me just how I'd intended.

"Okay now, Jack, give me the glass." I extended my other hand and motioned to Jack.

"Here," Jack said as he handed the shard over.

"Now give me *your* hand," I instructed.

"No way!" Jack shouted.

"Come on now, Jack. Give me your hand –"

"This is stupid. Let's just go get rid of these smoke bombs."

"Not until you give me your hand," I said, and this time I was more serious than ever. Reluctantly, Jack stopped his complaining and gave me his hand. I placed the glass in the middle of his pointer finger, pressed slightly and yanked the glass down into his skin.

"Damn it!" Jack whined.

"You're alright. It'll stop hurting in a minute."

"Shit! It burns!"

"Quit being a wuss," I barked, and for some reason, the word *wuss* seemed to toughen my friend up; he paused his swearing and stopped pacing from side to side and acting like his finger had been blown off.

Jack stood up straight, fighting off his pain in silence. "Now why did we do this again?" Jack asked me. He was still trying to get rid of the ache in his hand by shaking it.

"We're going to be blood brothers," I told him.

"We're going to be *what*?"

"Blood brothers. You know, just like *Tom Sawyer* and *Huck Finn*."

"I hope you know those guys aren't real," Jack said, sarcastically.

"I know that, damn it. But our parents can't keep us

away from each other if we're brothers. I mean – you're my *best* friend."

"I know, Jody."

"Look, all we have to do is rub both of our fingers together and we'll be brothers for life, even though we have different moms."

Jack stared at the ground, deep in thought, as if he had the hundred-yard stare. I began to think for a moment that I'd upset my friend or something, until he looked up and shot me a weak smile. Right then, at that very instant I knew he wanted to do it; so I broke the silence and teased, "By the way, my mom is way cooler than yours."

"No way. My mom is way cooler than yours!" he rebutted.

"Yeah, right. Your mom doesn't even let you stay up late to watch movies. My mom lets me stay up as long as I want on the weekends," I bragged.

"Oh yeah? Well your mom won't let you shoot your BB gun at your Memaw's bluebirds. My mom doesn't care about how many birds I shoot. She says I'm a good shot – just like my dad."

When the word *Dad* came rolling out of Jack's mouth, everything that was going on around me seemed to vanish. It was as if I had been scooped off into another dimension, light years away; I was now in a dream world that only let me see what I was thinking. I visualized my father, who was at that time living in Baton Rouge with his new girlfriend. It felt like I was there with them as they enjoyed dinner together at their kitchen table. I missed having a father, even though he wasn't worth a pot to piss in, just being able to say I had one made me feel normal, like all the other kids. I wanted a father to teach me how to shoot like Mr. Shawn taught Jack, but Momma told me that Daddy didn't love her anymore and she didn't know if he would ever come back around. I couldn't quite comprehend why he never did come back, it wasn't Hunter's or my fault so what was the big deal with being around us...?

"Jody? Earth to Jody..." Jack said and waved his hand in my face.

"What?" I asked.

"You had that same look on your face that you get when you're on the bus. You know, that spaced-out look."

"Yeah... I think I did space out for a second there. Sorry."

"It's cool. What were you thinking about?" Jack asked me.

"My Dad."

"Oh. I'm sorry."

"No, it's okay. I was just wondering what he was doing right now. I wonder if he's drunk and doing naked jumping jacks in his girlfriend's living room, just how he used to do them in ours," I mused, feeling that I had to throw something humorous in there, or else the conversation would have turned too serious and we would've never gotten rid of those damn smoke bombs.

"Oh yeah, I remember you telling me about that," Jack laughed.

"Oh my God, it was so funny. This one time, he'd just got back from drinking with his buddies out in Hammond and he walked in the trailer smelling like booze. Momma started yelling at him, calling him a drunken bastard and then Daddy looked over at Momma and said, '*I'm not drunk! Watch this shit!*' Then no joke, Jack, Daddy stripped down butt-ass naked in the living room and started doing jumping jacks, counting out loud like he was in gym class." Toward the end of my little story, I was trying so hard to hold back – it was like I

117

had a bag of laughs that wanted to open itself up in my mouth and consume my whole body.

"Oh my God, that's *so* funny, Jody," Jack laughed uncontrollably.

"I know. My Dad's a dumbass." After that final comment, laughter overcame us both and we collapsed to our knees, laughing loudly like crazed lunatics, fingers dripping with blood and all.

A couple of minutes later we regained control and stood up from the ground, facing each other.

"You ready?" Jack asked.

"Ready," I said.

We brought our fingers together and pressed them tight against one another. Our blood smeared together as we rubbed our fingers up and down until we were absolutely certain our blood was in each other's veins. We then brought our arms down to our sides and just stood and looked at each other.

"Are we blood brothers now?" Jack asked.

"Yep, and we always will be," I told him.

"Awesome!" Jack yelled.

"Sweet! Now let's go set those damned smoke bombs off in *Mr. I'm too Cool for School's* mailbox," I said.

"Let's do it!" Jack replied.

As we rode in the direction of the Oaks subdivision, I looked over to Jack and asked, "You want to start a gang?"

"You mean like those kids in the *Lost Boys* movie?"

"Sort of. Except we don't fight vampires. That's dumb. Vampires aren't even real. We'll just be a gang of troublemakers or something."

"Sounds cool to me. Too bad we couldn't have motorcycles, though. That would be *totally* awesome."

"One day I'll have one, but I doubt I'll get one any time soon."

"Too bad, huh? We could get so many girls if we had 'em."

"I know. But, Memaw would shit a brick if I was to ever get on one of those things. You remember when Pepaw had that big motorcycle in the back yard?" I asked.

"Yeah."

"Well, one day I was riding on the back of it with Pepaw and she came running out the house and throwing a fit. She told Pepaw she didn't want me on one of those death traps and he needed to get me off of it."

"I know what you mean. My grandmother is the same way. She doesn't even like when I slide in to home base. She thinks I'm gonna break my leg every time I do it."

"Yep. That sounds just like Memaw too. God, I hope I don't turn out like them when I get older," I said.

"Me either," Jack said.

"Anyways... so I guess we're a gang now, right?"

"Right,"

"So what are we gonna call ourselves?"

"I don't know... how about the Lost Boys."

"That name has already been used – twice," I said.

"Really? The movie was the first time I heard it."

"What!? You've never heard of *Peter Pan and the Lost Boys*?" I asked my brand-new blood brother.

"Oh yeah," Jack replied with a smirk, "those kids were a bunch of pussies, though."

"Whatever, Jack. They lived in the coolest tree house in the world, *and* killed pirates all day long. I would love to do that all the time. Kill pirates, save girls, hang out with friends, no parents – now *that's* the life for me."

"Damn. Too bad *Neverland* isn't real either."

"I know," I said as we turned onto Alvin Drive, the main street of the Oaks subdivision.

As we rolled down the street on our bikes, I took some time to check out the surrounding area just in case we needed to make a quick break for it. You never knew when shit like this was going to go sour, and for some reason I had a real nervous feeling in my stomach. I hardly ever felt this way when Jack and I were up to no good, but for reasons I couldn't explain I had that *Luke Skywalker* feeling as we continued to pedal.

The Oaks was called a subdivision, but in all actuality it wasn't. It was just a way for Mr. Benson to get more people to move here onto Rhine Road. The Oaks had four streets; Daniel, Alvin, Keith and Benson Drive, and was a huge man-made square of middle-class houses with streets that all interconnected at some point

It just so happened that our target, Chris Jacobs – the little ass-face that Jack and I hated so – lived on Daniel Drive. That was great news for us because it meant we only had three houses to watch out for, since there were no other homes on the right side of the street. The fewer the houses, the better chance Jack and I had of not being seen. We rode our bikes around the subdivision several more times, studying the neighborhood as if we were professional thieves, before rounding the corner onto Alvin Drive for the last time.

"Alright – the coast is clear. You ready, Jack?"

"I was born ready," Jack said boldly, and that made us both snicker again.

We turned onto Daniel Drive and rode our bikes into the woods behind the first house on the street. Chris Rogers lived in the second house, and that worked out perfectly because it meant we wouldn't have to run that far back to our bikes when we were done with our mischief.

We gathered our equipment; Jack took the matches and stuffed them in his pocket, while I snatched up the smoke bombs. We walked onto the pavement and hung a left toward Chris's house, talking to each other all casual, like we were just some regular kids hanging out. About thirty feet away from the mailbox, I slowed down my stride, and Jack pulled ahead of me. He approached the mailbox, reached up with his left hand, and pulled open its aluminum face. He kept on walking another twenty feet or so and stopped.

At this point, I was reaching into my pocket to prepare the smoke bombs for their departure. As I snuck up to the mailbox, I threw them in and continued on until I caught up with Jack again.

"Okay. They're in there," I said.

"This is going to be awesome," Jack said, excited.

"I know, I know," I said, keeping my voice to a near hush. "Here's the plan. We stand here and talk another minute or so, and then we'll head back over there. I'll light them while you look out."

"No way, Jody. They're my matches and smoke bombs – *I'm* lighting them."

"Aww – come on, Jack. Let me light 'em, please."

"No way," Jack was firm.

As disappointed as I was, I could see where the kid was coming from. I was very stingy and selfish with certain things that I possessed, so I really couldn't get too upset with him. I was pretty sure that at some point in our friendship I had been an ass to him, too.

"Okay, you win. I'll be lookout while you light those bad boys."

"Now that sounds like a plan to me," Jack said.

When we got back to the mailbox, I glanced around wildly, and to anyone who saw, I would have looked like a paranoid schizophrenic. I was watching everything around us so quickly, my attention bouncing between houses and objects was so fast that I couldn't have been locked onto anything for more than five seconds at a time and I was getting that funny feeling in my stomach again.

Jack brought his head up from the mailbox. "There's no mail in there."

"What!?" I exclaimed.

"Yeah, no mail is in there. The mailman must not have come yet."

"Damn it. *Now* what are we supposed to do?"

"We can come back later and do it," Jack suggested.

"I won't be able to come back. Momma said we're going to the store in a couple of hours, and you know how we like to stay gone forever."

"Well – screw the mail."

Jack pulled out the matches, took one out of the pack and swiped it along the side of the box. The acrid stink of sulfur hit my nostrils and in an instant I heard the smoke bomb fuses burning. Jack slammed the mailbox shut and took off like a rocket back toward our bikes.

"Wait up!" I yelled as I ran after Jack.

I was running so fast that I passed him and dove into the wooded area where our bikes were waiting. I laid there for a while, catching my breath as Jack came in head first to land only a few feet away from me.

"Did you light em' all?" I asked him.

"Only the ones you put in there, but yeah, that mailbox is smoking," Jack told me with a grin.

I leaned over and celebrated our successful mission by giving Jack a quick high-five before throwing myself back onto my bike.

I was pedaling out of the woods, back onto the road, when I glanced down the street and noticed the mail truck making its way in our direction. Jack came out of the woods on his bike and stopped right next to me. The mailman was making the right onto Daniel when he stopped directly in front of us and studied the mailbox that was now producing thick green and blue smoke. My throat dried up, and I do believe I heard Jack cut loose a nervous fart.

The mailman turned his head slowly and looked at us. The sweat on my skin turned cold and sent a shiver down my spine.

"Do you boys know who did that?" the mailman asked.

"Did what?" Jack asked stupidly.

"You boys know what I'm talking about."

As I stared at the mailman, I couldn't help but notice how creepy-looking he was. I used to think that all mailmen were old as dirt, already retired from a previous profession and were just doing the job to earn a little extra cash to top up their pension. But this guy wasn't old at all. In fact, he couldn't have been a day over thirty-five; his hair was long, dark brown, slicked back like a businessman's and tied in a ponytail. But the thing that disturbed me the most about the guy was that he looked like he hadn't slept in days and his voice was a deep baritone.

"You know, messing with people's mail is a federal offense. You can get five to ten years in jail – sometimes even more," the mailman informed us with a cold, matter-of-fact tone.

"It wasn't us, sir. We were just back here building a clubhouse in the woods. We were just on our way back to my house to get some more nails," I lied.

"Really?" the mailman replied.

"Yes, really," I nodded.

"Can you show me the hammer you've been using, then?"

I thought to myself, *who the hell does this guy think he is, Magnum PI?* And then Jack answered his question. "It's back there in the woods," he said. "But we really have to hurry up and get home. My dad locks his shed up soon, so we *really* need to get back."

"I thought you said you were going back to his house – not yours," the mailman said.

This guy was good at getting to the bottom of things. I knew he was trying to catch us out in our lie, but we weren't about to let that happen. Jack and I came to a mutual, silent conclusion that we were going to have to finagle our way out of this one, big time.

"My house *is* his house," I shot back.

"Yeah – we're brothers," Jack added.

"Really? If that's true, then where do you boys live?"

"I can't tell you that, sir. Our mother told us never to talk to strangers," I said.

"Well, you're talking to me now, aren't you? I wouldn't consider myself a stranger if I was in your shoes – but that's okay if you don't want to tell me," he looked back up the road to the smoldering mailbox and then back to us, "Well, I have to get going, if you boys find out who set those smoke bombs off in that mailbox, please let me know next time you see me. There could be a reward in store for whoever gives me some information."

"No problem, sir," Jack said.

"Good. I guess I'll see you boys around then," The mailman smiled.

I took a deep breath and released it slowly through my nose, and I thanked God that Jack and I had gotten out of that sticky situation without incident. We watched our friendly neighborhood mailman shift his little white truck into first gear and drive on toward the smoking mailbox. As he got closer to it, a woman – who we assumed to be Mrs. Rogers – came dashing from her house with a cup of water to extinguish the smoke.

As soon as the mailman stopped next to Mrs. Jacobs, I tapped Jack on the arm and urged, "Let's get the hell outta here!" And we came quickly to our senses and scurried off on our bikes.

Somewhere along the way between The Oaks and my house, Jack jettisoned the matches and the remaining smoke bombs into the woods – the day's stunt had almost been a failure, so we decided to take a break from the pyrotechnics for the time being and concentrate our efforts on other methods of destruction. I made a right onto Memaw's driveway while shouting goodbye to Jack, not slowing down at all. I parked my bike up against the tree next to the front porch and ran inside to see what Pepaw was up to.

***

"Jody!" Momma yelled, snapping me back into reality, "did you and Jack tear anyone's stuff up? You better answer me, boy."

I looked over at Pepaw, and even he was giving me the evil eye. I was really on the spot, I didn't know if I should tell them about the mailbox incident. For all I knew, if I told them the truth, I could end up in jail, just like the mailman said – five to ten years was a very, *very* long time, especially for a kid my age. Another reason I didn't say a word was because I couldn't be sure if the mailman had said anything about us to Mrs. Rogers or not, so I did what I did best, and I lied.

After I was done being interrogated by Momma and Pepaw, I went back to my room and played my video games. About thirty minutes later, Momma came into my room and turned off the TV.

"I want you to listen to me, Jody. I know you and Jack are off doing stupid stuff that you know you are not supposed to be doing. I know you've been lying to me recently, but you're not as good of a liar as you think you are. You need to stop doing bad things with Jack, son. I don't know who is the mastermind to all of y'all's little fiascos, but the shit needs to stop, or I swear to God you'll never play with that boy again."

"You can't do that to us," I said, "we're brothers now. Blood brothers – and *nobody* can keep us away from each other."

"Do you know how serious this is, Jody? Somebody was so angry with you that they came to our trailer to scare us. If you don't stop doing bad things, I promise you, I will call Renee and let her know everything. And I guarantee that she'll agree with me to keep Jack away from you."

"But Momma!" I whined.

"I don't want to hear it! Just get in bed, and think about what you could have done to bring this upon yourself and this family."

Momma backed out of the room and slammed the door hard enough to shake the whole trailer. I crawled in bed and buried myself under my Nintendo sheets with my knees tucked firmly into my chest. I couldn't stop wondering who it was that had been messing with our trailer. I also started to wonder what life would be like without Jack, and honestly I believe that was what scared me the most that night.

CHAPTER ELEVEN

BIKING ACCIDENT: 1990

After the trailer incident, life went on as it always does and the events of that night slowly vanished from my thoughts. I never actually got around to telling Jack about what happened that night at our trailer. Momma pulled me aside once in the Delchamps grocery store a couple of days afterwards, when I'd seen Jack running around on aisle three knocking shampoo bottles off the shelves. I went to take off after him and suddenly Momma grabbed me by the arm, stopping me in my tracks. "Don't you dare say a word to Jack about what happened the other night, or what we talked about," She hissed.

"Why not?" I asked, although I really should have known better.

"Because I said so, son. I don't want the rest of the street thinking there are some crazy lunatics running around."

"I won't say anything like that, Momma."

"Jody, I know how you are, and you turn everything

into a story. Remember when you convinced Alex that Ninjas were hiding in the woods behind his house?"

"Yes."

"And do you remember when you told all the kids in Mrs. Thompson's class that there was a ghoul that lived in the boys' bathroom, and if they sat on the toilet it'd eat them?"

"Yeah," I whined, even though that had been a really good fib.

"Did you know I was on the phone with Mrs. Thompson for over an hour, listing to all the rest of the crazy stories you'd told everyone in class once she got wind of your ghoul rumor?"

"No, I didn't know that," I said.

"Well I *was*," Momma spat. "Mrs. Thompson said kids in the school weren't taking shits anymore due to your little fabrication, and believe me, Jody, I don't want to have to explain to anyone else that you have an active imagination that runs away with you all the time. So keep your mouth shut and don't tell anyone about what happened, *not even Jack*."

"Okay, Momma," I said and went on my merry way, and I never did say a word to anyone.

Over the summer, Jack and I took a break from our terrorizing activities and focused all our attention to bike ramping. But I'm not talking about your average, everyday bike ramping; I'm talking about *country boy bike ramping*. We never actually had real ramps, instead we just jumped everything in sight, be it manmade objects such as culverts, or nature's naturally produced ramps, which were usually huge tree roots that shot up out of the earth.

Now that I think of it, there was never really all that much technique or skill involved in our new hobby, it just basically boiled down to which of us had the bigger set of balls. And there was nothing we wouldn't jump, and that's the reason my fearless ass wound up with a broken arm for the rest of the summer. For some odd reason, Jack wasn't with me the day I broke my arm, but I'll never forget how stupid it was of me to try to attempt the stunt I'd pulled that day.

Kyle Green was five years older than Jack and I, and just happened to be playing catch in his front yard with one of his buddies as I rode past them on my bike one late summer afternoon.

"Hey, Jody!" Kyle yelled across at me.

I placed my feet down to the hard pavement and brought my bike to a stop directly in front of his house.

"I've been watching you and Jack do a lot of crazy shit on your bike lately," Kyle said with what may well have been admiration.

"Yeah... so?" I prompted.

"Well," Kyle said, easing off his baseball glove, "I bet you can't jump this ditch."

"*This* ditch?" I asked and pointed my finger at the enormous gash that ran alongside the road.

"Yeah, *that* ditch," Kyle repeated, cutting loose a conniving smile. In the back of my mind, I knew I couldn't make that jump. The ditch was at least six feet wide with dull green, slimy algae growing in it and a ton of trash floating on top of its thin surface layer of grime; there was just no possible way a kid my age could do it. For one, I didn't have enough room to get up to enough speed; and for two, there was nothing alongside the road that could project me high enough into the air to clear the ditch. But, due to me being an incorrigible show-off, I often made incredibly bad decisions – and this time I would walk away with a permanent scar to remind me just how foolish pride can get the best of you.

"Oh, that ain't squat. I can clear that – no problem,"

I said confidently.

Even though I knew I was fucked before I even started, there was no way I was going to let Kyle punk me out and then run around telling everybody that I was a pussy. No way, Jack and I had worked too hard for our reputations, and I was not about to bring shame to our names in any way, shape, or form.

"Oh yeah?" Kyle provoked. "Then let's see you do it."

"Alright, watch this."

I brought my feet back up to my pedals, turned around and headed back down in the opposite direction to Kyle's house. Once I was far enough away, I turned the bike around and stopped in the middle of the street. My heart was racing, and I could hear Kyle screaming, "Come on! I gotta see this!" in the distance, but I tried my very best to ignore him. I thought to myself, *all you have to do, Jody, is pull up as hard as you can on your handlebars right after your front tire touches the grass. If you pull hard enough, you just might land on your back tire on the other side of the ditch.*

"Yeah, pull up as hard as I can and I'll make it," I said aloud to myself.

"Let's go! It's almost Christmas already!" Kyle screamed while his friend looked on nervously at the impending disaster.

I took a deep breath, said a small prayer and took off. I could feel the wind blowing through my hair as I pedaled faster and faster, all the while hoping like hell I was going to clear that ditch.

The next thing I remember was hearing Kyle shout, "Oh shit!" as I flew over my handlebars and head first into the opposite side of the ditch. My left arm struck the ground hard and snapped like a spring twig, the bones bursting from my split skin. I rolled over onto my back as fast as I could, half covered in clinging algae, smelling like sewage and stared with disbelief at my arm. Twin spikes of bone stuck straight out of my flesh, blood steadily flowing from beneath it, the bones yellow, not the stark white you see in the movies. When that image finally set in, I screamed and cried like a little girl. The pain washed over me, a hot, agonizing throb that began in my arm and shot through the entirety of my body, and I was overcome with panic. I scrabbled to my feet, jumped out of the ditch and ran home, screaming bloody murder with Kyle right behind me.

"You're gonna be okay, Jody. Everything is going to be okay," Kyle said, and I think he was panicking more than I was.

All I could do was wail loudly as tears fell down my face. Once we got to my trailer, Kyle placed his hands on my shoulders and helped lead me up the stairs. Momma opened the front door and came out, with Hunter not far behind. The little turd was sucking on a delicious Popsicle while I was in complete agony.

"Oh my God!" Momma shrieked as she caught glimpse of my grotesque, horror-movie arm.

"Miss Gayla," Kyle said, "he broke his arm while trying to jump a ditch on his bike."

"I knew it! I knew it," Momma ranted, "I told you, Jody. All that daredevil stuff was going come back and bite you in the ass, but oh no, don't listen to me, I don't know anything, I've just been on this earth twenty plus years longer than you, what do I know?!"

"Miss Gayla, he needs to go to the hospital," Kyle said.

Once Kyle's words got to Momma's ears, she stopped ranting and wrapped her arms around me tight.

"Owwww, Momma! Not so tight!"

"Hunter, go run and get Pepaw. Tell him Jody broke

his arm and we need to go to the hospital."

"Okay," Hunter said, and took off running.

Three minutes later, Pepaw came roaring up our driveway in his car. He parked right next to the porch where Momma and I were standing.

"Get him in, Sissy," Pepaw said through the window.

"Let's go, Jody," Momma whispered.

The car ride to the hospital had to be the most miserable road trip of my life. Pepaw seemed intent on hitting every single pothole on every road, and I was beginning to think he was doing it on purpose. With every bump came a new surge of white hot pain in my arm, and I screamed for Pepaw to slow down; and boy did he. Pepaw then slowed down to a crawl and I yelled at him again, but this time for him to *please go faster*.

"I'm sorry, Jody. What do you want me to do? If I go fast, the bumps make your arm hurt more, and if I go slow, you want me to go faster. So what do you want me to do?" Pepaw asked.

"Go fast, Pepaw. Please just get me to the hospital!" I cried.

Pepaw nodded his head, as if he was a genie granting my wish, and put the pedal to the metal, which sent me flying into the back of my seat. Momma continued to hold me tight as Pepaw hauled tail through the streets of Hammond at breakneck speeds, whipping around corners and running stoplights like they just weren't there.

That car ride seemed never-ending, but as soon as I looked over to Momma to ask her for the thousandth time when we were going to be there, Pepaw made a right onto the ER's entrance road. And within a matter of minutes, I was in the emergency room, still crying like a little girl, standing with Momma while Pepaw talked to the receptionist at the counter.

Instantly, the ER doors swung open and two orderlies came running out with a wheelchair, and Momma placed her hands on my shoulders and gently spun me around until my rear end was seated in the thing. The orderlies then trundled me into a white room with all types of medical equipment in it. They stopped halfway into the room, took me out of the wheelchair and placed me on the examination table. Momma walked into the room alongside a doctor who looked like he hadn't slept in months, grabbed a chair and placed it right next to me. The doctor approached and placed a pink towel under my broken arm while the orderlies came back into the room, this time bearing gifts. They rolled a cart in with them, covered with syringes and needles. I felt my eyes widen as I stared at the impossibly huge needle in the middle of the tray, and hoped that they wouldn't have to use it on me. The doctor barked orders to the two orderlies as I looked over to Momma.

"What are they going to do?" I asked.

"They're going to reset your arm."

"What does that –" but before I could finish, the doctor interrupted.

"All right now, buddy, my name is Doctor Borden. I need you to open your mouth up nice and wide and bite down on this as hard as you can, okay?" Dr. Borden instructed.

"Okay," I said, scared shitless.

I opened my mouth as wide as I could manage, and Dr. Borden placed a wooden bar in my mouth, about as thick as those oversized school pencils you sometime see the little kids carrying around – I never understood why kids used them, the bastards were so damned big it was damned near impossible to do any schoolwork with it. I bit down hard as instructed, and watched Dr. Borden move his hands down to my arm.

"I want you to bite down hard when you feel pain, okay?" Doctor Borden told me.

I nodded my head weakly, and rested it down on the table, gazing upward at the fluorescent lights above me.

"One... Two... Three!"

On three, I felt an excruciating pain shoot throughout my entire body as the doctor pulled down on my arm, trying to place the bones back together.

"*Arrrggghhhhh... arrrggghhhhh!*" I screamed while biting down on that fat chunk of wood.

"We're gonna try again, guys, get over here and hold his legs down. We have to keep him from moving. We gotta set this thing," Dr. Borden sounded grim.

The pair of orderlies ran over and held my feet down firmly on the table, and I shot Momma a look of anguish.

"Alright – be tough buddy – Two – Three!"

***

I woke up in one of the recovery rooms on the fourth floor of the hospital, having undergone surgery. I'd passed out on that last tug of my arm, courtesy of Dr. Borden, and was rushed into surgery because they couldn't reset the bones without slicing my poor arm. It turned out to be one hell of a break, and two metal pins had to be screwed in my arm just to hold the shattered bones together.

As my vision came back into focus after my drug-induced sleep, I looked down at my arm and saw the almost pristine, white cast – Momma and Pepaw had already signed it. I could have sworn my father had been in the room at some point while I was out, but maybe I'd dreamed it, all thanks to the anesthetics they had given me. But I felt deep down, pretty damned sure I'd seen my father standing over me while I was in that hospital bed. I could even remember what color hat he had on; it was a green John Deere, and I even remembered seeing him smile at me.

I sat up nice and straight in the bed, looked to my left and saw Momma sitting in the chair next to the lamp. She was reading an old magazine, but once she saw that I was awake, she put it down and came over to give me smooches.

"You're awake, Jody," Momma ran her fingers through my hair, "how you feeling?"

"Okay I guess. Was Daddy here, Momma?" I asked.

"Yes. He was here, but he had to go back to work," Momma told me.

"He came back. I knew I wasn't dreaming. I saw him standing right next to me."

"Yeah, he was here, standing right there, but he had to go. Sorry you didn't get to talk to him, but he did sign your cast."

"Really? Where at?" I asked, excited.

"Flip your arm over," Momma said.

I turned my arm over, which now felt like it weighed a million pounds, and read what my Daddy wrote.

Bubba-

Get better.

Dad.

My heart lit up like a Christmas tree when I read it, and I slumped down into my bed, making myself comfortable. I could feel a smile trying to sneak its way on my face. A part of me so desperately wanted my father to be a part of my life, and I just wanted to know that he truly loved me. Well, I quickly found out the hard way that you can want in one hand and shit in the other to see which one fills up first, because my father never did become part of my life. My smile quickly went away, and all I felt was disdain and anger for my father; I just wanted to go to sleep, and dream of a father who truly loved me.

The cast was still on when the school year began; my arm had to stay in a cast for almost the entire first half of fifth-grade, only having to be replaced twice due to my failure to follow instructions – the first when I got the original soaking wet, the second, when I tried cutting the infernal thing off because it was itching up a storm. Every photo taken of me on my tenth birthday, which was a pretty good birthday otherwise, shows me wearing that damned thing with my shiny braces – it's so embarrassing to look at them, even to this day.

CHAPTER TWELVE

A NEW YEAR: 1991

After the New Year, the doctors finally removed the cast and rescheduled me for surgery so they could remove the two pins that were in my arm. A month later, I went in at seven in the morning and I was out by one o'clock in the afternoon. The whole process felt like drive-thru surgery to me, done and over with in the blink of an eye. Once the operation was done, they monitored me for a couple of hours, and then I was free to go. And believe me, I couldn't have been more ecstatic that I would be able to finish the last five months of school feeling like a normal kid again, and it was straight into my fifth-grade summer with my good friend, Jack.

"Glory, glory, hallelujah," Jack sang, "my teacher hit me with a ruler, I met her at the bank with a loaded Army tank, glory, glory no more teacher!"

"Holy shit, that's pretty funny," I laughed along, "I got one too, wanna hear it?"

"Yeah, let me hear it," Jack encouraged.

"Deck the halls with gasoline, FA-LA-LA-LA-LA-LALA-LA-LA, strike a match and watch it gleam, FA-LA-LA-LA-LA-LA-LALA-LA-LA, watch the school burn down to ashes, FA-LALA-LALALA-LA-LA-LA, aren't you glad we play with matches, FA-LALA-LA-LA-LALA-LA-LA!"

"I *have* to use that one," Jack gasped through floods of tears, laughing so hard he could barely breathe.

We were walking down Rhine Road, heading back toward my trailer and singing the new tunes we'd picked up during the school year. As kids, goofy little songs are a pretty cool way of making the time pass, whether you're in school or not. Hundreds of such songs were passed around each year, and if I could've written down every one I'd heard at school, I'd have a book as thick as the Holy Bible itself. Still to this day, every time I hear a stupid song sung by little kids, it makes me feel alive and makes me wish that a child's innocence could last forever.

So eventually, Jack and I wound up in my backyard; which was about an acre wide and two acres long. Just recently, Pepaw had installed one of the first satellite dishes on the domestic market. That big, black bastard stood in the middle of my backyard and made our trailer look like it had NASA agents working inside it trying to locate aliens. It was pretty embarrassing now that I think about it, but the thing made us look rich, and that was good enough for me. And when kids asked where I lived, I told them to look for the big, expensive satellite dish, even though only Pepaw got the channels; but no one else really needed to know that.

Jack and I walked through the ton of pine needles that had fallen from the group of pine trees that huddled together in the middle of our yard. The trees were located roughly fifty feet behind the dish, and as soon as you thought they'd taken over the entire yard, there was a narrow opening that revealed the entrance to woods – which was where the drumming came from what seemed to be a lifetime ago. I hadn't ventured anywhere in the woods during the whole fifth grade year, because of what happened the last time I was fiddle-farting around behind Angela's house. Yet, even though what I'd stumbled upon had been intensely horrifying, my curiosity crept back as I stared into the tree line.

"Wow! Look, Jody," Jack said, pointing his finger next to one of the pine trees, "A *Clearly Canadian* bottle."

"Who put that there?" I asked him, "I sure didn't. I haven't played back here in the longest time."

"I don't know who put it here – can we go break it?"

"Shit yeah, we can!" I replied.

"Where do you want to go to break it?" Jack asked as he picked the bottle up from the ground.

"Let's go bust the window out of Kyle's momma's car. He's the reason I had to wear that damned cast all year."

"No way, they'd definitely know it was us." Jack paused and scratched his head, "How about Mrs. Ansen? That was the bitch who tried to tell my mom we were stealing plants from people's houses."

"But we *were* stealing plants, Jack," I stated.

"I know, but it's the fact that she tried to tell on us. You know what I mean?"

"Yeah, I know what you mean."

As we made our way back through the pines to my trailer, we saw a bluebird land on one of the pine branches. Jack and I both looked up and watched as it sat there and chirped its daily melody.

"I'm gonna hit that bastard with this bottle," Jack said boldly.

139

"Whatever, Jack. Look how high up it is. There's no way you can throw a bottle that high."

"Oh yeah? Watch me."

Jack walked slowly toward the bird, making sure he didn't make a sound on his approach.

"Don't get me in trouble, Jack. You know Memaw will shit a golden egg if she finds out you hurt one of her bluebirds."

"Be quiet!" Jack hissed.

I watched my friend as he moved a tad bit closer to the bird. Finally he reached his arm back, then accelerated it forwards to release the bottle high into the air. The next thing that happened took me by complete surprise, I still tell the story to this very day. Jack hit that damn bird and knocked it out of the tree, sending it fluttering a good thirty feet to the ground below. When the bird slammed into the ground, blue feathers floated on down behind it like late guests arriving to a dinner party. Jack and I stood there, amazed. I could barely shoot a bird with a BB gun, much less hit one with a bottle. It had to have been one of the most amazing flukes I had ever seen in my life.

As we snapped out of our trance, the bird began to hop away, trying desperately to make a break for it. Jack had undoubtedly injured the poor thing's wing when he'd scored this hit. We took off running after the bird, but Jack beat me to the damned thing, and before I could reach down to pick it up, Jack leapt into the air, bringing his knees deep into his chest and then brought his feet down hard onto the bird's body, killing it instantly.

"What the hell?" I gasped.

"What?" Jack asked innocently.

"Why'd you kill it?"

"I don't know, 'cause it was hurt, I guess."

"We could have tried to fix its wing instead of killing

it," I told him.

"Yeah, well – could've, should've, would've, but didn't."

"Whatever, Jack. What do we do with it now?"

"Let's take it to my house and skin it," Jack suggested.

"Gross! Momma says if you kill an animal, you're supposed to eat it. If you don't eat it, God will get mad at you and kill you – or something like that."

"– really?" Jack sounded nervous.

"Yeah – really."

"Well, when we skin it, we'll cook it, and *then* eat it."

"Sounds good to me."

"Alright then, let's go," Jack said.

At first, I had felt bad about the bird, but knowing that we were going to eat it put me at ease. I was never really cruel to animals, so this whole situation felt weird to me. Jack was a hunter; his dad took him all the time, so killing an animal wasn't something new to him like it was for me. In the end, I was just glad that Jack put it out of its misery, and I got over the incident pretty quickly too.

When we arrived at Jack's house, we made our way to his backyard, grabbed a steak knife from off the grill and returned to the edge of the woods behind the dog kennel Mr. Shawn had built. Jack and his father were huge raccoon hunters, and had some of the best tracking dogs that Hammond had to offer – I think they were *Redbones*, but that didn't really matter to me, I wasn't a big coon hunter, nor did I have any interest in becoming one.

I slung the dead bluebird onto the ground and Jack knelt down to begin the skinning. As soon as he jabbed the knife into the bird's stomach, we heard something shuffling through the woods; twigs and branches breaking as whatever it was moved, and all the dogs in the kennel set to barking and scratching at the back door.

"What was that?" I asked.

"I don't know," Jack said, scanning the area cautiously. "Shut the hell up, you damned mutts!" Jack yelled at the dogs.

As soon as Jack yelled, the barking ceased and we heard the noise in the woods once more. Rising from his knees, Jack threw the bird and the knife down to the ground. Something big was in the woods behind the dog kennel, and it *wasn't* an animal.

"Hello," Jack called out, "who's there?"

There was no answer, just more movement. Whatever it was, it was scurrying along the fence adjacent to Jack's next-door neighbors. I never did know their names, but they had the tallest wooden fence on our road.

"I have a gun, ya know!" Jack yelled his false bravado into the woods.

I watched the trees shimmy and shake along the fence as whoever – *whatever* – it was retreated to the other side of the woods. I strained my eyes to see if I could make out what was in there, but I couldn't see a damned thing.

"Jack," I whispered, "let's get on your trampoline and see if we can get a good look over the fence."

Jack said nothing, but nodded his head in agreement.

So, we ran over to Jack's run-down trampoline and began jumping on it until we could see over the fence and into the neighbor's backyard. I caught a good double bounce from Jack after a few jumps and went soaring into the air, legs flailing and all. When I got to the peak of my bounce, I caught a glimpse of a man looking over the fence right back at me. I couldn't see his face clearly, but I could tell that he was white, and was wearing dark clothes. On my way back down to the trampoline, a surge of fear pulsed through my entire body. Once my feet touched down, I stopped myself from bouncing and grabbed Jack by the arm.

"It's a guy!" I said.

"What?"

"It's a guy– and he's looking over your neighbor's fence at us."

"Well, who is he?"

"I don't know."

"What do you think he wants?"

"I don't know, Jack!" I yelled. "All I know is that he's *watching us*."

We both fell silent and stood perfectly still on the trampoline, listening and gathering our thoughts.

"I can go tell my Mom that we treed a squirrel, and she'll let me get my twenty-two out of the gun case," Jack said with fear in his voice.

"Then what? We go back there in the woods and hunt the guy out?" I asked.

"I guess," Jack said, "you got any better ideas?"

Jack glanced over his right shoulder at his neighbor's fence, as if he was expecting some hideous monster to come smashing through it at any second.

"Yeah, I do. We can call the cops and get him arrested for trespassing."

"But he's not on my property. You said he's over there on the neighbor's property," Jack muttered.

"Okay, but just give me another good double bounce, and if he's still spying on us, we'll go get your gun."

"Alright," Jack said, and began jumping once more on the trampoline.

I caught a good bounce from Jack a few jumps later and went soaring into the air once more. This time when I reached the peak of my jump, the strange man wasn't there. I landed back on the trampoline and looked over to Jack. "He's gone, man," I reported. So, we both stood there for a moment, listening intently to the silence that surrounded us.

"Who the hell was that, Jack? Why was he watching us?" I asked.

"I don't know. But if he comes back again, I'll get my Dad to put a bullet in his nosey ass."

CHAPTER THIRTEEN

THE MAN IN THE MALL: 1991

"Remember when we wanted to start a gang?" I asked my blood brother. Jack and I were walking down Rhine Road toward my trailer, bullshitting as usual. The black pavement under our bare feet blazed with heat; to any other kid, walking barefooted on this asphalt was nearly impossible. The scorching sun heated up the road and could seriously sear the skin clean off the bottom of your feet of you weren't used to it, but Jack and I were immune to the fire that stirred beneath us.

"Yeah I remember, but we never came up with a name," Jack said.

"What about the *Rhine Road Boys*?" I asked.

"Yeah – sounds good to me."

"Sweet," I exclaimed, "now all we need is a theme song."

"A theme song?" Jack grinned at me.

"Yeah. You know, like all the ones they have in the movies."

"Only blacks have theme songs," Jack said.

"Well," I paused and thought for a bit, "we can be the first white boys to have one."

"Cool, but I suck at making songs up," Jack replied.

"Don't worry; I'm sure we'll come up with something."

And no shit – by the time we got down to my front yard, we'd come up with a song that defined us perfectly and was so damn catchy I can still remember it to this very day.

"Ready?" I asked.

"Yeah," Jack responded.

So we started up the tune, a take on 90's rap grouping the style of *Snap*.

"At least we go out and get what's coming! The Rhine Road Boys ain't known for running! We'll egg your house and toilet paper your trees!

So you better get down on your knees and lick a couple of deez…

Balls that is! Fuck all of ya'll – whores, that is!"

"Awesome!" I yelled out loud.

Jack had a huge, dumbass smile on his face, and he raised his hand in the air to give me a high five. I raised mine too, but then quickly brought it down and punched Jack in the ribs. I took off running and laughing as Jack chased me into my front yard.

***

It was about a week before I started sixth grade when things took a turn for the worse in my family. I was playing Super Mario World on my new Super Nintendo that I'd received that last Christmas, when Momma came into my room.

"Jody, I need to talk to you."

"What for?" I asked, mashing buttons together and popping *Koopas* back into their shells.

"Pepaw's been diagnosed with cancer," Momma told me, very straightforward; never had she been that blunt with me.

I paused the game, put the controller down and stared up at Momma.

"What's cancer?" I asked hesitantly.

"It's a disease people get sometimes, and sometimes it's something doctors can't cure."

"So is Pepaw going to be okay?"

"I don't know, Bubba. It doesn't look good," Momma said and her eyes slowly filled with tears, which I knew that wasn't a good sign.

"Is he going to die or something?" I asked her, my voice trembling.

"Yes, Bubba," again, painfully to the point. "The doctors have no idea how much longer Pepaw has left to live. Some say a year, others say six months, but it doesn't really matter how much longer Pepaw has left; we all know what the outcome is going to be."

Suddenly, my mind felt like the whole world just stopped turning around me; I simply couldn't imagine my life without Pepaw, he was the only real father figure I had. The thought of him dying made my stomach queasy, and I reached out to Momma and began to cry. Momma wrapped her arms around me and wept as well.

We cried like that for God knows how long, but somehow it didn't really seem to be long enough, not for Pepaw. My heart still ached with sadness when Momma unlatched her arms from around me, and I couldn't stop the tears from falling from my face.

But eventually my eyes did stop crying, and I sat in my room in front of my Super Nintendo wiping snot from my nose. Momma was sitting behind me on the bed rubbing the back of my neck, trying to calm me down as much as she could.

"What do I say to him when I see him?" I asked.

"Just talk to him like you do any other time."

"But he's dying now, Momma. If I go talk to him I'll probably start crying."

"Well, how about this," Momma suggested. "How about you wait for him to talk to you instead? That way, you have some time to get yourself together and possibly think of what you want to say when you see him next time."

I didn't respond, I just nodded sadly and thought about Pepaw. I wanted to know what he was going to do with the rest of his time here on earth. I also wanted to know how he felt about the whole situation, but I wasn't really ready to ask about any of that just yet; there was no way I would be able to keep my composure, and I didn't want to come off as a sissy or, even worse, send Pepaw on an emotional rollercoaster because I broke down in front of him. I didn't want to do that to him, so I took Momma's advice about staying away until he approached me.

I came to the conclusion for the first time in my short life, sitting down in front of my small TV with the video game on pause, that death is the only thing that's certain in life. I hypothesized that from the moment we are born, we begin to die and yet on the other hand, we never know what life has in store for us. One could wind up married with eight beautiful kids, a millionaire, a single parent, a serial killer, or even the President of The United States, the possibilities are endless; there's only one thing that is certain in this so-called *life* – you *will* die.

And the life that you choose to live is up to you, and you alone.

So, I avoided Pepaw like the plague, diving behind anything and everything that would hide me every time I saw him. I felt like a complete asshole most of the time, but I still didn't know what to say to him. I felt terrible knowing he was dying, and I thought about how he must be feeling too. When I watched him from a distance, usually from under my trailer or up in a tree, I remember him appearing to be just fine. He would be out in his shop, sawing and sanding like he did every other day, and I began to believe at the back of my mind that it couldn't be as bad as Momma had made it out to be. And I thought to myself, *maybe this cancer thing would take his life quickly and painlessly.*

A week after Momma told me the dreadful news about Pepaw, I started sixth grade at a new school located in Tickfaw, a small town seven miles away from where we lived, a town mostly made up of white trash folk with a few poor black families here and there. I was so excited about being in a bigger school, but at the same time Pepaw's situation was dragging me down. Momma told me not to think about it too much, and be happy that I was now attending Nelson Middle School.

In Tickfaw, middle school consisted of grades six through eight, and all students had seven teachers, each one teaching a different curriculum. I thought this was cool, but some kids were absolutely terrified. Despite all the nervous kids who were throwing up in the bathrooms, afraid that an eighth grader was going to beat their asses on the first day, going to Nelson Middle School made me feel kind of like an adult, although if I'm honest, it did make me kinda nervous, just not like the kids who were barricading themselves in the lavatories.

My first-period teacher, Mrs. Phillips, warned us the very first day of school about what the teachers were expecting of us now that we were in middle school. She closed the door to the classroom as soon as the bell rang and walked to the front of the class. "This is not the fifth grade, boys and girls. You are not in elementary anymore. Your teachers are not going to tell you what books to bring to class, what day your homework is due, what week your first spelling test is and so on and so forth. You must take notes – and pay attention. If you can do this, your time here in Nelson Middle School will be a very easy one. Sixth grade is not hard, boys and girls, but it can be if you make it that way," Mrs. Phillips informed us with a smile on her face.

I glanced around the room to see if I knew anybody from last year, and the first person to catch my eye was none other than Angela. She was sitting a row over from me, and she was looking around the classroom too. I hadn't seen her all summer, even though she lived right down the street, and she looked different to how I remembered her. She had grown at least two to three inches over the summer, and had gotten her hair cut shoulder-length – and she was still the most beautiful creature I think I'd ever seen. Once our eyes met, Angela shot me a small grin, and butterflies invaded my stomach. I cut her a small grin as well, and then planted my blushing face back into my English book.

The bell rang shortly after, and I gathered my things from up off my desk, stuffed them in my book-sack and exited towards the door. I entered the hallway and it was filled with swarms of kids herding in all directions like cattle to the slaughter. I couldn't walk but two feet without bumping into someone and quickly I found the whole thing a bit overwhelming. Before I could get the strap from my book-sack over my shoulder, I felt someone tap me on the back. I turned around briskly.

"Hey, Jody," Angela said.

"Hey, Angela," I replied, quickly swallowing the lump of nerves that shot up into my throat.

"How was your summer?" she asked me.

"It's was okay, how was yours?"

"Well, we went to Disney World, and that was pretty fun. Then we went to visit some of my cousins in Mississippi. I didn't have much fun at my cousins' though. My dad stayed drunk with my uncle the whole time, and we hardly ever left the house to do anything. We mainly just watched movies and stuff."

"Aw, that sucks."

"Yeah, it sucked," she agreed.

Then there came an odd silence between us. I didn't know if we had just run out of things to say to each other, or if my breath was so bad it was making her not want to talk to me. I reached back, scratched the nape of my neck and looked at the faces of the other kids in the hall. I wanted to say something, but I wasn't sure what to say. I didn't want the conversation to end, but I wasn't going to be the one to strike it back up again.

"So, I heard that two summers ago there was some interesting stuff that happened across the street from my house while we were away." Mercifully for me, it was Angela who broke the awkward silence. "My Aunt Carol stopped by the house the other day and I overheard her talking to my mom about it. She said cops and big trucks hauled a disgusting old trailer out of the woods. Did you hear anything about that?"

"No – well – I – aww," I stammered, trying hard to keep the secret behind my teeth. "No, I didn't hear anything about it."

"Really?" Angela was curious, "'cause Justin Richardson told me that you guys were back there and found some dead cows."

My heart hit the bottom of my stomach, and I knew

then that my secret was out. The secret that even I, the mouth of the south who made kids believe Ninjas lived in the woods, had kept for so long – the cat was well and truly out of the bag.

"Justin said that? Huh, I don't remember seeing anything like that. It was a long time ago, anyways. All I saw was a spot that some of the older kids hung out at. We didn't see any crazy stuff like that. I bet Justin just made that up to scare you," I told Angela.

"It didn't scare me. I thought it was kind of cool how you guys got out of there. You're pretty brave."

"One – I'm not brave, Angela; I'll run away from my shadow if it startles me, and two – the story's not true. Don't listen to anything Justin tells you, okay? It's all bullshit."

"Well, *something* was pulled out of those woods," Angela pushed, rocking back and forth on her feet. "It looked like a T-Rex had come stomping out of there – the trees were all either knocked down or at least tilted over some."

"That's pretty funny." I grinned at the mental image. "You said a T-Rex came stopping out of the woods." I repeated, and then broke out into forced laughter, in the hope of changing the subject.

Angela started giggling too, and before we knew it, we were the only two kids left in the hallway, other than the stragglers hauling ass to make it to class on time.

"Oh! We're going to be tardy!" I said.

"What class do you have next?"

"Hold on, let me look at my schedule." I slung my book sack around to my front, unzipped it and reached in to grab my schedule. I pulled it out and opened it up.

"I have Math, room 306. Do you know where that's at?" I asked.

"Not a clue," Angela replied with a shrug of her

pretty shoulders.

I glanced back down and read through my classes once more.

"French? I'm taking French? What the hell!?"

"Welcome to the sixth grade," Angela said with a big smile.

The bell rang as soon as I flew through the door of Mr. Morris's math class just as all the other doors in the hallway slammed shut behind me. The entire class looked up from their desks and I shrugged my shoulders at them to gesture, *what the hell are you looking at?*

"Take a seat, son," Mr. Morris instructed. He was writing some mathematical equations on the chalkboard, the type of which that I had never seen before, and by the looks of it I could tell that Math was going to be a son-of-a-bitch that year.

I looked around to locate an empty desk, but the only one that was empty was the one right next to the dirtiest kid in school, Kent Lester. I shit you not, that kid smelled like ass; he must have never taken a shower or a bath in his life. It wasn't that healthy odor you get from good, honest exercise sweat, or anything close to that; Kent's stank was straight-up gorilla ass. Now, I've never lived in the jungle, or personally gotten up close enough to smell a gorilla's ass, but that was the closest thing my imagination could compare Kent to.

Later that period, I was sitting back in my chair doing some type of refresher multiplication test, and I suddenly felt a fart cooking up in the lowest bowels of my belly. I knew I was only getting the bubble-guts because I had forgotten all the times tables over the summer. I was so nervous, and I didn't want Mr. Morris to think I was an idiot, but that fart was inching its way out of my rear end and there was nothing I could do to stop it. So, I did the best I could to prevent the catastrophe of embarrassment and squeezed my ass cheeks tight together and begged God to not let it slip out.

Well, I guess I hadn't said my prayers good enough that morning, 'cause the gas came blasting out of my backside like the detonation at Trinity. It pounded its way out onto the plastic chair in full force, making a terrible sound so loud that it sounded like someone had stacked 12 bullfrogs on top of each other and stomped on them all at once. Laughter spread through the class, and Mr. Morris came storming over toward my and Kent's desks.

"Alright, who did *that*?" Mr. Morris demanded to know, although I think he had a pretty good idea.

I raised my hand slowly, eventually extending my pointer finger directly at Kent. "Kent did it, Mr. Morris. And it smells horrible!" I said.

"No I didn't! You did!" Kent yelled, his face reddening.

By this time, the class was uncontrollable with laughter, and I joined in. Now don't get me wrong, I knew what I did wasn't right, but I'll be goddamned if it wasn't funny.

In the long run, sitting next to *Stinky McStinkPants* turned out to work quite nicely for me because, every time I had to fart I would just point my finger at Kent and blame it on him; and it worked every single time.

It was two minutes before the bell rang for lunch, and I was finally going to be able to see Jack. Plus, everything Angela had told me about Justin was starting to creep back into my mind and I wanted to talk to him too. I knew I had to find Justin quickly because if I didn't, the whole school was going to find out about what happened a year ago.

The bell finally rang, and I made my way out of the

classroom into the hallway that led straight to the playground. I opened the double doors, and eyed the swarms of kids who were already playing outside; it must have been lunchtime for the eighth-graders as well, because I saw kids who were all at least four inches taller than everybody else.

The school's playground was completely fenced in, with no way in or out. Grass covered the majority of it, except for the hollowed out dirt pit that was underneath the monkey bars. As I looked around, I noticed two boys playing chicken on the rusted monkey bars, swinging their dangling legs in their attempts to wrap them around the other's and pull them from the bars. Directly in front of me was a group of girls huddled together, gossiping, and a fight was breaking out between some older kids at the far end.

Kids began bumping into me as I stood in the doorway like a dumbass, instead of getting out of the way. They ran by me to join their friends, throwing up high-fives and giving out hugs as if they'd been incarcerated for years and not just one morning. I looked around for Jack, but I wasn't sure if he had the same lunchtime as me: some kids had the lunch that was thirty minutes after mine, which was pretty cool since they got an extra ten minutes.

I made my way out into the middle of the playground, walking slowly as if I had nothing to do, but I was really trying to get a good look at all the kids' faces as they milled around – I didn't want to accidentally pass Jack up. But, after a few minutes or so of looking around frantically for my friend, I called off my search and decided to look for Justin instead. Then, much to my surprise, I spotted him standing over by one of his friends named Chase, trading baseball cards. I made my way over and placed my hand on the kid's shoulder. "Hey, Justin. Can I talk to you for a second?"

"Hey, Jody. Sure, hold on."

Justin turned to his friend, gave him some more cards and then turned back toward me. I noticed that Justin had grown a couple of inches since our excursion into the woods, and had slimmed down a lot too.

"Let me guess," Justin said, crossing his arms like a bouncer, "you want to know why I told Angela about the shit that happened in the woods."

"Yes, I do. What the hell were you thinking, man? That shit's going to get around to everyone."

"No it's not."

"Yes it is! If you told Angela, then how many other people is she gonna tell? And then, how many people will those people tell?"

"Damn, Jody. I didn't know it was that big of a deal."

"Well it is, Justin. Didn't your parents tell you not to say anything?" I asked.

"I didn't tell my parents," Justin said.

"What! You didn't tell your parents?!"

"Hell no! If I'd told them about what happened back there, my ass would've never left the house for the rest of the summer."

"I thought you did tell them, and that was why I hadn't seen you around in so long."

"No, that's not why I haven't been back over," Justin told me. And then his voice dropped to a near-whisper and he scooted up closer to me, "I haven't been back over because I'm scared out of my damned mind. I don't want to ever step foot onto Rhine Road again."

I took a step back and realized how badly that incident must have traumatized Justin. I had yet to think about how he was dealing with the situation, 'cause I was too busy trying to deal with it myself. I felt horrible about it, but there was nothing I could do about it now besides listen to what the poor kid had to say.

"I've been having nightmares ever since that day in the woods, Jody. It's been over a year, and I still don't want to go to sleep at night; I keep seeing those dead calves every time I close my eyes, and sometimes in my dreams they come alive and let out a God-awful scream. Then, every now and again, I think I see someone standing in the corner of my room, and all I keep asking myself is what if there really had been a crazy guy in the woods with us that day."

"We're not sure if there was *any* guy, Justin. I think we just got spooked, and who wouldn't have, man? I mean, Jesus, it was a slaughterhouse back there," I said.

"You're wrong, Jody – I think there was someone back there. I just know it. Did you hear about the Harvest Christian Academy, off Baptiste Road?"

"No."

"Someone put graffiti all over it. They drew circles with stars in them all over that Christian school, Jody. That's right by my house! I *know* someone was back there at the trailer with us, and I can't shake it from my mind."

I stood in silence, taking it all in. I didn't know what to say, but I knew Justin wasn't lying. Momma, Pepaw and I had driven past the Harvest Christian Academy a few weeks ago, and a fresh coat of paint covered the grey building. The staff had clearly painted over *something*, it was likely it was the weird graffiti Justin was talking about.

"Well, if everything you're telling me *is* true, then why are you running your mouth to everybody about what we saw?"

"I only told Angela, but that's because I think she needs to know. I didn't want to scare her, so I didn't even mention that we thought there was a guy back there. I just had to tell someone, Jody, and Angela really needed to know that those cows were killed back there. How would you feel if something bad like that happened across the street from your house and no one told you jack-shit about it? And if it takes me telling Angela about it to keep her away from there – then so be it."

"I'm pretty sure she doesn't play in the woods, Justin," I said, being sarcastic as ever.

"You never know. She could be a tomboy."

"Doubt it."

"Yeah, maybe you're right," he said, glancing down at the ground.

We stopped our conversation there, with a cursory glance around to see if everyone had been listening, and our minds temporarily drifted off into another place. I wasn't sure what Justin was thinking about, but I replayed the whole scenario at that God-forsaken trailer all over again in my mind. I did have some nightmares, just like Justin, but Momma really helped me get over those and the issue was pretty much dead to me. But just talking to Justin, the floodgates had opened back up.

"Are you sure you only told Angela?" I asked him.

"Yes," Justin replied.

"Did you tell Jack?"

"No, I thought he would've known about it already, being your best buddy and all."

"Well, he doesn't. And I'd like to keep it that way."

"You mean, you didn't tell *Jack*? I thought you guys were supposed to be best friends?"

"He is my best friend, but Momma told me to keep my mouth shut about what we saw. She didn't want people to turn it into something bigger than what it was."

"I never thought about it like that." Justin said. He rocked back on his heels with his head lifted up to the sky, then reached down to pick up his book-sack.

"So, you're not going to tell anyone else, right?" I asked him with more than a little menace to my tone.

"Don't worry, I won't tell anybody else," Justin said, "but you know what?"

"What."

"When I told Angela, my nightmares eased up a little. It feels like a weight has been lifted off of me."

"Well, I'm glad, but can we please squash this?" I asked, sincerely.

"Sure – if you do something for me."

"What?" I growled.

"I want you to do something for me," Justin said with a conniving grin.

"I can't believe you, Justin. What do I need to do to keep your trap shut?" I asked, throwing my arms up dramatically.

"I want you and Jack to come to the mall with me tomorrow. That's all," Justin said. "We haven't hung out in a long time and I think it would be fun."

I suddenly felt like a douche-bag for getting all fired up for no reason, but Justin had a way of doing that to me. He could get under your skin like you couldn't imagine; sometimes to the point that you just wanted to kick him square in the balls. I never saw him use his wits in a bad way though, it was always for something good, or fun.

"Let me ask my mom. I think she'll be okay with it, but I'm not sure if Mrs. Renee will let Jack go."

"If you're going, I'm sure Jack will be coming, too. You guys are like conjoined twins," Justin grinned.

"Yeah, but I'm the handsome one."

"Keep telling yourself that," Justin said, letting a smirk loose on his face. "I'll give you a call tonight, so make sure you ask your mom if you can go as soon as you get home. And don't worry, Jody, we've kept it a secret this long, it's not gonna get out of hand."

"Thanks," I said and walked away from him, knowing that the bell was about to ring. "I'll ask my mom tonight. Talk to you later on, then."

"Alright," Justin replied and headed toward the double doors that lead back into the school and shortly after he went in, the bell rang.

***

Once I got home, I asked Momma if I could go to the mall with Justin. She approved, and the phone rang shortly after. I answered the call.

"Hello?"

"Hey, Jody, it's Jack."

"What's up? Can you go or not?" I questioned.

"Yeah, I can go, but what the hell is there to do at the mall?"

"I don't know, but we'll find something to do. I'll talk to you later."

"Alright, bye," Jack said.

I hung up the phone and jumped up and down with joy. I had only been to the Hammond mall twice, and both times had been with Momma and Hunter. This time, I wouldn't have Momma making me follow her around like a dog; I was beginning to feel like a big kid, and not a little baby who had to go everywhere his Mom went.

"You better not act like a damned fool tomorrow, Jody. If I find out you acted like an ass, you'll never go anywhere without me again. Understand?" Momma told me in her stern voice.

"Yes, Momma," I said, secretly rolling my eyes at her.

The next day at school went about the same as any other day before it – long, boring and full of stupid teachers. By the second day of French class, I knew I'd never want to meet a Frenchman; French class sucked major dick, and to top it off, my French teacher had the worst smelling breath ever. So, not only did I have to smell the stinky kid in math class, but I also had to endure the French teacher's shit-breath. By the end of that class, I swore to myself that I would never ask the teacher another question again, because when I did, she'd come over and get all in your face to explain what you needed to know. I simply couldn't handle it, so I decided that if I needed to ask a question, I would just lean over and ask Krystle, the girl that sat right next to me.

Krystle was short, thin, with dark brown-colored hair cut into a neat bob hairstyle. She always wore glasses and multi-colored scrunchies in her hair, but was nonetheless very pretty. Krystle had yet to ask a question the whole two days that we'd spent in class together, and she *always* completed her work before any of us were even halfway through it. I took that to mean she was smart, and boy, was I right. When I asked people throughout the day if they knew anything about her, I found out that Krystle was actually *the* smartest girl in our school – was always on honor roll, and had never made an F in her life.

I wished I could say that about me, but I'd be lying to you; there's no telling how many times I tried turning an F into a B, or an F into an A on my report card on the bus ride home from school. Come to think of it, I don't know why I kept on doing that, as it never worked. Momma was always able spot the correction, and tore my ass up for it – but whatever, it gave me something to do on the bus. Now, however, I was pretty confident I wouldn't fail French if I got Krystle's help.

When the release bell rang, I got to the bus as fast as possible. I sat near the back with Jack, and when the bus cranked up, we began picking on this nerdy kid who sat in front of us. I can't remember his name, but I do remember the angry red rash he constantly had around his lips. It looked something like poison ivy, or a nasty case of ringworm. If I'd known what an STD was back then, I would have told you the kid had herpes – the gift that keeps on giving. For all we know, he could've gotten that rash from sucking on the rubber end of a plunger, but Jack and I thought of something way better than that.

"Hey – hey, kid – pssst," I hissed.

"What?"

"Have you been sucking on a cat's ass?" I asked him, trying to keep the laughter from busting out of my mouth.

"No," he replied.

"Oh, yeah you have," Jack butted in. "A nice, big, juicy, alley cat's ass."

"Nothing like sucking on some cat ass, right, Jack?" I joked.

"Meow – meow – smooch – meow. Ahh, sucking on cat ass."

"Nothing like some cat ass, I tell ya. Best dish Louisiana has to offer! Why, I think I'm going to go home and suck on my cat's ass, too!" I said.

"Me three!" Jack spat, and an explosion of laughter spread throughout the bus.

Some of the kids were turning blue in the face from laughing so damn hard and soon our Mick Jagger look a-like bus driver, Ms. Kenton, was screaming at the top of her lungs once more, telling us all to shut the hell up.

"Leave me alone or I'm going to tell my parents!" the

boy whined at Jack and me.

"No – no – not your parents! *Please no*, not your parents, anything but your parents!" I mocked, grabbing at my heart like I was dying.

"Do your parents serve cat ass for supper?" Jack deadpanned.

And that's basically how the rest of the bus ride went – with me and Jack making cat sounds for the rest of the way home, and we didn't stop pestering that poor kid until he got off the bus, and when he did, he was in tears.

Jack got off the bus about ten minutes later, and I decided to get off with him. Once the bus doors closed and it drove away, Jack and I turned around and gave everyone who was left on it a big middle finger. We giggled together and gave each other a high five before I took off running home.

Several hours later, Jack and I were standing at the end of my driveway waiting for Justin and his dad to come pick us up for our trip to the mall. Momma had just given both of us the *don't fuck up* speech, but we really hadn't heard a thing that came out of her mouth; we were both just so excited and ready to go out on our own without parental supervision. A couple of minutes later, Justin rolled up with his dad in their Chevrolet. The door opened, and we hopped right in.

It took about fifteen minutes or so for us to get to the mall, and when we got there Justin's dad gave us all the same *don't fuck up* speech we'd received from Momma; Jack and I hypothesized that all parents must have to study and memorize that dialogue before becoming a parent. Hell, Justin's dad's spiel was almost identical to Momma's, except for the *god damns*; Momma normally used *fuck* or *shit* instead.

"I'll be back in an hour and a half, boys. Ya'll need to

be standing right where you're standing now, no later than eight fifteen. Understand?"

"Yes, Mr. Richardson," Jack and I said.

"Love you, Dad," Justin said.

"Love you too, son. Be good."

"I will," he replied.

As the truck pulled away, I felt the excitement building in the air like some crazed pyromaniac was inside our souls, stacking loads of Black Cat fireworks on top of each other. And once the taillights vanished into the distance, we all yelled and jumped around as if we had just won homecoming queen.

"This is going to be *awesome*," Justin gushed.

"*I know, right?* So, what do you guys want to do first?" I asked.

"Let's go up to the sporting goods store. There's always something cool to look at in there," Jack suggested.

"Sounds good to me. You in, Justin?"

"I'm up for anything right now. This is so *awesome*."

"Tell me about it. Let's go," I said.

The Hammond Mall wasn't grand, or as great to see as some of the other malls out there in the big, wide world, but in the small town of Hammond it was as good as it was going to get. The outside design was pretty bland, and in desperate need of a new paint job. It was all grey, with multiple patches of paint missing in some areas, and split off into three sections with only two floors.

Dillard's was on the right-hand side on the first floor, JC Penny was all the way in the back section of the mall on the second floor, and the movie theater could be found in the farthest left-hand corner. So basically, the building was shaped like a giant H. I don't know if the architects built it that way because it was located in

Hammond, or if that was just the way it ended up. Nevertheless, it was *our* mall, and we loved it.

We high-tailed it up the stairs and through the electronic doors at the main entrance, stopping in the walkway to take a look around and study the lay of the land. A Kay Bee Toys was up on the second floor, the corndog stand (that Jamie ended up working in) was to the immediate left and the elevator was dead in the center. Stretched overhead was a walkway for the second floor that connected with each of the other sections of the mall. Guardrails had been placed on each side to prevent the clumsy or the suicidal from falling over, but I could see kids hanging over the sides anyway, dropping pennies into the fountain that bubbled below. There were also numerous, smaller stores lined up and down both sides of each corridor in the mall, but we three had no interest in most them. There was a gift shop that was *really* expensive, a gag shop, an arcade on the top floor, a Chik-Fil-A next to the entrance of Dillard's, a sporting goods store and a music store across from the arcade. And that was it; any other stores in the Hammond mall were completely pointless as far as we were concerned.

"Sporting goods store, right?" I asked.

"Yeah – it's up on the second floor," Jack said.

"Well, let's get going," Justin said.

We made our way over to the elevator, pressed the button and waited for it to arrive. When it did, the doors opened up and there were a pair of college kids in there making out. When they realized the door was open, they stopped wiggling their tongues in each other's mouths and rushed past us, giggling. We stepped into the elevator, pressed the number 2 button and rode it up to the second floor.

"Did you see the tits on that girl?" Justin asked us.

"I sure did. Those babies were huge," I said.

"I'd like to suck on them jokers," Justin smirked.

"That's not the only thing I'd like to suck on," Jack said.

"What else is there to suck on besides her feet?" I asked him.

Justin chuckled, and Jack turned red in the face from embarrassment. I didn't mean to embarrass him, but we never really talked about girls that much so when we did, we were ruthless, and I think that made Jack a little uncomfortable. I could definitely say that Jack was a shy one when it came to girls.

"Ewwww. You don't mean you want to suck on her *muff* do you?" Justin asked.

"What's a muff?" I pried.

"It's a pussy. You know – the hairy thing between girls' legs."

"I thought that was called a vagina?"

"That's the word the doctors use for it. Everyone else either calls it a pussy, muff, hair pie, or meat wallet," Justin declared with confidence.

"What the hell is a *meat wallet*? That's sounds disgusting," Jack said in repugnance.

"I don't know, but I hope I never see one. The name sounds horrible enough," Justin concluded.

We walked out of the elevator and turned right, heading toward the sporting goods store, laughing and joking as usual. Once we got into the store, Jack looked around at the prices on every single squirrel-hunting gun they had. I don't know why he wanted to look at all of them, because Mr. Shawn already had an arsenal in the house big enough to hold off a small Army. But, if that's what floated Jack's boat, that was fine with me.

Once Jack was done looking at the last gun, we wandered across the hall to the arcade; the place I'd wanted to go to the most. As we walked in, a guy on his way out bumped into me so hard that I collided into Jack. Justin quickly extended his arm and caught me by the shirt, preventing me from hitting the floor.

"Whoa! You alright, Jody?" Jack asked me as he regained his balance. "Can't you say *excuse me*, asshole!" Jack yelled out after the guy.

As I straightened myself up, I stared at the man, and instantly was overtaken with fear. He'd stopped dead in his tracks and was now staring directly into our eyes. He wore a long, black jacket, and black clothes from head to toe. But what had created the surge of fear through my body was the design that was on his t-shirt; it was that same circle with the star in it that I had seen in the trailer that fateful day.

And once my eyes drifted up from the guy's shirt to his face, I began to analyze him, the first thing I noticed was that he had a harelip that ran from the top of his upper lip all the way up to his right nostril. His hair was brown and he looked skinny, standing around five foot ten, with jet-black eyes that reminded me of a sharks. The guy looked *real* mean, and Jack had just called him an asshole.

"It's okay, sir," I said nervously, "it was my fault. I didn't see you coming out. I'm sorry."

He just stood there – no reaction, no apology, nothing; he just stared the three of us up and down. I looked over at Justin and could see that he was scared too; the terrified look on his face said everything.

"Let's get the fuck out of here, okay guys?" Justin mumbled.

"No! He can apologize for –"

"Shut the fuck up, Jack! Forget about it. Let's go," I urged.

I grabbed Jack by the shoulders and pulled him into

motion with me. Justin followed right behind us and we headed into the arcade; I glanced back over my shoulder to see if the guy was still standing there, but he was gone. As we got further into the arcade, it was dense with hot, sweaty bodies. Children were playing games and waiting for tokens, others standing by waiting for an opening to play. I dragged Jack up to the *Mortal Kombat* arcade and only then did I let him go.

"Jesus Christ, Jack! Why'd you pop off to that damned psycho?" I spit.

"Because the bastard almost knocked both of us down. Who the hell does he think he is?"

"I don't want to know *who* he is," Justin said as he stared directly into my eyes. "Did you see his shirt, Jody?"

"Yeah, I saw it."

"What was that on his shirt?" Jack asked us.

"What does that damned symbol mean?"

"I don't know, Justin, but did you see that scar on his face?" I asked him, I was getting nervous all over again just by talking about the guy.

"He looked crazy – just standing there and staring at us; it made me feel weird," Justin said, his voice was shaky now. "I wonder if he had anything to do with those calves."

"What calves?" Jack was confused.

"It's nothing, Jack, don't worry about it," I placated, trying to quash his interest in the conversation.

"Maybe we should fill Jack in, Jody," Justin suggested.

"Listen, damn it! Stop bringing that shit up, Justin. It's over and done with. We don't need to bring Jack into it, either. He wasn't *there*, so it's not his problem. Plus, I couldn't really give two shits about who that guy was, or where he's from, or even if he did have something to do with what we saw in the woods." I didn't realize it at the time, but my voice was raised above the general cacophony of the arcade. "Just because somebody's wearing a symbol, doesn't mean they had anything to do with what happened. We don't even know what it means. It could be the new symbol that means *I love pussy,* for all we know. Right now, I just want to go home," I ranted.

"Would someone please tell me what the fuck is going on?" Jack asked furiously, grabbing me by the shirt, twisting it in the process.

I grabbed Jack's hand, yanked it away from my collar and looked deep into his eyes. I knew he was upset – I would have been, too, if it were me; there were no secrets between Jack and I – *ever*. We told each other everything, but because of the incident in the woods coming out like this, I felt like the worst friend anyone could ever have.

"He's back," Justin whispered.

I broke eye contact with Jack and looked over at Justin. "What?"

"He's back – he's over there, watching us," Justin said quietly.

Jack and I simultaneously turned our heads and looked across to where Justin was pointing.

"Jesus Christ," Jack muttered under his breath.

There the guy was again, standing behind one of the arcade machines not more than twenty feet away from us. The neon lights from the arcade reflected off his face to give it an eerie glow and cast dark shadows around the harelip to create a deep, black crevasse on his face.

"What the hell is he doing?" Justin asked in a whisper.

"I have no clue. Let's just start walking the hell out of here," I suggested.

"Sounds good," Jack agreed and we turned around in unison and began making our way out of the arcade.

Once we were out, and had walked a few feet, I turned around to see if the guy was behind us.

"The son-of-a-bitch is following us," I declared, with panic in my voice.

He walked quickly, his back ramrod-straight; the guy had excellent posture and reminded me a little of *Michael Myers* from *Halloween*, only without the mask. Visions of the symbol that was displayed upon our stalker's shirt flashed around inside my head; some from the trailer wall.

"Turn in here, turn in here!" Justin gabbled and he grabbed Jack and I by the wrists, his hands slick with sweat.

Justin steered us left into the *KB Toys* store, and the three of us hurried in. As soon as we stepped foot into the store, we noticed that there were only a few adults – and most of them were in line checking out – and a shit load of kids were running around everywhere. We continued on, maneuvering through the bins of toys and the little kids that filled the main floor, and finally made our way up the middle aisle, coming to a halt by the *Ninja Turtle* toys.

"We need to tell an adult," Justin said.

"I'm for it. Let's go tell the guy that works behind the register," Jack added.

"Alright, I'll go," I offered.

I turned to go tell, but before I could move, our sinister pursuer shot down the aisle and grabbed me by the arm. I screamed, and caught the attention of everyone in the store. Justin reacted first, and kicked my assailant in the shin as hard as he could. The man slung me to the floor as if I was nothing, which knocked the wind out of my body. Dazed, panting, I looked up and saw the man attempt to grab Justin, but Jack rammed him in the stomach, sending him falling backwards into a shelf filled with super soakers and G.I. Joes.

"Get up, Jody! Get up!" Jack yelled at me.

I was still winded, but I was finally catching my breath. The next thing I felt was Jack and Justin gripping me from under the arms and pulling me to my feet.

"We gotta go!" Justin shouted in my ear.

I knew that this was serious; whoever this guy was, he was out to do us harm.

"You okay, buddy?" the cashier asked, looking like he was in well over his head. He'd finally come from around the counter, and as I looked around, all the adults were holding their children close to them and watching as our attacker rose up from the ground like a weird kind of zombie coming back to life.

"Beat feet!" I screamed, and Jack, Justin and I dashed out of the toy store, not thinking twice and without looking back.

I ran so fast through the mall that my lungs were beginning to burn, I was bumping into people left and right, and I could hear some of them yelling at me, but I couldn't give two shits; a goddamned lunatic wasn't chasing them. I could hear Jack's feet hitting the floor behind me, so I knew he was right there with me, but I didn't know if Justin was keeping up.

I got to the elevator, pressed the button and the doors opened wide. I ran into the elevator, and poked my head out to see where everyone was. Jack stumbled in first, but Justin was still a few feet behind, with the guy in close pursuit. People stared hard at us, like we were a bunch of out-of-control hoodlums, simply running amuck with no parental supervision.

Justin's face had turned pale, but at the same time there were bright red circles consuming his cheeks. The man was right behind him, shoving people out of his way in his attempt to catch Justin. It was then that I thought *why the hell am I taking the elevator instead of the stairs?* – but it was too late to change that decision, because Justin was coming in hot.

"Hurry up!" Jack yelled at the kid.

I prodded again at the first floor button just as Justin dove into the elevator, smacking his head up against the metal wall. And as the doors closed, the man slipped through at the very last second and they shut firmly behind him.

He grabbed Jack by the throat and rammed him hard into the elevator wall, Jack's face turning bright red. I was terrified, didn't know what to do, my body shaking uncontrollably.

"You're going to give me some blood, you little cocksucker!" the man screamed loud and harsh in Jack's face. "Did you really think you and your friends were going to get away from me? Huh? I'll fucking take your life, boy!" He glowered down at Justin, who was scrabbling to his feet, and kicked the poor kid square in the chest. Justin let out a whimper of pain and went right back down to the floor.

The man then glared over at me, and all I could see was pure evil etched upon his face; the only emotion showing was pure rage as fire flashed in his eyes. I honestly thought we were going to die in that elevator, but then the man threw his head back and let loose with an agonized scream and when I glanced down, I saw that Justin was biting into his calf muscle.

At this, my adrenaline kicked in and washed all my fears away. I knew that we had to fight back, but most importantly, I had to help my friends.

I let loose a battle cry, screaming it at the top of my lungs; Justin released his bite and screamed as well, then sunk his teeth back into the man's calf. I jumped onto the man's back, wrapped my legs firmly around his waist and bit him as hard as I could on the back of his neck. The guy screamed bloody murder and released Jack from his grip.

As soon as I tasted blood in my mouth, I spit it out into his hair and jumped off his back. Jack spit in the man's face, and then kicked him hard between the legs. This sent our attacker to his knees with excruciating pain, and he bellowed like a wounded dog. He then got a swift kick across the face, courtesy of Justin, his nose now bled profusely, and blood poured out and onto the floor.

The elevator stopped, the doors opened up and we jetted out, leaving the man bleeding and on his knees inside. We didn't look back once, we just hauled ass out the main entrance of the mall and didn't stop until we were in the middle of the well-lit parking lot.

"Is – he behind – us?" Jack gasped, out of breath.

"No. I think I busted – him up – pretty good back there," Justin said as he took in big gulps of air. "Thank God – I took those Karate classes."

We stood there in the parking lot, caught our breath and decided to go wait across the street at the Taco Bell for Justin's dad. We had only been at the mall for thirty minutes, but it was thirty minutes that we would certainly never forget.

We crossed the street; I slung open the door to Taco Bell and made a beeline for one of the empty booths. I walked over, planted my ass on the cushioned seat and waited for my friends to do the same. Once they were all seated, Jack began to tear up.

"You alright, Jack?" I was genuinely concerned, my blood brother rarely cried.

"I couldn't breathe, Jody," Jack told me, "I couldn't

173

breathe when he was choking me. I thought I was going to die."

"Well you *didn't*," Justin said, firmly. "You made it out okay. We're *all* okay now."

"Why did this happen?" Jack asked, placing his hand on his forehead.

"I don't know. Maybe it's because we popped off to him," I offered.

"I don't think that's why; I think he was just some Looney Toon, probably on drugs or something and decided it would be fun to bully us around a little," Justin said.

"A *little...?*" I said dramatically. "He tried to kill us, Justin!"

"Enough," Jack said quietly. "Can we please stop talking about it now? We don't know *why* he did it, but it happened. And now it's over. I just want to go home."

We fell quiet, realizing how serious the situation had been. We had escaped a mad man and lived to tell the tale; and it was one that we were going to keep between ourselves.

"Should we tell our parents?" Justin asked.

"No," I replied, knowing what the immediate reaction from Momma would be. "Jack?"

"No. We can't tell them anything. If we do, they'll freak, then we'll never be able to go anywhere by ourselves again. Ya'll know I'm telling the truth."

"I know," Justin agreed.

"You're right – we won't say a word."

I stood up from the table, stretched and walked up to the front counter.

"Where you going, Jody?" Jack asked me.

I didn't respond, I just kept on walking, pretending that I hadn't heard him.

"Welcome to Taco Bell, how can I help you?"

"Do you have a pen and piece of paper?" I asked.

"Sure, hold on," said the employee.

After a minute or so, he came back with the pen and paper I'd asked for. I looked around and noticed that we were the only ones in the place, so I asked the question that had been burning inside of me since that day in the woods. I grabbed the pen and drew the circle with the upside-down star in the middle of it.

"What does this symbol mean?" I asked the guy.

"Ummm – are your parents with you?" he asked.

"No, they're not. Can you please tell me what this means?"

The employee let out a deep sigh and looked over at his co-workers who were joking on the food line, throwing lettuce and cheese at each other. The cashier leaned over the counter. "I can't believe I'm telling you this," he said, shaking his head. "You're serious?"

"Yes. Please," I pleaded. "Please, tell me what this symbol means."

"It's a pentagram," he said, softly.

"A *pentagram*?"

"Yep."

"What does it mean, though? I couldn't care less what it's called."

"Listen," the cashier told me, "I don't want to scare you, kid, but people who are into witchcraft and Satanism use it. They wear it on their clothes, draw it on their belongings and so on and so forth. It's a way they express their religion, like good Christian folk use the cross. Although, some just do it 'cause they like the attention it brings them."

"What's *Satanism*?" I asked, a tad perplexed at the information.

"It's people who worship the devil, but not like you may think; if I explain it to you, you'd only get confused

175

– but I guess I can try."

He took the paper from me and turned it upside down.

"You see how the tip of the star is pointing up?" he said.

"Yes." I nodded.

"That's the symbol for Witchcraft. Pagans and Wiccans use this symbol. Now," he turned the paper upside down again, "you see how the tip of the star is pointing to the *bottom* of the circle?"

"Yeah."

"This is the symbol that Satanists and devil worshippers use."

"Devil worshippers?" I asked him, nervously.

"Don't get me started on *those guys*. They have the worse bad reputation for picking up the troubled seeds around here."

"How do you know that?"

"Well, I'm a Satanist," he said quietly with a nervous glance over his shoulder. "I hear things within our congregation."

My skin turned cold and my stomach felt sick; I felt puke rush up into my throat, but I held it back. I couldn't believe that this man was a *Satanist*. He looked just like a regular person to me; clean cut, well groomed, you name it. I guess the word *Satan* just scared the hell out of me.

"You okay, bud? Don't be scared. I'm not going to hurt ya. Here, you want some water?"

I shook my head no, swallowed the puke that was threatening to escape from my throat and decided to ask him another question, "Do you guys – hurt kids?"

"No way!" he exclaimed. "Who told you that?"

"No one, sir. That's just what I thought."

Justin and Jack walked up behind me and joined in

on the conversation. They had been standing behind, eavesdropping to the conversation and I hadn't even realized it.

"The reason he, I mean, *we* think that, sir, is because in the mall, a guy wearing a shirt with that symbol on it tried to hurt us," Justin explained, his voice still a little shaky.

"What? Are you kids okay?"

"We're okay," Jack assured him.

"Listen guys," the employee said, leaning even further over the counter, "there are some crazy people in this world, from all different types of religions and faiths. And whenever you see this pentagram – either on TV or in the newspapers – it's never about something good. You need to be careful around here, guys. Stay away from strangers, and always stick together when you're out and about. Got it?" he asked.

We all nodded our heads in agreement.

"You want me to call the police for you?"

"No, sir!" we said in unison.

"Okay then – here," he slammed down three large plastic cups on the counter. "Get yourselves something to drink, and don't forget what I've said."

We all nodded our heads and wandered over to the drink machine to fill up our cups. My nerves had dissipated and I felt as if I could finally put something in my stomach without the fear of it coming back up again. I moved over to Jack and wrapped my arm around him. "You okay, man? You're not mad at me, are you?"

"A little bit. I just can't believe you kept a secret from me. You know I never would've told anyone," Jack said.

"I know, Jack, but Momma put the fear of God in me. She told me if I said anything to *anyone* she'd beat the shit out of me."

"I know what you mean. Your mom's ass whippings

are pretty brutal," Jack replied with a grin.

"I know. Tell that to my ass sometime," I joked.

"Thanks, but no thanks," Jack giggled.

"I promise I'll tell you *everything* once I get back from the bathroom."

"You gotta pee or something?"

"No. I just still taste that crazy guy's blood in my mouth from when I bit him," I explained.

"Yeah, you really should go to the bathroom and wash your mouth out," Jack suggested. "You don't want to get AIDS or something from him."

"Good idea."

Upon my return from the bathroom, Justin and I spent the remainder of our time in *Taco Bell* getting Jack caught up on all the details. By the time we were finished, we had to head out to wait for Justin's dad in the parking lot. We got up, threw our trash away and exited the building, leaving behind what had happened to us at the mall in the trash as well.

CHAPTER FOURTEEN

SCOTT

"Way to go, Scott! *Way to fucking go!*" Rebecca yelled as she turned out of the mall parking lot onto the main road that ran through the middle of Hammond.

"Stop yelling, goddamn it," Scott fired back, "I know I fucked up. You don't have to keep reminding me!"

"Yes I do, you piece of shit! Your little fiasco with the kids is not going to go over very well with Mitch. He's going to blow a gasket when he finds out what you did. Do you realize, Scott, that if I hadn't been there, you'd probably be sitting in the back of a squad car right now?"

"Yes, yes, yes! I know, I know, so could you please shut the fuck up?!"

"Don't you tell *me* to shut the fuck up! You're out of control, Scott. We should have never taken you in with us!" Rebecca slammed on the brakes, throwing them both forwards. "You're too much of a liability – you stay jacked up on cocaine all the time, you don't listen to

Mitch, you're sloppy with your work *and* you're going to get us caught!" Rebecca screamed at the guy, jerking the wheel to the right to avoid a head-on collision from the opposite lane.

"Watch your driving, for fucks sake!" Scott yelled, pulling the lower part of his shirt up to his sore nose to stem the bleeding.

"Now those kids are going to go to the cops to give them a description of you – and then we're all fucked! You hear me? *Fucked!*"

"Shut up! You've said this all before, Rebecca, and I'm tired of hearing it."

"I'm tired of having to repeat myself to you. Why don't you ever listen, Scott? If you did, you wouldn't get into half the shit you do."

"I didn't mean to do that to those kids, okay! I just overreacted a tad and took things a little too far. But they shouldn't have popped off at the mouth to me. That little blonde-haired bastard was the one I wanted the most – for mouthing off to me –twice," Scott growled, his voice partially muffled by the firm grasp he had on his nostrils.

"It doesn't matter if they popped off to you; that's what kids do. But if you hadn't been jacked up on Coke, you probably wouldn't have reacted the way you did. You could've just ignored them and walked away, Scott, but you didn't. We've already shook em' up enough, and *they* haven't been snooping around either – but *you* have, haven't you, Scott? Do you remember, or were you too fucked up at the time?"

"Yeah, I remember. What's the big deal?"

"The big deal, Scott, is that we told you not to go back to their homes, but you did anyway. Why can't you just stay away? You always do what Scott wants to do, but this time, you got your ass kicked by the same group of middle school boys that you keep trying to terrorize." At this, Rebecca gave a snort of derision; Scott really was a complete asshole when he was high.

"You fucking bitch! Don't you fucking talk to me like that," Scott screamed. He reached down into his coat pocket and pulled out a knife. He lunged towards Rebecca. He brought the knife up to her throat and began poking it at her smooth, flawless skin and said, "You see, bitch, if I wanted to, I could have killed them right then and there, just like I could kill you – right here, right now!"

"Put the knife down, Scott. I can't drive with that fucking thing in my throat." Rebecca said firmly. She remained sitting perfectly straight, hands at ten and two, the only hint of nervousness the beads of sweat forming on her brow.

"I'll take the knife away after you say I *could have* killed them, right then and right there." Scott's eyes were bloodshot and wide; the blood on his face was now dried and formed a long red line from his left nostril, all the way down to his chin, "Say it, you fuck!"

"Okay, okay! You could have killed them, Scott! Right then and there!"

"Thank you," Scott said. He withdrew the knife from Rebecca's throat and placed it back in his jacket pocket.

"You crazy son-of-a-bitch, wait 'til I tell Mitch what you just did to me! He's going to kill you for this!"

"No, he's not," Scott said. He threw his body back into the seat and stared out the window. "And you know why?" Scott asked, his eyes half rolled into the back of his head. He un-zipped his pants and pulled out his penis; stroking the limp thing up and down with one hand. "'Cause you're gonna give me some of that good ol' wet pussy of yours. Ain't that right, baby?"

"Fuck you, Scott. Fuck you!" Rebecca spat.

"I'm just playing with you, baby," Scott joked and placed his member back into his pants, zipping them up quickly. "Please don't tell Mitch, please! I don't have anywhere else to go. I'm sorry, I'm so fucking sorry," Scott cried.

Rebecca looked at the man with a tiny amount of sympathy in her eyes. What he said was true; when they'd taken him into their group, Scott was a lost soul. He was living the sad life of drug addiction and isolation, but with them, he had a clear purpose; to fulfill the Devil's work.

"Don't worry. I won't tell Mitch you fucked up again, but that's as long as we don't see a sketch of you on the news tonight. If we do, I'm telling him everything."

"Oh, thank you, baby. *Thank you*," Scott whined.

"Shut up, and stop calling me baby." Rebecca focused on the road, looking straight ahead and contemplating what to do next. "I've got to tell Mitch that we have to lay low for a bit. After this, it'd be best if we hid our faces for a while. Shit got a little too out of hand in the mall."

"We couldn't have gotten a kid tonight anyway. The arcade was too crowded. Too many sets of eyes, maybe next time we'll get one," Scott told her.

"Next time isn't good enough, Scott. We needed one tonight, and Mitch was *very* specific about what he wanted," Rebecca stated and turned left onto West University.

"I know what he wanted, but there weren't any boys in there that young. We should've gone back to the place we were at last week. Now *that* was the hotspot. And boy, you remember how sweet that little pussy was?" Scott squealed as he tapped Rebecca on the shoulder and punched the roof of the van in excitement. "Makes my teeth hurt just thinking about how good that twat was."

"It was sweet, wasn't it?" Rebecca said and she shot a sinful grin at Scott.

"Hell yeah, but let's not talk about it right now, alright? It gets my dick all hard every time we bring it up."

The conversation stopped there as Rebecca thought of what she was going to say when she got home to Mitch. Scott was beginning to come down off his high, and was slowly passing out in the passenger seat. Rebecca reached over to him and gave him a good shake. "Stop dozing off, Scott. We're almost back to the house."

Scott jolted awake and began moving around restlessly in his seat. "Can we please stop and pick up some more Coke? I can't keep my fucking eyes open anymore."

"No, goddamn it," Rebecca snarled. "Now listen up. Wipe the fucking blood off your face and let me do the talking when we get inside. Understand?" Rebecca asked, but Scott was already fast asleep.

They continued to drive for another ten minutes or so, then Rebecca flicked the right turn signal up turning onto Leslie Drive, a street that was less than four miles away from Rhine Road.

CHAPTER FIFTEEN

THE NAIL INCIDENT: 1991

Two months passed, and the incident at the mall eventually faded away from our conversation, dwindling from our thoughts like the leaves falling from the trees.

Fall was coming; the days began to get shorter, the nights longer, and my entire front yard was covered with pinecones and pine needles, along with myriad other leaves that had escaped the clutches of the surrounding trees. The sweet smell of honeysuckle was replaced by the aroma of seasoned oak that carried itself on the crisp wind; fragrances of autumn that invaded every corner of my world. And it didn't matter if you were in a car, or even inside your house, those scents always crept through the smallest crack and up into your nose.

Every time I took a step, leaves crunched under my feet to make any attempt of a stealthy approach on Jack – or anybody else – near impossible. Then there was the blue October sky in all its glory and in my opinion, it looks completely different than any other month's sky. It almost had a different feel to it; like it was enchanted or something; to this day, fall and October are my favorite times of the year.

Not only was I excited about the change of season, I also had my eleventh birthday on the thirtieth of the month, along with my favorite holiday the day after: Halloween. It was the only holiday in the world that expected kids to do bad things, and believe me, Jack and I didn't intend to disappoint.

Justin had quit hanging out with us after the mall incident, and started hanging out with Chase Newman a whole lot more. Every time Jack and I saw Justin, he pretended to be too cool to talk to us, and went back to hanging out with his *new* best friend. In the end Jack and I said screw it, realizing that two wheels are as good as three, and paid no attention to him. I didn't blame Justin for not wanting to hang out with us anymore; it seemed like every time we were together, something horrible happened.

Anyways, Jack and I had taken a good hiatus after my eleventh birthday. Of course we had done some bad shit on Halloween, but that really didn't count, it was a given. We were never too bad around Thanksgiving time, though, but that was only because we had too many family members running around all over the place and it was easier to get caught.

One mid-afternoon a few days after Thanksgiving, Jack and I decided to start up our reign of terror once again. During the fall and winter months, the liveliness of the neighborhood tended to slow down, and the only kids outside playing were Jack and me; it was like everyone except for us had gone into hibernation. The only other kids we saw every now and again were Kyle and Lucy, but they rarely came out of their house anyway.

Like people say though, it's always calm before the

storm – and the storm was definitely on its way.

Around three thirty or so one afternoon, I was playing around in Pepaw's shed, digging around in the toolboxes, when I found some nails in a plastic bag. In an instant, I'd conjured up a plan for what to do with my new and exciting find, and I just *knew* Jack would love it. I grabbed a handful of the nails and ran from the shed, hoping that Pepaw wouldn't see me. Once I got in front of my trailer, I glanced up the road toward Jack's house, and saw that he was already on his bike and heading my way. I took off towards him with a sprint, maneuvering my way across the pine needles that covered my front yard and stopped next to the road. Jack rolled up with his hair looking like an untamed mess, and stopped right next to me.

"What's going on?" Jack asked, picking up on the excitement in my face.

"Check it out man; I got some nails from Pepaw's shed, and –"

"And?" Jack interrupted.

"If you'd let me finish, I'd tell you what I want to do with them."

"Let me guess – you want to build a clubhouse."

"No, damn it! I want to pop some tires with these babies!" I exclaimed.

"Now, that's what I'm talking about!" Jack shouted, as his mood suddenly switching from *I don't care* to *Let's do this!*

Jack got off his bike, walked it over to one of the big pine trees in my yard and leaned it up against its smooth trunk. He trotted back over to me with a look of sheer mischief on his face, as I was knelt down counting the nails I'd spread out on the ground.

"So, how are we going to do this?" Jack asked.

"You see that hole over there in the road?"

"No – where?"

"Right there, dumbass!" I said, pointing my finger across the road.

Jack followed my finger with his eyes and searched for the landmark. "I don't see shit, Jody," he said.

"Damn it," I grumbled. I stood to my feet and walked to the road, "this hole *right here*."

I bent down and slammed my index finger into a tiny hole about half an inch deep, certainly no wider than an inch; the circumference probably the same as an eraser on a pencil.

"We're putting the nails in that little hole?" Jack was curious.

"Yes. We're putting them in there – 'cause look." I got down on my stomach and lay alongside the road. "You see," I explained, "this little hole is lined up perfectly with where a car's tires pass. If we stand the nail up in the hole and maybe stick some dirt around it to keep it steady, it might just go into someone's tire. And then – BOOM! They're having a bad day." Grinning, I got up from off the ground and dusted myself off.

"Ha-ha! Genius, pure genius, I tell you." Jack clapped his hands together with glee. "How the hell did you spot that tiny hole?"

"I was out here checking the mail the other day and I just happened to see it. It wasn't until I got the nails that I remembered it, though."

"Awesome. Let's do it," Jack insisted.

We got down on our knees. I held the nail up and Jack stuffed the dirt around its base. Once it stood up by itself, we ran into my front yard, hid behind one of the trees and waited for a vehicle to pass. A few minutes later, we heard our first victim and pure joy shot through our bodies.

"Can you see who it is? Can you see?" Jack was almost beyond himself with excitement.

"Hold on," I said. I poked my head out from behind the tree and caught a glimpse of some multi-colored piece of shit, which I'd never seen before, rattling its way along the road. "It's some piece of shit jalopy," I reported back to Jack, "I think it's on fire, too. Smoke is shooting out the back of it."

"Oh – that's one of Mr. Rhine's friends," Jack told me, "my dad went coon hunting with him once."

"Well, with a car like that, I hope he can afford a new tire," I joked, and we laughed like maniacs.

"Shhh – listen for the pop!" Jack said as he composed himself.

"Oh my God, I can't take all this excitement," I said.

We waited as the car got right upon us, then – nothing. The pile of junk just kept on going right down Rhine Road, all four tires still inflated. We got up from behind the tree and walked out to the road.

"I'll be a son-of-a-bitch," Jack said, scratching his head. "The damned nail is still standing up."

"What? It didn't stick into that guy's tire?" I asked in total disappointment.

"Nope, it's still here."

"Damn it! Well, let's go hide and wait again. Maybe the next car will hit it."

"Okay," Jack agreed, and we went back behind the tree.

We waited for a good five minutes for another victim, and once again the nail didn't penetrate the car's tire.

"Maybe we need to put some more dirt around it – you know, to keep it sturdier?" Jack suggested as we stood over that nail, gazing down upon it as if we were about to scold it for not doing its job. We packed the hole with yet more dirt; hell, we even threw some spit in there hoping it would add some support once it dried. After we were done we went back, yet again, to our hiding spot.

"You ever think about what happened that day at the mall?" Jack asked me.

The question had come straight out of left field. I wasn't expecting to hear it from my friend at all, but I knew Jack was serious; his tone of voice said it all.

"Every now and again, I guess. How about you?"

"Yeah, every now and again too, I suppose. I have a lot of nightmares about it though, and sometimes I don't get away from him. I just stand there in that elevator and let him choke me until I die," Jack told me as he brought his knees up tight to his chest and crossed his arms on top of them. "I don't know if I'd still be here if it wasn't for you and Justin."

"Don't talk like that, Jack. There were too many people in that mall to let that asshole kill someone."

"Oh yeah, then why didn't anyone stop him from chasing us, huh?" Jack asked.

"I don't know, maybe because it all happened so fast. One minute we were in the toy store, then the next thing you know, shit was going crazy inside the elevator."

"Yeah, but someone still should've helped us," Jack said, staring blankly down at the ground.

"I know, Jack. Look," I said as I placed a hand on his shoulder, "what's done is done, man. That yahoo is probably locked up in jail somewhere getting his asshole shaved by Brutus The Butt Shaving Beefcake."

Jack started giggling, and by that, I knew we would soon be off the topic, which suited me just fine because quite frankly, I didn't like talking about it at all, either; it was something I wanted to forget and put behind the both of us.

"He's probably in jail, huh?" Jack said.

"Totally. The cops don't keep lunatics like that on the streets for long. They have a special little place to put those people."

"Hey," Jack said, springing to his knees, "another car is coming – I hear it!"

And *voila*, our serious conversation ended and we were focusing once more upon the nail. It's funny how a child's mind works sometimes; I didn't understand back then, and I still sometimes can't understand it today. Kids can be talking about the most serious things one minute, and the next they're back talking about stupid kid stuff. It's bizarre, but I guess that's just how it is; I'm learning that now with my own offspring.

"Here we go baby, here we go!" I said, rubbing my hands together like a madman.

"See who it is!" Jack demanded.

I leaned over to take a peek at who was approaching, and felt my eyes widen as I looked upon Mr. Shawn's truck.

"Aww shit," I muttered.

"What?" Jack asked.

"Oh, fuck…"

"Oh fuck what?!" Jack spat.

I brought my head back around and stared directly at Jack's face. "Dude, we are so screwed – it's your dad."

"My dad?" Jack asked, shockingly, leaning over me, taking a look-see for himself.

"Holy shit, it *is* my dad," Jack gasped, "he must've gotten off work early today. He normally doesn't get home until dark."

"Maybe he'll miss the nail just like everyone else has," I said, trying to give Jack a little hope.

"Let's run out there and stop him," Jack insisted.

"Should we?"

"Yes, damn it! Let's go."

We both clambered to our feet and ran toward the road, our arms waving up and down to try to get Mr. Shawn to stop.

"Hey, Dad! Stop! Stop!" Jack shouted.

"Mr. Shawn! Hey! Stop! Wait!"

We were jumping up and down alongside the road as if a Christmas parade was passing us by, and Mr. Shawn was Saint Nick himself. As he got closer in his Ford Ranger, he caught sight of us jumping up and down like a bunch of faggots at a dildo show, but didn't show any signs of slowing down or stopping. He just began waving at us with a presidential wave, you know, all nice and proper like the ones you see on TV. He had a huge smile on his face as he passed us, which lasted right up until his front right tire just ran right over the nail.

A small *POP* was heard and Jack and I quit our jumping up and down, slowly backing away from the road. And then we watched with our mouths hanging wide open as Mr. Shawn drove all the way home.

"I can't believe he didn't stop," I said.

"He is going to be *so* pissed off," Jack blurted out. "I'm not owning up to this one! Fuck that, he'll tear my ass up if he finds out I had anything to do with it."

"Well don't say anything. It'd be suicide if you did."

"Don't worry; I'm taking this one to the grave, that's for damned sure," Jack reassured me.

"So – you want to put another one in the hole?" I asked, hoping that Mr. Shawn hitting the nail hadn't foiled our plans.

"Might as well. I'm not going home until it gets dark now. Once Dad realizes that joker's flat, he'll be out there changing it and cursing up a storm, and I don't feel much like helping."

"You're an ass," I told him.

Jack jokingly pushed me off the road and walked over to the nails that we'd left on the ground. He picked one up and placed it into the hole. I gathered up some more dirt and was helping Jack get the nail situated, when someone honked a horn off to our right. It wasn't a loud horn, but it was loud enough to get our attention since we were facing in the opposite direction. We both looked over and saw that it was the mailman. We stood up and I surreptitiously swung my foot around to knock over the nail so he wouldn't see it.

"Shit, what the hell does he want?" I asked, aloud.

The mailman pulled his rinky-dink mail truck over to the right-hand side of the road, put on his four way flashers and turned off the vehicle. He rolled down his window and signaled us over with a wave of his hand. Slowly, we walked across to him, hoping that he hadn't seen us putting the nails on the road.

"You boys wouldn't happen to be putting anything sharp on the roadway, now would you?" the mailman asked us.

The man's voice was so deep, it would have intimidated any kid who hadn't perfected the art of lying into spilling the beans about what they were doing, but thank God Jack and I were seasoned veterans.

"No sir, we weren't doing anything like that at all," Jack spoke up first.

"I don't believe you," the mailman said coldly.

"Well I *don't care*," I was furious; I was tired of this guy trying to intimidate Jack and I every time he had the chance to. I know what we were doing was wrong, but I was already beginning to develop a problem with authority and decided that this guy just needed to leave us the hell alone. "You're not my dad, and you're not my mother either." I realized just how cocky I must have sounded. "So why don't you get the heck out of here.

It's none of your business what we do, so why don't you start up your little piece of shit truck and leave us alone."

Jack looked over at me in complete shock. He couldn't believe I had just spoken to an adult that way, and I was pretty surprised at myself too – I rarely used cuss words when arguing with adults, but there was just something about this guy that sent me over the edge.

"Let me tell you something, you little foul-mouthed fool," the mailman said maliciously, "you had better watch how you talk to me, you understand? You and your friend here – that's right," he nodded slowly, "I *know* he's not your brother."

"So what, creep? What's it matter to you?" I demanded.

"It matters to me because you're a pair of conniving little liars on a destructive path that's going to get you into a whole world of trouble. You have no respect for your elders, and you need to be disciplined! Maybe I should walk up there to your five-star trailer and tell your fat-ass mother what you're doing out here. Would you like that?" he growled.

"Fuck you, weirdo," Jack spat. "Why don't you get the hell out of here before we call the police and tell them you're harassing us?"

"You little bastard! You're not going to speak to me that way!" the mailman roared, and flung open the truck's door.

Jack and I jumped back a little, but still we stood our ground as this monster of a man stepped out of his vehicle and cast his giant shadow over us. He walked toward us, red in the face, extremely pissed off and with murder flashing in his cruel eyes.

Then I felt someone yank me back by the shoulder.

"Is there a problem, sir?" Pepaw asked.

I was standing behind Pepaw, Jack quickly joining me.

"Yes, there's a problem," the mailman spat, "I saw these kids putting nails on the road and trying to pop people's tires. When I rolled up and asked them what they were doing, that one right there," he pointed directly at me, "used foul language and I'm not going to take that kind of lip from a little boy!"

"You swore at us, too –" Jack blurted out, but Pepaw quickly reached back and covered up my friend's mouth with his hand.

"I'm sorry for the way the boys behaved. I will personally take care of them. I'm sorry they troubled you," Pepaw said, kindly.

"What's your name, sir?" The mailman asked Pepaw, standing mere inches from his face.

I swallowed a sour lump of nerves as I watched in anxiety, hoping that Pepaw would knock him out.

"My name's Jerry Jones, and yours?"

"Mitch Moreland," the mailman replied, backing away slowly from Pepaw as he spoke. "You won't be around forever to protect them, old man, so you'd better teach them some manners while you still can."

"Oh yeah," he continued after a small pause and nodding his head knowingly, "I know you're sick. You see, I deliver your mail, and I see all the doctor bills you got coming in from the hospitals, Jerry. Looks like you're not doing so well," he glanced down at me and Jack. "Next time this happens – 'cause I'm sure there'll be a next time – he won't be here to save you. I just want you both to know that."

"I'm going to give you to the count of three to get back into your truck, and then I want you to finish your run, and get off this street. Do you understand me, Mitch?" Pepaw asked, coolly.

"Aye aye, Sir!" the sinister mailman growled. He shot one last chilling glance back at Jack and me, and then got into his vehicle, and continued on down the road.

"I want you to run home, Jack. You can play with Jody tomorrow," Pepaw said.

"You're not going to tell my parents about what happened, are you, Mr. Jones?" Jack asked nervously.

"No son, I'm not going to say anything to them. You just run along home, okay?"

"Yes, Sir," Jack said. "Later, Jody."

"Later, Jack," I said and looked up at Pepaw.

"Are you mad at me, Pepaw?" I asked him.

"No, Bubba, I'm not mad at you. I was actually just on my way over to talk to you, since we haven't talked in a while, but once I saw that the situation was getting a little out of control, I figured I had to step in."

"I know."

"You been okay?" Pepaw asked me, "We didn't talk much during Thanksgiving."

"Yeah, just been playing with Jack and doing the whole school thing."

"I remember those days," Pepaw said, looking up into the sky. "Those were some of the best times of my life; I had great friends, and I did very well in school. That's important, you know, to get good grades and a good education. It'll help you be successful later on down the road in life, believe me – but friends are important too."

"I know, Pepaw, Momma told me the same thing."

"Good," Pepaw said with a warm smile, "that means she listened to me while she was growing up, 'cause I gave her and her brother that exact same lecture."

"How have you been, Pepaw?" I asked, even though I was scared to hear his response.

"Well, Jody, to be honest with you, it doesn't look

good for me right now," Pepaw told me with his usual bluntness.

"What do you mean?"

"The doctors say the cancer has spread all the way down into my stomach, and the chemotherapy isn't working anymore, so it looks like my time here has gotten a little shorter. That's why I was coming to talk to you, Bubba, I wanted to give you the news myself."

"Why are you telling me this, Pepaw? I really don't want to hear it," I said angrily. I could feel myself getting sad, but I quickly turned that sadness into anger. "I *don't want* to hear about how you're dying. I don't even want to *think* about it."

"But it's okay, Bubba. Really, I'm okay with it, and we really should talk about it. Dying is a part of life, and you shouldn't be afraid of it. It's all part of God's plan. He knows everything from the moment you are born, to the moment you die. I'm not afraid to die, Bubba, because I know I've lived a good life and there's a better place waiting for me."

"Heaven, right?" I said sarcastically. "But we won't be there with you! So how can it be a better place! Me, Momma and Hunter will still be down here, and Memaw is going to fall apart without you, Pepaw – you're her *everything*! Jesus, you're *my* everything! What are we going to do without you?"

Tears flowed down my face and showed no signs of stopping, but I could feel the anger within myself at the same time; it was as if my body was confused on which emotion to express, so it had decided to do both.

"Jody," Pepaw said as he walked right up to me and placed his hand under my chin, "you're going to go on and do great things in your life," he said, his eyes filling up with tears, "I have no doubt about it; the entire state of Louisiana can't possibly hold all the potential you have. I'm not worried about you, Bubba, but you will have to watch over your brother, and you'll need to be there for your mother. You'll be the man of both households when I leave, so you have to stop doing bad things, and get on the right track, son. A lot of responsibilities will come your way when I'm gone, and you have to be ready to face them with your head held high, just like I would expect you to do."

"I don't want you to die, Pepaw! I don't want you to go, please don't go!" I cried and ran into his arms.

Pepaw wrapped them around me nice and tight, and then dropped to his knees so he could be eye level with me. "I love you, Jody," he said, and I felt his words go straight into my heart.

"I love you too, Pepaw," I sobbed, clinching my fingers into his back.

"I'll always be with you, and I'll never forget the times we shared together. I promise." Pepaw whispered into my ear, and then he broke down in tears.

We cried there alongside Rhine Road on our knees, holding each other tightly, and wept together for the last time.

Pepaw died four days after Christmas.

***

I remember riding back from the hospital in New Orleans where Pepaw passed away, and Momma bawling at the top of her lungs with grief pretty much the entire journey back.

"That cancer can't chew on my Daddy anymore! He's off to a place where there is no pain! Oh, my God, please give me the strength!" Momma yelled at the roof of the car, tears running all down her face.

I sat in the back seat, quietly crying and trying not to

pay Momma any attention; she needed to let all the built-up emotions out, just like I did that day with Pepaw by the road. I was heartbroken, and a part of me died that day along with Pepaw. I can't explain it, but something about me changed the moment he passed away. We got back to our trailer late that night and went straight to bed. I could hear Momma crying through the walls, and I placed a pillow over my head to drown out her heart wrenching sobs. Once I fell asleep, I had a dream about Pepaw – well sort of, it was more of a *memory*, really.

I was riding on the back of Pepaw's motorcycle, a Harley Davidson of some sort, circling around the yard while Momma, Uncle Jerry and Memaw sat on the back porch of the house watching us. Hunter was chasing Rambo around the yard, and every time Pepaw and I would pass him, I would make a funny face and he would run after us. We went around the yard a couple of more times and then came back around to the back porch.

"You think Hunter would like to have a ride, Bubba?" Pepaw asked.

"Sure. I'd think he'd love it."

"Hunter-man!" Pepaw called out, waving him over to us.

My little brother came trotting along without a care in the world, and stopped next to the bike.

"You wanna take a ride, Hunter?" Pepaw asked.

"Yeah!" Hunter said, nodding his head a million miles an hour.

Pepaw reached down, picked Hunter up, and placed him between his legs at the front of the bike.

"Jerry Jones, don't you put that baby on that bike! You'll give me a heart attack!" Memaw shrieked.

"We'll be alright, Teddie. Just sit down and let the

big boys play," Pepaw shouted back with a mischievous grin on his face.

Memaw flung her hands down to her side and planted herself back into the chair she'd been sitting in, copping an attitude. I looked over at Uncle Jerry who waved over at me, and then turned the gesture into a thumbs up.

"Alright, you boys ready?" Pepaw asked.

"Yeah!" Hunter and I exclaimed.

We took off on the bike, going slowly at first, but eventually we picked up some good speed. I leaned forward on the bike and let the wind hit my face and it felt great; almost as if I were flying just like Peter Pan.

"Hold on!" Pepaw instructed.

I held on to his waist, wrapping my arms around him tight, while Hunter gripped the handlebars. Once Pepaw saw we were as secured as we were going to get, he revved the throttle all the way down, and we took off like a rocket ship through the yard. Even over the noise of the engine, I could hear Memaw letting little shrieks slip out every time we rounded the corner by the back porch. Momma had a smile on her face and she was waving to us, and Uncle Jerry threw a fresh chew of tobacco inside his lip.

And that was the last thing I saw before Pepaw dumped the bike over, and we all went sliding sideways through the yard.

My life flashed before my eyes, Hunter was thrown from the bike and I was trapped beneath it with Pepaw on top of me. I could feel the heat coming off the pipes onto my skin, so I quickly shifted to avoid getting third-degree burns. Hunter had landed a good three feet away from us, but he was standing up and looking upon us like we were lifeless. Pepaw shimmied out from under the bike, got to his feet and lifted the Harley off me with just one hand. I was amazed at this feat, I honestly thought he was gonna turn green – like the Incredible Hulk. Once I was freed, Pepaw slung himself back on the bike, made sure I was okay and then extended his hand to me.

"Don't be scared, Bubba. Come on, get back up here," Pepaw said.

I just stood there and looked at my grandfather like he was crazy; there was no way I was getting back on that bike. By now, Memaw and others came running around the corner, still screaming their heads off at Pepaw as if we had just died.

"I told you not to ride those babies on that bike!" Memaw screeched.

Pepaw ignored her and kept his eyes focused on mine. I could tell he was a little embarrassed about what happened, but he wasn't about to let it get to him. Momma ran over to Hunter – who was perfectly fine, not a scratch on him – scooped him up in her arms and asked him if he was all right. Pepaw still kept his eyes connected to mine, not breaking that contact for a second.

"Riding a bike is a lot like life, Bubba. Sometimes you may fall off, but you always have to pick yourself back up to get to where you're going," Pepaw said. He smiled as I extended my hand to him, and he yanked me back up on the bike.

"Now, you want to go fast or slow?" Pepaw asked me.

I thought about it for a second, and then leaned forward. "Fast, Pepaw. I wanna go fast!" I exclaimed.

"Alright, fast it is!" Pepaw laughed.

We shot out into the yard once again on the motorcycle, leaving everyone eating dust and Memaw yelling bloody murder.

That was the last dream I had of Pepaw for many

years, but it was a memory that I would hold onto for a lifetime.

We buried Pepaw two days after the wake, in his hometown of Vivian, Louisiana. He was buried toward the middle of the cemetery and right next to his head stone was one for Memaw; when her time came, she was going to be buried next to Pepaw where they could be together once more. I thought that very weird at the time, but it makes perfect sense to me now that I'm married. Love is a powerful thing, and I believe it follows us over to the next life. I don't think the feelings you have for all your loved ones disappear once you're gone, but that you carry them like baggage to the other side – just call me an old romantic.

As I stood over Pepaw's grave, I began to cry once more. Momma walked up behind me and slowly turned me around to face her.

"Don't cry, Bubba," Momma said.

"I can't help it."

Momma leaned down in front of me so that she could look into my eyes. "You know what Pepaw told me before he died?" Momma asked.

"No," I said as I wiped the tears from my face.

"He said – Sissy, don't you cry for me when you visit my grave, because I'm not there. I'm somewhere better. A place where I can look down upon all of you, waiting for the day we can all be together again. And on that day, when we do set eyes upon each other again, it will be the most glorious day ever – that's what he told me, Bubba," Momma said.

She went to walk away, but I grabbed her by the hand.

"Momma."

"Yes, Bubba."

"I'll be looking forward to that day too," I told her.

"So will I," Momma said gently, as she pulled me into her arms.

CHAPTER SIXTEEN

GAME OF THE YEAR: 1992

After Pepaw's death, the majority of our family was still melancholy and all doom and gloom, except for me and Hunter. My eleventh birthday was decent, and ringing in the New Year was okay, I guess, and Momma kept us busy with sports and extra activities after school which made our sorrow fade away a tad quicker.

Momma signed me up to play Biddy Basketball at Nelson Middle School which started in mid-February and tried getting me on the same team as Jack, but decided at the last minute that I needed to enjoy playing with other kids. Regardless, I was stoked and couldn't wait to start playing.

Memaw was still having a hard time with missing Pepaw, but Momma was there to comfort her during her times of need. Any time Memaw needed something, Momma was there in a jiffy, and eventually Memaw got better, although she was never quite the same.

The last time I had seen Jack, other than at Pepaw's wake, was at school and on the bus after Christmas break. Momma told me Mrs. Renee was keeping him away until our family had time to heal, which was very respectful, but this was the time I needed Jack more than ever. Being with him was like being in a different dimension – I felt no pain or sadness and if something was bothering either of us, we would each get it off our chest by spilling it to each other. I told Momma I wanted Jack to start coming back over, and she had no objections; I think that deep down inside, she knew I needed my friend.

It was about a week into February when Jack and I got back to our normal routine of doing stuff together. We began training up and practicing for basketball every day and we were getting pretty good – as good as white boys can get down south, anyways. Mr. Shawn nailed a homemade basketball goal up in a tree next to the gravel driveway and every day Jack and I would practice our asses off. The goal had a wooden backboard, a rusted-up ring, and a chain net that wasn't that much better than the hoop it hung on, but it was all we had at the time, and we loved it. Of course, we would parade up and down Rhine Road, practicing our dribbling skills and occasionally stopping off in the driveways of those fortunate enough to have a real basketball goal.

And come to think of it, no one ever seemed to mind, maybe because they saw we were doing something productive, rather than our usual destructive nature – and sometimes you got to feed the beast, know what I mean? We'd practice for hours and hours every day to better ourselves as players, although in all honesty, we didn't really need it because we were already two of the highest scorers in the league.

On the last game of the season, Nelson Middle School's gym was packed to the rafters with kids and families filling the bleachers, stuffing their faces with hot dogs and snicker bars from the concession stand. In the crowd, some were covered in blankets, others in flannel as they eagerly awaited the final games of the season; the gym was indoors, of course, but the Tickfaw public school system couldn't afford a damn heater for the place, so you had to fight off the cold the best way you could.

So, it just so happened that Jack's team and mine were facing off against each other, which made it a game I would never forget. It would turn out to be one of the best basketball games I'd ever play in my life, and although I was heartbroken that Pepaw couldn't be there to see me play I knew deep down he was watching, cheering me on from afar.

The buzzer rang, ending the first quarter and I stood up from the bench, removed my jacket and glanced over at the score – we were down by twelve – and ran out onto the court. I normally played first string point guard, but Coach wanted me to start off on second string to help bring in some points in the all-important second quarter. I glanced over to the opposing teams' bench, and lo and behold, here came none other than my blood brother, running onto the court like he owned it. I shook my head; it was a bad idea to put us up against each other. Nonetheless, I made my way up to half court, stopping in the middle of the big green circle with Jack.

"What's goin' on, loser?" Jack asked me with a shit-eating grin.

"Nothing much, douche bag, just about to whoop the shit out of you and your team."

"We'll see about that," Jack said, still grinning.

The rest of the teams formed a circle around us – pretty soon, Jack and I were going to be jumping ball against each other.

"Come on, Jody! Get the ball! You can do it!" one of

my teammates gave the war cry.

Jack's team yelled out their encouragement to him, too, and then the referee entered the circle with the basketball, twirling it on his finger like he was Michael Jordan. "All right, gentlemen, I want a clean jump, and no funny stuff," the ref said. He stuck the whistle in his mouth, gave it a good, hard blow and threw the ball in the air.

I leapt from the ground as high as I could, my right arm fully extended, fingers stretched as far as possible and smacked the ball in the direction of my teammates.

"I let you get that," Jack said smugly, and took off after my team.

I ran down the court and signaled for the ball. It was passed to me, but before I knew it, Jack was on me like white on rice.

"Where ya gonna go?" Jack asked as I turned my back to him and kept on dribbling.

"I'm going left and to the goal."

"No, go right and to the goal. That big guy over there's a retard and has no skills whatsoever."

"Sweet," I said and shot off to the right. Jack was quickly picked off by one of my teammates and I went right for the big kid, spun around him and scored a lay-up.

The crowd went wild.

I got back to half court as soon as Jack brought the ball down. I ran up to him and he put his back to me, dribbling the ball closely to the court.

"Go to my left. I'll fake a fall," I whispered.

"Sounds good." Jack spun left and I went down, faking one of the best falls of my life. As I pushed myself up from the court, I heard a roar of applause and I knew that my friend had scored.

That's how the second quarter went down, with Jack

and I giving one another helpful hints; although occasionally our competitive sides would come to the fore and we would actually play hard against each other. When we did that, neither of us scored, but hell, we knew each other's moves all too well.

Late in the fourth quarter, one of my teammates got fouled and went to the free-throw line. Jack and I retreated to the half court line to make a wager.

"I bet five bucks he doesn't make it," Jack said.

"I bet you ten dollars he makes one of the two."

"Blow me. You don't even have ten dollars," Jack was derisive.

"And your sorry ass doesn't have five dollars."

"Whatever, let's just see what happens," he said, rolling his eyes.

And so, we stood back and watched the dumb kid miss both free throws.

"You owe me five bucks!" Jack said as he ran back to his team.

"Hey, Jack," I yelled after him, and when he turned around I bellowed, "lick a nut!"

Jack smiled, reached down, grabbed his crotch and gave it a good squeeze while at the same time thrusting it at me. I laughed at that, and couldn't stop for the remainder of the game.

In the final moments, the clock counting down each second, I searched the crowd for Momma, spotting her in the middle of the bleachers. She was sitting next to Mrs. Renee and they were talking about God knows what and sharing a bucket of popcorn together. I looked a couple of rows up from Momma and saw Angela sitting with Krystle; heads together and giggling as per usual – they had recently become really good friends. And when I glanced back at the confounded clock, the buzzer sounded.

We'd lost – again; final score 42-34.

Jack had scored twenty of those winning points, and I had scored sixteen of the losing ones. Nevertheless, it was the best basketball game I played that season, and it was my second highest scoring game of *all time*.

The court was overrun by people giving out hugs and kisses, *congratulations* and *maybe next time son*, you know, the typical shit parents say after a game. What did catch me by total surprise was the hug I got from Angela, when her skinny little arms wrapped around my sweaty neck, I initially had the urge to push her away – 'cause I knew I stunk – but didn't want to, I liked it way too much.

"Good game, Jody," Angela said as she slowly released me from that delicious hug.

"Yeah, good game, Jody," Krystle chipped in.

"It wasn't all that good, but thanks." I gave them a half-smile. "Did you guys watch the entire game?"

"Well, we sort of had to. Krystle's parents aren't picking us up 'til four."

"Oh," I said, disappointed – I was kind of hoping Angela had been there just to see me play.

"You and Jack are crazy. We saw you guys cutting up at the half court line. What were you guys talking about?"

"Oh yeah, that, umm – we bet on that kid making the free throw shots. And he didn't, so Jack won."

"How much do you owe him?" Krystle giggled.

"Owe him? I'm not giving Jack one red cent. It was just a joke anyways."

"Well HA-HA, you guys shouldn't be so mean all the time," Angela said, giving me a coy nudge on the shoulder.

"We're not mean," Jack butted in with that shit-eating grin of his. He was back from celebrating the victory with his team. "We just tell it like it is."

"Hey, Jack," Krystle said, blushing slightly.

"Hey, Krystle," Jack replied, trying not to look the girl in the eyes. "So, what's going on?"

"We're just over here to say congrats to you, and better luck next time to Jody," Angela replied.

"Oh – I see how it is! Now who's being mean?" I faked annoyance and gave Jack a nudge in his ribs with my elbow.

"I said you shouldn't be mean all the time, there's nothing wrong with it every now and again," Angela flashed that perfect smile of hers – the one that never failed to make me go all weak in the knees.

"Well, maybe we'll try to be nicer," I promised.

"No you won't. You guys will still stay the same and keep living up to your *Bad Boys of Nelson Middle School* reputation," Krystle added.

"Is that what people call us?" Jack sounded surprised.

"Hell, don't look at me, I didn't give us that name, *they* did," I said.

"Yes, Jack," Krystle said, moving a little closer to him, "that's what everybody calls and thinks of ya'll; they say you guys think your poop doesn't stink."

"You can say 'shit' around us, Krystle, we won't tell on you," I joked.

"Wow, you guys are so cool 'cause you curse. Did you hear that Angela? They said *shit*,'" Krystle dripped sarcasm.

"Yep, I heard it. They're such rebels!" Angela joined in, and they both giggled.

"Alright, cut the jokes. I know ya'll just didn't come over here to bust our berries, so what's up?"

"Well, Angela wanted to come over here because she likes –"

"Krystle!" Angela squealed and grabbed Krystle by

the wrist. "We gotta go, guys – see ya later!"

"Bye Jack, bye Jody!" Krystle tittered as she was unceremoniously dragged away from us and across the basketball court.

"What the hell what was that all about?" I asked Jack.

"Seriously, man? You don't know?" Jack beamed at me like the cat that got the mouse. "Angela *likes* you."

"Get outta here." I punched Jack in the arm.

"Uh huh, oh yeah," Jack sung as he dry humped the air in front of me. "You know what this means."

"No I don't, sure you're gonna fill me in though."

"It means – um huh," Jack cleared his throat, "Jody and Angela sittin' in the tree, F-U-C-K-I-N-G,"

"Aww, get out of here with that!" I grimaced, fanning Jack away from me as if he was a bad fart.

"First comes love, then comes marriage, then comes Jody pushing a baby carriage!" Jack finished his rhyme, and we busted out laughing.

"Seriously though, Jody. I think Angela likes you – you should ask her out."

"You mean, like ask her to be my girlfriend?" I must have sounded real dumb.

"Yeah, like they do on the soap operas," Jack said.

"I don't know, I'll think about it."

"Come on! I know you like her," Jack pressed.

"Can we not talk about this right now?" I asked him. I was sort getting embarrassed, and that was a rare thing for me.

"Alright – whatever you say," Jack said. There was a slight pause and then, "Jody and Angela sittin' in the –"

"You bastard!" I snapped, and then chased my best friend in the world around the gymnasium.

I eventually caught up with Jack by the concession stand, which was on the far-right side by the boys' bathroom, located next to the bleachers. I put him in a headlock and took him to the ground laughing. Jack quickly got out of that and rolled on top of me. As I rolled over to my belly, I got a good look up into the bleachers, and I noticed a man in a black coat sitting in the upper left hand side.

"Jack, let go!" I said, panicking.

"Not until you say uncle."

"Let go, damn it!" I demanded, and Jack let go.

"What's your problem?"

I rolled over to my back to face Jack.

"Look in the bleachers, top left," I instructed.

Jack took a look, and I watched his face go in an instant from flustered to terrified.

"Is it *him*?" Jack asked.

"I don't know, you tell me."

Jack studied the man the same way a tiger scans its prey, slow and steady and waiting for the perfect moment to go in for the kill.

"I can't tell from here," Jack said, "we need to move closer so we can get a look at his face."

"You can go get a look at his face, I'm staying right here."

Jack squinted hard, trying to get a good look, 'cause if it was who we thought it was, he would have that distinctive harelip. But, before Jack could look any further, he was pulled up to his feet by his mother.

"What the hell are you doing on the floor, boy? You trying to embarrass the hell outta me?" Renee asked him, her voice sharp.

One thing about Mrs. Renee I forgot to mention – she was absolutely hysterical when she went off on one of her rants. Everything from the way she talked, to the way she dragged out her punctuations and also her mannerisms, were all way too funny. Having said that, I was too scared to laugh at that moment in time because the man who'd tried to kill us was in the gym. And he was watching us.

"Gayla," Renee motioned Momma over, "can ya believe they're over here rollin' around on the goddamned floor like a pair of animals?"

"Get your ass up, Jody," Momma said harshly as she walked over to me.

"I swear, you boys are gonna give me hemorrhoids. Let's go, Jack," Renee vented, as she waited for her errant son to get to his feet. "See ya later, Gayla. I'll call you later tonight to see what time you wanna go walking."

"It won't be until I get this nut and Hunter into bed tonight, so I say around ten o'clock," Momma replied.

"Alright then, you just call me when you're ready." Renee went to leave, but turned back as if she'd forgotten something. "Oh, Gayla, Shawn was wondering if it would be alright if he took Jody coon hunting tomorrow night?"

"That's fine by me," Momma said, casting her *you'd better not act the fool anymore today or you won't go* look at me. "What time do you want him at yours?"

"They normally start loading the trucks with the dogs around eight, so I say send him down around seven-thirty. But make sure he's dressed warm, 'cause he'll be out there 'til about three in the morning."

"Don't you worry, he'll be good to go."

"Alright now, talk to you tonight. Let's go, boy."

Mrs. Renee picked Jack up under the arm and escorted him from the gym. I knew Jack was still terrified at what – who – we'd seen, because he hadn't gone ape-shit crazy when he found out I was going hunting with him. Instead, he showed no sign of emotion and as he was led out of the gym by his mother, I watched as he kept his eyes focused on the bleachers, trying to stall his mother in order to get one last good look to see if it *was* that same guy from the mall. Renee, however, just kept on walking straight out the double doors.

"You ready to go home, Jody?" Momma asked me. I knew we were leaving because she was putting her jacket on, so it was a rhetorical question.

I stared back up into the bleachers, but I didn't see the man. Then I looked over towards the exit doors and caught one last look of him before he left, but still I couldn't tell if it was the same guy. So, I just shrugged it off and decided to wait and ask Jack if he had gotten a better look at him.

CHAPTER SEVENTEEN

WHISPERS IN THE DARK: 1992

The next night, I bundled up in a flannel jacket, rubber boots, a pair of worn-out pants with some long johns under them and headed over to Jack's house. Momma dropped me off in the driveway and gave me a kiss goodbye as I rushed up the gravel toward the house.

Three trucks were already there; one was Mr. Shawn's (with a new tire!) and the other two were F-150's with deer racks bolted to the front bumpers. Turned out to belong to some of Mr. Shawn's friends from work, and I could hear them rummaging around in the back yard.

I went in through the side door that was under the carport and walked into the kitchen. Mrs. Renee was stuffing coolers full of beer and treats, and Jamie was sitting at the table playing with a Polly Pocket playset.

"Hey, Jody," Jamie greeted me.

"What's going on, Jamie? Where's Jack?"

"I think he's still in his room getting dressed."

"He's not ready yet?"

"Don't think so. He's been acting weird since yesterday though, I don't know why."

"Oh," I replied, and figured that Jack must've gotten a good look at his face – and it had been our guy. "Well, I'll talk to you later, Jamie."

"Later."

I headed down the hallway to Jack's room and gave his closed door a rap with my knuckles. I heard Jack say *come in* so I opened the door, let myself in and closed it firmly behind me.

"Did you see his face? Was it him?" I blurted out, anxiously. '

"No, I wasn't able to get a good look at him. How 'bout you?" Jack was gloomy.

"I couldn't tell, either." I paused and looked over at Jack. He was sitting on his bed tying his shoes and looking depressed. "What's the matter, man? You okay?"

"I think I'm still a little shaken up from yesterday, that's all. When I saw that guy in the bleachers, I felt like I was gonna hurl."

"Do you still feel sick?"

"No," Jack looked up at me, "but I'm scared alright. I had nightmares again last night."

"Hey, man," I tried to reassure, "it probably wasn't him anyway. Most likely some poor schmuck who just so happened to look a bit like him, that's all. Nothing to worry about, trust me."

"You sure?"

"Yeah, and besides, what the hell would the crazy harelip guy be doing at the school gym?"

"Looking for us?" Jack offered, and the thought sent shivers down my spine. "If it was him, Jody, he was there looking for us."

I took a step back and thought about what Jack had

215

just said. It did make some sense. We'd kicked the shit out of the guy and left him bleeding in the mall elevator. If that had happened to me, I'd want to find the kids who beat my ass and give them some kind of payback. Although he'd have to be some special kind of lunatic to come to our school, since he did already try to kill us.

"That's bullshit," I tried to sound brave. "If it *was* him, he had every chance to do something, and he didn't. The guy from the mall is either in jail, or dead somewhere on the streets."

"I hope so," Jack said.

"Jesus, can you not be any less excited about this hunting trip? You're starting to make me worried."

"I'm sorry, Jody, you're probably right."

"Damned right I am!" I put Jack in a headlock and gave him a quick noogie, "Now let's go pump some coons full of lead!"

"Alright, alright," Jack stood up from his bed and walked out of the bedroom with me following right behind him.

Renee was filling mugs with tea, and let me tell you, Mrs. Renee could make *some* tea. It was the perfect mix, not too sweet and not too bland; it made you crave more the second you took that first big gulp. She filled four thermoses full of it and another four with either coffee or hot chocolate. As we helped Renee finish packing all the goodies into the cooler, I heard Mr. Shawn bringing the dogs around to the trucks. I glanced out the back door – which was one of those big sliding-glass affairs – and saw Mr. Shawn walking Jack's favorite dog, Scarlet, to the trucks. She sniffed enthusiastically at the ground, sweeping her head side to side like she'd already picked up a scent. Jack and I darted out the side door and I watched as my friend ran up to his dad and knelt down in front of Scarlet.

"Scarlet!" Jack said, sweetly and kissed his dog's face.

Scarlet kissed him back with an assault of licks, sending gobs of drool running down his chin to make it look like Jack was the one drooling. She jumped up on her back legs, lunged forward and took Jack to the ground. He wrapped his arms around her and the two of them rolled around in the gravel.

"Quit horsing around, Jack," Mr. Shawn ordered, "I gotta get her strapped into the back of the truck. You and Jody can ride with her on the way out to the camp."

"Okay, Dad." Jack gave Scarlet one last smooch and got to his feet.

Mr. Shawn walked Scarlet around to the back of his pick-up, lowered the tailgate and lifted her up into the cab. She sniffed around the back of the truck as Mr. Shawn closed the tailgate and walked around to the side to connect the end of the leash, snapping it onto one of the tie-down hoops.

"Alrighty, Scarlet. You better tree us some good-sized coons tonight, 'cause you're riding first class on the way to the camp," Shawn gave the dog a good rub on the head, and walked back to the house. "You boys can start bringing the stuff out," he called over to me and Jack.

When we got back inside, Mr. Shawn's buddies were filling their rifles with ammo; one man was loading a .22, another a 4-10. Mr. Shawn opened up his gun cabinet and pulled out a beautiful Remington rifle. Its body was wooden, immaculately lacquered, and it had a long barrel with a scope mounted on top.

"I'm gonna get me some coons with this baby," Mr. Shawn said, looking at his gun with pride, "isn't that right, Jack?"

"Oh yeah, Dad, you're gonna make their day with that thing," Jack replied with a reassuring smile.

Once the big boys were done loading their rifles and shooting the shit, the rest of Mr. Shawn's friends went outside to gather up the dogs – another six from the kennel – and loaded them into the back of their F150's. Once they were done, they came back inside to make last-minute checks on their equipment. Mr. Shawn got up off the couch, walked into the kitchen to give Mrs. Renee a small kiss goodbye on the cheek. Five of the men headed to the pisser to empty their tanks, and Jack and I decided to go empty our bladders on the lawn.

"You boys ready?" Mr. Shawn asked, and we nodded our heads in excitement, "Well, go on out there to the truck. We're all about done in here, so we'll be out in a minute."

Jack reached over, pushed me into the kitchen table and then ran outside, hollering like a lunatic. Mr. Shawn stood there shaking his head, probably already regretting inviting me along.

As I came running out of the house, my rubber boots almost flew off my feet. If you've ever worn rubber boots, you know that they're not designed for running by any means. Nonetheless, I ran up to Jack, who stood next to his Dad's truck, frozen solid like a statue.

"Jack? What's the matter?" I slowed up and walked quietly up behind him.

My friend didn't respond and when I looked over his shoulder, I saw why.

Scarlet hung off the side of the truck with her leash wrapped tightly around her neck. Her tongue was hanging out of her mouth, moving along in the cool breeze. I looked closely at her and saw that blood was pouring from her neck, running all the way down her belly and dripping onto Jack's boots. I could see the inside of her throat, the white and pink tissue split open and the cut was almost to the bone.

"Scarlet..." Jack muttered.

My heart beat fast and sour chunks of vomit made their way up my throat. I backed away from Scarlet, and I heard someone whisper my name from the darkness. Jack quit looking at his poor, dead dog and snapped his neck hard to his right; he'd heard the voice, too.

"Jack – pssst – you wanna play –" wafted towards us in the wind.

The voice was faint, almost inaudible, and impossible to tell where it was coming from. It was pitch black in the yard, the only light a shallow glow from the front window.

"Jody –" the voice whispered tauntingly, "I see you – come and play with us –"

I looked nervously around the yard and grabbed Jack by the wrist; I needed to know he was there as I was petrified. Jack scanned the yard, trying to locate the source of that eerie voice. I focused my eyes on the fence to my right, the one that Jack's neighbors owned, horrified, I saw a shadow making its way along the fence and toward the road.

"Jack," I whispered, "someone's by the fence."

"Somebody's across the road, over in the woods, too."

I moved my attention to the tree line across the street. There was another person, draped in some kind of dark, heavy robe. They just stood there on the edge of the woods, not caring that they'd been spotted. I glanced back to the fence and scrutinized it all the way to where it ran into the ditch, and I saw a shadow leap over it to join the other one at the wood line. Jack and I stared wide-eyed at their empty, dark faces, hoping they were simply figments of our imagination, until slowly, they faded away into the woods and disappeared into the night.

"Help!" Jack screamed, breaking the silence, "Daddy, help!"

"Mr. Shawn, help!" I echoed, finally finding the courage to scream.

Mr. Shawn and his buddies came running out with fully loaded rifles ready to fire.

"What's wrong, boys?" Mr. Shawn's voice was filled with anxiety.

"Two people were here – one in the yard and the other across the street. They killed Scarlet, Daddy! *They killed her*!" Jack cried and ran into his father's arms, sobbing.

"Check the woods across the street, guys!" Shawn barked to his friends, and in instant they were off down the driveway, across the street and into the woods. Shots were fired moments later, which made us all jump.

"What exactly did you see, Jody?" Mr. Shawn asked.

"Two people, wearing thick blankets or something, they said our names, but it was hard to see them, they looked like shadows."

"Come here, Buddy," Mr. Shawn said to me, nudging Jack a little to make room for me.

I stepped over to him and he brought me into the hug with Jack, and I instantly felt safe. Jack was still sobbing, and when he took his face away from his father's chest to wipe his tears, I saw that Mr. Shawn's shirt had a big wet spot on it. I looked over to Scarlet and my heart ached. She just hung there, her throat sliced open and bleeding as my poor friend wept for his loss. Jack reached out from the comfort of his father's hug, and ran his fingers through the fur on Scarlet's head, and then Mr. Shawn turned us away and brought us back in the house.

"Get the goddamned police on the phone," Shawn growled, as he sat us down on the couch. "Did you hear me, Renee?"

"What's going on, Shawn? Why's there shooting outside?" Mrs. Renee was frightened.

"Just get the damned police on the phone!"

Renee said no more and did as Shawn had asked.

"Sit here, boys, and *don't move*," Mr. Shawn instructed, and took off out of the living room. And this time he took the Remington with him.

I sat there on the couch for a while in total silence and completely zoned out. I couldn't help but replay the events in my racing mind, over and over again. Why would someone do such a thing to a poor dog? Who the hell had been whispering our names? The only sound that I could hear was Jack's sobs; he had curled into a fetal position and was letting out uneven, heavy breaths.

Another shot rang out into the night. It startled me, but Jack didn't even flinch. I quit staring at him, because watching him cry reminded me too much of losing Pepaw, and I got to my knees on the sofa, pulling the bay window curtain aside to peer out into the front yard.

Without warning, a man in a thick black robe with a cow skull for a face threw himself into the window. I fell backwards off the couch and saw the masked man lift up Scarlet's severed head in his hand, as if he was revealing some glorious gift. I squeezed my eyes tight shut and screamed for Mrs. Renee.

I looked back at the man and I saw his eyes through the skull's sockets; he waved at me and then threw Scarlet's head at the window.

I screamed so loud that I tasted blood in the back of my throat. Jack sat bolt upright and stared at the blood splatter upon the glass and the weird man retreating into the night. Jack, too unleashed a blood-curdling scream.

"Oh my God! Shawn, where are you? Shawn! Look away, Jody, look away!" Renee cried as she dashed in and rushed over to Jack and me, taking us to the comfort of her bosom.

The blue and red lights from the police cars parked up on Jack's front lawn drew the attention of the night's travelers along Rhine Road. Some cars slowed down as they drove by, others hung their heads out the window to rubberneck, while others simply zoomed past and paid us no attention.

Mr. Shawn had called Momma and then ushered Jack and I back to Jack's bedroom once the police arrived, and there we sat in silence. I stepped away from peering through the window and walked over to the door. I pressed my ear hard up against it and eavesdropped on the conversation that was taking place in the kitchen. The cops were saying something about a similar incident over in Albany; only there, the residents didn't actually see anyone. They'd awoken the next morning to find a whole bunch of dogs beheaded and drained of their blood. Listening to that made me even more uneasy, so I quit and lay on the bed next to Jack, who was in a deep sleep and looked kinda dead himself.

An hour or so passed, and once the interviews were done and statements taken, Shawn, Renee and Momma came into the room to get us. All of Mr. Shawn's buddies had left, and the house was once again quiet. We went into the living room, and the first thing I looked at was the window, but someone had washed away the blood already. Our parents sat us down on the couch and turned on the TV, without saying a word. Shawn escorted Jamie to her room, and after about twenty minutes, he came back and stood before us.

"I'm going to go bury Scarlet in the back yard under the oak tree," he spoke solemnly. " When I'm done, you can go out back and say your goodbyes."

Jack didn't say a word. He just sat on the couch and

began crying again. Momma walked into the room and rubbed Jack on his leg to try to comfort him, but it didn't work, I doubted that anything would.

Mr. Shawn left us there and headed outside. I watched him through the bay window as he walked over to Scarlet's headless body, gently picked her up and carried her away. The sound of metal striking the cold, hard ground followed a few moments later as Mr. Shawn buried Scarlet beneath the tree. At this, Jack cried even harder and Mrs. Renee walked over, sat beside him and squeezed him tight.

Jack loved that dog, and Scarlet loved him right back. She'd many great times with Jack, just as many as I'd had with Rambo, and my friend's bond with her was incredibly strong; it was like a part of him died that night with her, and I totally understood.

Momma and I said our goodbyes to Shawn and Renee and left. I didn't say goodbye to Jack, it just didn't seem like the right time. I knew that when my friend was ready, he would let me know.

When we got home, Memaw was sitting on the couch with Hunter, rocking him back and forth and waiting for Momma to tell her the details, but she didn't say a word when we stepped in.

And when she did ask, Momma simply told her that a fire had broken out in the kitchen; but it was put out before the fire department responded, and the police had just showed up to take a report. Placated, Memaw's face went from worried to fine in a matter of seconds. She gave us all a kiss goodnight before she walked home. Hunter wanted to play with me, but Momma swiftly intervened and told him just to go play in his room, since I wasn't feeling good.

"You going to be alright, Bubba?" Momma asked me.

"I don't know, Momma, maybe."

"You want to talk about it?"

"Do the police know who those people were?"

"No – they don't, but they believe that it's some gang from Albany."

"I know. I heard a cop telling ya'll about what happened out there, when I was in Jack's room."

"So you were listening?" Momma asked.

"Yeah," I looked down at my feet, and I guessed she was probably mad at me for eavesdropping, but at least I was being honest. "Are they going to catch them, Momma?"

"I don't know."

"Are we safe?" I really wanted an answer to that.

Momma looked around and picked Hunter's stuff up off the floor, avoiding the question.

"Momma," I said, making sure I had her attention. *"Are we safe?"*

Momma came up from the floor with a handful of Hunter's toys in her arms and looked right at me.

"I don't know, Bubba. We just need to keep an eye on things around here, okay? The cops gave me and Renee a detective's phone number, in case we need to call him, you know, if we see or hear anything that's out of the ordinary." Momma paused. "We can't tell Memaw though, Jody, she can't handle something like this right now. Not so soon after losing Pepaw."

"We all lost Pepaw," I was angry. "So what about Memaw? She needs to know what's going on, Jesus – the whole street needs to know, because something like this can happen to any one of us next! What about me, Momma? I was the one who saw everything that happened tonight. I was the one who watched a man throw Scarlet's head into the window. I'm never going to forget what happened tonight – ever! We need Pepaw more than we've ever needed him, but he's gone, and there's nothing we can do."

"I'm sorry, Bubba. Come here," Momma held out her arms.

"Leave me alone!"

"Jody, don't talk to me that way."

"I hate this place and I hate Pepaw for dying, because now he's not here to protect us – and Daddy won't help us either, because he's too busy fucking his new bitch!"

Momma slapped my face, and I spun around like a tilt-a-whirl. Although her strike was firm and deliberate, it still didn't take away the pain I was feeling – it actually pissed me off more.

"You're not going to use that kind of language with me, son! I'm not one of your little friends who thinks you're so cool – I'm your *mother*, and you will not speak to me this way!"

"Why don't you hit me again so I can call the police?" I tried to sound brave.

"You can call them all you want, son, but when they get here, I'll beat their ass too," Momma said.

"You hate me!"

"I love you, Jody, and I'm trying to help you through all of this. I know you're scared, and there's nothing wrong with that. We'll get through this together."

"No one can help me, not even you! I can help myself!" I yelled and stormed off to my room.

"Get back here, Jody," Momma called after me. "Get over here – *now*!"

I ignored her and continued onto my room. I went in and slammed the door shut and before I made it to my bed, I collapsed to my knees.

"Why did you take him, God? Why did you take my Pepaw? *Please* give him back," I prayed and stared up at the ceiling, expecting God to show his face. "I'm in trouble, and I know it. I don't know what to do, though.

I'm so scared, and I think those people are gonna be back, and when they come, they'll kill me, and if not me, then someone important to me. Please, help me, God."

When I was done praying, I crawled into my bed, covered up with my sheets and cried myself to sleep. Every dream I had that night was about my own death at the hands of the man with the cow skull over his face.

When morning came, I lay awake in my bed and gazed blankly at the ceiling, not moving, or thinking about anything that had happened the night before. Something was wrong with me – I felt numb, yet filled with anger. I had changed overnight, and not for the better, believe me.

After that morning, my life began to spiral out of control.

CHAPTER EIGHTEEN

LIFE IN THE FAST LANE: 1992

It takes time for wounds to heal, and Jack and I sure had plenty of those that needed curing. I knew that I was emotionally scarred from what I had witnessed that night and though Jack was too, he was showing it in different ways. He stopped playing with his dogs, and began killing small animals; birds, stray cats, stray dogs, it didn't matter to Jack, if it wasn't human, it got shot.

As for me, I became ever more disobedient toward Momma, Memaw – and any other adult, for that matter. I would constantly talk back, and got my ass beat on plenty occasions for it, but it had no effect on me. I had sprouted to about five foot six inches, and had grown meaner toward my brother and peers too.

I remember all too well the last basketball game I played at Nelson Middle School…

I was guarding a point guard who was running down the court, clearly hoping to dribble a fake and go around me. I was near the sideline, close to the guy's parents and friends who were cheering him on, and as he tried to pass me, I bent down, pushed my shoulder forward and forced it hard into his pelvis. The poor kid went flying over my shoulder and landed on his neck. The crowd stood up and screamed *foul* at the referee – one parent, a balding man with a ruddy face, stood up from the bleachers and yelled at me, like I really gave a shit what *he* thought. I gave Baldy the middle finger, and the rest of the crowd broke out into outrage.

I was taken out of the game, of course, but I honestly didn't care; I'd inflicted pain upon my opponent and that thought made me smile. The downside was that my stunt landed my ass in a psychiatrist's office early the following month, and Mrs. Renee and Mr. Shawn waited to see my results before they placed Jack there, too.

"I want you to draw me a picture of how you feel right now," the psychiatrist requested.

"Can't you tell how I feel by just looking at me? I don't want to be in this office drawing damned third-grade pictures about my feelings," I growled at the shrink.

"Why are you so angry, Jody? Is it because of what happened that night with Jack's dog? Or is there something else that's making you behave this way?"

"How much longer do I have to be in here?" I asked, rudely.

"As long as it takes to get some kind of answer out of you."

"Well," I said, slapping my hand on my knee and throwing myself back into the couch, "how about I ask *you* some questions instead?"

"Go for it," said the shrink, giving me one of those smug smiles, as if he'd got me cornered.

"Who the hell were the people who killed Jack's dog?"

"I can't answer that for you, I'm sorry. That's something you should maybe ask the police." He looked around the room, leaned backed and then asked nonchalantly, "can we talk about your father, perhaps?"

"Fuck my father," I snapped.

"Hey, I know a divorce isn't anything easy to go through, especially for a kid your age. You're going through a tough time in your life right now, where you need a father figure, and it's hard, I know. Your father doesn't call, he doesn't send birthday cards – he doesn't do anything. And I do understand your grief and anger when it comes to your Pepaw. I know you were close with him, and he took the place of your father. I know you need someone to talk to right now, Jody, and I'm your man."

"I don't think any of this has anything to do with my father. He's been gone since I was in second grade, so why would it bother me now?" I asked; he had broken me down into opening up, and I felt my blood boiling beneath my skin.

"Because you're coming of age, and you have all these hormones and feelings racing throughout your body, and sometimes it gets so out of control that you start behaving differently."

"So, you think the way that I've been acting is – is because I'm starting puberty?" I asked, looking at the shrink as if he was a retard with a PhD.

"That could be one of the factors," He nodded, sagely.

"*Wow*," I dripped sarcasm. I stood up from the couch. "You might as well give me one of those plaques you have up there on your wall, *doctor*, because *I* could've told *you* that."

I stormed out of the room, not once looking back at the man who didn't give two shits about what was going on in my life. Dr. PhD just wanted to waste time and money beating around the bush, talking about daddy problems and stating the obvious about childhood adolescence; practically the same shit you learn in Sexual Education classes.

I met with Momma in the hallway and she asked me how it had gone in there.

"It was a waste of time, Momma. Can we just go home, please?"

Momma didn't say a single word to me; we simply walked out of the office, got into the car and went back home.

Over the rest of the school year, I found myself in Saturday detentions more than any other kid in the school – besides Jack of course. And even though our behavior had worsened, our parents didn't keep us from each other; I think they were hoping that Jack and I could solve our problems together, but sadly, that wasn't the case. We hadn't mentioned once the incident with Scarlet, we'd buried that memory deep in the back of our minds and had no intention of digging it back up. What we did do, however, was act out our bad feelings, because causing chaos and mayhem were the only things that seemed to help our problems go away; and we loved every minute of it.

The last day of my sixth-grade year, I worked up the nerve to ask Angela to be my girlfriend. I saw her cleaning out her locker after the final bell rang and I approached her, all queasy and unsure.

"Hey, Angela."

"Oh, hey, Jody."

"Look, I'm going to go straight for it, okay?" I took in a deep breath.

"Straight for what?" Angela looked at me as if I were about to mug her.

"Umm – will you go out with me?" I bit my bottom lip and looked down at the floor.

"It's about time you asked me," Angela grinned. She grabbed my hands, giving them an excited squeeze. "I thought I was going to have to ask you – since it seemed like you never would."

Angela's hands were soft and fragile, and I rubbed them with my fingers in small, shaky, circles. "So, the answer is yes?"

"*Yes*, I would love to be your girlfriend," Angela beamed, and I figured I'd just made her day; hell, it had sure made mine.

"Thank God you said yes," I let out a sigh of relief. "'Cause –" I pointed over to Jack, who was lurking behind one of the lockers, "– if you'd said no, I would have caught shit all summer long from him."

"There was no way I was going to say no to you," Angela said sweetly, and I felt my heart light up, something I hadn't felt in a long time.

I felt something else too; it was growing uncontrollably down in my pants. I tried to imagine the nastiest girl in school naked on a beach drinking a diet Coke and stuffing her spotty, fat face full of ding-dongs – but it didn't work and I officially had a boner. I let go of Angela's hands and I felt the little guy begin to soften up. I looked into her eyes and thanked God she hadn't noticed the tent I'd made in my pants.

"Well, can I have your phone number, you know, so I can call you this summer?" the words hurried from my mouth in a blathering torrent.

"Sure."

Angela reached into her locker, pulled out a pen and paper and wrote down her number for me.

"Thanks," I stuffed Angela's number into my front pocket, "I gotta go now, but I'll call you soon."

"Okay."

"Alright, then," I said, not really knowing what to do next. So, I made a daring move and reached over to give her a hug and before I could get one arm around her, Angela kissed me on the cheek.

"See you this summer," Angela smiled as she shut her locker door and scurried over to her friends. Immediately, they all swarmed around her with giggling joy and praise, and I saw that Krystle was amongst the throng. She looked over at me from the group and gave me a simple wave.

"The whole school is gonna know ya'll are going out in no time," Jack said as he sidled up to me.

"You think so?"

"I give it five minutes – tops."

And no shit, my good friend was right. In what seemed to be a blink of an eye, the entire school was congratulating me on my new girlfriend, and I was getting everything from high fives to jealous looks from the other girls who were obviously pissed that I hadn't asked *them* out.

Yes sir, that summer was going to be the best one yet.

Or so I thought.

CHAPTER NINETEEN

MOUTH OF THE SOUTH: 1992

Having a girlfriend changed a lot of things that summer between Jack and I, but surprisingly, it wasn't all for the worse. It kept the two of us out of a lot of trouble, but of course we still had time to find it when the fancy took us. When we weren't at the movies, mini golf, or taking trips out to the fun park in Baton Rouge, we dished out our bits of havoc around the neighborhood; lighting mailboxes on fire and shooting animals were our favorites, the latter using the BB gun I'd stolen out of Pepaw's old gun closet. Before we set off to scout the neighborhood for pets – strays or otherwise – Jack would hop on the handlebars of my bike, stuff the gun under his shirt and give me the big thumbs-up, and no pets on Rhine Road were safe.

We rolled up into the Oaks one day and spotted a big-ass Golden Retriever digging around in a trash can. Jack jumped off my handlebars, lay down on his belly, took aim and pulled the trigger. He did it so fast – the entire maneuver had to have been less than twenty seconds flat – and *poof*, that BB was heading for its target. The gun bucked in Jack's hands and we watched the BB strike the dog square in the balls. The poor bastard went to his knees and dragged his sack across the grass, howling like a banshee. Laughing, Jack and I got back on the bike and took off in absolute hysterics.

"Did you see that fucker dragging his balls across the yard?" Jack could barely speak and was decidedly red in the face from laughing.

"Oh my God! My stomach hurts!" I howled.

"I didn't mean to get him in the balls," Jack said, "I think the wind took the shot."

"Where were you aiming?" I giggled.

"His ass!" Jack bellowed, and laughter claimed us again.

A week later, Jack beat up some kid who lived a few streets over. He was riding his bike down Rhine Road and stopped to chat with us near the entrance to the Oaks. Next thing I knew, a punch was thrown, and the kid soared up into the air and landed on his back in the sewage ditch across the street.

Apparently the dumb kid had called Jack a motherfucker, or some such – must have been something *really* insulting, because Jack would never have randomly beaten up on some kid; that just wasn't him. Still, I couldn't help but wonder if Jack was still having problems with what had happened to Scarlet. We still hadn't talked about it, ever; the subject was forbidden fruit and we both knew it. The change I noticed in my blood brother made me wonder if he saw a difference in me.

That summer, I was officially labeled the *Mouth of the South* by kids and adults alike. Shit, even Momma started calling me it!

I turned into the biggest shit talking soon-to-be-twelve-year-old in Tangipahoa Parish and I was damned proud of it. I would argue with the devil himself, along with anyone who pissed me off or got in my way. I wasn't a great fighter, not at all, I was a bit of a weenie, truth be told, but my mouth usually ran people off; they thought that if my bark was as big as my bite, I would surely be a force to be reckoned with. My mouth started a lot of shit, but thank God it was able to get me out of a lot too.

One day, Jack and I were riding down the street and we noticed a condom on the side the road, still in its little foil wrapper, clearly someone didn't get lucky last night. Of course, we stopped next to it, and Jack clambered off my handlebars, tore the rubber packet open and stretched the contents out.

"Holy shit," Jack was shocked, "you think our dicks will ever fit into something this long?"

"Damn, that thing's fucking huge!" I gasped.

"Yeah."

"How do you put 'em on?" I genuinely had no idea, I guess I'd been too busy goofing off in Sex Ed' class.

"No idea," Jack admitted. He brought the rubber up to his mouth and blew it up like a balloon – a *ribbed* balloon, incidentally. "Shit! It's made a funny smell around my lips, and now they've gone all numb."

"Well, stop blowing the damned thing up, then."

"Good call," Jack muttered as he licked his lips to see if he could feel them.

Just then, a car pulled out of the Oaks and made its way towards us. I glanced over at Jack and he had that look on his face – that *I'm about to do something I probably shouldn't do* look of his. As the car approached, Jack placed the blown-up contraceptive over his genitals and dry humped the air. The elderly

235

couple in the car stared at us in complete disgust as Jack viciously thrust his pelvis at them as they drove by. "Suck it, baby! Suck my dick!" he yelled after the car.

I knew it was horribly wrong, but really I couldn't help but laugh, after all, the look on the old lady's face had been priceless.

After they'd passed us, I picked up my bike, Jack jumped on the handlebars and we made our way down along Rhine Road; Jack with the blown up rubber still in his hands, yelling and screaming a whole host of obscenities to the world in general.

It took Angela and Krystle a figurative act of congress to talk Jack and I into going to the mall with them one late summer afternoon. They had gotten us to go to the movie theater, but that was attached to the far side of the mall, so to us it was just the theater and hence not the place where we'd almost been murdered in an elevator.

The girls called my house and asked Momma if we could go with them, since they knew Jack was staying the night at my house. We hadn't been inside the main mall since the incident, and we didn't really want to go back, but women have a way of convincing you to do shit you don't want to do, even at the tender age of eleven.

So, reluctantly, Jack and I agreed to go, but we made a pact beforehand to stay on our toes and stick to each other like glue. Angela's dad came and picked us up about an hour later, rolling into our driveway, honking his horn. Jack, Momma and I went out to greet them, and as Momma made small talk and thanked him for taking us to the mall, Jack opened the sliding door to the van.

Krystle was sitting primly in the third-row seat with Angela, so Jack and I got in and settled in the comfy seats in the center row. After Momma was done bullshitting with Angela's Dad, we pulled out of the driveway and headed off to the mall. To regular kids like Angela and Krystle, a trip to the mall got them all excited and giggly, but for Jack and I – well, we remained silent the whole trip up there.

Once we got there, Angela's dad pulled up to the main entrance and dropped the four of us off. He was taking the van to get an oil change and told us to meet him at the Taco Bell across the way in about an hour and a half.

Things went smoothly this time around, we walked around with the girls, window shopped and sauntered into a couple of clothing stores that at any other given time Jack and I wouldn't have stepped foot in. That entire time, though, we kept a wary eye open, scanning every department store before going in, and we never turned our backs to anyone. After about an hour of wandering around looking at stuff none of us could have afforded, the girls were ready to head over to Taco Bell. Jack and I had no objections to that; we were both relieved to have survived our second trip to the mall without incident.

We crossed the street carefully and when we got into the parking lot, Angela took hold of my hand. I got that funny feeling again in my pants, but quickly got it under control. Jack opened the doors for us – such a gentleman – and we went inside. There were only three people inside; one under the advertisement for the new Taco Salad, eating alone, and a young couple, mid-twenties maybe, sitting by one of the windows that looked out towards the mall.

"I'll go grab us a booth," Krystle said and weaved her way through the tables and chairs.

"You want something to eat, Jody?" Angela asked.

"No, I'm good. I didn't bring any money anyways."

"That's okay, I'll get something for you. My dad gave me twenty dollars."

"Can you get Jack something, too, then?" I asked, I didn't want to leave my best friend flapping in the wind.

"Sure."

"Thanks."

I walked over to the booth and joined Krystle and Jack, who were having a conversation about school.

"You think we'll get a new French teacher next year?" Krystle asked.

"God, I hope so," Jack replied, "I can't stand that twat we had last."

"Me either."

"Angela is getting us both something, Jack," I butted in.

"Cool, what's she getting?"

"I have no idea, but it's free."

"And beggars can't be choosers."

"Sometimes they can," Krystle chimed in. "But that makes them a selfish ass-wad. My Uncle Frank is like that. You give him free mashed potatoes, and he'll ask you where the hell the gravy's at."

"What a dick," I said.

"Yeah, tell me about it," Krystle grimaced.

I looked over to Angela, and she was getting our food pushed over to her on one of those cheap turquoise trays by none other than my old friend, the Satanist.

I was delighted to see him again, since there was something I had to ask him; hell, I knew I'd get a sensible answer from him. I made my way toward the counter in a trance-like state, so damned nervous because although I wanted answers, I was shit-scared of what they might be.

Angela turned around with the tray in her hand and

smiled at me as if I was going to take the load off her hands – I didn't. I walked right by her and knocked on the counter to get the guy's attention. I heard Angela let out a frustrated sigh and she stormed off to the booth.

"Hey, buddy. Goodness you got big! What's going on?" he asked politely.

"I need to talk to you," I was blunt, in no mood for pleasantries.

"*Oookaaay,*" the guy behind the counter said, "about what?"

"Please, could you step outside? I have something very important to ask you."

"Look, kid, I'm on the clock still, and I can't –"

"Please," I begged.

He took a serious look at me, then at the clock on the wall in the lobby and then back down at his own watch.

"Alright," he agreed, "you got ten minutes, and this better be good. Go wait out back by the dumpster. I'll be there in a minute."

I said no more and walked back over to the booth where Jack was busy stuffing his face with a burrito supreme. I grabbed him by the shirt, pulling him to his feet "We'll be right back," I said to the girls, and Jack and I left out the main doors, Jack's mouth still full of beans, meat, cheese and sour cream.

"What the fuck, Jody? You trying to make me choke to death?"

"I don't want to hear it right now, Jack, just follow me."

We walked up to the big blue dumpster that had the letters BFI on the side of it. I waited to hear Jack's old joke of how the abbreviation meant *Black Family Inside*, but he remained silent. Cardboard boxes were scattered on the ground around the dumpster, with rotted lettuce and the stench of curdled refried beans polluting the air.

The cashier came out the back door, lit a cigarette and walked up to us.

"So, let me hear what's so important that I had to take a ten-minute break for two middle schoolers that I haven't seen in over a year. Hell, I don't even know your names."

I wasted no time and told him about that night at Jack's house, and once I got to the part about what the people had been wearing, and what they'd done to poor Scarlet, the Satanist cashier was sucking on his cigarette like it was going to run away from him. And before I knew it, he was lighting up another one. As I regaled the cashier, I looked over at Jack, who paced back and forth in front of the dumpster and I could tell that he was crying a little.

When I was done telling the cashier everything about that night, he stood there and looked upon us with pity.

"So now that you know everything, I want you to tell me who, or what these people are, if you can," I finished up like a half-priced courtroom lawyer.

"Have your parents not talked to you about any of it?"

"Look, sir, we're not stupid kids, but our parents seem to think we are. I figure they don't want to scare us, but by them not telling us shit, it's just making things worse. We need to know what's happening. Why were they wearing those robes? Why was the guy who killed Scarlet wearing a skull mask? Are we in danger?"

"You want to know the truth?" the cashier asked us, his tone straightforward.

"Yes," Jack broke his silence, "I want to know who killed my dog."

"Look," the guy said, placing one hand on each of our shoulders. "Those people are part of a cult, a group claiming to be Devil Worshippers. But they're not your typical breed, this bunch of lunatics have been running between Hammond, Albany and Ponchatoula for the past couple of years, stirring up the shit pot. Do you guys watch the news?"

"No," we said, I mean, what eleven year old watches the damned news?

"A lot of talk show hosts have been doing specials on this kind of stuff recently. Everything from murderous cults to the occult seems to be on the tips of everyone's tongues these days. Have you guys heard of Hurtado Mendoza?"

"Isn't he a big news guy from New Orleans? I've heard my mom mention him a few times," I said.

"Yes, that's right. He came to Hammond about three months ago to do a special on the occult, and on his first night in town, his equipment van was trashed and someone had left a wooden box on the hood. When Mendoza opened it, there was a note inside telling him to back the fuck off – along with a cow's heart. Boy, let me tell you, his ass was out of here the next morning."

"That's crazy," I was disgusted by the story, the memory of the butchered calves flashing through my mind.

"I know what a *cult* is," Jack chipped in. "It's a bunch of wackos that get together and do sex stuff and stupid shit – my dad told me all about the Manson Murders. But what's an *occult*?" Jack asked.

"Let me break it down for you so it's easier to understand," the cashier said, taking another deep drag on his cigarette. "The occult is a secret religion people have been studying since the beginning of time. It was first mentioned in the Bible and people that were suspected of practicing it, your necromancers, fortunetellers, psychics and the like, were stoned to death in public because it was all considered the way of

241

the Devil, according to the Good Book.

"Nowadays, it's still looked down upon by normal society, but Satanists like me study it anyway – we believe that it holds the truth to everything that people are too scared to see. The occult has a bad rap because of people like those who killed your dog."

"If the Bible says it's wrong, then why take a chance studying it?" I was getting completely overwhelmed with all this information.

"I have my reasons, kid, but I'm not about to discuss my beliefs with two eleven-year-old boys."

"We're about to be twelve," Jack stated proudly.

The cashier paid him no attention and went on, "The problem you two boys are facing is one that we've always had here in Hammond – *Devil Worshippers*. Over the years, beliefs like the occult, Satanism, and Devil worship have attracted some of the most out-of-control youths and adults across America. Things have gotten completely out of hand, so out of hand that it's caught the attention of the media and the police. I'm not going to lie to you boys, there is a problem in this small town of ours, and like I told you before, stay safe, stick together and don't talk to any strangers."

"Do these so-called Devil Worshippers kill kids?" I asked. I really hadn't paid attention to the history lesson he'd just relayed, I just wanted to know if we were in any real danger.

"There have been reports, yes, but that's not what true Devil Worshippers are about, but I think the group running around these parts are capable of it though. A kid was offered as a sacrifice in the small town of Cumberland, Iowa the other day; I saw it on the news." He sucked harder on his cigarette. "He'd been hog-tied and stabbed to death in an old run-down mill out in the middle of nowhere. The cops found his body and found enough evidence to point them to a group of so-called Devil Worshippers active in the area – they were arrested and are now awaiting trial.

"People do some unspeakable things in this world, boys, you'll see that when you get older, but I want you to know something else..." he looked at Jack and I with fear in his eyes. "There was a boy who was kidnapped from that very mall just yesterday; did you guys hear about that?"

"No, sir," Jack's voice was shaky.

"You boys should read the paper and watch the news more often, instead of those dumb cartoons. Things are getting pretty bad around here. He was taken from the arcade up on the second floor in the mall. The police are still looking for him."

"My God," I gasped. "Do you think the people we saw are the ones that took him?" I asked.

"I don't know, can't say for sure who it was, but I do have my suspicions."

"What do you think we should do?" I asked him.

"The best advice I can give you is to avoid any trouble with these people. Seems to me like they're using your street as one of their stomping grounds."

"But we don't know who they are; the police have no clues either," Jack threw in.

"Just lay low until these people are caught, boys. For shit's sake, they were in your yard, and they know where you live – I don't mean to scare you, but you did want the truth. Stick together and you'll be fine – and call the police if you think you're ever in danger, it's much better to be safe than sorry. I gotta go now," he squinted down at his watch. "Your parents aren't gonna come up here later on and chew my ass for telling you all this stuff, are they?"

"No, sir, we won't say a word to anyone," I

promised.

"Good. You boys take care and remember what I said." And with that, the cashier flicked his cigarette to the ground, stomped it out and went back inside.

Jack and I stood there in total shock, trying desperately to process the information that he'd just dumped on us. Deep down in my soul, I had already known these people were evil, but up until now, hadn't known exactly *what* they were. But now we knew everything our parents had been too scared to tell us for fear of terrifying us even more.

CHAPTER TWENTY

THE BOMBSHELL: 1992

The rest of that summer, Jack and I laid low, mostly focusing on basketball. Memaw had bought me a real basketball goal, and we had it put up behind my trailer. Mr. Shawn helped lay down the cement and I gazed upon that hoop as if it were Jesus Christ himself up on the cross. The backboard was a light grey and had red lightning designs in each of the four corners, which gave it a hip nineties look. Jack loved the goal too, and once Mr. Shawn said the cement was dry, we'd shot hoops on it 'til nine o'clock at night.

We had stopped terrorizing the road – temporarily – which was pretty hard for us; it was like weaning a Meth addict off of his drug of choice. We would get urges to break shit, and the feeling to light things on fire, but when we thought about what the cashier at Taco Bell had told us, we didn't want to go around pissing off the wrong people.

One night, I was watching *The Burbs* – Tom Hanks is

so damned funny in that movie! It's a comedy, but the part in which Tom Hanks' character imagined his next-door neighbors to be a group of homicidal maniacs kinda got to me a little – too close to home for comfort. As it transpired, Hanks' character wound up in a huge barbeque pit, strapped down while a guy in a black robe stood over him with a knife.

There were other people in black robes around the pit, most of them wearing masks, and of course that made me think of the night at Jack's house. When the main guy – whose robe bore a symbol uncannily like the pentagram I'd seen – brought the knife down, Hanks let out a goofy scream and then he woke up; it had all been one of those bad movie dreams.

I'd turned the movie off at that point, as I realized that it most likely had basis in some sick kind of truth.

I told Jack about the movie the next day, and we tried to think of people in our neighborhood who fit the profile of a Devil worshipper.

"Mr. Freeman who lives down at the beginning of the road looks like a creep. He could be one," Jack suggested.

"No, too old." I replied, "Even though I didn't get a look at the guy's face that night at your house, I could still tell he wasn't old."

"How?"

"By his eyes, that's how."

And that's how it went the rest of the summer, us living in fear and with constant paranoia of who might be what. We'd make our assumptions about the people we thought weird, and those we saw outside of their houses; we truly believed at one point or another, that they all could be Devil worshippers, but as the saying goes – when you *assume*, you make an *ass* out of *you* and *me*.

Summer ended, and I began what would be my last year at Nelson Middle School. I didn't know it yet, but my life was soon about to be flipped upside down again, and in more ways than just one.

Two months into the school year, and about a week before my twelfth birthday, Momma dropped one of the biggest bombshells on me; I guess I returned the favor later in life when I joined the Army, but whatever, that's just how life goes sometimes.

I was playing *Street Fighter* one evening, doing my best not to get shocked by Blanka, and Momma walked into my room with a look on her face that I knew couldn't be good. "Jody," she said, "I have to talk to you about something."

"Can it wait until I beat this guy?"

"Please, Jody," Momma insisted. She reached over and took the controller from me, "this is serious."

"Aww – you just let Blanka win!"

"Could we please talk for a second?"

"About what?"

Momma looked away from me as if she didn't want to say what was eating her up, but I saw her work up the courage to force it out.

"Memaw is thinking about moving to Baton Rouge."

"And?"

"We're gonna go with her."

"What?!" I yelled, completely over taken by shock. I jumped to my feet. "No way! I'm not going anywhere. I'm staying right here."

"You can't be like that, Jody, Memaw needs us."

"I don't care! I'm not moving to Baton Rouge!"

"Listen to me, Jody," Momma said quietly and sat herself beside me on the bed, "ever since Pepaw died, Memaw has been wanting to get away from here. There are too many memories here, and she can't get over losing Pepaw. Being in that house every day doesn't make things better for her, so she wants to start a new life somewhere new, closer to Uncle Jerry."

"And she can't do that by herself?" I asked angrily. I could feel myself beginning to tear up; the thought of leaving Jack and Angela was heart-wrenching.

"No, she can't, Jody, and neither can we. We can't make it here by ourselves – we'd be eating off the streets in less than a week because we have no money."

"Can Daddy help more?" I suggested.

"He already does, son, but it's not enough. We can't live off of four hundred dollars a month. It's impossible."

"Is that the only reason why you want to go, Momma, huh? Because we don't have any money?"

"My mother needs me, Jody, and my daddy told me to take care of her. I plan on doing that for him," Momma said, and she was tearing up, too.

"Well, Pepaw told me to take care of ya'll, too. You don't see me ready to pack up and leave town."

"I'm sure he did, Bubba, but you're not getting the big picture. Memaw is miserable here."

"Well I'll be miserable if we move from here. I promise you that!"

"Jody," Momma spoke calmly as she tried to diffuse the tension that sparked between us, "I think it would be better for all of us. With everything going on around here, I really think it would be for the best."

"Maybe for ya'll, but not for me," I said. I threw myself onto the floor and faced myself away from her.

"Look, Bubba. If Memaw decides to go, we're going to be there with her every step of the way. Just be prepared," Momma ended our conversation and left my room.

I didn't want to go – end of story.

Everything I needed was right there in Hammond; there was absolutely no need for me to go anywhere. And even if there was a group of lunatics stalking us, I didn't care – I was tough, and I could handle it!

If only I had known what was going to happen; I would have left right then and there.

The floodgates of my self-destruction had been reopened by Momma's unsettling news.

***

After my birthday party, Momma had dropped me and Jack off at a haunted house in downtown Hammond. We went in, scared out of our minds and when the first guy jumped out and spooked us, we took off running through the place like *Speedy Gonzales*, screaming at the top of our voices like silly little schoolgirls. We neared the exit, and a guy in a monkey suit jumped out in front of us.

"Holy shit!" Jack screamed.

"Kick that motherfucker!" I yelled back, suddenly very angry.

Without hesitation, Jack landed a flawless jump-kick right in the middle of the guy's chest, and Monkey Man flew backwards and landed hard on his ass. Jack and I just trampled over him and proceeded to the exit, not looking back once. We laughed about it when we got out into the parking lot, but I did wonder why I'd gotten so angry; haunted houses were usually a blast for me, but this time it had felt different – something was very wrong.

I took out my frustrations on everyone, beginning with Angela. I ignored her at school, and I never answered her phone calls. I was suspended from school two weeks after the haunted house incident – I got caught hitting a teacher in the head with my notebook while walking down the hallway. I'd only done it because she'd been in my way as I was attempting to get around the horde of annoying kids in the hallway. I just gave the old gal a good pop to move her out of my path, and when Momma got the call from the principal she was furious.

Momma grounded me for a week from Jack, and that was a big mistake on her part. Jack began sneaking out of his house to come see me, and when Mrs. Renee found out, she punished him, keeping him away from me. And after the punishments were all served and Jack and I got back together, we were so angry with our parents that we turned against them. We decided then and there to cause as much pain and destruction as we possibly could and wreak havoc on those who tried to stop us; everything the satanic cashier had told us seemed irrelevant, and so the rebellion began.

And boy, what a ride it was.

We began riding our bikes further and further each day, and soon we were so far away, no whistle Momma could ever blow would have reached our ears. We didn't care if we got in trouble, we just wanted to have as much fun as we could before I left. Momma had told Jack's Mom about us moving, and from what Momma told me, Mrs. Renee didn't want us to go either, although she did understand why we had to. Jack didn't seem to let it bother him for the time being, and each time I brought it up, he'd change the subject and turn his focus on the positive; which was me still being around, for the time being at least.

I stole a can of spray paint out of Pepaw's shed one day and brought it out to the road, where Jack was waiting for me. I had just recently discovered that Pepaw's shed had a shit load of goodies in it, so whenever I needed something that would help us to cause mischief, that was my first port of call. And I'd always end up looking over at Pepaw's old table saw and tear up.

"That's what I'm talking about," Jack was beside himself with excitement.

"I know. I found it behind some plywood. What do you wanna go do with it?"

"We could tag up Kyle and Lucy's mailbox?"

"No. They'll know it was us."

"You're right."

"How about tagging some trees instead?"

"We could, but people drive by too fast, they might not see it."

"Well, how about the street, then?" I asked.

"Sure. Let's go down in front of the field between my house and yours. We'll do some tagging there."

"Sounds like a plan to me."

We walked down Rhine Road about a good sixty yards and stopped in the middle of the street. The field that sat between our houses was used to make hay, but during the fall the grass began to die off and it now looked like a brown graveyard full of straw, with some rebellious strands of green still trying to hang on until winter. We looked around to make sure no one was watching, and Jack grabbed the can from me.

"Whoa, what are you doing?" I blurted out.

Jack didn't respond. He just shook up the can, and I watched as he sprayed the letters *RRB* and under it to the left, his own initials, *JLM.* Jack stood up when he was done and handed me back the can.

"What the hell does that mean?" I asked.

"Rhine Road Boys, remember? That's who we are – forever and always. It doesn't matter if you leave, Jody, because we'll always have this mark here on the road to let everyone know that we were here. This will always be our road, no matter who takes our place. Right now, we run this fucking street, and we always will.

I understood what Jack was saying; he knew I was going to leave, but wanted to have a piece of me stay behind. Even though it was just some stupid initials and a childish gang name, it meant something to us; it meant the world.

Jack and I sat awhile and admired his creation. This was my home and it would always be in my heart, and I decided that I, too wanted to leave my mark. I hunched over and sprayed squiggly lines under the *RRB,* and then my initials to the right of Jack's. Then we stood over our work, looking upon it as if it was a masterpiece from Da Vinci himself.

It was a peaceful moment, when time stood still with the both of us, and the cool, fall wind blew swiftly through our hair. Jack and I had been there for each other through thick and thin, and the thought of me having to leave was ripping me apart inside. As we stood there, silently side-by-side, I did my very best not to think about life without my best friend and blood brother.

CHAPTER TWENTY-ONE

FIRST BREAK-UP: 1993

The school year was flying by faster than any other so far, and next thing I knew I was spending my last New Year's on Rhine Road with my family. We brought it in with fireworks, bottle rockets, black cats, M-60's, Roman Candles and the ones everyone in the South called *Nigger Chasers*; the ones that were long like candles that whistled extremely loud and shot off in one direction.

We popped so much shit that night, you'd have thought there was a goddamned firefight going on in the front yard. I had a blast while popping the fireworks, but once we were done and Jack went home, Momma and me went back inside and she told me for sure that we were leaving as soon as school was over.

Happy fucking New Year.

Momma told me Memaw had already put a down payment on a house and there was no way she was going to back out of it now. I got angry again, but when I thought about living in a house instead of a trailer, I did get a little excited, although not enough to make me happy about the whole thing.

After Christmas break was over, I played basketball with Jack out front, and I finished up the basketball season in March, scoring over twenty points in my last game; the most I had ever scored in my life –I actually made it into the town newspaper! Momma cut the section out, and I believe she still has it to this day.

Once the season was over, the next couple of months were filled with yet more repercussions over my bad behavior at school. I had grown at least another two inches, sprouted more hair on parts of my body, had a full set of pubes (which I was real proud of), had underarm hair that looked like I had Chewbacca in a headlock and finally, I had gotten those goddamned braces off.

I was at the peak of my adolescence, and testosterone was coursing through my body like drunken college kids in the streets of Florida during Spring Break. Momma understood that, and knew I was becoming a man, but it was hard for her as a single parent; especially with an ex-husband who never helped. My behavior got so bad that Momma stopped disciplining me; she was just so numb and worn out from all my shenanigans; I was out of control, there was no denying that at all, but there wasn't anything she or anyone else could do about it. All she did was keep grounding me from Jack and that only fueled the fire.

Jack and I, over the next couple of weeks, began doing whatever the fuck we felt like, playing very much by our own rules. There was not one thing you could say or do to us to break our reckless spirits and it rubbed everyone the wrong way. It didn't matter how many times Jack and I got called down to the office for harassing Cat Ass Boy, or how many Saturday detentions the teachers gave us; none of it mattered.

Simply put, we'd become the type of kids that all parents hope and fear that theirs won't turn out to be. Our friendship was so strong that we had become untouchable when together; we were hoodlums and our egos were so damn huge, we really began to think that our shit didn't stink. Yep, Jack and I were the Rock Stars of Nelson Middle School, and they could say whatever they wanted to say, but mere words barely penetrated our eardrums.

The kids that were jealous of us tried kicking our asses, but we either fought back together and beat the shit out of them, or just ran off at the mouths and kept them at bay. And I had gotten so bad that Angela actually broke up with me. I'd just come out the boy's bathroom because I'd flushed a full roll of toilet paper, trying to overflow the lavatory, when I bumped into Angela.

"Jody," Angela said quietly, "I need to talk to you."

"Well go ahead and talk, I'm right here."

Krystle stood behind her, giving that moral support that girls need during times like these.

"I can't go out with you anymore."

"Why the hell not?" I sounded angry, but in actuality, I was hurt; first break-ups are tough.

"My mom says I can't be going out with a kid like you anymore."

"A kid like me?" I asked, "What am I, a fucking vampire or something?"

"It's not that, it's just…"

"It doesn't matter, Angela. If we're done, then we're done. I only have a couple of months left here anyways, so it wasn't like we were going to last forever. Shit, that doesn't happen in real life."

"Why," Angela said, biting her bottom lip, "do you

have to be such an asshole about this? You think you're so cool, Jody, but you're not. You're looked upon as a bully and a foul-mouthed heathen, and that's why I can't go out with you anymore. My parents won't have it."

"I didn't do shit to your parents, so why are they so pissed at me?"

"Everyone knows what you and Jack do, Jody. This is a small town and everyone knows everybody. Do you remember throwing an egg at a blue car on Rhine Road last week?"

"Yeah, I popped that joker right on the windshield," I said proudly.

"Well, that was my aunt and she told my mom."

"She didn't see me throw it, so how did she know it was me?"

"Because you left your bike on the side of the road. My aunt asked who rode a blue and silver bike, and my mom knew exactly who she was talking about. Maybe you should hide your getaway vehicle better next time, Jody?"

"Whatever," I said, and flung my hands up into the air. "I don't give a shit if she saw me, who cares?"

"I don't want to stand here all day and argue, okay? I just wanted to tell you in person instead. I'm sorry, Jody."

I could feel the rage burning inside me, but I didn't know how to express it. I had been dating Angela since the summer, but the relationship didn't really start getting serious until the new year. I didn't know what had pissed me off most, the fact that she was breaking up with me, or the fact that her parents thought I was a *heathen*.

"Well, I'm not. I'm happy, you know why?" I gave her my best sarcasm.

Angela's face was gloomy and I could tell she was

hurting too, but I didn't care; I really wanted to say something hurtful just so I could feel better.

"Why, Jody?" Angela was emotionless.

"Because now, I can finally ask out all the other girls who've been dying to go out with me. And to be honest, you're quite boring and I'm glad it's over. Maybe the next girl will let me feel her tits." I turned and walked away.

I looked back once after I got halfway down the hallway and saw Krystle hugging Angela. Angela was crying and I pretended I felt better, but it was a lie; I was heartbroken.

Less than a week later, I began dating a hotheaded redhead named Laura who was very attractive, but most importantly, she lived in Independence – a small town that bordered Tickfaw. To me, that meant one thing – her parents knew nothing about me. I didn't think Jack and my reputations had traveled that far, but then again, I could've been wrong. Thank God I was right, because I really hit it off with Laura, and I liked her a lot. I wasn't really over Angela yet, but Momma told me there were too many other fish in the sea, and that I shouldn't tie myself down to one young lady at such a tender age. I never actually told Laura that I was moving away anyway, but she ended up finding out by word of mouth at school.

I wanted to just slip out of town unnoticed and say goodbye to the only person who really mattered: Jack.

CHAPTER TWENTY-TWO

BEGINNING OF THE END: 1993

The Louisiana heat swept quickly across the state, coming around the corner faster than an outbreak of chicken pox in a kindergarten class. And before I knew it, it was hot as hell again and there was a little less than a month left in the school year.

My time here was coming to an end and to make things worse, Laura asked me to the end of the year dance. Yes, *she* asked *me* – who said chivalry isn't dead? I didn't want to go, though, because I knew I couldn't dance. To be honest, I still can't dance – all I do is gyrate wildly behind girls and dry hump their asses, and that's about it.

I knew Jack wouldn't want to go either, because dances were never really our thing. I told Momma I didn't want to go – but she told me I was going whether I liked it or not. The dance was in two weeks, and she suggested that I start watching *MTV* to learn some moves; she said if I didn't, I'd look like a stiff out on the dance floor.

So I took Momma's advice and watched the damn music videos. I watched one by *Ace of Base,* studying them as they danced around, pop-locking and two-stepping all over the place, wearing their trademark loose denim jeans and *ADIDAS* sneakers. I tried swaying from side to side like the girls, but it really wasn't going so hot; I was fucked and I knew it. But, that didn't stop me from trying to learn at least *something.*

I practiced for the next two weeks – everything from the *Running Man* to the *Roger Rabbit* and, believe it or not, I eventually got them both down pretty good. I went out into the living room to show Momma my new moves, and she gave me kudos for having learned them so quickly; I was stoked and ran out of our trailer to go show Jack.

Once I showed Jack my new dance moves, which I proudly preformed out on Rhine Road, he scratched his head and looked at me as if I had lost my mind.

"So that's what that thumping sound was. I heard it every time I came over to your damned house – I thought it was your Mom chasing you through the trailer with the belt again."

"Nope, it was just me practicing my moves," I confessed.

"You're really serious about this dance shit, huh?" Jack asked.

"Yep."

"Why?"

"I don't know," I said as I walked over to my bike. "Maybe it's because it's my last dance here, or maybe because I didn't want to look like a retard around Laura."

"Makes some sense, I suppose. I'm not even going to dance when I go."

"You're going?" I asked.

"Well, yeah. You didn't think I was going to stay home and play with myself while you go to the dance and hang out with all the hot girls, did ya?"

"I was hoping you were going to come," I told him.

"I was thinking though, since you're about to move and this is the only dance we've ever been to at Nelson together, maybe we can ride our bikes to the dance – no kids have ever done that before; we can go out in style. What do you think?"

"Are you crazy? Momma and Mrs. Renee will never let that shit fly. The school is seven miles away, they bitch when they find out we go two streets over."

"It can't hurt to ask," Jack said. "Maybe they'll let us do it. We'll play the *Jody's about to move* card on them, and see how it goes."

"Good thinking – let's ask them."

Renee said there was no way in hell it was going to happen but, to our surprise, Momma said she didn't mind. Renee ended up recanting her statement which led to her agreement, and I was thrilled about it; it's not every day a twelve-year-old kid gets to ride his bike to the end of the year dance; in a small town like Hammond, we'd be seen as total legends. Jack would be on the handle bars and I would arrive sweating and breathing heavily after hauling his rear all the way to the school – it was going to be *epic*.

Not too long after our request for the ride of our lives, people started showing up at the trailer, since it was for sale. Even for being as ugly as it was, our home sold quickly, ending up with a young, newlywed couple out of Hammond. Shortly after that, Momma, Hunter and I began moving all our belongings over to Memaw's house; it didn't take us all that long, since we didn't own all that much stuff. Plus, some of the beds stayed in the trailer for the young couple to keep; Memaw said they needed them more than we did, and that she was going to buy Hunter and I brand new sets once we moved in to our new house.

When we finally got settled in at Memaw's, I decided I wanted to stay in Uncle Jerry's old bedroom, which was the room next to the front door. Momma and Hunter took the guest bedroom, but most nights Hunter ended up sleeping with me anyway. Memaw stayed put in her room most of the time, reading and catalog shopping; and that's how it was in Memaw's house – everyone just doing their own thing.

***

One night, I went to the kitchen to get me something to drink, and when I opened the refrigerator door the light from inside lit up the room like a lantern in a cave, casting small shadows throughout the room. When I looked to my left, Memaw was sitting at the kitchen table. Her eyes were pink and her nose was runny. She tried wiping her eyes, but I knew she was crying.

"What are you doing up, Memaw?" I asked her.

"Nothing, sweetie. I just can't sleep."

"Yeah. Me either," I said.

I pulled a chair up next to her, sat down, cracked open the Coke I had taken from the fridge and gulped it down my dry throat.

"It's just hard with your Pepaw being gone. I haven't had a good night's sleep since he died," Memaw told me, wiping the shiny tears from under her eyes.

"I know. I miss him too," I sympathized.

There was a short moment of silence, – so quiet, I heard the crickets chirping outside.

"You remember when Pepaw brought you home that

electric drum set?" Memaw broke the silence.

"Yeah. I still play it." I cracked a small grin. "I remember he taught me how to hold the sticks underhand like a jazz drummer – but I wanted to hold them overhand, like a rock and roll drummer."

"Pepaw loved jazz." Memaw sported a small smile, too. "Anyways, you need to get back to bed. Don't you have school in the morning?"

"Yeah, but we're not doing anything. It's the end of the year, and all we do is sit around and stare at each other."

"Oh. Well that doesn't sound too educational," Memaw said.

"I know, but what's there to teach?" I asked.

"I'm sure there's something them teachers could be teaching ya'll." Memaw said. She stood up and went over to the refrigerator.

When she opened the door, the cold, crisp light spread throughout the kitchen again, giving everything a golden glow, and Memaw's skin went from a translucent white to yellow mustard, and the stove shone like gold, as if touched by King Midas himself.

I happened to glance over to the backdoor window that Pepaw had installed himself, and I caught sight of a shadowy figure. I jolted back, sending my chair dragging across the floor, and spilling my Coke in the process. Memaw let out a shriek and looked over at me with one hand over her heart and the other on the closed refrigerator door.

"What is it, Jody?" Memaw was clearly startled.

"Nothing – nothing," I said, bending down to pick up my Coke. "I just thought I saw something in the window," I confessed, bringing the half-empty soda can back up to the table.

I took one more glimpse back at the window, and

whatever had been there before was gone. I hurried over to get the paper towels out of the pantry to clean up the mess I'd made, my heart beating a million miles a minute. And by the time I had ripped the plastic wrapping off and unraveled the towels, Memaw was back in her chair at the kitchen table with her eyes fixed on the door.

"What did you see, Jody?" There was no emotion in her voice.

"I don't know. It was probably my eyes just playing tricks on me, it's late and I'm tired," I told her, trying hard to cover up the fact that I was still shaken up.

Truth was, I didn't know what I had seen – it had all happened so fast. There were only two logical possibilities: it was either the figment of my imagination, or one of *them*.

"I saw something on the back porch, three days before Pepaw died," Memaw confessed, and her words chilled me to the core. "It was around five in the afternoon, and I saw a shadowy figure standing on the back porch. I even called out, but it didn't move or reply. At first, I thought it was your uncle, 'cause I was expecting him around five-thirty; but it wasn't him. I felt weird, and a cold chill rushed through my body, and it felt to me as if I was staring Death right in the face."

I tried swallowing as Memaw regaled me with her terrifying experience, but I just couldn't; my throat was bone-dry once again. Eventually, I forced myself to speak.

"You don't think you saw Death standing on the back porch, do you, Memaw?" I asked her, my voice quiet.

"It was either Death, or a demon of sorts, that's the only thing I could compare it to. Who really knows what either looks like?" Memaw shook her head. "But one thing's for sure, whatever that thing was, it wasn't friendly."

"How could you tell?"

"I felt it in the air. Like something just wasn't *right*."

"What happened then?"

"It went away, eventually. I turned around to pick up the phone to call Uncle Jerry, and when I turned back, the shadow thing was gone."

"Why are you telling me this, Memaw?" I asked her. I bent over with the paper towels to clean up the spill.

"I don't know, Jody," Memaw said. She looked down at her feet, stared at them briefly, and then rose up from the table. "Go ahead and go to bed, sweetie; I'll clean the rest of that up for you. You need your rest."

"Thank you." I handed her the paper towels.

Before I walked out of the kitchen, I turned back and gave Memaw a small kiss on the cheek. "Love you, Memaw."

"I love you too."

I said no more and left the kitchen, not even thinking about looking back at that door.

That night, I stayed awake for hours with my covers pulled up to my nose, thinking about what Memaw had told me and what I had seen at the door, it was all so scary to me. What creeped me out the most was that both of us had seen something so similar, and in the same spot, but at different times. I tossed and turned the rest of the night, hoping that whatever I saw was something human, and not spiritual; you can kill a man, but I wasn't sure on how to take on Death or a demon, and for the first time in years, I was scared about something other than the Devil worshippers.

***

It was the day before the dance, and I remember it

being hot as hell. The love bugs were everywhere – flying around and being the nuisances that they were every year. Jack and I just swatted the pesky bugs away from our faces, or caught the ones that just wouldn't go away and squished them.

Jack had heard through the school grapevine that there was a creek by Rhine Road, not too far away, up through the woods toward Albany. It sounded like a good idea to go try to find it since we were tired of jumping in ditches to cool off, so we decided to embark on a new adventure.

"Where is this creek supposed to be at?" I asked him as we made our way toward the bend in Rhine Road. Jack was, as usual, riding comfortably on my handlebars.

"When we get to the bend up here, we have to ditch the bike and head left through the woods," Jack told me. "It's a bit of a hike, so I hope you're up for it."

"I'm always up for *anything*, you know that."

"Good. Now hurry up – it's hot as balls out here."

"Well, *your highness*," I replied, "why don't you get your ass off the handlebars and let *me* ride up there for a change."

"Aw, come on, Jody. We're almost there."

"Whatever," I said, "but you're riding me back when we get done swimming."

"Deal," Jack said.

We got to the bend in Rhine Road where it turned right and swept down toward Angela's house. There, we stopped. To the left was the old, beaten-down driveway that I had seen with Justin that fateful day.

"I wonder what's down that driveway," I pointed towards it.

"I dunno," Jack shrugged his shoulders.

"Didn't you say we go left at the bend?" I asked him.

"Yeah, but I don't remember anything about a driveway. The kid did say we had to go through the woods, though." Jack pointed over at the woods across the street.

"Who the hell told you where this creek was at?"

"I can't remember his name." Jack scratched his head. "It's that kid that used to get off the bus right before Angela."

"You mean Jacob McKenny?" I really hoped that wasn't the guy.

"*Yeah.*" Jack snapped his fingers like he just solved a math problem. "That's the guy."

"You know he doesn't like us," I was blunt.

"Really? Why?"

"Oh gee, I don't know, Jack, maybe because I punched him in the back of the head one day when he was getting off the bus."

"Oh yeah, I remember that," Jack said. He placed his hand under his chin as if deep in thought. "But you know what?"

"What?"

"He told me about this place *before* you rocked his noggin."

"Oh. Well then, that makes everything better, then." I played the smartass.

"I think he was telling the truth; he said his Dad has taken him fishing back there a couple of times. But I can't remember how he said to get there. I know it's kinda in that direction," Jack said, his finger fully extended to the left, "but which way do *you* want to go?"

"Let's see." I uncrossed my arms and stretched out my right. "Eeny, meeny, miney, moe."

"Aw, come on with that shit, Jody," Jack laughed a little, "which way?"

"Let's go *through* the woods," I decided.

"Woods it is, then," Jack concurred, and we set off.

I stashed my bike in a set of bushes about thirty feet into the wood line. The smell of sap and pine needles was overwhelming in the oppressive heat and we were literally *pouring* with sweat. I soon heard the buzzing sound of the countless mosquitoes as they discovered we were in their territory, and they quickly launched their hungry assault upon our bloodstreams. Jack and I began to run, frantically swatting and slapping our skin along the way.

Eventually, the onslaught from the mosquitoes died down and we were able to slow down. "I hate those damned things," Jack grumbled, he had a pissed-off look on his face.

"No shit. Why do our parents even pay the bug man to drive up and down the street spraying that mist stuff into the air? It doesn't kill 'em, so why waste the money?"

"Good point," Jack agreed. "At least they're gone now."

"Yeah, *for now*," I stated the inevitable; the damn things *always* come back.

We pressed further into the woods, unclear at some points if we were even headed in the right direction, but we kept on going anyway. The trees did their best at blocking out the sun, but were not winning the fight, and streams of sunlight managed to escape through the leaves and down into the woods; and it was beautiful, as if we were walking through a painting. White and blue flowers were scattered all over the soft ground, and we'd run into small piles of vivid green moss as we made our way through the woods.

After walking about another five minutes, the woods suddenly became thicker; briar patches and clusters of poison ivy appeared like unwanted guests at a dinner party. I tried my hardest to squeeze through the briars without being cut, and to my surprise, I did manage to come out on the other side unscathed. Jack, on the other hand, wasn't so lucky. I could hear him let loose some choice cusswords every now and again as the vicious thorns pierced almost every part of his body. I just hoped that my blood brother could make it through without getting that dreaded double dose of pain – poison ivy inside a deep cut; I'd had that once before, and it wasn't a fun time. As soon as we made it through the thickest part of the woods, Jack and I stopped in our tracks to re-orient ourselves.

"Shhh – you hear that?" I asked him.

"What?" Jack responded.

"Sounds like running water to me."

We stood a moment, acclimating our ears to the eerie silence. A handful of birds were chirping, but once we blocked those out, we heard the soothing sound of running water.

"We're here!" Jack yelled, and took off like a bullet.

"Wait for me!" I called out, but Jack ran at full pelt, yelling like a crazy person.

We ended up at a small hill that overlooked the creek; its steep decline dipping down into the copper-colored water. The only things on the way down the hill were small branches, roots and thin, wiry weeds that stood around about a foot high. The hill we stood upon on was at least a good twenty feet up from the creek, but the murky water that flowed steadily below looked deep enough for us to jump straight into.

And so, Jack and I pulled off our shirts and shoes and hung them from one of the branches conveniently provided by a nearby tree.

"You ready?" I asked, my heart pounding with

excitement.

"You?" Jack nodded.

"Oh hell, yeah," I said.

I wiped my sweaty palms on my shorts and placed my strong foot behind me, like a track star waiting for the shot to be fired.

"One... two..." Jack counted.

But before he could finish I yelled, "three!"

I pushed off with my right foot, and felt myself falling through the air. I brought my left leg up into my chest and landed a near perfect can-opener into the water. And when I came back up, Jack was resurfacing as well, shaking his head like a dog to clear the water from his hair.

"Man this water feels good!" I gasped.

"Yeah."

"I'm glad the water was deep enough. We would've been fucked if it wasn't," I said, realizing what we'd just done wasn't the smartest thing to do.

"No shit," Jack said with a wide grin.

We swam downstream for a while, until the water became shallower and we were able to stand up. We had hit a small mud bank in the middle of the creek; with all sorts of rocks and sticks accumulated upon it, as well as a few fish skeletons. I stood up on the mud bank and let the coolness of the stream roll over my feet. I leaned my head back and looked into the overlapping branches that hung above me, and they looked like they were trying to wrap themselves around each other. It all provided good cover from the sun, but hot rays of sunshine still pushed their way through.

"This is awesome, huh?" Jack breathed.

"Yeah, it sure is. I'm really glad we found it."

We waded back into the deeper part of the creek and swam down a little further, scouting for another place to jump off. We stopped in a dark part of the water and I went under to test out the depth, resurfacing quickly to give Jack my report.

"I can't touch the bottom right here. This is a good spot," I told him as I trod water.

"And that looks like a good spot to jump from." Jack pointed to a small cliff on our right.

We swam over to the cliff and pulled ourselves up by the tree roots that grew from the side of a monstrous piece of earth. It felt like climbing a mountain instead of a cliff, so I made sure I had proper footing before moving up to the next root or flat edge that lay within reach. It took about five minutes for us to make it up to the top, and when we stood there we were sweating again. I walked over to the edge and looked down.

"Holy shit. This one looks way higher than the other one," I said.

Jack walked over and poked his head over the side and when he was leaned over, I grabbed him by the waist and gave him a good shake.

"Stop, asshole! You'll make me fall!" Jack barked.

"Come on, I won't let you fall. You should know me better than that."

Jack took one more glance down at the creek. "I didn't think it'd be this high."

"Well, it is. And the only way down is to jump. You game?" I asked my friend.

Jack just nodded his head in agreement, but I could tell he was truly nervous about this one.

"You want to do it together, or do you want me to go first?"

"Together," Jack said boldly.

"Okay, then let's do it."

We both walked up to the edge of the cliff and Jack glanced over at me.

"You sure it's deep enough?" Jack asked.

"I'm *sure*," I said with confidence. "Rhine Road Boys for life, right?" I said with a quick grin.

"Rhine Road Boys forever," Jack replied, and I heard some confidence back in his voice.

"You ready?" I asked.

"Always," Jack replied.

We didn't even count to three that time – we just jumped.

I came up from under the water laughing and spraying dark brown water out of my mouth, and when I looked over, I saw that Jack was laughing, too. I was glad that we both were okay, and now we had massive bragging rights; it had been one hell of a drop – it had made my balls rise up into my stomach on the way down – but now, we were safely in the creek again, treading water.

"Wow," Jack said. "What a drop."

"I know, but wasn't it awesome?"

"Yeah, it was pretty awesome," Jack agreed.

As we talked, I felt something rub up against my legs. At first, I thought it was Jack, since he was floating only a few feet away.

"Are you kicking my legs?" I asked him.

"No. Were you rubbing against mine, though?"

"I was not," I protested, "That'd be so gay."

"Well, *something* was rubbing up against me."

"Me too."

Suddenly, and as if from nowhere, a water moccasin – one of Louisiana's most venomous snakes – popped his head out of the water right between me and Jack, and I damned near Hershey-squirted myself.

"Snake!" Jack screamed at the top of his lungs, but I was already halfway back to the shallow part of the creek.

I swam as fast as I could, and when I was able to stand, I ran. I made it back to the mud bank, my heart pounding like a jackhammer. Jack came running up close behind me, red in the face from laughter. "Oh my God! You should have seen the look on your face. It was hilarious!" Jack ragged on me. "You looked like Jesus running on water."

"Shut up," I joked back, my heart still thumping. "Those damned things can kill with just one bite."

"I know," Jack said, taking a seat on the mud bank, "but it really was funny as hell."

"It was pretty funny," I agreed, "I think I shit on myself though."

"That makes it even *funnier*!" Jack bellowed, and he rolled around on the mud bank with laughter.

I laughed along, until I got to the point where I couldn't breathe; it was one of those really good laughs you get once in a while. I really hadn't shit on myself, but I was damned close – like I've said before, I hate snakes.

Once the last bit of laughter was out of our system, we made our way back up the creek from where we'd entered. We scanned the bank for our shirts, and finally we laid eyes on the hill we came down.

"I think we came in through there," Jack said.

"You sure?"

"Yeah, pretty sure. But where the hell are our shirts?"

"Maybe they fell off the branches?"

As we made our way over to the hill to climb back up, I heard the bushes up top shuffle around.

"Quiet," I commanded, and Jack stopped dead in his tracks.

We heard the sound of people walking above us – couldn't tell how many, but I was sure there were at least two. A dog barked, and we heard the sound of muffled voices. We stood there, perfectly still and watched as our shirts went flying over our heads and into the creek.

A female voice then spoke, "looking for these?" The voice didn't sound like an adult at all.

"Who's up there?" I yelled.

We listened at more shuffling and movement above us, until finally, our mystery guests revealed themselves.

Krystle came sliding down into the creek, with Angela following hot on her heels, both wearing long shirts that went almost to their knees. And as they made their way toward us, the dog up top began barking again, like he was warning them to stay away.

"Be quiet, Shadow," Angela demanded, and the dog fell silent.

"Were you guys scared?" Krystle was trying to hold herself back from laughing.

"No," Jack said, although I think we could all hear the relief in his voice. "Takes a lot more than our shirts getting thrown into the creek to scare us."

"Whatever. You guys *were* scared. I don't care what you say," Krystle said, crossing her arms, clearly proud of getting somewhat of an upper hand on the two of us.

"What are you doing here?" Jack asked them.

"I'm staying the night at Angela's," Krystle said, as if that somehow answered his question.

"How did you guys find this place?" I asked.

"Wow, got any more questions?" Krystle snapped.

"My dad has taken me back here a few times," Angela answered.

"Plus, we saw you guys going into the woods, and decided to come look for ya'll."

"Well, you found us, but we're leaving now," I said, trying not to look at Angela.

"Aw – come on, Jody. Please don't leave," Krystle begged me. "We came all this way 'specially to find y'all."

"We gotta get back home," I said sharply. "My mom is probably going ape-shit crazy right now wondering where I'm at. We've been gone a long time, so I'm sorry, we can't stay."

"That's too bad," Krystle was disappointed.

I didn't make eye contact with either of the girls as I began climbing my way back up to the high ground. I turned to look back, to make sure Jack was following me, but he hadn't moved an inch. He was just standing there with his jaw hung open like an old man at a strip joint, watching Krystle and Angela peel off their long shirts to reveal their bathing suits.

This caught my attention as well, and I watched as the girls threw their long shirts on the bank, giggling in the process as they walked side by side, avoiding the deep part of the creek. Both wore two piece suits – Krystle's black-and-white striped, and Angela's, multi-colored.

I snapped my fingers loudly and Jack jolted out of his trance. "Come on, Jack, let's go," I said.

Jack stood stock-still and shook his head.

"*Come on,* Jack," I growled and bit my bottom lip.

I knew I was acting rude, but if any other girl besides Angela had shown up with Krystle, I wouldn't have wanted to leave quite so badly. Our relationship hadn't ended on a good note; I was a total asshole to her when we broke up. But, I was only twelve years old and I didn't know how to deal with my feelings, let alone relationships, so I'd acted like a complete douchebag.

"They're in their bathing suits," Jack whispered up to me.

"I can see that, Sherlock Holmes," I whispered back.

"I'm not going anywhere."

"Don't be a prick, Jack."

"I'm not; didn't you *see* Krystle in her bathing suit?" Jack asked me.

"Yeah."

"She looks *so* hot."

"So?"

"I think I'm gonna go talk to her."

"Damn it, Jack. Momma's going to beat the hell outta me if I don't get back soon. She's probably blue in the face blowing that whistle of hers right now."

"You should have stolen that whistle off her years ago like I told you."

Angry at Jack, I threw my arms down to my sides and took several more steps forward, but I couldn't do it. I really wasn't too concerned about getting in trouble; I was just using it as an excuse to get away from Angela. I still liked the girl, regardless of the fact that I had a girlfriend already.

I let out an aggravated sigh and turned back.

"Come on, Jody," Jack pleaded with me, "I'd stay if you wanted to go talk to a girl."

"I know," I said, feeling like I wasn't being the greatest friend.

"Well, you gonna get back in?"

"Sure."

I got back into the creek and Jack threw his arm around my neck.

"Thanks, Jody."

"You're welcome, but this better be worth it," I joked.

We caught up to the girls and Jack quickly went to work on Krystle. As I watched him flirt with her, I thought back to not so many years ago when he didn't even like talking about girls – and now he was putting expert moves on Krystle. While all this avid flirting was going on, Angela never strayed more than five feet away from Krystle, and I hoped it wasn't because of me.

We'd had a bad break, there was no getting around that, but I didn't like feeling like I had leprosy or something equally unpleasant. So, as Angela kept her distance from me, I returned the favor and ended up being the goober trailing the three of them as we all swam back up the creek. Although I was confined to bringing up the rear, it wasn't all bad, for every time the creek became shallow, we all had to stand up. This meant, of course, that I would get a good look at the girl's backsides – especially Angela's – and several times I think she even caught me checking her out.

As we got closer to the small cliff that Jack and I jumped from earlier, Jack and Krystle started roughhousing in the water. Jack picked Krystle up by the waist and threw her into the deep end of the creek. Angela just stood by and watched the shenanigans, and all I could do was sit back and laugh, because yeah, it was funny. Jack beat on his chest like *King Kong* and leapt on top of Krystle, and she'd let out one of those high-pitched screams that all but made your ears bleed, and then dunk his head under the water – it was a joy to watch, seeing my best friend in the world looking so damn happy.

Once Jack and Krystle got tired from goofing around, we all swam in the deep end under the cliff where we'd seen the snake.

"Did you guys go up any further than this?" Krystle asked.

"Nah. This is the spot where a snake screwed everything up for us," Jack said.

"Oh my God! There was a snake swimming in the creek with you guys?" Angela squealed.

"He wasn't swimming *with* us – he just sorta showed up and ruined the party," Jack replied.

We all laughed – except for Angela; I guess she had a worse phobia than me when it came to snakes.

"Let's go up a little further and see what's down there, Jack," Krystle suggested.

Jack shot me a nervous look. I knew full well what was going on, and I think Jack did too, because he had the *what the fuck do I do now* look written all over his dumb face.

"Um – Jody, you want to come too?" Jack asked, blushing.

"I'd rather stay here," I played it cool.

"Okay," Jack said, "but if I find something cool up there, I'll be sure to come back and get you."

"Sounds good," I said and dove under the water.

When I came back up, I wiped the murky water from my face and saw that Jack was walking ahead of Krystle a little. She was not too far behind, walking backwards and shooing Angela away with her hands like she was a bothersome fly. Angela stomped her feet and walked away with a flustered look on her face. Moments later, Jack and Krystle made it around the next bend of the creek and then they were completely out of sight. Angela stood in the middle of the creek, arms crossed, frustrated and not wanting to be left alone with me.

I took a deep breath, swam over to the shallow end and stood up. I ran my fingers through my hair, spiking it up. I knew that if I actually talked to Angela, I probably wouldn't like what she had to say to me, but I was dying to say something to her. So, I sucked it up and walked over to her.

"Hey," I said quietly.

"Hey," Angela replied, keeping her back to me.

"So, you're still mad at me?" I went straight for the elephant in the creek, so to speak. "Is that why you haven't said a word to me this whole time?"

"What do you think, Jody?"

"I don't know," I raised my voice a tad. "We haven't said a word to each other since we broke up."

"And you think I should've been talking to you?" Angela uncrossed her arms and adopted a defensive posture. "You said a lot of hurtful things to me that day, Jody. Things I haven't forgotten. And then, breaking up with me after we'd been together for so long, you asked Laura to go out with you!"

"*You* broke up with *me*, remember?" I hissed, "I wasn't the one that wanted to break up. I believe it was because your Mommy and Daddy forced you to do it?" I thought I sounded smart, like they do on the soaps, but I guess I was coming off as more of an asshole.

"I didn't want to," Angela said her eyes glossy. "But I did. And ever since we've split, I've had to watch you walk through the halls holding hands with Laura like I never even existed!"

"It's not like that."

"Then tell me what it's like," Angela demanded, "do you not really like her?"

"Of course I like her."

"Well then, tell me how *much* you like Laura. Tell me how long y'all stay on the phone talking to each other on the weekends," Angela ranted. "Tell me *anything*."

"I haven't stopped thinking about you, Angela," I yelled, silencing her rant. "Just because I'm going out with Laura, doesn't mean I don't have feelings for you. I think about you *all the time*."

"And I think about you all the time," Angela said and started to cry. I walked over and placed my hands on top of her slim, bare shoulders.

"I didn't mean any of those things I said to you, I was angry. There's been some things going on in my life for the past couple of years that you wouldn't understand."

"We've *all* been going through things," Angela retorted; she had stopped crying.

"No doubt about that," I agreed wholeheartedly, "look," I brought my hand under her chin and raised her face until she was looking me dead in the eyes, "I'm so sorry that I hurt you, Angela. Can you not be mad at me anymore, please?"

"Sure," Angela said, letting loose a long sigh.

"Good, now come here," I smiled warmly at her.

I pulled Angela into a tight hug and she wrapped her skinny arms tightly around my waist. As our bodies pressed closely against another, I brought my head down to her shoulder and squeezed her tighter. Her hair smelled like raspberry, and I felt her heart beating against mine as I swayed with her in my arms, like we were dancing a slow dance and time seemed to stand still.

I felt Angela's arms loosen around my waist and she leaned back as we continued to rock slowly from side to side. The sun was blazing hot on our bodies, and dragonflies buzzed and skittered over the water, searching for small insects. She brought both her hands up to my face and ran her fingers through my spiked hair.

"Kiss me," she breathed.

"Okay." I licked my lips and hoped that she wouldn't notice that I was nervous, and conjured up the intestinal fortitude to lean in for the kiss. As I did so, a frantic splashing in the distance broke my concentration. I heard Jack scream loudly at the top of his lungs and I opened my eyes and let go of Angela, focusing my attention on Jack and Krystle, who were running towards us with panic etched upon their faces.

"Run, goddamn it! Run!" Jack yelled.

Krystle looked absolutely terrified, and I could see

that she was crying.

"Jody, what's going on?" Angela asked me, her face filled with dread.

"Run, Jody! It's him! It's *him*!" Jack cried out.

I turned to Angela. "Don't ask, just run – *now*!"

Angela didn't say another word; she just took off running full-speed. I stood my ground and waited for Krystle and Jack to get closer. My body was pumping with adrenaline as I watched them draw nearer, and I finally saw whom they were running from.

Of course, I recognized him instantly. It was our old friend with the harelip – the same man we'd hoped was dead or locked up. He was running on the edge of the bank, trying to catch up to Jack, and I saw that he had something clenched tight in his hand.

My body went into autopilot as Krystle ran past me, her sobs louder than the splashes she made. I turned and began running, with Jack closely on my heels, sending fat splashes of cool water against the back of my legs and spine. I heard a shout of anger from our pursuer and I knew he was getting frustrated.

"You gotta run, Krystle!" I yelled as I caught up with her.

"I can't go… any… faster," Krystle panted, tears flowing down her cheeks.

"Take my hand!"

Krystle did so, and once I had a strong grip on her, I pulled her along with me. The poor girl was terrified and out of breath, and I wasn't going to let that maniac get his hands on her; but Krystle really was going to have to push it.

Fifty yards later, my arms were fatigued from pulling Krystle through the water, and I felt like I was dragging a dead body. No matter how hard I tried, we just weren't moving fast enough. Suddenly, I felt Krystle speed up, and when I looked back, Jack was pushing her. His hands were placed in the middle of her back, shoving just enough to give Krystle the extra boost her weary legs needed. And like that, we all ran through the creek, panting and gasping for air and hoping against hope that we would make it out of there safely.

The sound of our pursuer could still be heard from behind us, and when, reluctantly, I glanced back, I saw that the hare-lip guy was now in the creek. He was gaining on us, and I saw clearly that the thing in his hand was a large knife.

As we ran, we bounced back and forth between the bank and the creek. When we knew deep water was approaching, we would run onto the bank. There, I swung my free arm from side to side to knock the low hanging branches and bushes out of my way. Ahead, I saw Angela jump from out of the wood line into the creek, making her way over to where Jack and I had entered what seemed like a lifetime ago. I tugged hard on Krystle's hand as she slowed down again; I didn't know how far back the man was and really didn't want to.

As we came out of a small of patch woods alongside the bank, Angela was already up top with her dog, slumped over him and desperately out of breath. Then I remembered about the deep spot that Jack and I had jumped into, and I bore left.

"Hurry! He's right behind ya'll!" Angela yelled at us from above.

Our bodies sunk to waist level in the murky water and it felt like I had cement shoes on, but nonetheless, we safely made it to the other side and were finally able to stand up and make our way up the bank. Shadow was up top, barking furiously, and Angela was hanging a helpful hand down the side of the hill for us to grab. We threw Krystle into the side of the muddy incline and she crawled her way up the hill, with much encouragement. "Come on, Krystle, you gotta hurry!" Angela cried.

"I'm – trying," Krystle whined.

I heard a splash come from behind me and I turned to see the harelip man standing where we'd emerged from the wood line. He was holding his beloved knife to his side and breathing like a steamroller. Just like the previous time our paths had crossed, the guy wore all black clothes, and I'm positive his shirt said *MEGADETH* on it. He placed one hand on top of his knee and bent over to get air, and I turned back around and saw that Krystle was almost to the top of the bank.

"Go, Jack," I said.

"Are you sure?" Jack asked.

"Yes, now, *go*." I yelled, and I pushed Jack toward the hill.

Jack began crawling up the steep incline, and I faced our enemy. He was walking slowly in our direction and watching Jack make his way upwards. And then he spoke, "No matter where you run, I'll catch you." He brought the knife up from his side. "No matter where you hide, I'll find you." He then pointed his knife directly at me, his eyes crazed. "And when that day comes, boy, I'll kill you. And who knows, today might just be the day."

I was in a trance. I felt as if the man's menacing words had been injected directly into my bloodstream to leave me paralyzed. I simply *couldn't move*, I couldn't think and I felt warm piss running down my legs. I'd never been more terrified in my short life, and I just wanted to cry; I didn't understand why the ugly man wanted to kill me – I was just a kid!

"Let's go, Jody, get your ass up here!" Jack yelled.

I snapped from my daze at the sound of Jack's voice,

and the man walked slowly forward, like a lion cornering its prey.

"Please, Jody, *hurry*!" Angela cried.

I looked one last time into the black-clad man's maniacal eyes and made my dash up the bank, hoping I would get away.

The man sprinted after me.

"Oh my God, Jody, he's coming," Krystle screamed.

"Faster, faster!" Jack yelled.

I dug my fingers and toes deep into the muddy earth as I made my way up, the sound of movement coming up behind me, closer, then closer still...

There came an almighty *splash*.

I dared to twist my head around and saw that our would be killer had fallen into the deep part of the creek. He splashed around furiously, still maintaining his focus on me and, cursing up a storm. I returned to climbing my way up the bank, and when I neared the top, Jack extended a hand down to me. I hauled myself up several more feet and finally grabbed hold of Jack.

"Lift your legs, lift your legs!" Jack yelled into my face.

I turned my head to the side and looked down just in time to see the man bringing the knife down toward my legs. I bent them up quickly, trying to bring my heels into my buttocks, but I just wasn't quick enough. The knife sliced through the side of my foot like butter, and I felt a wet burning sensation there.

"Pull me up!" I screamed.

Jack yanked with all his might and I felt myself moving up the incline as roots and sticks dug hard into my heaving chest. Once I was a few pulls higher, I brought my feet back into the muddy side of the slope and gave myself a big kick off and finally I had made it to the top. Not without injury, though, my heel was peeled open, raw and bleeding profusely.

Shadow was barking like *Cujo*, warning off the hare-lipped lunatic that had chased us, and as I laid flat on the solid ground, trying to catch my breath and ignore the dull throbbing in my slashed foot, I thought that it was the most glorious sound in the world.

"What the hell are you doing?" Krystle sounded angry.

"Get up, Jody. We gotta go – we're not out of here yet," Jack added.

I nodded and tried to stand up, but the man grabbed me by my bloody foot and I fell forward onto my stomach.

"Help me!" I cried out, and my three friends jumped to my aid.

Krystle and Angela grabbed under my arms, and Jack went to work punching at the man's hand, even though the blows he took from Jack didn't seem to faze him at all, and he pulled me back down over the edge. I kicked out violently with my free leg to get the guy to let me go, but it simply wasn't working – hare-lip man had a death grip on me.

But then, like a knight in shining armor, Shadow jumped in and chomped down hard on the man's arm, shaking his head as if he were worrying a rabbit. The scream my assailant let loose was one of shock and extreme pain as the dog's canines sank into the soft flesh of his wrist, and he released my foot.

Finally free, I scrambled to my feet and limped over to Jack. Shadow was still viciously mauling the man's wrist, and blood poured out of the ragged tear in the flesh, pooling thickly onto the ground. Snarling, Shadow pulled back on the guy's wrist like he was playing with a chew toy, and then the man's torso shot up over the edge of the hill. He swung the muddy knife into the side of

Shadow's neck, sending blood squirting out like a punctured water balloon. Shadow let out a loud yelp, released his bite and collapsed to the ground.

"Shadow!" Angela screamed.

"Run!" Jack cried, grabbing Krystle by the hand to drag her along with him.

"You can't worry about him now, just go!" I told Angela.

We all ran into the woods, hoping we would make it out alive. Jack had Krystle by the hand most the way and I was running next to Angela. The open wound in the side of my foot was slowing me down, but I still managed to move at a good speed. We eventually came out onto Rhine Road, breathing like Olympic track runners after the four-hundred-yard relay race. A car was making its way around the bend, and the elderly gentleman inside it gave us a wave. Not one of us returned it. Everything that just happened to us was something you'd expect to see in a horror movie, only it was real, and we had survived.

***

"What the fuck happened back there, Jack?" I asked as all four of us sat beneath a huge pine tree across the street from the woods.

The traffic on Rhine Road was moderate at the moment, so the best place for us to figure things out was in plain sight. I didn't think that harelip guy would be stupid enough to attack us in broad daylight alongside the busy road – he'd made the mistake of trying to get to us at the busy mall and that had failed spectacularly.

"Me and Krystle were around the corner of the creek and we saw two people dragging something through the woods down to the creek. We tried hiding behind one of the oaks alongside the bank, but they heard us – and you know what happened next."

"What were they dragging?" Angela asked, she was still real shaken up, her eyes red from crying.

"It looked like a black body bag to me," Jack told us. "I'm not a hundred percent sure, though."

Krystle agreed with my friend. "It was damned sure big enough to be a body bag."

"You gotta be shitting me," I muttered. "You guys seriously think they were dragging a dead body to the creek?"

"I think so," Jack said, he looked drained.

"Why else would that guy have tried to kill us?" Krystle asked. "People don't try to kill you if you spot them taking out the trash."

"We dealt with this guy a long time ago," Jack confessed. "We were in the Hammond Mall and he attacked us for no reason. And now, he pops up in the middle of the woods. It's fucking weird. I don't understand it."

"I think we stumbled upon something we weren't supposed to see today," Angela whispered, drawing out attention.

Silence fell as we watched Angela wipe tears from her face, and we all knew it was true.

"Did you get a good look at the other person?" I asked Krystle and Jack.

"It was a girl," Jack told us.

"A girl?" I replied. "Well, did you recognize her?"

"Not at all. I didn't even see her face, just the back of her head," Jack answered.

"Are we going to go call the police now?" Angela sounded impatient.

"I don't know," I told her, looking around at everyone's faces. "Maybe we shouldn't say anything."

"What?" Angela spat. "You don't want to call the police after some manic tried to kill us all? Are you crazy?"

"I think it will only make more trouble for us if we do," I explained. "Jesus, guys, if what ya'll are saying is true, then that means we are probably witnesses to a murder. Don't you think if they found out we called the cops, they'd hunt us all down and kill us for sure? We might have made it away this time, but what about the next time? We need to lay low and not tell a soul."

"That guy tried to kill us, Jody," Krystle said. "He murdered Shadow, and got a piece of you in the process."

I looked down at the cruel gash in my foot; it was still bleeding.

"This is bad," Jack said, his eyes serious. "And I'm pretty sure they'll know where we live, so maybe we *should* call the police this time."

"What do you think, Angela?" I asked.

"That man killed Shadow," Angela said and began to cry again. "We need him to be caught and put in jail, so yes, we need to call the police. I don't care if there was a body in that bag or not, we have to do something about this."

Krystle scooted up next to Angela and wrapped her arms around her shoulders.

"Krystle?" I crossed my fingers, hoping that she would be the one to agree with me.

"We should call the cops, Jody."

"Fine," I said. I stood up, wincing at the sharp pain that shot through my foot. "But I don't want to bring you two into this any more than you already are," I said to the girls. "I need both of you to try to forget about what just happened; I know it's hard, but you *have* to do it. Ya'll better get to working up a good story before y'all head back home, too. Your parents are going to know that something's wrong, so you'd better be ready to do the best lying of your lives."

"I know it's hard, Angela." Jack reached over and tapped Angela on the foot. "I've lost a dog too, but it will get better, and the pain will eventually fade – but you need to say that Shadow got hit by a car or something. I know it sounds like an asshole thing for me to say right now, but it's all I got. You got to have a good story."

"I'll do the story telling," Krystle assured, squeezing Angela tighter. "You guys just make sure you call the police so they can catch that sick bastard."

"You got it," I said, giving off a convincing smile. "Now head home and never tell a soul about this."

Krystle and Angela nodded. Even though I was being harsh with them, they knew I was doing my best to protect them. They both stood up and said their goodbyes.

"You might want to go to the hospital and get that looked at," Krystle pointed down to my foot. "And remember to thank God that you're alive."

"I will."

The girls left and Jack and I waited until they were a good ways down the street before we made our way back home. As we walked, every sound, from the buzzing of a bee, to the growl of a passing car made us jump. I thought that we weren't being followed, but I couldn't be positive. We remained silent awhile, but then, I began to cry.

"Just what the hell is going on around here?" I sobbed, hopping on my good foot as the wounded one left a trail of blood on the road. "I could have died, Jack. That son-of-a-bitch would've killed me if the dog hadn't taken him."

"I know, but he *didn't*," Jack placated.

"I'm scared, man."

"I am too."

An awkward silence fell between us as tears trickled down my cheeks. I thought back to our pursuer's face, that mask of pure hatred and rage; it made my stomach turn and my head throb.

"Do you think he was one of the ones that killed Scarlet?" I asked, wiping the tears from my eyes as I fought to get my emotions back under control.

"Yeah, I do," Jack told me. He lifted his head up to face the sky, trying to fight back his own tears. "And that's how come I said they know where we live."

"You think he'll come for us?"

"Him and anyone else he wants to bring along," Jack sounded scared.

"Jesus Christ, what are we going to do?"

"I don't know, but you were right, we're not calling the cops."

"Huh? I thought you wanted to call them," I was shocked – I hadn't expected Jack to go along with my suggestion.

"I only said it 'cause the girls were around, but you're right. We can't say a word. That would only make things worse. If those people think we called the police, it'll only get them more pissed off at us."

"You really think so?"

"It doesn't matter if we call the cops, Jody. Angela was right; we witnessed something today that we shouldn't have. The police can't help us now. Whoever those people are, they're going to come for us. And when they do, I hope there's a telephone close by, or somebody that can help us. That's the only way the police are going to catch them."

"You think this is going to turn out badly?"

"Yeah, I do," Jack told me and stared off into the distance. "It's been a long time coming, and what happened today just put the icing on the cake."

Jack spoke to me as if he was an adult, all full of wisdom and understanding, yet he was merely a kid who stood only half an inch shorter than myself.

"This is too much, Jack. I can't deal with this shit; maybe we *should* call the cops." I felt weak in the knees; all I wanted to do was lie down and sleep.

"Listen to me, Jody," Jack was angry. He placed his hand in the middle of my chest and stopped me dead in my tracks. "Did you not hear anything I just said? The cops can't do shit for us, they wouldn't even know where to start."

"We'll tell them about the body. They can start there," I suggested. The reality of it all was setting in and I knew we were in over our heads.

"If it was a body, do you really think it's still there now?" Jack asked me, his face returning to its normal color.

"No."

"Thank you, so now you see my point."

We stood there in silence, letting the situation run its course through our young minds. The sounds of an early summer could be heard, and the heat coming from the asphalt smelled of melted tar.

"Remember what the guy at Taco Bell told us?" Jack asked.

"Which part?"

"If we stick together, we'll be fine," Jack reminded me.

"I really hope so, Jack. I really, really hope so," I sighed.

***

By the time I made it back to Memaw's house, I had conjured up a story about what had happened to my foot. I was going to tell Momma that I was in the creek, swimming around innocently, and cut my foot on a broken glass bottle buried in the mud.

It was somewhat truthful, so when I told the fib, Momma took it hook, line and sinker, then loaded up into our ever-faithful *Geo Metro* and drove me to the hospital. On the way I remained silent, my thoughts spinning with what may happen next, and wondering if we really should've called the police. I didn't know what to do, but I wish I had said something to Momma instead of keeping it inside – because that turned out to be one of the biggest mistake of my life.

CHAPTER TWENTY-THREE

DANCING THE NIGHT AWAY: 1993

It was the day of the dance, as well as my last day at school, and I woke up with my foot throbbing with pain. I'd received several stitches, and I wasn't sure how much dancing I would be doing. I got up, brushed my teeth, got dressed and went to eat breakfast. After I was done, I made my way out to the road to catch the bus for the last time.

When the doors swung open, Mrs. Kenton was sitting in her seat and looking the happiest she had all year. I said good morning to her as I boarded, but she didn't respond, just looked at me with a loose grin plastered on her face. I made my way to the back of the bus, where Jack, Krystle and Angela sat, and planted myself down with them. This was the first time Krystle had ridden our bus, and since she had stayed the night with Angela, she was soon to experience Mrs. Kenton's rage – and would probably be happy that she didn't have to ride this bus ever again.

"How are you feeling?" Jack asked me.

"Alright I guess. I didn't sleep good last night."

"Me either."

Krystle and Angela sat beside us in the last seat on the left, looking as if they hadn't gotten their forty winks either.

"You think they told Angela's parents?" I whispered into Jack's ear.

"I don't think so," Jack said, speaking in his best church voice. "I think our secret is safe."

"Did they ask if we called the cops yet?"

"They haven't said a word," Jack told me as he glanced over at the girls.

The bus ride was fairly quiet the rest of the way, except for Mrs. Kenton going ape-shit crazy on a kid for playing his *Gameboy* so early in the morning. When we got to school, the bus doors opened up and we all went our separate directions. Angela and Krystle, to my surprise, moseyed over to us.

"Did you call them yesterday?" Angela's face was pale.

"Yeah," I lied, "we told them everything."

"Good," Krystle said, "I hope they catch that lunatic."

"Me too," Jack agreed.

"What did you guys tell your parents, Angela?" I asked.

"Krystle told them that when we were swimming in the creek, Shadow got swept away by the current and drowned," Angela said gloomily.

I knew it was hard for her to talk about losing her dog, but I wanted to make sure our story was concrete.

"They believed us, too," Krystle said.

"Perfect," Jack said. "Now just make sure you don't say a word to anyone else."

"Don't worry, guys," Krystle said. "The secret is safe with us, but you guys need to lay low for a while."

"Don't worry, we won't be playing in the woods or swimming in that creek anytime soon," I reassured.

I heard more bus engines revving as they pulled up to drop more kids off. Laura's bus was here, and I had to go greet her when she alighted. "I gotta run, guys," I made my excuses as I made my way toward my girlfriend's bus, "I'll see ya'll later."

"Later," Krystle and Jack replied.

Angela just stared at me, emotionless. I knew she was upset that I was going to Laura after what had happened between us at the creek. We'd had a moment, a good moment, but a mad man had interrupted it; and I wanted to walk over to Angela, kiss her and ask her to be my girlfriend again, but I knew she was forbidden fruit to me, as I was to her. No matter how much we wanted to be with each other, we both knew it would never happen. She was destined to be the first love that had escaped me, slipped right through my fingers like sand sifting through the ocean. I would have done anything just to hold her one more time, but I guess the universe had other plans for us.

Dutifully, I sauntered over to greet Laura; she immediately grabbed my hand and held it tight as we walked toward one of the entrances to the school.

The day went by quicker than any other; probably because it was my last at the school. The big secret of me moving away really wasn't that much of a secret anymore, so everyone and their brother made an effort to come to say their goodbyes, even though I would see a majority of them at the dance. Nevertheless, they still felt the need to say farewell, even the kids who I thought hated me, which came as a shock.

When the bell rang at the end of the day, we lined up

like cattle and herded ourselves back onto the school buses. My last bus ride home was like a college party, but on wheels; kids were throwing their notebooks out the windows, spitballs flew everywhere, fights broke out and Mrs. Kenton screamed out in vain for everyone to knock it off. Finally, I got off at my stop, walked as fast I was able, no thanks to the cut on my foot, and went inside Memaw's house to get ready for the dance.

"You and Jack still plan on riding to the dance with your foot like that?" Momma asked, concerned. "Me and Renee can give ya'll a ride up there."

"Don't worry about it, Momma. I'm not gonna let a dumb cut stop me from going," I told her as I unwrapped the bandage from around my wound. "Jack's going to let me ride on the handlebars most of the way anyway, so it won't get aggravated that much."

"Ya'll aren't taking separate bikes?" Momma sounded surprised.

"When's the last time you've seen Jack on a bike?"

"I can't remember."

"That's because he's been riding on my handle bars for the last year. He never got a new bike after his last one got all messed up from ramping."

"Well excuse me then, Sir," Momma said playfully. "Then ya'll go ahead and do what ya'll gotta do to get to the dance. Just make sure those stitches don't pop out." Momma walked away and headed toward the kitchen, while I limped over to the bathroom to take a shower.

When I was done scrubbing myself from head to toe, I dried off and began re-wrapping my bandage. When it was on I didn't limp as much, as it provided good support to my foot, as well as a decent amount of pressure to the wound; I was definitely going to have to keep it on if I wanted to try dancing tonight.

As I entered my room, I checked the clock and

realized I still had a few hours before I had to start getting ready, so I played video games and listened to *The Cranberries* – their song "*Zombie*" is still one of my personal favorites – blasting it loud on the stereo.

As I tried to focus on beating my game, I suddenly found that I couldn't concentrate. I felt a weird pressure, like someone was sitting on my chest. I turned off the game and threw myself on my bed, *The Cranberries* still playing in the background. My pillows welcomed me with their cool, soft faces, but even they were unable to comfort me.

In a flash, I began to shiver and shake, my mind racing with the events of the day before, and then the time before that... and so on. Images of the harelip man danced around in my memory like a bibulous vapor floating about in an empty room. My mind was trying hard to put the pieces of terror together to see if any of it made sense; everything from the drums in the woods, the murdered calves, the mall, the day Jack and I saw someone skulking next door from the trampoline – to Scarlet, and lastly, the events from yesterday.

Of course, I didn't know who the harelip guy was, and I'd never seen him but twice in my life; and both times he was trying to kill me. Jack mentioned a woman being there at the creek, helping the guy drag *something* towards the water, but I didn't have a clue to who *she* might be. As I thought about all this, somehow, I slowly drifted off to sleep.

***

I jolted awake, sending my stereo remote falling to the ground, as Momma came busting into my room.

"What are you doing sleeping, boy?" Momma asked me, surprised. "You need to get dressed right now, 'cause the dance starts in a few hours, and I don't think you and Jack will make it there in time if you don't leave now."

"What?" I asked, still groggy.

"I said you need to get going. Here," Momma said, throwing me a purple, collared shirt and a pair of black Marithe Francois Girbaud jeans. "That's what you're wearing to the dance."

"I hate that purple shirt," I whined, rolling onto my stomach.

"Shut up, son. You look good in it, and those jeans ain't cheap! Now get dressed. I'll go give Renee a call to make sure Jack is ready."

Momma then left the room and I got up to get dressed. I looked over to the clock built into my CD player; six o'clock. I had been asleep for almost three hours! I got dressed, spiked my hair with gel, sprayed some cologne and off to the bathroom I went. I had shit breath from my nap, so I brushed my teeth and gargled with some mouthwash. Soon as I was done doing all this, I carefully put on my black Reeboks, trying my best to avoid aggravating the gash in my foot, and then went into the kitchen, where Momma and Memaw awaited.

"Wow! You look so handsome," Memaw gushed.

"Look at Bubba," Momma boasted. "All dressed up and ready to go." She was smiling from ear to ear, in that way parents do when they see that their kids are growing up.

"Pepaw would've loved to see you dressed so nice," Memaw sounded happy.

"I know," I really didn't know how to reply to that without bursting into tears. "Is Jack ready, Momma?"

"Renee is bringing him down in a few minutes. Go get your bike ready."

"Okay," I said, and went out the back door.

As soon as I'd brought the bike around to the front porch, I saw Jack pulling up in our driveway with Renee. I went back in through the front door and waited for my friend to come inside. Jack looked sharp, wearing a buttoned up white shirt with Levi blue jeans and sporting a combover that he didn't look too happy about.

"Did your Mom make you wear that shirt?" I asked him.

"Yep," Jack said. "Did your Mom make you wear yours?"

"Yep."

"I hate button up shirts. Nerds wear buttoned up shirts."

"Well, do you want to wear *this* purple nightmare?" I asked him.

Jack took a good look at my shirt. "I'll keep this one."

"That's what I thought," I said. "At least you're not wearing a shirt that looks like you skinned *Barney* and made a shirt out of him."

"True, but if I had a calculator and some pens in this pocket, I'd look worse than you."

"Well, I have those in my room; you want me to get them?" I joked.

Jack responded by punching me in the arm.

Momma and Renee sat us down and gave us one of their speeches. We were told not to fuck up, not to stray from the route we had told them we were taking, not to go anywhere other than the dance, blah, blah, blah.

"We'll be at the gym at ten o'clock to pick ya'll up," Renee announced.

"What!?" Jack and I exclaimed.

"Ya'll heard us. We'll be at the gym to pick ya'll up. Ya'll ain't riding back during the goddamned nighttime. You could get hit by a car or something," Renee said.

"Aww," I whined.

"Jody," Momma snapped. "We're letting you ride up there, but not back. So, don't press your luck, son, or we won't let you ride up there at all. Just be outside the gym with your bike, so you can load it up in Mr. Shawn's truck, by ten o'clock. Me and Renee will be waiting out there for ya'll."

"Aww – alright," I grumbled.

"Now ya'll boys need to get going," Renee told us.

We got up from off the couch and walked over to our mothers to give them a kiss.

"I love you, Bubba," Momma said as she planted a kiss on my cheek. "Now you be safe and have fun."

"I will," I said, and then Jack and I were gone.

***

Thirty minutes into our bike ride, we were already a little over halfway there. We cruised up and down the backcountry roads to the school, excited, happy, and full of ourselves. We passed houses and trailers of all shapes and sizes, and low-slung trees hung over the roads, and provided us with shade as we made our way to our destination.

Jack had brought a SONY FM radio tape player along, and it played music loud enough for us to listen to as we rode along. I grasped the radio firmly in my hands as I sat atop the handlebars, enjoying the warm wind rush across my face. We listened to the radio stations at first, B-97 FM mostly, and when a song came on we didn't like, Jack had me hit the play button to start the mixed tape inside. As the tape played, *Stone Temple Pilots's* song *Plush* blared while we sat back and enjoyed the bike ride, making rapid progress toward the school.

We only had about three miles left when Jack asked if I would switch with him. I could tell he was beat, so I traded places, in hopes that I would actually be able to do it without my foot hurting too badly. As I started pedaling, the pain shot through my entire body and I thought I wasn't going to be able to carry on, but after a few minutes, my foot went numb and the pain drifted away. As we made the right onto the street that brought us into Tickfaw, I remembered that there was an overpass ahead.

"You, ass!" I yelled to Jack.

"What?"

"You get to ride down the other side of the overpass," I complained.

"So what! I rode your crippled-ass over more than halfway."

I couldn't really argue that, Jack had ferried me on the handlebars for over four miles, so I had no recourse. I sucked it up, pedaled us up the overpass and pulled over to the side once we reached the top.

"Man," I said, wiping the sweat from my brow. "That was a smoker."

"Take a breather, then. We don't have much further to go anyways."

"I'm gonna be all sweaty when we get to the dance. Laura probably won't want to dance with me."

"Everybody's gonna get sweaty eventually," Jack said. "The gym is gonna be filled with damned near every kid in school tonight, and you know it stays hot as hell in there."

"You're right about that," I agreed, stretching my back out until it crackled.

Jack walked over to the guardrail and peered down onto the highway. I put my bike down and joined him to take a peek for myself. Below us, the traffic flowed like running water in both lanes. Down in front of us, on the right-hand side of the highway, was a sign that said *HAMMOND-10 miles*, this was the interstate that took you in and out of Amite and up into Mississippi. I watched as an eighteen-wheeler approached and then disappear under our feet, shaking the ground beneath us. I looked over at Jack, who was busy spitting over the side into oncoming traffic, and that's when I noticed a small red pick-up truck making its way up to the overpass.

"Stop that, Jack," I barked, "a truck's coming."

Jack stepped away from the guardrail and put his back to it. We put on our best innocent faces as we heard the truck approaching.

The red pick-up sped to where we were standing with loud rock music echoing its way out of the cab – I do believe it was *Alice in Chains*. We watched as the truck flew past us and made its way across the overpass, where it came to a sudden, screeching halt. The smell of burning rubber invaded my nostrils, and the unexpected halt in the truck's motion arose my suspicions.

"What the hell?" Jack was nervous.

"Maybe they saw you spitting over the edge."

"They were too far back to see that."

"Well, I don't know," I said, and my heart sped up.

The reverse lights for the truck came on, and it rolled backwards. I swallowed a lump of dry nerves as I watched the vehicle make its way back towards us. Then, without any warning, the brakes were hit again and the truck came to another screeching halt about sixty feet away from us. Jack scooted closer to me as the pick-up sat there with its engine running. Stickers – everything from radio stations to funnies were plastered over the back window, making it impossible to see inside the truck, let along who was driving the thing.

Seconds passed, and then the reverse lights shut off and the truck slowly began to drive away. Jack and I looked on as it continued down the overpass, and didn't move from our spot until the truck had become a small, red dot in the distance.

"I don't know what that was all about, but we need to get to the dance – fast." I said.

"Do you think it was *him*?" Jack was panicked.

When my friend's words sunk in, fear paralyzed my body.

"I don't know, but we don't *need* to find out," I said. I picked my bike up from the ground. "Now, get on and let's go!"

Jack hopped on and we made our way down the overpass, free-rolling along at breakneck speed. When we reached the bottom and our momentum died down, I resumed pedaling.

"Keep a look out for that truck," I said. "If we see it again, we'll ditch the bike and run to someone's house for help. Okay?"

"Got ya."

Jack remained on constant vigil the rest of our trip, and I was a bag of nerves the whole time. Every street we turned down, every cross street we went through, I expected to see the red truck parked to the side of the road with the harelipped man leaning up against it, waiting on us. That thought made me pedal faster and before we knew it, we were at the dance.

***

I rode my bike up to the fence that surrounded the gym. My front tire smacked into it so hard, the fence rattled and sent vibrations all the way down to the end. Jack hopped off the handlebars and placed the radio player up against the fence while I positioned my bike. When I looked down the fence line, I noticed two more bikes leaning up against it; apparently we weren't the only kids to have ridden to the dance. I walked along with Jack, who was still looking around frantically for the red truck, to the gate where two adults stood sentry.

"You boys ready for a good time tonight?" the older looking man asked us with enthusiasm.

"Sure," I replied as we scurried past him and paid him the least amount of attention possible.

I really didn't mean to be rude, but I just wanted to make it inside the gymnasium where it was safe, where we'd be surrounded by friends and teachers; the thought of that made me feel a lot better. I certainly didn't have time to stand there and shoot the shit with a total stranger and pretend to be super excited about the dance when there was a distinct possibly that someone was following us. I just wanted to get out of sight, and out of mind.

Quite a few kids were standing out by the entrance to the gym as Jack and I walked up, some passing around cigarettes while others were handing out breath mints in the hope of getting their first kiss. As we wove through the small group of people, I heard music bouncing around the gymnasium; it was *What is Love?* by *Haddaway.*

We stepped into the gymnasium and checked out the sea of people who were dancing to the thumping music. It was extremely loud and hot, almost to the point where I wanted to turn right back around and leave, and I could see that virtually everyone was sweating profusely, just as Jack had predicted.

To the immediate left was the DJ. He had his equipment and a quartet of enormous speakers parked under the basketball goal. He danced around like a goof with his headphones on, bouncing his arm up and down with the beat of the song. Directly in front of him was the crowd of dancing kids, and I actually caught a glimpse of stinky-ass Kent Lester shaking his tail feather like he could really dance.

I looked over to my right and chairs were set up all the way down the wall for the losers who didn't have dates, or for those who didn't want to dance. And just a few feet in front of that Wall of Shame stood the refreshment table; I couldn't quite see what was on it, but I did spot a glass bowl with an insipid, red liquid in it.

As my eyes circled the gym, I spied the chaperones. Many of them were teachers, but there were a few parents who'd been brave enough to take on the responsibility, and I cringed when I thought just how embarrassing it must be for the poor kids, and thanked God Momma hadn't volunteered.

Jack and I shuffled through the constant onslaught of bumps and slams, until finally we came upon the refreshment table. It was just punch in the glass bowl, and there were a few snacks and dips scattered across the table. Chips, dip and a few baby carrots had managed to find a new home on the floor in the short period of time since the dance had begun, and I couldn't wait to see what the place would look like by the time Momma and Renee came to pick us up.

"You seen Laura yet?" I asked Jack, and it felt like I was yelling.

"No, not yet," Jack shouted, loudly. "Have you seen Krystle?"

"No."

"Let's go check out the bleachers. They might be over there."

"Okay," I replied.

We made our way toward the bleachers, skirting behind the dancers this time instead of attempting to go through them. Then, I saw Laura. She was standing with her arms crossed, as if she was irritated at something. She wore an all-black dress that went to her knees, and I thought she looked beautiful. I knew she'd be mad because I hadn't met her at the door like I'd promised, but I figured she'd just have to get over it.

"One hot-blooded red-head coming your way," Jack forewarned as Laura stomped over.

"Where have you been, Jody?"

"I'm sorry I'm late. Jack and I rode my bike up here, so it took us a while," I explained.

"Justin and Chase rode their bikes up here too, and *they* were able to make it here in time," Laura copped an attitude.

"What?" I blurted out.

Jack stood there with a pissed off look on his face.

"You heard what I said," Laura spat.

"Justin and Chase rode up here, too?"

"Those one-uppers," Jack bitched, swaying from side to side in agitation. "They just had to go and steal our idea."

"What's the big deal?" Laura asked us.

"The *big deal* is that we planned this a long time ago. It was supposed to be our big bang to go out on for the school year," I explained.

"This is bullshit," Jack muttered, biting his bottom lip.

Just then, when the timing couldn't have been any worse, Justin walked up behind Jack and grabbed him by the shoulders. Chase stood a few feet behind him, and Jack turned swiftly to face them.

"What's up, guys?" Justin asked, with a big smile on his face.

"You stole our fucking idea," Jack yelled above the music, within inches of Justin's face.

"Whoa– whoa–" Justin backed away from Jack, his hands held up in front of him. "I didn't know it was against the law for us to ride our bikes up here."

"You know me and Jody planned on doing it first, but you had to try to beat us to the punch," Jack growled.

"I don't have to explain anything to you, Jack," Justin said coldly. He placed his finger in the middle of Jack's chest, "you're just pissed because we beat you up here and now you can't go around bragging about it like you're some hot shot."

"Get your damned finger off me," Jack warned him.

"What are you gonna do if I don't?"

I stepped in before things could get out of hand; I didn't want either of us to get thrown out of the dance for fighting. We had ridden all the way up here and I didn't want to sit outside for the next three hours with mosquitoes feeding off me while we waited for Momma and Renee to pick us up.

"Calm down," I said, pushing them away from each other.

"You need to tell Jack to calm down," Chase decided to play one of the tough guys.

"Who asked you to speak, *faggot*?" I snapped, shooting a quick middle finger in the kid's general direction. "I know I didn't, so keep your damned mouth shut."

"Don't talk to him that way!" Justin barked.

The inevitable, all-out, testosterone laden verbal argument ensued, followed by a number of hard shoves between Justin and Jack. One of the chaperones magically appeared and grabbed Jack and Justin by the wrists.

"Cut it out, gentlemen," he said calmly. "I don't want to throw ya'll out of the dance, but I will if ya'll keep this up."

Jack shook his wrist free from the chaperone's hold, glared one last time at Justin and made his way over to the bleachers. I didn't say anything more to Justin or Chase, and I turned to follow Jack.

"Where are you going?" Laura asked as I walked past her.

"I'll be right back."

My girlfriend threw her hands down to her side in a huff and stomped off to join the crowd on the dance floor. I made my way up to Jack, who sat glumly in the fourth row of bleachers, and sat down beside him.

"Don't let those assholes ruin this for us," I said.

"We should have never told Justin anything. It should have stayed a secret," Jack said, picking strips of paint from the bleachers. "Guess it didn't impress as many people as we thought."

"It doesn't really matter if people thought it was cool, and I don't care if Justin and Chase stole our idea. All that matters is that we did it together, Jack, and that's something I'll remember for the rest of my life."

Jack quit peeling the paint and looked over at me; he finally had a smile on his face. "I'll never forget it, either," He said quietly.

"Good," I said, slapping my hands together, "now let's go back down and do what we came here to do."

"And what did we come here for?"

"We came to dance, dipshit," I told him as I stood up and thrust my pelvis back and forth like some maniacal Elvis. "I didn't practice all these sweet dance moves for nothing."

We made our way onto the dance floor and we soon stumbled upon Krystle, Angela, Laura and a bunch of other girls and their boyfriends, all dancing in a circle. Angela took a quick gander at me, and went right back to dancing. The guys walked up to us and made with the usual handshakes and high-fives. They then reminisced about all things that I had done that year, and it felt to me like I was already gone. Still, I cut loose with them, throwing in some fake laughter at each story, and then I casually inched myself away and into the crowd of dancing girls. I was ready to put my dance moves to the test, despite my aching foot, but just then the music stopped and the DJ shouted into his mic.

"Is everybody having a good time tonight?!" he called out. At this, the gym erupted with yells and shouting, and it was deafening. "Alright, I wanna see everybody on the dance floor for this one!" The DJ shouted, slamming down the microphone.

"Party peopllllle!!" yelled the rapper on the record, and I recognized the song immediately – *"Whoomp! There it is."* The funky bass groove kicked in and the gym erupted with shouts as everyone danced in unison.

"Oh my God, I love this song!" Krystle shouted, and without warning, she grabbed Jack by the hand and pulled him towards her.

I was glad to see that the horrors from yesterday had been erased from Krystle's and Angela's memory, albeit temporarily – it's amazing what being amongst friends can do. They seemed fine now as they danced their hearts out, and Jack looked over at me, shrugged his shoulders and began dancing as well. I laughed, but was abruptly stopped when Laura yanked me over and rubbed her rear end seductively upon my boy parts.

I fought back the boner that tried to push its way out of my pants, somehow finding it within myself to control it. Jack on the other hand, didn't look like he was doing so well. He'd dance close up against Krystle, then he'd yank himself back and dance by himself – it was hysterical. Even though every kid in the gym was country as you could get, they sure the hell could dance. You can't blame kids for dancing dirty; it's one of those things that's inevitable.

When the song ended, everyone was winded and the gym was starting to smell like musk, perfume and fruit punch all mixed together. Laura had evidently forgotten all about being rude to me earlier, she was now holding my hand tightly as we made our way with the group over to the bleachers. There, we stood in a big circle, joking around and gossiping as the next song played.

I, on the other hand, wanted to go dance. I liked the feeling I'd gotten earlier while dancing with Laura, and I wanted to get it again – errant boner notwithstanding. Several of the other kids in the group told me how much they were going to miss me, and that I must swear to stay in touch with them after I moved. I just nodded my head and made promises to them that I knew I wouldn't keep; though, many years later, I found most of them again on social networking websites.

For over an hour, we danced away to the *Electric Slide* and *The Freeze*, busting out many other dance moves while the DJ switched songs. I'd introduce the Running Man and Roger Rabbit to everyone when I got tired of bouncing and just swaying from side to side. *Naughty by Nature's* song "*Hip Hop Hooray*" came blasting from the speakers, and the entire gym waved their arms from left to right as one; it was fun, but once the song was over, the mood in the gymnasium went in a new direction.

The atmosphere changed drastically as the dance music stopped and the first slow song of the night played. It was *Boyz II Men's* number-one hit single "*End of the Road*," and I skimmed through the crowd of non-dancers, who were all awkwardly attached to the wall. I came to the conclusion right then and there that I might have learned some sweet dance moves in a short period of time, but I had totally forgotten to practice slow dancing. My stomach boiled with freshly-cooked nerves, and soon I was feeling as if liquid magma had filled the floor. And then Laura wrapped her arms around my neck.

"Will you have this dance with me?" Laura asked, jokingly.

"Sure," I said. I looked around for Jack, hoping he would come bail me out.

I placed my arms on Laura's hips, mimicking what the others in the gym were doing and began rocking slowly from side to side, and in an instant, it reminded me of the day before when I'd held Angela in the creek.

"I'm sorry for the way I acted earlier," Laura apologized.

"Don't worry about it. I shouldn't have shown up late."

"You don't have to apologize. I was just upset that everyone else's dates were here before mine. I just wanted to spend as much time with you as I can before you move."

"Well, here I am," I said and gave her love handles a gentle squeeze. "You got me in a choke hold, so I'm not going anywhere any time soon."

"I'm sorry," Laura laughed, releasing the tight grip her arms had around my neck. "Let's try it this way."

She freed her arms from my neck, only to bring them down around my waist, pulling me closer into her. I readjusted myself and placed my arms around her neck, turning it into more of a hug. The ballad played on and we danced together, spinning slowly, enjoying our youth while getting lost in the moment. Laura rested her head upon my chest and when she did, I felt her warm breath rolling sweetly across my collarbone.

I scanned the gym as we slowly spun, and I locked eyes with Angela, who was dancing with Chase only a few feet away from me. She looked heartbroken. At that very moment, all the feelings I was experiencing with Laura dissipated, and I knew I wanted to be with Angela, and I wanted more than anything to give her that kiss she'd asked for the day before.

When our eye contact was broken, I saw Jack and Krystle kissing. My heart lit up like a Christmas tree, I was so happy for my friend. I was witnessing another chapter in his life open up before me, and I realized I wasn't going to be around to be a part of it. I looked away so no one would think of me as a creep for watching them and I laid eyes on Justin, who was dancing with a pretty, auburn-headed girl named Paige. He just nodded his head and gave me a quick thumbs up from behind her back; evidently, he wasn't pissed at me anymore, either. It's funny how kids fight; one minute they're at each other's throats and then the next, they're best friends again. The innocence of childhood is an amazing thing indeed.

"Aren't you going to kiss me...?" Laura asked softly, looking up from my chest.

"Umm... I..." I stuttered, trying to come up with something on the fly, but instead of lying, I took a deep breath and told her the truth; something I hadn't done in a long time, "I don't think it would be a good idea."

"Why?"

"Listen, I really like you, Laura, but –I like you more as a friend," I was very straightforward.

"What?" Laura was understandably confused.

"Please don't get mad at me."

"You like me more as friend than as a *girlfriend*,"

Laura snapped, releasing her hold from my waist. "Is that what you're telling me?"

I shrugged my shoulders in agreement. I knew shit was about to hit the fan.

"Why are you telling me this now, Jody?"

"I don't know," I said, suddenly feeling a bit ashamed. I backed away from her.

If I had known that telling Laura the truth about the way I felt would've turned out like this, I should've just stuck to my original plan of lying to her.

"You know what, I don't want to know. Just stay away from me, okay? We're finished!" Laura yelled and stormed off across the dance floor, knocking couples loose from one another's arms as she pushed by.

The song continued to play, and for a short time, I felt like I was standing in front of the crowd naked, embarrassed and very red in the face. Laura's shouts had raised some attention, and many of the kids were staring at me, most specifically Angela who had a troubled look on her face; I usually like being the center of attention, but not in *that* way.

Finally, the song ended, and I came back to reality as the DJ struck up the next tune; *"Rhythm is a Dancer."* The atmosphere returned to normal and the kids migrated back to their friends and made ready to shake it after the intro of the song was over. I saw Laura exiting the gym doors – most likely heading to the pay phones to call her mother for a ride, and Justin hurried over to me.

"What the hell happened with Laura, Jody?"

"Let's just say we're not boyfriend and girlfriend anymore," I told him, agitated. I and turned to walk away, but froze in my tracks…

He had found us.

Standing by the stairs that lead up the bleachers, less

than thirty feet away from where I stood, was the man who'd tried taking my life the day before. He wore black clothes, and that trench coat that he had worn at the mall. His eyes were filled with malice, and they were fixed directly on me.

"He's here," I mumbled, petrified.

"What did you say?" Justin was puzzled.

"He found us."

"What are you talking about?" Justin asked, "who?"

I took hold of Justin's arm and steered him around until he faced the guy. At once, Justin's skin turned cold – I felt the tiny goose bumps rise up on his forearm.

My head spun, and I felt as if something had sucked the breath from my lungs and I struggled to speak to Justin. "What... do we... do?" I spoke quietly.

"Let's go, umm – tell one of the chaperones."

Justin had answered my question, but I didn't comprehend what he'd said. I watched the man with the harelip as he made his way slowly along the wall of the gym, not once breaking eye contact until he disappeared amongst the crowd of losers that hung out by the bathrooms.

"We need to go tell one of the parents – *now*," I said, and as I turned around, Jack's body collided against mine.

"They've come for us," Jack was frightened, his face colorless, "I told you they would."

"*They?*" I asked, panicking.

"The woman standing over by the refreshment table, with the man with the harelip," Jack pointed behind himself, towards the table. "She keeps looking at us."

"The woman with him at the creek?" I asked.

Jack's face dropped and I thought he was about to throw up. "Turn around," he groaned.

When I did, I saw the man with the woman that Jack

had seen, and she was casually making conversation with one of the chaperones as they made their way back toward us. She had on dark blue jeans and a long-sleeved black shirt, and certainly didn't resemble the hare-lipped lunatic that was with her in any way; she was well-groomed, her hair was nicely combed, and she was actually very pretty. The man shot looks of hatred at us, between fake laughs with the chaperone and his accomplice, and I guessed they had gotten into the dance by posing as parents. The man's eyes penetrated my soul as he stared with fierce intent at me. I could feel his boiling rage, and I knew that he was here to finish the job – to silence Jack and I once and for all.

"They're not gonna leave here tonight without getting their hands on us. You know that, right?" I told Jack, the fear making my voice tremble.

"We need to leave," Justin stressed.

"And go where?" I asked him. "We need to just wait here for Momma. When she gets here, she can take us to the police."

The woman was now done talking with the chaperone and the pair split up, heading in opposite directions. They made their way around the gym, just like all the other chaperones, pausing to make small conversation every now and again. Kids danced into us as we stood rooted to the floor and they yelled at us to dance, or get the hell out of the way. I didn't know where the girls had gone, but I was glad, I didn't want these people to know that Angela and Krystle were here too. We watched as they made their rounds, circling us like sharks, waiting for the opportune moment to strike. They were blending in very well – too well.

"They're going to do something soon if we don't do something first," I said.

"Then what do we do?" Justin asked me.

"You stay put, Justin," Jack instructed, "they're not here for you."

"How do you know?" Justin asked, I could tell in his voice that he desperately wanted that to be true.

"I just do," Jack told him.

Then, I had an idea. "You're probably right, Jack," I agreed. "I'll bet they're only here for us – and possibly the girls – but I have an idea."

Jack raised a quizzical eyebrow.

"Justin?"

"Yeah."

"I need you to go find Chase, and both of you need to go over by the DJ's table."

"Okay, then what?" Justin looked scared.

"When the shit hits the fan, you just make sure you stall them while Jack and I make it outta here."

"We're gonna run for it?" Jack was shocked.

"It's the only way. If we stay here, we put everyone in here in danger. What if that lunatic starts slicing up kids on the dance floor while trying to get to us? You think you could live with that?" I asked my friend.

Jack didn't answer.

"Don't worry, we'll stall 'em for you," Justin reassured. He was as nervous as hell, but I knew he would come though.

"What time is it, Jack?" I asked.

"Nine o'clock," Jack looked up from his *Casio* watch.

"Think we can make back home before our moms leave to come pick us up?"

"I don't know, Jody," Jack said nervously, walking in place while talking. "That's pushing it, but maybe."

"Alright then," I said. I felt sick, but I had to stay strong, that's what Pepaw would have done. "Justin, go get Chase. Jack, follow me."

We said no more. Justin went to look for Chase, while Jack and I made our way into the mob of kids on the dance floor. I searched for Krystle and Angela as fast as I could. I knew our unwelcome guests were closing in on us. We twisted and turned our way through the sweaty kids, moving as fast as we could, until I finally happened upon Angela. She was dancing, but when I made a bee line for her and grabbed her firmly by her shoulders, she immediately knew something was wrong.

"I need you to listen to me," I told her, noticing that other kids had stopped dancing and were listening. "Are your parents picking you up at ten?" I asked her.

"Yeah, they'll be here."

"Are you going straight home afterwards?"

"Yes, but what's going on, Jody?"

"Just listen," I replied, shaking her a little. "If my Mom shows up here at ten, let her know that Jack and I left early because some kids wanted to beat us up. She'll be pissed, but just tell her that, okay?"

Angela said nothing, she just listened to me, her eyes wide with fear.

"We gotta go, just promise me you'll tell her."

"I promise."

As I walked away, I saw the man coming through the crowd toward us. Jack stepped in front of me and made his way through the kids and on towards the refreshment table, so I followed him. Once we were at the table, I stopped to make myself a drink.

"What the fuck are you doing, Jody?" Jack asked.

"Are Justin and Chase by the DJ table?" I asked, my heart pounding.

Jack stood on his tiptoes, leaned left and came back down.

"Yeah, they're there."

I grabbed the ladle that was in the fruit punch, filled

it to the brim and poured it into one of the foam cups that was on the table. I held it tight and backed up against the wall behind the table. All we could do now was to wait for the harelip guy and his lady accomplice to attack; we both knew it, but said nothing.

Jack walked over to me and I could see that he was in total disarray. I looked left, there was no one coming, and only a handful of kids stood in our way of the exit. But when I looked right, the woman and harelip man were making their way toward us; keeping tight to the back wall. As they drew closer, the woman glanced around the gym in each and every direction, doing her best not to appear suspicious, and I knew in my guts that the two of them were getting impatient, sloppy and ready to strike.

They came closer and closer, and before I knew it, the two of them were less than six feet away. The man shot a sinister look my way, and as I watched, he reached into his trench coat...

"Eat shit, motherfucker!" I yelled out as loud as I could. This garnered curious attention from the kids and adults in the gym, all of whom looked on, startled as I threw my cup of punch in harelip's face, and he stopped dead in his tracks.

With the man and his sinister companion distracted, Jack and I seized the opportunity and made a mad dash for the exit. I heard the woman yell something as we ran, but I couldn't make it out, and I was way too scared out of my mind to care much. The chaperones and kids we ran past looked just as scared as we were, although I doubted that it had registered with them that we were in trouble, and by the time they figured it out, we would be long gone.

"Do it now, Justin, do it now!" I screamed as I flew through the exit with Jack close by.

I heard a loud *thud*, followed by screams, hollering and a whole bunch of ruckus bellowing from the gym; Justin and Chase had come through on delaying the woman and harelip man from pursuing us. Jack and I sprinted out through the gate, and made our way towards my bike. I grabbed it by the handlebars, pulled it up from the fence in one swift motion and threw myself on it.

"Get on!" I barked at Jack, and in his panic to do so, he left behind the FM radio.

Before I pushed us off into the night, I took a fleeting look back at the gym. The staff had turned the lights on, and I saw that the adults had the man and woman held up at the door, and were trying to calm them down. My plan had worked perfectly, up until Justin and Chase appeared, trotting out of the gate and heading for their bikes.

"What the fuck are ya'll doing?" Jack roared at them. "Get back inside where it's safe!"

"It's not safe... anymore, Jack," Justin panted, all out of breath. "We stopped them, but... we need to go now... before they get away from the gym!"

"Well get moving!" I hollered.

The four of us set off together, fleeing into the dark Louisiana night.

CHAPTER TWENTY-FOUR

LIVING ON A PRAYER: 1993

We rode as fast as the night would carry us, twisting and turning through the back-country roads. Traffic was minimal, thank God, but when a vehicle did show up, their blinding headlights meant that we had to pull over to the side of the road so they could pass; I didn't want to get hit by a car – I already had enough to worry about.

"We need to take the next road on the left," Justin instructed. "We can't go back home the same way we came."

"Why?" I asked.

"They knew we were at the dance, so I'd guess they had to have followed us there, or at least knew our route."

"I don't know any other way home," Jack said glumly. He played lookout on my handlebars, constantly checking behind us for a tail.

"Don't worry," Justin reassured, "I do."

We pressed on and faithfully followed Justin's orders,

never second-guessing him once. I had no clue where we were, but Justin seemed pretty confident. Poor Chase, the kid who'd just got sucked into all this, he'd hardly spoken a word since we took to the streets on our bikes. He was a thin kid, with dark brown hair and a wide nose; I didn't know him, and hadn't spoken to him until that night.

"I can't keep up," Chase panted. He slowed down on his bike, breathing in deep gasps of air like a beached perch, "I can't do this!"

"You need to suck it up, Chase," I retorted. I glowered over my left shoulder at the kid. "We can't slow down now. If we do, we're *dead*. These people are *crazy*."

"Ya'll should've stayed in the gym," Jack was reproving, "we didn't need to get anyone else involved."

"Too late for that now, Jack," Justin threw in. "*We're* a target now, just like ya'll. When I threw myself under that ugly guy's feet, a knife fell out of his coat when he tripped. He told me he was gonna kill me, and I think he would have if Chase hadn't dragged me away – and then one of the chaperones came over and we just ran."

"I'm glad ya'll got away," I said, pedaling the bike faster, sweat running down my temple. "But you really shouldn't have come with us."

Justin didn't respond; but I could tell that he knew I was right. Even though the harelip man knew who Justin was – hell, he had kicked Justin in the stomach in the mall's elevator – he hadn't come to the dance tonight to kill him. He'd come for me and Jack, but so far, his plan had been a failure.

The roads became harder to see, and several times we passed the ones we needed to turn onto, gliding right past them as we rode on through the darkness. Every time Jack would yell *car*, we'd ditch the bikes on the side of the road, jump the ditch and lay flat on our stomachs. I felt no pain in my foot, since it had gone completely numb, but my legs were cramping up and I knew I wouldn't be able to pedal for much longer. So, I asked Jack to switch, and I became the lookout.

Before I knew it, we were turning onto Rhine Road from its farthest end. This meant that Angela's house would be one of the first we'd see on the right, and I wanted to stop there to make sure she'd told Momma what I'd told her to say. I knew my ass would be grass when I got home. It would be the last good ass-whooping I'd get on Rhine Road, but I was fine with that.

"What time is it, Jack?" I asked.

"10:17."

"Pull in to Angela's driveway. I need to know what she told Momma so we can get our stories straight."

Jack snorted, loud enough for me to hear it. I knew he just wanted to get home – I did too, but I *had* to know what Angela had said.

We rolled into the driveway and I leapt from the handlebars, running towards the window on the bottom floor, as it was the only one with a light on, other than the flickering TV glare that came from an upstairs window. I guessed that the window on the bottom floor was Angela's room.

When I got closer to the porch, I tiptoed like some pervert prowler trying to get a peek at some girl's boobs, and stepped quietly onto the porch. I pressed my back up against the house and shimmied my way down to the lit room. Once there, I took a quick look over at the road and saw that Jack, Justin and Chase were close by. I took a deep breath and leaned over just enough to get a look into the window.

Angela and Krystle were sitting on the floor going

through a bunch of music CD's. I lifted my hand up and tapped gently on the window. The girls looked up, scared, but once they saw it was just me, they relaxed some. Krystle closed Angela's door, while Angela made her way over to the window. She fought with the lock that held the window shut tight, but then there came a resounding *click*, and the window slid upwards. Angela poked her head out.

"Thank God you're okay. I was really worried about ya'll," Angela whispered loudly, no doubt relieved to see that we were still alive.

"Shhh – I don't want your parents to know we're out here," I hissed.

"Sorry," Angela made with an apologetic face.

"So, what happened after we left?"

"It was chaos," Angela told me. She glanced back at Krystle, who had her ear pressed up to the bedroom door, listening out for Angela's parents. "The whole place went totally nuts. The chaperones moved the kids onto the bleachers after the lights came on, and some of the parents had that lunatic held up by the door, but they couldn't hold him for long. He left with some woman shortly after that."

"Did Momma show up?" I asked, nervously.

"Yeah, she did."

"Was she pissed?"

"Oh yeah."

"What did you tell her?"

"I told her ya'll left early because some of the eighth graders tried beating ya'll up."

"Was everyone still in the bleachers when she got there, or had things calmed down by then?" I asked, beginning to feel like a *NYPD Blue* detective.

"Everything was back to normal, except that the gym lights stayed on for the rest of the time."

"Good," I breathed a sigh of relief.

I offered a silent prayer that one of the chaperones hadn't gotten to Momma to tell her what had actually happened in the gym; I wanted to be the one who came clean to her about what was going on. I knew that once the truth came out, Momma would want to comfort me instead of whoop me. I felt Angela slide her hand over mine, and my heart sped up with delight as her smooth skin caressed my fingers.

"Why didn't you tell me they were there?"

"I don't know," I tried to avoid her eyes. "I guess I didn't want you and Krystle to freak out. Both of you have enough to deal with."

"And so do you." Angela squeezed my hand tighter. "I don't want you to get hurt, Jody."

"I won't."

"Promise me."

"I don't do promises," I said, and I thought that sounded really grown up.

"You made *me* promise, so now you owe me one – please, promise me," Angela demanded.

"Okay," I squirmed, "I promise... I won't get hurt."

I took a moment to look Angela in the eyes, and I got hopelessly caught in the moment – the earth quit moving, the night fell silent, and I knew that if I didn't act then, I may never have the chance again.

I ran my fingers up Angela's neck, slipping them around to the back of her head and buried them in her sweet smelling hair. I placed my other hand gently upon her cheek, took a deep breath and brought my lips to hers. I could feel that I'd taken Angela by surprise, but that's just how I wanted it to be; I wanted to leave her breathless. My lips were a little dry, but Angela's were moist and warm, and as we kissed, she placed her hand on the back of my neck. We held the kiss for a few more seconds before parting.

"You don't know how long I've been waiting to do that," I told her.

"I'm sure you've been waiting just as long as me," Angela whispered.

"I gotta go now."

"Okay," she said glumly. "Will I see you again before you move?"

"I'll make sure I find my way over here," I assured her. "Maybe I'll be able to get me another one of these kisses."

Angela's face lit up like Times Square, and she planted a fond kiss on my cheek. With great reluctance, I let go of her, turned and jumped off the porch. I spun around for a brief second and gave her a wave goodbye, which she returned with a sad smile.

"Let's go, lover boy," Justin whispered.

I ran towards Jack, who was sitting on the bike with a thin, knowing smile on his face, maybe he felt the same way I'd felt when I saw him kissing Krystle. I said nothing about it, clambered back onto the handlebars, and watched Angela's window as we made our way up the street. I could see her jumping up and down, holding hands with Krystle like they were a couple of giddy pre-schoolers; that kiss had made her night.

We made it down the last bit of straightaway before we hit the bend in the road before home. The night was calm, all except for the rolling of our tires on the pavement. I could hear the crickets chirping merrily in the woods, the mosquitoes buzzing around our heads with malicious intent, and the frogs croaking their nighttime lullabies. The wind felt cooler as it rushed upon my face and filled my ears with a seashell sound.

Then, less than a hundred yards before the bend, I heard something that didn't quite fit. I twisted my head to one side and squinted around Jack. It was the unmistakable noise of an engine, and it was coming from a menacing, black shape that was rolling up the road behind us. I knew then that we were in trouble, and before I could give out a warning, the high beams switched on and the engine revved like some great, mechanical beast.

"Get off the road!" I yelled, startling Jack and the others.

The wheels of the vehicle squealed as the driver put the pedal to the metal, and Jack turned the bike sharply to the left, sending us rolling down a small hill into the bushes at the side of the road – and his instinct saved our lives.

Justin and Chase rolled down the hill, stopping a couple of feet in front of us. They ditched their bikes and hid in the bushes. The vehicle ground to a sudden halt, and the reverse lights popped on. Jack and I low crawled on our bellies like soldiers, and came to a rest in a thick bush only several feet away from Justin and Chase. I was scared out of my mind, we'd thought we were in the clear, thought we were home free, but had been so dreadfully wrong. I watched the vehicle as it came to a stop straight in front of us. The driver cut the engine and lights off, a door opened and I heard feet touch the asphalt.

"Yoo-hoo," a voice taunted, "where are my little tough guys at?"

I couldn't think, my mind was spinning way too much for that. I heard whistling in front of me, an eerily out of place, upbeat tune, and then I heard a second pair of feet make contact with the asphalt.

"Stop making this so hard on yourselves," a deep voice boomed into the night. "If you don't come out, we'll just have to come in and get you. And you don't want that to happen, boys."

I've heard that voice before - but where?

Suddenly, the moon made its presence known from behind the darkened clouds, providing us with much-needed illumination, and when I looked over at Jack, his face was one of absolute terror. I glanced over at Justin, who had a hand over Chase's mouth to keep him quiet. Poor Chase looked like he was about to wail. Justin looked back at me as if he were waiting on my direction, but I still couldn't reason, let alone take command. In frustration, I pulled at my hair, as if that would kickstart my brain.

"Come out, goddamn it!" a voice yelled out impatiently.

Banging hard against the vehicle came next, and I knew they were trying to scare us out of hiding. And now that it wasn't completely dark out anymore, I saw that the truck was the red one we'd seen earlier on the overpass.

"I'm going to give ya'll to the count of three, sort of how your Grandfather did to me – remember that, boy?" the deep voice asked.

In that instant, I knew who the owner of that sinister, baritone voice was –the fuckin' mailman – and he was one of *them!*

"Go in there and get the little bastards," came the woman's voice from inside the vehicle. "Quit playing around with them, for fucks sake!"

I watched as the men's feet moved closer to the side of the road. They were about to come in after us, and suddenly I felt the urge to cry. I put my face into the palms of my hands and began weeping. I felt Jack scoot over to me and place his arm over my back.

"We need to run, Jody," Jack whispered. "If we don't, they're gonna catch us for sure."

I snorted back the tears and I felt thick, warm snot run down my throat.

"Where do we go?" I asked, wiping the snot from my nose, "there's nowhere to run to, Jack."

"There's that driveway at the bend in the road. The one we saw yesterday, remember?"

"Yeah."

"Maybe somebody lives down there. They can help us."

"One," the mailman counted, his voice in the night cold and menacing.

"I'm fucking scared, Jack," I admitted, my whole body trembling.

"I'm scared too, Jody, but we gotta run if we want to live," Jack said with tears running down his face. "I think they're really going to kill us."

"Two," the mailman raised his voice.

I peered out through the bushes, and saw a set of grubby sneakers on their way down the hill towards us. I looked to Jack and he nodded his head; he was good to go. I grabbed a stick from under the bush and threw it at Justin. It hit the kid in the leg and he turned to me. Silently, I moved my lips, forming the word *run*, which he acknowledged. As the mailman made his way down the hill, I reached over and clasped Jack's hand.

"THREE!" the mailman yelled.

"GO!" I screamed, as I shot up from the earth with lightning speed.

Jack and I darted by Justin and Chase, who were only just picking themselves up off the ground. I heard the popping and rustling of branches, leaves and twigs as one of the men entered after us – I didn't know which one and the truth is, I really didn't care. I just ran and ran until I came out by the pine tree that Jack, the girls and I had conspired under just the day before. I continued to run until I crossed the street, and then kicked it into second gear as I made it onto the overgrown driveway.

"Move your ass, Jody!" Jack yelled out. He was right behind me, but I could feel the presence of someone else, too.

The truck's engine started up, and when the lights came on, it casted four shadows upon the ground -- the one in front was mine, to my right was Jack's, on my left was either Justin or Chase, and last but not least, furthest back was the giant shadow of a man.

"Help," I cried out, "HELP US!"

"Somebody help us!" Justin echoed, and I knew it was him behind me, and not Chase.

I pumped my arms hard and hustled down the driveway that was illuminated by the truck's high beams. I heard its engine roar and dared a glance over my shoulder for the first time. Chase was nowhere to be seen, and Mitch – I'd remembered the mailman's name – was flagging down the truck. He climbed in and it rolled steadily up the driveway.

There was an overgrown field surrounded by a rusted barbed wire fence to my left, its towering grass a light blue hue under the moonlight, and the dark woods were to my right. And as we ran blindly into unchartered territory, an old, raggedy house appeared in the distance like a gift from the night itself.

I raced toward the house, with the sound of the truck's engine getting ever closer, and I spied a small shed off to the side, on the very edge of the woods. I was torn between the shed and the house, deciding at the last second to run to the house.

At the house, I raced up the front stairs and grabbed the doorknob. I jiggled it furiously as Jack and Justin stumbled into me, desperate to get the thing to yield.

"Open the damn door, Jody!" Justin screamed at me.

"Hurry up, they're coming –" Jack urged.

"I can't open it!"

"Move!" Justin took charge.

I stepped out of the way and Justin kicked in the front door, sending it slamming up against the wall inside the house.

The truck hurtled along the driveway, made a hard left which sent its back end fish-tailing. The truck's fat tires flung up clods of dirt and mud, which soared through the air as the truck came to a rest mere yards in front of us. The passenger door was slung open and Mitch the Mailman stepped out. His hair wasn't in a ponytail like when we'd had our altercation on Rhine Road; he wore it perfectly straight, down his back like a woman's. His face was pale in the harsh glare of the truck's lights, and he had a ferocious countenance that fair chilled the soul.

The woman was driving the truck, and when she cut the engine, the headlights faded and everything turned black. The headlights had been our friend thus far, having helped us navigate to this decrepit sanctuary, and now the only light that was provided by the moon.

"Get in, Jody!" Jack bellowed at me from inside – he and Justin were already in the house.

I ran in and slammed the door shut behind me. Jack searched the nearest wall, looking for a light switch, stumbling over unseen objects that were concealed by the dark and scattered across the floor. The room was damned near pitch black, but as my eyes adjusted, I could make out that we were standing in the living room of a crumbling house. There was a long table of sorts in the center, draped with a black sheet. A mantle was behind that, which was home to several dark-colored candles. The smell inside the house was cloying, sour; it

329

made my nose twitch and I took soft, shallow breaths to avoid inhaling the stink any more than I had to. It reminded me of rust and salt and stale piss – it was gross.

"The lights don't work," Jack reported, frantically wiggling the light switch.

"Where's Chase?" Justin was worried.

"I don't know," I replied, fighting back the dismay in my voice.

A rock smashed through one of the large, grimy windows, raining glass over Jack's back. He groaned loudly and grabbed at his neck, where the glass had lacerated his skin.

"Come outside, boys," Mitch teased. "You forgot someone!"

I looked at Justin. "They must have caught Chase," I mumbled.

"Oh God, please no –" Justin whimpered and broke down for the first time that night. Tears welled and ran their course down Justin's face, and he fell to his knees, as if he were ready to pray.

Jack walked over to him. "Get up, Justin," my friend demanded, grabbing Justin's biceps to help him to his feet. "We don't have the time for this."

"I can't," Justin cried, swaying like a drunk. "We're gonna die… we're *all* going to die."

"Don't say that," I said, and felt myself starting to cry as well.

A rock busted through another window, only this time it came from somewhere further back in the house. It became apparent that the crazy people outside were circling the house, playing with us like a cat plays with a mouse – perhaps hoping they would catch us trying to escape out the back door.

"Help!" a voiced cried from outside – it was Chase.

"Help me, Justin! *Please!*"

"Shut your fucking mouth, twerp," we heard the harelip man snarl, and that was followed by a loud slap.

"Pick him up, Scott," Mitch instructed.

The harelip man's name was Scott - finally, after all this time, I knew the ugly bastard's name!

"Rebecca?" Mitch's voice echoed out through the darkness. No response. "Rebecca!" he called once more, but still there came no reply.

Jack, Justin and I stood in the darkness of that musty, stinking old house and tried to listen to Mitch and Scott talking – but their voices were too muffled for us to make out much more than the odd, disjointed word. But, loud and clear was Chase's forlorn sobbing, his heart-wrenching whimpers penetrating the old walls. Then, from inside the house, we heard a long, drawn-out squeaking noise – the sound of a door closing on rusted hinges; evidently, there was someone in the house with us, and it wasn't Mitch or Scott.

"We gotta move," Jack said, desperately looking over his shoulder towards the sound, "and we gotta move now."

"Okay, we'd better stay low," I suggested. I dropped to my hands and knees, "they won't be able see us through the windows."

Justin was still on his knees, the trail of tears glistening on his face.

"Come on, Justin," I urged, and took off crawling.

It was a rough, hardwood floor, filthy with dirt, sand and mud, which stuck to the palms of my hands as I shuffled after Jack. We moved along as quickly and as quietly as we could, making our way past the long table and heading towards what I guessed was the kitchen. I took a quick look behind to make sure that Justin was following us, and I spotted something dark – darker even than the room itself – moving across the floor behind him. I blinked and whatever it was went way, so I dismissed it as a trick of the inky shadows and I went back to crawling.

We made it to the kitchen, and the floor turned to tile, which was even filthier than the hardwood. There was a door to the left, sporting a rusted golden chain and a deadbolt held it shut; the only thing that separated us from the monsters outside. A stench invaded my senses, it smelled like bad plumbing, or festering mold, hanging in the air like some malevolent spirit.

I crawled further into the kitchen, placing my back against the cabinets beneath the sink. I paused, taking a deep breath to try calming my nerves and looked on as Justin crawled into the room. He came to rest next to me, slamming his back against the cabinet and shutting a small, half-open cabinet door so loudly that Mitch, Scott and whoever was in the house with us had to have heard it.

"Shhh!" Jack hissed, standing up warily.

He tiptoed over to a drawer; grasped it and pulled it open as quietly as its corroded runners would allow. I heard a thump from the living room. Jack shut the drawer and threw himself down to the ground, his breathing labored. It was then that I noticed he was holding an old steak knife close to his chest. Another thump came, then a couple of hard bumps on the outside of the house. I focused my attention back towards the living room. It sounded like a blind ghost was walking around in there, a clumsy one at that. Suddenly, the door shook violently and in unison, the three of us screamed.

"Open the fucking door, Rebecca!" Scott yelled.

"Jody!" Jack screamed.

Rebecca lunged up from the floor and grabbed my throat in her long, powerful fingers. She'd been crawling behind us and was covered in a thick black cloak – the nebulous shape I thought I'd seen earlier and ignored. Her fingernails dug deep into the soft skin around my trachea and I began to panic as my airway was restricted. I flailed my arms wildly, my hands snagging in her hair – I pulled hard on it. Rebecca's head snapped backwards and she screamed with anger.

"Let him go, you bitch!" Justin screamed and kicked the woman in the side of her face.

She released me and I let go of her hair, stumbling to my feet and gasping for breath. Justin scrambled to his feet, but Rebecca lunged forwards and wrapped her arms around his legs, which brought him right back down to the ground with a winded yowl. Acting instinctively, I jumped on the woman's back and punched her in the back of the head as hard as I could, again and again.

I rained as many blows on Rebecca's head as I could, and Justin managed to wiggle his legs free of her grasp. Jack ran over, and pulled me off of the woman. I was severely winded and my knuckles were black and blue from pounding her skull, and throbbing with pain.

Exhausted, I fell to my knees. Rebecca crawled across the floor, moaning with pain and rubbing the back of her head. Before I could catch my next breath, Jack brought the knife up above his head and walked over to Rebecca.

"Jack, *no!*" I cried.

Too late.

The steak knife arced down fast and dug into Rebecca's shoulder. She unleashed an un-Godly scream and flailed around on the filthy tiles. Jack stumbled backwards, his eyes wide with shock and fixed on the steak knife that stuck upright in the woman's back and pressed himself up against the kitchen door. I threw myself against the cabinets once again, and clamped my hands over my ears to muffle the screams.

"Let's go before the other two come in!" Justin said, scrabbling to his feet.

A piercing smash of glass reverberated from the living room, and seconds later, Mitch stepped into the kitchen with a look of complete surprise on his face.

Neither Jack nor I could move, but Justin was ready to make a run for it. He shot me a regretful cast and tried to barge his way around Mitch, but sadly, his strategy didn't work out so well for him.

Mitch grabbed Justin by the collar and slung him hard into the kitchen wall, showering chunks of damp plaster onto the dirt-strewn floor, and Justin slumped to the ground, unconscious.

Rebecca was still screaming and flopping along the ground like a fish out of water, trying desperately to grab at the knife in her shoulder. Mitch knelt down and yanked the knife out of her, taking no trouble to spare the poor woman any further pain. A shrill squeal shot from Rebecca's lips and Mitch rolled her over to her back.

"You're going to be okay," Mitch growled, as if Rebecca's agony was an annoyance to him. "Which one of the little bastards did this?"

Rebecca was crying like a little kid, blood making the back of her cloak glisten wetly in the wan light, and between sobs, she pointed to Jack.

Mitch glanced over at my blood brother, who was still pressed up against the door and clearly terrified out of his mind. The mailman took two strides forward and grabbed Jack by both ears. Jack whimpered with pain and Mitch brought his knee up into Jack's stomach, forcing every ounce of breath from his lungs. Jack fought for breath and collapsed to the ground in a fetal position, weeping uncontrollably.

"Scott!" Mitch yelled up at the ceiling. "Get your ass in here! We got a problem!"

I felt decidedly ill; my body temperature dropped, my skin felt cold and clammy, my head throbbed like a mad thing and I began dry heaving, the sour taste of bile and the fruit punch burning the back of my throat.

Mitch stomped over to me and grabbed my purple, sweat-stained shirt, and pulled me to my feet. I tried in vain to get away from him, but he was far too strong, his huge hands were like meaty vises, unmovable and inherently tough. Our eyes met briefly and he gave me a sinister grin as I struggled against him, as if this were mere sport for his own delectation.

He released one hand from my shirt, stretched his arm out wide to his side, and showed me his palm before bringing it forwards, hard across my face. The slap stung like an electric shock, and set my ears to ringing. He pulled that massive hand back once more, but this time, his hand turned to a fist, and all I remembered was seeing dancing stars behind my eyes right before I hit the tiles.

***

I woke up on the living room floor with my hands and feet duct-taped together and my jaw throbbing with pain. I was pushed up against the mantle that lay directly behind the long, covered table in the dead center of the room. The candles on the mantle had been lit, and they illuminated the entire room with a ghostly orange, flickering glow. Justin was leaning up against me on my right, still out cold and Jack was to my left, wide awake and duct-taped just as I was.

Once he saw I was conscious, Jack looked at me as if expecting me to help, but there really was nothing I could do. I noticed his eyelids were bright pink, his eyes a tad glassy – he looked horrible.

I scanned around the room and saw that Chase was with us – tied up too. He'd been placed far away from Justin, Jack and me, up against the crumbling wall farthest across the room. Chase was the only one of us with duct-tape wrapped tightly around his mouth. For some reason Mitch, Rebecca and the hideous Scott wanted to keep the kid quiet.

What I saw next made me wish they had kept the candles unlit, for all around that long table, the floor was stained with dried blood.

It looked to me as if someone had taken a bucket of the stuff and dumped it all over the hardwood; most of it permanently stained a dark, brownish-red; most of the puddled globs of blood were flaking away, much the same as old, spilled milk.

I forced my eyes away from the floor and peered around the room, eying warily the pentagrams that were spray painted on all of the windows that were unbroken, and the myriad dense cobwebs that spanned high up across the corners of the room. There was a thick layer of dust on the windowsills, in which sat the fat, flickering candles.

Over by the entrance to a hallway that led to the back of the house, there sat a huge drum, which I guessed to be the source of the rhythmic beats Momma, Hunter and I had been so terrified by.

I examined the long table once more, noting that the cloth covering it was solid black, and covered in desiccated blood stains, and my guts sank at the realization of what those stains could mean.

Scott and Mitch came back inside the house through the busted-up front door. "She'll be fine, as long as I get her over to Daren's real quick," Mitch said, running his fingers through his long mane of dark hair. "You think you can keep these four under control while I'm gone?"

"Not a problem," Scott said with a snarl and a sideways glance at me.

"Good."

"Woo-hoo!" Scott shouted out and jumped into the air. "You boys are gonna wish you'd never shown your faces around here."

"Please... don't kill... us," I sobbed, breaking my silence.

"Shut your fucking mouth, boy!" Mitch hollered. He strutted over to me like some malevolent drill sergeant and squatted down to eye-level, resting his buttocks on the back of his heels. "You never should've gotten involved, son. But you did and now you're going to pay the price for your stupidity."

"Please, sir, for the love of God, please let us go," I implored, my eyes brimming with fresh tears.

"God?" Mitch asked, cocking his head to one side like an inquisitive puppy, "There is no God – only the Devil. *He* is the only God."

"Please – please," Jack prayed, staring heavenwards as he squirmed closer to me.

"You can pray all you want to, gentlemen," Mitch lectured as he gazed over to Jack, "but no God will save you tonight, because your asses belong to me and *my* God – and we want your blood." Mitch got slowly to his feet, his huge frame towering over. "So I'd save your breath for your screams."

Mitch then motioned Scott over to Chase. "Have your way with this one first," he said without emotion, "and do what you wish with this one," he pointed at Justin's unconscious body. Then he turned slowly around, his menacing demeanor aimed squarely at Jack and me. "But don't touch these two; I have something special planned for them when I get back," Mitch growled.

"Not a problem," Scott said with a sadistic leer.

"I'll be back in ten minutes, tops."

Mitch walked away and made his way back outside. The sound of the truck's engine firing up resounded through the windows, fading quickly into the distance. Jack and I began crying hysterically as our imaginations ran riot with thoughts of our promised fate.

Scott sauntered over to Chase and grabbed him by the hair. Chase's cheeks puffed in and out as he was pulled to his feet, and I knew the poor kid was hyperventilating. Feeling helpless, I brought my tied hands up to my face and wiped my tears away.

"Come on, you little fuck," Scott growled as he dragged Chase along by the hair, the kid hopping along as fast as his bound legs would allow, "we're gonna have some fun!"

All of a sudden, Justin's body began twitching and shaking, like he was having a seizure or something, but as I watched his eyelids attempting to open, I knew he was just waking up.

"Justin," I muttered, "come on, Justin, wake up."

Justin quit shaking and slowly opened his eyes.

"Well look who's awake," Scott said, acting all surprised, "seems you woke up just in time for the party." Scott kicked Justin in the chest and sent him hard into the mantle. The ugly guy then lifted Chase up onto the table and rolled him over on his belly – I could hear Chase's muffled screams from behind the duct tape that sealed his mouth.

"Leave him alone!" I yelled.

A swift kick to the side of my head from Scott sent me tumbling into Jack's lap.

"All of you need to keep your motherfucking mouths shut, or I will take out your intestines and feed them to you!" Scott screamed, his voice thick with menace.

Chase was doing his best to roll from the table, but Scott grasped his legs and pulled him halfway off the table. Chase was now bent over the table with Scott standing right behind him. I pushed myself up from Jack's lap, back to upright, and Scott turned to face us.

"If any of you try to get away, or even think about escaping, it will only make things worse," Scott snarled. He then reached into his inner trench coat pocket and pulled out a knife – the same one he'd sliced my foot open with – which he brought down hard into the table right next to Chase, making all of us jump.

Scott removed his coat and threw it to the side of the table. He leaned forward, wrapping his hands around Chase's waist, sneering over at us and moments later, Chase's pants and underwear were down around his ankles.

Chase's screams bellowed out, his terror in the hands of the monster palpable. Scott brought his hands around front of him and unfastened his own pants, and in the blink of an eye, he too stood before us with his pants to his knees. Scott turned to one side for a split second to grab his knife, and I shuddered to see that his penis was semi-erect.

Scott lined himself up directly behind Chase, and I watched in horror as he brought the knife down hard into Chase's back, not once, but five times. And each time the knife entered the kid's flesh, Chase's body lunged forward with the impact, his legs straining, calf muscles bulging. Done with the knife, Scott laid it down gently on the edge of the table, all the while Chase's agonizing screams reverberated throughout the old house. Scott moved his right hand around and began masturbating – and while most boys do it, sitting there under the mantle all tied up and watching a grown man doing it mutilated my soul; it was like watching a train wreck – I wanted to look away, but couldn't. None of us could.

Scott shifted his hips back and then advanced, but Chase's butt cheeks were locked tightly together. Scott leaned over, pulled Chase's head back by his hair and ripped the duct tape from his mouth, and agonized cries filled the room.

"Stop fighting it!" Scott screamed. He leaned forward and punched Chase in the back of the head as the poor kid screamed and tried to break free.

"Stop it!" Justin yelled.

"You're killing him!" Jack squealed.

Scott ignored them and spat on his penis, pausing a moment to spread some of the spit on Chase's anus with his hand. And then he thrust forward.

Jack leaned his head up against my shoulder and cried like he'd never stop, and I cried along as the sounds of Chase's pain filled our ears. The acrid stink of feces and blood wafted over to us, and I threw up, hot, stinging bile that squirted from my mouth and nose to splash noisily on the floor. I glanced over at Justin and saw that he was in complete shock; he didn't even look like Justin anymore.

"You like that, baby?" Scott grunted, grabbing his knife once more and stabbing Chase over and over, until Chase's cries faded to nothing more than soft whimpering. I knew then that he was dying, bleeding out, and there was absolutely nothing any of us could do for him; the best we could do was sit and await our turn to die.

I turned to Jack.

"Pray," I whispered.

Jack nodded his head okay and closed his eyes. I looked across to Justin, but his eyes were already closed and his lips were moving silently.

I leaned my head back and prayed to God. I asked him to forgive me for everything I'd done wrong in my life. I asked him for a quick and painless death, even though I knew in my heart that it wouldn't be. I asked for Momma, Hunter and Memaw to be able to live long and happy lives. I told God to let Pepaw know I would soon be on my way to see him...

Just then, there came the noise of something hitting the floor with a dull, metallic clatter. Startled, my eyes flew open – I hadn't even gotten to say *Amen*.

As it turned out, I didn't need to; God had just answered my prayer.

There, on the floor and unseen by Scott, lay the blood-soaked knife, a little more than a few inches behind his feet. I felt a weird energy flow through my body, like the time I stuck my fingers in an outlet just to see what would happen. My mind began to be working again, racing ahead of me despite the atrocities happening in that old, derelict house; I found the will to survive again, and I knew that if my friends could see that, then just maybe it would rally them to fight back.

I thought no more, and acted purely on instinct. Leaning forward quietly, careful to not make any sound at all, I extended my tied hands towards the knife. Jack and Justin looked on, silent and wide eyed with terror, and shifted uncomfortably against their restraints. Straining, I slid my hand over the hilt of the knife and picked the thing up, it felt cool and slick against my sweating palm, its freshly honed blade glinting keen in the candlelight.

I kept my eyes on Scott, praying that he would not realize that his precious knife was missing from the table. Grasping the knife, I sat back slowly, the faint moans and groans from Chase prickling my ears, and stretched my upper thighs to place the sides of my knees upon the floor. I sliced through the tape that held my feet together; it was off with only two strokes. I reached over to Justin and he extended his hands to me. I cut through the tape on his wrists and handed him the knife so he could return the favor.

With both of my arms free, I hacked away the remainder of the tape on Jack and Justin, quicker than you could shake a stick at. I then grabbed my two friends by their napes and pulled them into me.

"When I stand up, I'm gonna jab this knife into the ugly bastard's fucking neck," I snarled quietly. "And when I do, run like hell out the back door." I said no more and stood to my feet, feeling just like one of my imaginary ninja assassins; Jack and Justin followed suit.

Scott had yet to look over to check on us, the sick bastard was otherwise occupied. So, I crept up behind him, with the knife held tightly against my chest, the fear in my heart turning quickly to pure, burning rage. I knew full well that if I didn't incapacitate – or better yet, *kill* – him, that would pretty much be the end of me.

I also figured that it'd be far easier to get away from one maniac rather than two; Mitch hadn't come back yet, I hadn't heard his truck pulling up at the front of the old house, so I guessed we had time on our side. I worried he'd be back soon enough with our surprise, and I had no intention of hanging around to see what that was.

I brought the knife away from my chest and lifted it high above my head. Scott was a good four inches taller than me, so I had to make sure I had the right amount of leverage to actually do some damage. I moved in closer as he violated Justin's dying friend, my heart pumping hard with adrenaline, anxiety and anger. I lifted the knife up a little higher, standing firm on my tip-toes, and then slammed it down as hard as I could into Scott's jugular.

I yanked the knife out of his neck and staggered backwards. Scott was squealing like a stuck pig, and I felt like He-Man. Scott's shrill, womanlike scream gargled and bubbled from his blood-filled throat. As he slumped forward over Chase's body, scarlet arcs jetted from the ragged hole in his neck like water from a split hose. He clamped a hand to his neck in a vain attempt to stem the bleeding, but all that achieved was fine sprays of blood splattering every which way, some of it splashed my face, making me gag.

"Let's go, damn it!" Jack yelled, happy I'd done enough damage to our captor to ensure he wouldn't be chasing us again any time soon.

I held onto the knife as Jack pulled me in front of him and pushed me into motion, my legs finally deciding to work. I was shocked to the core at what I'd just done, but I was glad I did it – that son-of-a-bitch more than deserved it.

Justin turned into the hallway first and sprinted his way down the hall. Jack and I followed behind closely, but before we got halfway down the dry-rotted hallway, I heard a sound behind us that chilled me to the bone.

It was the unmistakable noise of a circular saw, the kind Pepaw used in his shed. It was accompanied by a scream of pure, unadulterated fury from Mitch the mailman as he stormed into the house – he was back.

"Get the door open, Justin!" I barked, my voice squeaky. "He's coming!"

Justin screamed at the top of his lungs for help again as he raced towards the back door, I felt Jack's hand still on my back as he pushed me forward.

"Go damn it, go!" Jack was panic-stricken.

I ran down the dark hallway as the horrendous sound of that saw gained on us, its high-pitched buzzing shrill in my ears. Then Justin was at the door, fiddling with the knob with trembling hands shaking, his sweaty palms failing to find their grip.

I was only a few feet away from him. "Open the door!" I cried, and before I crashed into him, Justin wrenched the door opened and ran out into the night.

We all charged out of the back door, but the second my foot hit the ground, Jack stepped on my back heel and I fell flat on my face, the knife spinning out in front of me.

Jack stopped to pick me up.

"Shut the door, *shut the door*! I yelled, my voice high with panic.

Jack left me on the ground and turned towards the door, seeing that Mitch was almost to it. The man wore a heavy, black robe that covered him from head to toe, with Devil horns that stuck out on both sides of its hood, and he looked terrifying.

Mitch carried the cordless circular saw out in front of his chest, and he had a look of vengeance on his face. Undeterred, Jack made it back to the house and slammed the door shut just in time, the saw blade ripping right through the rotting wood, stopping just inches from Jack's ear.

"Help me, Jody! I can't keep it shut on my own!"

I scrabbled to my feet and ran over, grabbing the doorknob and pulling back with all my strength. Justin was nowhere to be seen.

"Justin!" I called out.

The saw's blade spun relentlessly as it quickly turned the door into sawdust, hacking chunks from the wood as if it were of little substance.

"Justin, we need help!" Jack screamed.

We could hear Mitch's angry shouts from behind the door, loud even over the noise of the saw. He yanked the saw from the slice it had just made and slammed it into the door again at a different spot. Sawdust blew out from the blade and fell down the back of my shirt, and the warm, woody smell reminded me of the days I'd spent watching Pepaw working in his shed.

I looked behind me as I pulled my weight against the door, with hopes of seeing Justin rushing heroically to our aid, but he was nowhere to be seen. Instead, I saw several old tree stumps and a couple of 2x4 boards next to an old chicken pen that was all rusted up and falling apart. The knife I had dropped was there in the grass, and a little further on from that – mere yards away – embedded in one of the tree stumps, was an axe.

The saw quit spinning and Mitch yanked violently on the door, screaming at us like a crazy person. "Let go!!" he yelled, "let go of the fucking door!"

My body was yanked forward on his pull, my arms were getting fatigued.

"Don't let go!" Jack implored, his eyes scared and tearful.

"I can't hold it much longer!"

Mitch's next tug pulled me forward even more and I let go of the knob, and once Jack realized I'd let go, he did too. The door swung open halfway, and Mitch pulled the saw from out of the ruined wood, his face twisted in an ugly, reddened grimace.

Immediately, I turned tail and ran towards the chicken coop as the dreadful sound of the circular saw started up again, with Jack close behind. I dashed over to the pile of boards next to the rotted chicken pen and grabbed one of the smallest 2x4s, turning to face Mitch.

"Aaaargh!" Mitch screamed at me from beneath his hood, his voice barely human, almost as if the man was demonically possessed. He stood there, legs open wide in a defensive stance, the circular saw spinning by his

345

side, his face an image of pure hate.

My adrenaline kicked into overdrive. "Come on!" I yelled at him, bringing the board up like a baseball bat, all ready to fight for my life.

Mitch faked a lunge forward with the saw, toying with me, and I was stupid enough to take the bait. I swung at him with the board, and as it came close to connecting with his ribs, he hopped back and bum-rushed me. My scrawny arms weren't strong enough to bring the board back around fast enough to take another swing, and Mitch rammed me with his monstrous shoulders and sent me crashing to the ground.

Instinctively, I pulled the 2x4 over my chest for protection as Mitch stepped forward and pressed his foot into my testicles. I howled like the Rougarou and Mitch pressed the saw down into the board, preventing me from moving at all.

"Ohhh – God!" I screamed in pain and pushed up even harder on the board.

"Scream, boy!" Mitch snarled, his lip curled in a cruel sneer.

I had little choice; my poor testes had at least two hundred pounds of grown man stomping on them. Sawdust flurried about my face as the saw cut through the 2x4 like butter, and my vision blurred as my eyelashes collected the dust.

Mitch released his foot from my testicles and brought his knee up to his chest. He then stomped on the board, splitting it in two, and my boney chest caught the rest of the impact from his size twelve. It felt like I'd been hit by a train, and I rolled over to my side, coughing and wheezing.

Mitch took one hand off the saw, grabbed me by the back of my pants, and rolled me over. He fell to his knees on top of me, shimmying forward and placing both knees on my arms so I couldn't move – just like I used to do to Hunter when we play fought. Part of Mitch's robe, cloak, or whatever the damn thing was, covered some of my face and I could only see out of one eye.

"Eat this!" I heard Jack's victory yell.

A long, thick stick smashed into Mitch's chest, knocking him off me and to one side, but he stopped himself from crashing to the ground. Jack had caught the guy off guard, but that hadn't been enough to knock him out. Jack quickly realized that his plan hadn't gone his way, so he rained a flurry of blows to the side of Mitch's head.

In the blink of an eye, Mitch grabbed Jack by the arm and pulled him into a head butt. There was a sickening, dull *clunk* and Jack fell down beside me, dazed and confused. Mitch found his balance and raised the saw up over his head.

"Be pleased, my Lord, as I give you the blood of the innocent. Bless upon me the power of Darkness!" he raved like a madman.

I felt Jack place a shaking hand on my chest. I turned to look at him; his nose was busted, most likely broken, and he was crying. I knew then that my friend was reaching out to me for his final minutes of comfort; Jack knew we were about to die. Everything else faded out for me, and I felt like I was underwater – and, mercifully I couldn't hear the crazed incantations that Mitch was spouting; I felt at peace.

I reached for Jack's hand and squeezed it tightly as I closed my eyes. The circular saw buzzed above us, and all I could do now was pray; pray for Mitch to bring the saw into my chest and end my life as quickly and painlessly as possible.

I embraced the end.

"Hail Satan!" Mitch cried out as he brought down that dreadful blade.

"No!!" Justin screamed at the top of his voice. My eyes flew open and I saw the kid running full pelt behind Mitch, swinging an axe with all of his might.

With a sodden thwack, the axe hit home, square in the crazed mailman's armpit.

Blood spurted from the wound, spraying high and raining down on our faces. Justin yanked the axe out from Mitch's body, there was a gross crackling sound and a fresh gush of warm blood covered me, filling my mouth with the taste of melted pennies. Yowling in agony, Mitch dropped the saw, and I could only look on in horror as it tumbled towards my face. Last second instinct had me rolling on top of Jack, and I heard the saw hitting the dirt an inch or so behind my head.

Mitch collapsed to his side and then onto his belly, crying out with the excruciating pain that wracked his huge frame, his voice deep and resonant in the darkness. Slowly, he inched his way across the grass, pulling himself towards the entrance to the woods with his uninjured arm, his other dragging limply alongside him.

Justin brought the bloodied axe up once more and swung it down into Mitch's ankle, peeling the flesh right off the bone, and damned near severing Mitch's foot. I grimaced at the sound it made, something akin to a thick, cypress branch snapping, and when I looked up at the axe, there were raw shreds of Mitch's skin hanging from its weathered blade.

I rolled off of Jack and struggled to my feet, my testicles still pounding a dull ache all the way up to my stomach. I limped over to the chicken coop, bent down and picked up another decent-sized 2x4, just as Justin dropped the axe and threw up over by one of the tree stumps.

I returned to Mitch and watched him blubber like a scared little kid as he tried to crawl into the woods. I felt nothing but pure hatred for the sick bastard. So, I whacked him across the back with the 2x4, preventing him from hauling his bloodied body one more inch.

He rolled over, onto his back. "Stop, goddamn it!" Mitch begged, and in that instant he looked like nothing more than our mailman. *"Please stop!"*

It's odd how the tables can turn so quickly, how the hunter can become the hunted, the predator the prey, and this monster of a man who was mere seconds away from taking my life, was begging for his. "I'll give you anything you want, just let me be." Mitch bleated, snot bubbling from his blood-splashed nose.

"Anything?" I asked, my throat painfully dry.

"Anything, just walk away and leave me be!" he blubbered.

Suddenly, heartache, pain, anger and a sense of injustice flowed through my heart, and I acted upon all of it.

"I want my Pepaw back!" I yelled at the devil-man. I cracked the 2x4 across his throat, crushing his trachea in an instant. He at once made wet, gurgling choking noises, and a fat rivulet of blood flowed from his mouth. "I want my Mom and Dad back together!" I screamed and struck him again, this time in his belly. "And I want *you* to bring Chase back!" at that I brought the wood down hard on Mitch's forehead, peeling the skin down to the cracked bone.

I stared awhile at the steady flow of blood that ran from our assailant's head, watching as it poured into his half-closed eyes and on down his sallow face. I walked away, out of breath, but not quite satisfied. I looked back at Jack, who stared over at Mitch. My best friend's face was unreadable to me at that moment, and I only realized what malevolence lurked behind the darkness in his eyes when he reached down to pick up the circular saw.

"What are you doing?" Justin asked him, nervously, as he wiped the dribbles of vomit from his lips with the back of one hand.

"Giving this son-of-a-bitch what he deserves."

I looked over at Mitch, who was barely recognizable, a deserving victim of his own evil. His breathing was shallow and labored, frothy bubbles of blood forming at the corners of his mouth, popping as they jostled against one another. I glanced over at Jack.

"Just leave him be. We need to get out of here and call the cops. Let them haul this child-killing piece of shit off to jail – if he's still alive when they get here."

Jack didn't respond, just walked straight on by me, and towards Mitch.

"Jack!"

My friend – my *blood brother* – spun around and looked at me, snapping out of his trance.

"You don't have to do this," I told him.

Jack was crying, the moon illuminating the tear trails on his face like they were a line of diamonds. Saying nothing, Jack turned away from me and walked slowly towards Mitch.

I made my way back by the house. I turned only when I heard the saw roar to life, and saw that Justin was on his knees, weeping uncontrollably, his body shuddering with great, wracking sobs. Then, a colossal weight crashed into me from behind. I fell to the ground, winded yet screaming with everything I had left in me.

Scott fell on top of me, holding one hand over the ragged gash in his neck, the other on my throat. In the moonlight, he looked like some terrible, bloodless Vampire; he was sickeningly pale, the veins in his face standing blue and proud through his translucent skin. He'd clearly lost a lot of blood due to the stab wound, and even in my panicked state, I couldn't help but wonder how the guy was still moving. Wriggling beneath his huge, stinking weight, I managed to shove a finger into the ugly fucker's eye socket, wincing as it squished into the soft orb and Scott yelped out loud in agony. I shoved my finger further into the socket, and felt his eyeball shift.

"Get off him, you piece of shit!" Justin cried, bringing the axe back into action.

The blade struck the middle of Scott's back, the impact so solid, I felt it through Scott's body. The man opened his mouth to scream, but no sounds came – only clots of thick, dark blood.

Taking advantage of his weakened state, I easily pushed the harelip man off me. He fell over to his back in the cool grass, moaning and twitching in torment, a fresh surge of blood draining out through the wound in his neck. I crawled across to him and clambered atop his frail body. "Why couldn't you just die!?" I screamed loud and harsh in his face.

Scott muttered, his lips barely moving, and I thought he was saying *help*; he reached a hand up towards me, as if begging for mercy. Unmoved, I slapped it away.

The sound of the saw got louder, and when I looked up, I saw Jack standing over us. Jack lowered the saw, stopping inches away from Scott's face, and I saw that the once terrifying harelip guy was pissing his pants as he struggled to form his final words.

"I can't do it." Jack said quietly. He was breathing heavily, and looked particularly gruesome with dark splashes of blood covering his face and white shirt.

Without thinking, I reached up and placed my hands

on top of Jack's. Together, we brought that saw down – slowly.

Justin came over, sliding on his knees until he was next to me, and placed his hands on the saw as well; he had a crazy, maniacal look in his eyes. The three of us pressed the buzzing blade into Scott's skull, blood drenching our hands and showering our bodies as it spurted and arced. With his remaining vestiges of strength, Scott let out a high, piercing scream of abject agony as the saw's blade ate its way into his ugly, twisted face.

"This is for Chase!" Justin screamed at the dying man, his voice charged with raw emotion.

Scott's body shook violently, his arms thrashing wildly as the saw carved through the bones of his skull, sending pinkish-gray putty spraying through the cold night air.

"Ahhh!" I yelled out at the top of my lungs. Blood and brains filled my open mouth, and I just spat it out as the pungent stink of burnt flesh filled my nose.

"Die!" Jack cried at the man, who was pretty much on the verge of doing just that. He released the trigger on the tool and we eased it out of Scott's face, wiggling it a tad as the man's chewed up face bones clung to the bloody blade.

Jack let the saw drop to the ground. I climbed off Scott and collapsed to the ground next to Justin.

Scott was dead.

We had killed the man – *murdered* him.

We hadn't been forced to end his life, but we had decided to anyway. Whatever innocence we'd had left in us was now gone forever. I could feel it in my darkened soul.

The night fell quiet again, and I listened to the sound of running water, which contrasted with Mitch's weak, crackling coughs; the creek was directly behind us, the place that had led us all to the events that had taken place that night. I began to cry as I looked up at the twinkling stars, and Jack made his way over, and we all embraced one another, happy the nightmare was over and thrilled to be alive.

***

As we walked back down the long driveway that had led us to the house of horrors, battered, bruised, bleeding and drenched in blood, I saw blue and red flashing police lights over by the corner where we had ditched our bikes.

"We have to tell them we killed Scott in self-defense," Justin said.

"Why?" I asked him.

"Because we could spend the rest our lives behind bars if they find out the truth."

"What's the truth?" Jack's voice was whisper-weak.

"That we *murdered* him in cold blood."

We all fell silent. We knew that what Justin was saying was true; we could have easily left Scott to bleed to death from his wounds, but in the heat of the moment we'd decided to play God and take his life.

"Deal," I said, "Story is, he came out, took me down, you hit him with the axe, he was still choking me, and that's when we all took the saw to him. Got it?"

"Got it," Jack agreed.

"Justin?" I asked again.

"Yeah," Justin said, wiping tears from his face. "Just remember that we're going to have to take this to our graves, guys"

We said nothing more and made our way toward the flashing lights. What Justin said was true; we'd have to

353

live with what we'd done for the rest of our lives.

All our parents were standing at the bend with over a dozen cops. Mr. Shawn noticed us first and ran toward us, followed by the others, and we were hugged tightly, even though we were covered in blood, and Momma and Mrs. Renee were crying hysterically.

"Oh my God, Bubba, what happened to you?" Momma shook my shoulders, and stared at my blood-spattered face in horror.

I noticed two people standing back from the crowd, holding hands, their faces sick with worry; Chase's Mom and Dad.

One of the cops walked up to me. "Son, my name's Officer Rogers, can you tell me what happened to y'all? *Why* are ya'll covered in blood?"

"They killed him," my voice was unintentionally loud, and caught the attention of the gathered people. "They killed Chase," I started to cry again. "Then they tried to kill us, but they didn't – we made it."

Chase's Mom let out a chilling, heart-wrenching wail and collapsed to her knees. Her husband tried to catch her before she hit the ground, but he was too slow. As the poor lady's knees collided with Rhine Road, my heart broke for her, and I felt her suffering. Unable to keep myself composed any longer, I broke down into a complete and utter mess and wrapped my bloody arms around Momma. I couldn't think, or speak; all I could do was cry.

"How did you boys manage to get away?" the lead investigator asked Jack.

"We fought back," Jack told him from the safe place of his father's strong arms, "And we killed him."

CHAPTER TWENTY-FIVE

BLOOD IN THE WOODS: 1993

We didn't move to Baton Rouge as originally planned, due to the ongoing investigation, the upcoming trial and medical treatment I had to receive for my testicular injury; after the crazy mailman's assault on my groin, my left testicle was severely swollen, and I was taken to the doctor for fear of losing it. Turned out, the ultrasound discovered a blood clot on my testicle, and I was immediately placed on a whole host of medication. There were days where I couldn't walk or get out of bed in the morning, but eventually the swelling did go down and the clot dissolved.

By this time, though, our incident had hit the local news and papers. Somehow, it failed to make national headlines, but it hit home to every parent in Hammond, New Orleans and Baton Rouge.

They ran the story on the news as

BLOOD IN THE WOODS

And in the local newspaper, *The Daily Star*, as:

"SATANIC CULT BROUGHT DOWN BY 3 YOUTHS AFTER ESCAPING GRISLY MURDER HOUSE"

They used the word *Satanic* in most of the headlines to attract more attention to the new moral panic – '*The Satanic Panic*' – which was sweeping the nation. The tabloid press made out like Jack, Justin and I were heroes, and of course, people wanted answers about what had really happened that night, as well as the names of the kids involved.

Thank God, the police were very supportive and protective of us; we were safeguarded from the media and newspapers, but those who lived on Rhine Road had a good idea that it was us who'd been involved in the whole damn mess; and small town gossip travels faster than the dead.

It transpired that Rebecca had been arrested at Mitch's house a day later. Mitch – the mailman no one ever suspected of wrong doing – died in the hospital from his wounds three days after that, and I didn't feel the least bit sorry for him when I heard, in fact I was actually angry that I hadn't gotten to watch him die like his murderous, hare-lipped friend.

Countless evidence had been recovered from the old, disintegrating house linking Rebecca to other missing children, which she conveniently blamed on the recently-deceased Mitch, at the same time throwing some guy named Daren under the bus. Meanwhile, Jack, Justin and I had to go through the mandatory counseling – provided by the state, of course – and I got some plump woman named Mrs. Wilson, who was actually pretty cool. I opened up to her a lot, and she really helped me get over the mess in my head over those next few months, reiterating that we did what we had to do to survive.

But, deep down in my soul, I knew the truth, and I felt foul. I even felt as if I couldn't pray to God anymore, because I figured he'd not be too happy with what I'd done – I was lost and confused, and sometimes felt like I had no soul at all.

By the end of the summer, thanks to swift southern justice, the case was closed, the trial over and we were informed that there'd be no future statements required from the three of us; Southerners love their quick justice, much like Texans love the death penalty.

After receiving the news, I smiled for the first time since summer began. The state didn't want to put us up on the stand in court, and the killing of Scott was ruled to have been in self-defense. I was glad that Jack and Justin's statements didn't contradict mine, we had all told the exact same story – I guess if we hadn't, we'd all be in prison or juvenile hall.

We were just kids, and we'd been through enough, and the state of Louisiana understood that. The counseling was obligatory and extended until we hit fifteen years of age, just to make sure that the three of us remained in good mental health and didn't go off on a killing spree of our own. That was fine by me because I really did want to recover from the incident and I knew that just talking to Momma about it wasn't going to solve any of my problems.

The evidence collected and statements made by Rebecca and Daren were all that was needed to slam their sick, child-killing asses behind bars for life. Those whose children had been murdered at the hands of the satanic group had filled the streets in downtown

Hammond on the day those two were sentenced, and the last thing I heard was that the police in Hammond, Ponchatoula and Albany had discovered the remains of over ten children, with the full cooperation of their newly booked prisoners. It was heartbreaking, but at least those poor parents could put their babies to rest and gain some closure.

After that, Momma forbade me from following the case, and I was only too happy to comply.

CHAPTER TWENTY-SIX

SAYING GOODBYE: 1993

The movers had finished packing everything up on a Sunday morning, and Memaw wanted to roll out by noon to our new home. Momma told me to go run out to the street to check the mail one last time, to make sure the box was empty before we left. I ran out to the road and saw Angela's van coming my way. I stepped off the road to let them pass, but to my surprise, Angela's dad stopped the van next to me. The side door slid open, and Angela got out.

"Hey," she said.

"Hey," I replied. "Sorry I haven't called or anything, I kinda had some serious things going on."

"I know what happened, Jody."

"You do, huh?" I rubbed my head, feigning surprise.

"I'm sorry about what happened to you," Angela was sincere.

"Don't worry about it. They're all either dead or locked up for good in prison now."

Angela's eyes began to well up, and she wiped a

solitary tear from her eye. She casted a furtive glance back towards her father.

"What's wrong?" I asked her.

"Am I ever going to see you again?" Angela let out a sad sigh.

"I don't know," I was honest with her. "There are a lot of bad memories here that I'd like to leave behind. But there's also a lot of good ones that I want to hold on to," I let out a light laugh. "I never thought I'd be saying that. I never thought I'd want to leave. I loved it here."

"If I could leave with you, I would," Angela said, biting the bottom of her lip as she fought back her tears, "just never forget me okay? 'Cause I'll never forget you, Jody."

I wrapped my arms around Angela's waist for the last time.

"I won't forget you. *I promise.*"

Angela squeezed me tight and kissed me gently on the lips. Then she let go of me, climbed back into her father's van, and slid the door shut.

As they drove away, she waved to me through the rear window, a forced smile on her tear-streaked face. I waved back and watched as the van disappeared around the corner of the street, gone forever.

That was the last time I saw Angela.

I stood there awhile and listened to the sound of the birds chirping their joyful songs, and breathed that hot, humid country summer air deep into my soul. As I stared down the street toward Jack's house I saw their car coming my way; Momma said they'd be coming by the house to see us off, so I ran back inside to prepare myself for saying goodbye to Jack.

"Hunter-man, you got everything you're taking?" Momma called out to my little brother.

"Yep!" Hunter replied, and darted out the front door,

heading for the car, where Memaw waited patiently.

Moments later, Renee, Jamie and Jack came through the door.

"Come here little Miss Jamie, and give me a kiss goodbye," Momma said, flinging her arms open wide. Jamie ran into Momma's arms and she squeezed her neck tight.

Jack was restless, walking around with his hands in his pockets, pacing the floor like some expectant father. "Can I use the bathroom?" he asked.

"Jack, you know you ain't got to ask me, boy," Momma joked. "Go use it if you got to."

"Thanks," Jack said, making his way to our bathroom.

"Come give me a hug, Jody," Renee demanded, "Mr. Shawn said to give you one for him, too, since he can't get off work."

I smiled at Mrs. Renee and went in for my hug, she held me tight for what seemed an age, before finally releasing me.

"Jody," Momma said, "go make sure I didn't leave the hair dryer in my room."

"Okay," I said, and made my way toward her empty bedroom.

When I opened the door I saw Jack was standing there, dead center, with his arms crossed. He was crying.

"What's up, man?" I asked the all too obvious question.

"I'm gonna miss you, Jody," Jack said, wiping his eyes with his arm.

"I'm gonna miss you too," I choked up on my words.

"You're like a brother to me, and now I'm losing you. I know you'll never come back," Jack sniffled, "now what am I supposed to do?"

My friend's words were crushing my heart, and it

made me cry, too. I placed my hands on his shoulders. "We'll always have each other, Jack," I tried to remain strong. "We'll *always* be best friends, no matter what comes along in our lives. I'll never forget the times we had together, not for the rest of my life. I'm sure I'll tell my kids stories about us one day, and hope they can find a friend just as good as you."

"Same here," Jack said, sucking back the snot that was oozing out of his nose.

"I'll never forget you... *ever*," I sobbed and pulled Jack into a hug. "As long as I live, you will be my best friend, and you'll know where to find me if you ever need me."

"I know," Jack nodded, his tears soaking through my shirt.

We had been through so much together. Almost every amount of joy and happiness we'd experienced so far in life, it had been together. The good, the bad, the happy, the sad, we'd been through it all side by side. I knew that I was losing the one friend in my life that I would never be able to replace; no matter who else came along, they wouldn't be Jack; we were like one soul that lived life through each other.

I let go of Jack and backed away. I extended my hand to him one last time for a shake.

"Rhine Road Boys forever, right?" I said.

"Rhine Road Boys forever – and always," Jack replied and placed his hand in mine.

Once we were done saying our goodbyes, Jack and I left Momma's bedroom and went outside. Momma gave Renee a final hug and Jack a quick peck on the cheek before getting into the car. I sat myself in the back seat and stared forlornly out the window at Memaw's house; I was already missing the place, and we hadn't even left yet. Memaw started up the car and backed up out of the driveway. Renee, Jack and Jamie walked off, back toward the road.

"Alright," Memaw said, "ya'll ready to get going to our new home?"

Hunter was the only one to respond, he was a little kid and most things got him excited. I just sat there and said nothing.

As Memaw pulled onto Rhine Road for her very last time, I looked back at Jack and gave him a wave. He returned it, as if he'd been waiting on it. I saw Mrs. Renee drape an arm around him, and Jack immediately began crying. As we picked up speed down the road, I watched with watery eyes and heartache as my best friend – my *blood brother* – disappeared into the distance.

I had lost the most important friend I would ever have in my life, and a part of me died as we made the left onto Hardline Road, which then took us out toward the Interstate; leaving is never easy, no matter how old, or young you are, but this was my farewell – another chapter in my life closing out; even though I didn't want it to.

EPILOGUE

OVER THE YEARS: 2008

Over the years after leaving Hammond, I rarely returned to Rhine Road. Mine and Jack's friendship became less and less each year, and by the time I was in ninth grade, we hardly heard from one another anymore, and everyone else I knew in Hammond fell off my radar completely.

Jack was busy with baseball and football at Albany High, while I was running track and playing in the drum line at Tara High, in Baton Rouge. Once in a blue moon, Jack would call, or I would call him, but it was never the same after I left. Time and distance tore us apart, and we eventually settled for what new friendships we made.

Even though right now isn't the best time for a reunion, since everyone is trying to keep the pain of losing Jamie at bay, I'm glad I'll get to be there for Jack in this time of tragedy. The road ahead for his family is going to be hard, but they'll make it through – I just know they will. Mourning and sorrow come together like peanut butter and jelly when you lose someone like

Jamie, a person who was so special and who touched so many hearts, it's impossibly hard. All we can do is accept our fates with our heads held high and drive on and never forget what those we lose leave behind; Jamie's memory will always be kept alive.

Earlier today, before coming to Rhine Road, I went to Chase's grave and placed a pack of baseball cards I'd bought from the local convenience store on his headstone. As I was walking away, I noticed his mom and dad's headstones were next to his, their faces blank. Chase's folks weren't dead, but when they did pass away, they would be buried next to their son – a son who had been taken away from this world far too soon.

It took me back to the day Memaw purchased her plot next to Pepaw. Even with thoughts of impending death, people hold on to the hope of reconnecting with their loved ones on the other side. I think that's beautiful, and I pray that it's true, and I hope when Chase's parents do pass, they find him waiting with open arms.

Upon reaching my car, I was in tears and could barely hold myself together; I really do wish I could've saved him.

As for Justin, I never saw him again after I left Hammond, even though I never forgot the kid. I'd ask Jack over the phone how Justin was doing, but he'd lost contact with him as well. We three carried a dark secret; one we all seemed to have learned to deal with rather well. I always kept my old friends in my memories, though, and it wasn't until recently that I found them all on the internet and we began communicating again.

I believe it was Justin whom I contacted first, and when we spoke on the phone together for the first time in many years, it was as if we had just met for the first time. At some point during that initial conversation, he informed me that Alex had passed away. I was speechless to find out that Alex ended up going into the Marine Corps and had died while serving his country in Iraq. I wished Alex Godspeed, like I did for all my fallen brethren in the Armed Forces, and hoped his mother was keeping herself together.

We'd ended the phone call promising each other that we would stay in touch more often. Justin wanted me to stop by his house in Hammond the next time I was around. It never happened, though, life kinda got in the way.

As for Krystle, she married, became a librarian and had two adorable little boys. Angela married as well, she also has two sons, and still resides in Hammond. I've only spoken to Angela and Krystle through *MySpace* so far, but they want to get together and have lunch next time I'm around, although I doubt it will happen.

I open my eyes to the sound of children's laughter, as two young boys race past me on their bicycles. They're late getting home, as I see that darkness has set in. I focus my attention for the moment on the stars that twinkle and shine above me, and get lost in their beauty.

I've been here in my old driveway for well over three hours now, dwelling in memories past. I turn and watch the kids as they make their way down Rhine Road, and several yards before Jack's old driveway the night swallows them up, and they are gone.

I would give almost anything to go back in time and be where they're at now, there are so many things I'd do differently. I was a murderer at twelve years old, no matter how you look at it, whether it was legally self-defense or not. I know what my soul tells me, and it tells me that I was wrong. We should have walked away that night, but you can't go back, not ever. What's done is done, and what's lost is gone forever, whether it's someone's life, innocence, or their very soul.

I know that I've never fully recovered from the incidents that took place all those years ago. Even after bringing myself here tonight, hoping that returning would put my heart and soul at peace, I've only proven myself wrong. I remember when Justin said we were going to have to take what we'd done to our graves, and he couldn't have put it any better; I now realize that maybe when I'm dead and gone, that's when I will finally have my peace, but of course, that all depends on whether what we did was right by God.

I'll leave it in his hands.

I walk over to my car and reach into my pocket to pull out my keys. My wife is probably wondering where the hell I'm at, so I need to hurry up and get back on the road. I stick the key into the lock, turn it and open the door. I plant myself in the driver's seat, and look through the bug-smeared windshield at my old front yard. There I see memories of Jack and I playing happily, full of innocence and joy. My chest tightens, my eyes water and imagined apparitions of everyone I knew while growing up here invade my mind like moths to a flame.

I grip the steering wheel and squeeze it tight. My youth was taken away from me and my innocence was stolen. Although my childhood was filled of well-rehearsed lies and deceit, it was also filled with love, friendship, trust, faith and compassion. I don't understand why I should feel so torn; I guess I never will.

I scream at the roof of my car until I feel my face heat up. I place my head between my arms on the steering wheel, and tears roll off my face and soak into my denim pants. I start the ignition, place the car in reverse and back up onto Rhine Road. Sometimes it's best not to live in the past, but no one ever said you couldn't carry the wonderful memories from those times along with you and hold them dearly to your heart. I guess that's what I do need to hold onto – the friends, the love, the happiness and nothing else.

I press my foot down on the pedal, closing out this chapter of my life on my own. All that remains is the future, but you can always return to the place of your last happiness, which this place truly was. I turn onto Hardline Road, whispering a fond goodbye to Rhine Road, and leaving the nightmares of my youth behind.

THE END

About the Author

J.P. Willie was born in Covington, Louisiana to parents Gayla and Joseph Willie on October 30th, 1981. He graduated from Tara High School in Baton Rouge, Louisiana and joined the United States Army on October 20, 2000. While serving in the Army, he was stationed at: Fort Bragg (North Carolina), Caserma  Ederle (Italy), Mannheim (Germany), Fort Benning (Georgia), Schofield Barracks (Hawaii) and Fort Polk (Louisiana). He served two combat tours in Afghanistan with the 82nd Airborne Division and the 173rd Airborne Brigade. He will retire from the Military in October of 2020.

His first novel, Blood In The Woods, was published by Fear Front Publishing on December 26, 2016. The story is inspired by true events from his childhood and is terrifying readers across the globe. He decided to leave Fear Front Publishing on March 1, 2017 for personal reasons and quickly self-published the novel on April 5, 2017 due to high demand. His first short story, *Welcome Home, Rougarou* reached #5 for short reads on Amazon.com. J.P. enjoys writing Horror, Thrillers, Supernatural Fiction and Dark Fiction. He is working on his first novella, *Hot Summer Savior*.

<u>Other HellBound Books Titles</u>
<u>Available at: www.hellboundbookspublishing.com</u>

Worship Me

Something is listening to the prayers of St. Paul's United Church, but it's not the god they asked for; it's something much, much older.

A quiet Sunday service turns into a living hell when this ancient entity descends upon the house of worship and claims the congregation for its own. The terrified churchgoers must now prove their loyalty to their new god by giving it one of their children or in two days time it will return and destroy them all.

As fear rips the congregation apart, it becomes clear that if they're to survive this untold horror, the faithful must become the faithless and enter into a battle against God itself. But as time runs out, they discover that true monsters come not from heaven or hell…

…they come from within.

No Rest For The Wicked

A modern day ghost story with its skeletons buried firmly in the past.

From beyond the grave, a murderous wife seeks to complete her revenge on those who betrayed her in life; a powerless domestic still fears for her immortal soul while trying to scare off anyone who comes too close; and the former plantation master - a sadistic doctor who puts more faith in the teachings of de Sade than the Bible

When Eric and Grace McLaughlin purchase Greenbrier Plantation, their dreams are just as big as those who have tried to tame the place before them. But, the doctor has learned a thing or two over his many years in the afterlife, is putting those new skills to the test, and will go to great lengths in order to gain the upper hand. While Grace digs into the death-filled history of her new home, Eric soon becomes a pawn of the doctor's unsavory desires and rapidly growing power, and is hell-bent on stopping her.

Shopping List 2: Another Horror Anthology

Once again, HellBound Books Publishing brings you an outstanding collection of horror, dark, slippery things, and supernatural terror - all from the very best up and coming minds in the genre.

We have given each and every one of our authors the opportunity to have their shopping lists read by you, the most wonderful reading public, and have the darkest corners of their creative psyche laid bare for all to see...

In all, 21 stories to chill the soul, tingle the spine and keep you awake in the cold, murky hours of the night from: Erin Lee, The Truth Artist, John Barackman, Serena Daniels, M.R. Wallace, Isobel Blackthorn, Pamela Morris, Alex Laybourne, Jason J. Nugent, Josh Darling, Jovan Jones, Nick Swain, Douglas Ford, Craig Bullock, Craig Bullock, Jeff C. Stevenson, PC3, David F Gray, Sergio Palumbo, Donna Maria McCarthy, David Clark & Megan E. Morales.

The Big Book of Bootleg Horror 3:
By Invitation Only

A very, very special edition of our anthology series - proceeds going to the awesome Alzheimer's charity *Hilarity for Charity*.

Only invited authors are featured - some of the biggest names in today's horror scene!

Contributing Authors:
Jack Ketchum, Michael Bray, Jeff Strand, Chad Lutzke, Eddie Generous, Lance Tuck, Wade H. Garrett, Richard Chizmar and Billy Chizmar, James H Longmore,
Jaap Boekestein, Iain Rob Wright, Michael McBride, Edward Lee, David Owain Hughes, Ray Garton & Benjamin Blake

Demons, Devils and Denizens of Hell Vol, 2

The second volume in HellBound Books' outstanding horror anthology fair teems with tales of Hades' finest citizens – both resident and vacationing in our earthly realm... -

Compiled by the inimitable P. Mattern and featuring: Savannah Morgan, Andrew MacKay, Jaap Boekestein, James H Longmore, Stephanie Kelley, Ryan Woods, James Nichols, P. Mattern, Marcus Mattern, Gerri R Gray, and legion more...

The Big Book of Bootleg Horror 2

The second volume in HellBound Books' flagship horror anthology - this one bursting at the seams with even more fantastically dark horror from the cream of the rising stars in today's horror scene!

Featuring: Tracey A. Cross, Elizabeth Zemlicka, Shelby Thomas, Matthew Gillies, Spinster Eskie, Stephen Clements, Ken Goldman, Nathan Robinson, K.M. Campbell, Cody Grady, Sebastian Bendix, Leo X. Robertson, David Owain Hughes, Timothy McGivney, Kane Gordon, Todd Sullivan, Mike Mayak, Edward Ahern, Rose Garnett, Jaap Boekestein, Brandy Delight, Stanley B. Webb, D. Norfolk, and Thomas Gunther.

J.P. Willie

**A HellBound Books LLC
Publication**

http://www.hellboundbookspublishing.com

Printed in the United States of America

Made in the USA
Coppell, TX
29 July 2020